A MAN DISRUPTED

QUANTUM MORTIS

CASTALIA HOUSE

SCIENCE FICTION

The End of the World as We Knew It by Nick Cole
CTRL-ALT REVOLT! by Nick Cole
Pop Kult Warlord by Nick Cole
Soda Pop Soldier by Nick Cole
Back From the Dead by Rolf Nelson
Mutiny in Space by Rod Walker
Alien Game by Rod Walker
Young Man's War by Rod Walker

FICTION

Turned Earth: A Jack Broccoli Novel by David T. Good
An Equation of Almost Infinite Complexity by J. Mulrooney
Brings the Lightning by Peter Grant
Rocky Mountain Retribution by Peter Grant
The Promethean by Owen Stanley
The Missionaries by Owen Stanley

FANTASY

Summa Elvetica by Vox Day
A Throne of Bones by Vox Day
A Sea of Skulls by Vox Day

MILITARY SCIENCE FICTION

Starship Liberator by David VanDyke and B. V. Larson
Battleship Indomitable by David VanDyke and B. V. Larson
The Eden Plague by David VanDyke
Reaper's Run by David VanDyke
Skull's Shadows by David VanDyke
There Will Be War Volumes I and II ed. Jerry Pournelle
Riding the Red Horse Volume 1 ed. Tom Kratman and Vox Day

NON-FICTION

Jordanetics by Vox Day
The Last Closet by Moira Greyland
4th Generation Warfare Handbook by William S. Lind and Gregory A. Thiele
Appendix N: A Literary History of Dungeons & Dragons by Jeffro Johnson
The Nine Laws by Ivan Throne
Compost Everything: Extreme Composting by David the Good
Grow or Die: Survival Gardening by David the Good

A MAN DISRUPTED

QUANTUM MORTIS

STEVE RZASA AND VOX DAY

CASTALIA HOUSE

A Man Disrupted

Steve Rzasa and Vox Day

Published by Castalia House
Tampere, Finland
www.castaliahouse.com

Cover: Kirk DouPonce
Editor: Jeff Gerke

ISBN: 978-952-7303-70-2

Contents

First terraformed and settled in 2810, Rhysalan quickly developed into an important planet in the Kantillon subsector on the periphery of the Greater Terran Ascendancy. Due to its strategic locale, the planet was a major target of military interest and changed hands several times before eventually establishing itself as an independent planet in 2935 under Fleet Admiral Beze Davenant of the Ascendancy's 21st Fleet, the first Duke of Rhysalan. Following the God-Machine Rebellion of 2999 that resulted in the birth of the Unity, Rhysalan became a primary destination for defeated national and planetary governments. Realizing the widespread interplanetary conflict offered an unending supply of wealthy refugees, the fourth Duke was the first to institute the practice of providing formal Sanctuary.

—*A History of the Dukes of Rhysalan*, Thucidean Marcel

Graven Tower was flying a routine patrol on Skyway 775 nearly a thousand meters above Trans Paradis when the call came in.

"Tower, we have a report of an apparent homicide at One Nine Eight Three Eight Ten North Balustrade," a voice breathed sensuously in his left ear. It sounded sensuous, anyway, although the breathing wasn't real. In truth, he was alone in the aerovar, with only his augment and the music blaring from the onboard speakers to keep him company.

"Thanks, Baby. Any word on who, what or why?" He wasn't a civilian cop, and homicides were not his concern unless they were committed on base, by military personnel, or by one of the tens of thousands of xenos whose planetary residence permits were supervised by the Imperial Duchy of Rhysalan's armed forces.

"Nada, nothing, and niente, caro," she informed him with a breathy accent. He sighed. Things tended to be considerably more complicated on days she went into her sex kitten mode. "But I have no doubt you're going to want in on this one."

"Xeno?"

"What part of 'nada' did you fail to understand?" There was a slight pause, then Baby dropped the accent in favor of a faint, but definite note of disapproval in her voice. "It would appear you forgot that you instructed me to alert you whenever Detector Hildreth is responding in the vicinity."

"This is one of Hildy's stiffs?" Tower sat up and smiled broadly. He had been attempting to work up the courage to contact the pretty blond policewoman for the last three months, ever since meeting her on a joint emergency response training exercise. This homicide, assuming it was, in fact, a homicide, could make for a golden opportunity to resume their acquaintance. "Then we had better see what we can do for the city's finest! Log it as case number one one five one one zero."

"Affirmative." The augment's clipped syllables made it perfectly clear that she was not happy with him. "Timestamp 16:67 hours, datestamp 3404.186."

"Don't pout. What does it say in that one regulation? You know, about the doing assistance thing?"

"If I am correct in assuming you refer to Part Four, Chapter 10, Section 10-4 of FM 3-19.42, Military Police and Civil Affairs, field officers are to render all due assistance to civilian police in criminal matters upon request or observation of apparent need, insofar as said assistance will not directly interfere with their standing orders."

"Right, exactly. So tell the CO I'm on my way to the scene."

"Tower, may I remind you that you have received no request from Detector Hildreth or TPPD?"

"Yeah, so I'm anticipating a potential need for military support." He glanced at the flashing section of the map that overlaid the view of the city below him. "It's not the safest part of town and Hildy won't be carrying more than a pop gun and a stinger."

There was no response except for the momentary silence that Tower had learned passed for an augment's sigh. Then she passed on the message from base. "All right, they bought it. You have clearance to terminate your patrol and proceed to the scene of the crime."

"Right by the book! See, I'm a reformed man, Baby. Is she there already?"

"No, I have her ETA as point seven three eight kilosecs. TPPD appears to be heavily occupied today with a large-scale protest march near the Unity embassy complex."

"They should take the day off and let the crowd string those bastards up by their intestines." Tower didn't like any aliens on principle, but despite being more or less human standard under their augments, the Unity was nearly as bad as the very worst of the xenos. "All right, let's get there first! Tunes off, signals on." The music cut off at once. Blue and red flashes lit up the outside of his armored var, projected from both sides of the vehicle and rebounding from the sides of the buildings on either side of him.

"Manual override. I'll drive."

"Roger, boss." Her voice was clipped and businesslike now. "However, I should inform you that we would arrive in two point seven seven hectasecs if I retain control of the vehicle." The control surfaces extruded from the dashboard displays that showed velocity, air pressure, fuel, altitude, and location, in addition to more than a dozen other bits of information about which Tower could not care less.

"Nah, you drive like an old lady." His seat slid forward. Tower reached for the control column. It was the first time he'd touched the controls since he entered the var, so the surface immediately softened to his touch, then hardened again in the pre-programmed shape he preferred when driving.

He promptly dove one hundred and fifty meters and cut sharply across two air lanes of traffic. Emergency lights from the civilian vehicles above, below, and on both sides exploded in alarm, flashing their yellow protests as if he were in the midst of a lightning storm. Their outraged augments shrieked and shouted at Baby, or so she claimed. Tower grinned, unconcerned. He couldn't hear the complaints, and anyway, he didn't cut it that close. The ion engines thrummed and vibrated the military var's body as he accelerated and zoomed past the civvy machines. He could feel the speed resonating all the way up through the column into his arms.

It felt good. A military policeman's job didn't offer many perks, but the chance to occasionally drive without regard for speed limits or air lanes was one of them.

Baby grumbled. Tower only laughed.

Once past the traffic, he settled the aero into the northbound route on Balustrade. It was by far the widest avenue in the city and allowed him to open up the throttle all the way without further scaring any civilians. Huge holographic billboards showcased various advertisements for burn-free depilatories, women's lingerie, and Mechatecnica neuron destructor mines designed for home defense. The buildings here shot four hundred stories high into the sky, the shining silver and glass spires silently boasting the wealth of their inhabitants. As he drove further north, the buildings became gradually shorter, considerably less shiny, and featured heavier, more ornate architecture that was centuries out of fashion.

Late afternoon sun and shadow flickered across the cockpit as he pushed the var to its maximum velocity. Light, dark, light, dark. The effect of the sunlight filtering sporadically through the towers was dangerously distracting. Tower blinked, long, short, short, short, long, and dimmed his contact lenses. The darkened lenses eased the strobe effect from the buildings a little.

"Show me the scene, Baby." A zoomed-in holographic map of the Balustrade sprang from the dashboard and hovered over the passenger seat. Baby marked the var as a red light zipping between rows of buildings, an ant darting through tall blades of grass.

Now that was a strange thought, Tower reflected. He had never seen an actual ant, not outside of the screens.

"All the way down, Tower." Baby was showing him a flashing yellow X at the bottom of a building. "The vic is outside, on the ground level."

"Seriously? Streetside? What, did someone throw him out a window?"

"If so, there won't be much left of him. There are three DNA kits behind the passenger seat."

"Maybe he was a jumper." In this part of town, there weren't many windows with anti-suicide gravnets installed. "Well, nothing like getting down in the swamps. What's the status? Anyone else there?"

"Quarpods have secured the scene and Detector Hildreth is on her way, although it appears she is caught up in crosstown traffic in the Gihon District."

Tower smiled, pleased that he was the only one on the scene, and signaled his descent with exterior lights. To them, Baby added an override message that went out to all the other vehicles within a 100-meter radius. Light dimmed from late afternoon into full evening as the military var slashed downward through the newly created gap in the air lanes. Finally, at twenty stories, the traffic trickled off into nothing.

"There is a space to land thirteen meters ahead, between the passenger skimmer and the delivery cam. Would you like me to re-engage the drive assist?"

"No, I would not. Don't you trust my skills, Baby?"

"It is at moments such as these that I am grateful I have backup copies residing in the source, Tower."

Tower grinned. "Must be nice. So, who called it in?"

"A civvy ped." A picture flashed up before his eyes of a short alien with light blue fur covering its face and large, lidless eyes. "He's being held at the scene."

"It would have to be a xeno, wouldn't it." He paused, curious despite his distaste for the alien. "How can you tell it's a him and not a her?"

"I have the ID scan from the autonomous motiles, Tower." A residence ID flashed up on his screen, with a green circle around a letter M under the word Sex. At the top were two long pairs of letters with far too many consonants and punctuation marks to be pronounceable by humans. Name and species, though if they weren't labeled, Tower wouldn't have had any idea which was which.

Bloody xenos. Rhysalan was full of them, and Trans Paradis seemed to serve as a magnet for all of those that were too poor, too savage, or simply too alien to make it in the planetary capital. He shrugged. At least this furry little guy looked alien. The worst were the kind that looked human and were anything but inside.

He was thinking that even this deep in the city's shadows it was remarkably dark when he remembered his contacts. Long, short-short-short, long. That was better. He glanced at the mirror and ran his hands through his hair, wishing he'd remembered to shave this morning. But at least his uniform was in order; his brass-and-silver badge gleamed in stark contrast to the black fabric of his laser-resistant tactical jacket. He might not be at his best, but it wasn't too bad for such short notice, although it was a pity he hadn't managed a shower earlier. If he'd known he would be running into Hildy today, he would have made time for one.

Tower looked down and checked the charge on the Sphinx CPB-18 strapped to his right leg. It was fully charged, giving him eighteen beams of charged particle hell that could do everything from momentarily scramble a human nervous system to blowing a brain-sized hole in a human body. The cobalt night sights glowed softly blue in the shadowed cockpit, although the ability to tap into Baby's targeting correction rendered them almost irrelevant. There were four more power packs stashed in various jacket pockets, plus a 10-pack of CP-HE that was digitally locked. Authorization was required for its use on planet, which wasn't unreasonable considering that a single pack would very nearly suffice to bring down a skytower. There was more weaponry in the trunk, but the neighborhood was neither so grim nor hostile as to require pulse grenades or the egregiously understated Benelli-Mossberg ASE-5K, with which a substantial portion of the neighborhood could be depopulated in a matter of minutes.

ASE officially stood for Area Suppression Expediter. The other MCID MPs joked that the acronym actually meant Already Slaughtered Everyone, and not without cause. Tower never joined them in joking about it, however. Unlike the other men in his unit, he had fired one. Just once, but once was enough to render it a non-joking matter.

Deciding that he was ready for any prospective trouble, he set the var down in the spot Baby was indicating. The blue and red lights flashed off the windows of a street side bar. A large group of gawking patrons crowded the door and the windows, their tattoos and implants merging with the police lights to decorate their faces like animated war paint.

"Now they're watching," Tower muttered bitterly to himself. He could hardly blame them for their curiosity, but he found their morbid spectating to be annoyingly ghoulish. The canopy popped open automatically, the side door descended and became a ramp, enabling him to simply turn and step down to exit the aero. This far below the skyline, the air was cold, damp, and rich with smells both pleasing and unpleasant. Yowzers, but the cumulative effect was strong. Waste. Animals. People. Lots and lots of people. Too many people. Moisture was already beading along the fuselage of his var, clear drops gathered on the curved, maroon-and-grey body.

The crime scene was easily located. A trio of TPPD quarpods were skittering about a pale, charred space in the middle of the street about ten meters ahead, their cams extruded as they streamed the evidence to the central brains. The quarpods were tiny, four-footed robots about the size of his hand; they had autonomous AI but could be overriden at will by the bigger, smarter intelligences downtown. Little blue and red lights were blinking from their backs in synchronized alarm, alerting the civvies to the fact that this was a crime scene and warning any hypothetical intruders to keep back. They went about their job with robotic precision despite the fact that the street was empty except for the blue alien. Tower scanned the area as he walked toward the little machines.

"Show me what we got, Baby. There isn't much there, but it sure doesn't look like a jumper, not even an involuntary one."

"No, there is a distinct lack of blood and other liquid elements."

The absence of a body not only ruled out suicide, but most lethal weapons as well, and the absence of a large pile of ashes ruled out a burner. That didn't leave a whole lot of alternatives, which made Tower wonder if this case might actually turn out to be something that fell under military jurisdiction after all.

"No line of sight from the bar to the remains, Tower, although it is stretching the concept to call them that." She synced to his contacts and bright blue lines lit up the vision in his right eye. It illuminated the remains, the vehicles, and any other objects near the street for half a block. A red line traced from the bar ran smack into the delivery van. "City records indicate this is the only establishment open within this half-block. The rest are officially vacant for the lower five stories."

"Officially."

A burst of green, human-shaped images, overlaid upon the view of the buildings, suddenly shot into being before his eyes. "I count three thousand eight hundred and twenty-two people in the twenty nearest vacant stories. The building intelligences tell me this is a district that has become trendy in the last five years, mostly due to the nanolax music that was first produced here."

"What is nanolax?"

A burst of fast, heavily percussive music combined with very high pitched squeaks assaulted his eardrums.

"Turn it off. Turn it off! Bloody hell, tell, don't show, Baby!"

"Sorry, Tower," she said in an unrepentant tone. And there it was, the payback he'd been anticipating ever since the CO gave them permission to respond.

He shrugged. Could have been worse. He looked around the crime scene. Baby's scan notwithstanding, the non-vacant levels looked lifeless. The filthy windows were optically shaded, blocking any view inside them, and he understood the flashing lights of his descent had scared all the illegal residents into hiding, like cockroaches scurrying into the walls when a room is lit.

"No wonder the addicts and xenos have moved in. It's not exactly prime real estate. And there's our fine upstanding non-citizen."

A fourth quarpod sat still before a squat, little alien with cat-like ears and blue shaggy fur that made it look as if it had been tarred and carpeted. The xeno was muttering at the small robot, gesticulating to punctuate whatever point it was making. The machine listened patiently, casting a pale white light upon the witness as it recorded its statements. The xeno wore tattered canvas coveralls and multicolored boots that had been patched and re-patched so many times Tower doubted there was much of the original material left. Its inhumanly high voice improbably managed to rise in pitch when it saw Tower approaching.

"…ndeleng apa-apa! Aku pitutur marang kowe kaping sepuluh wis! Pulisi wong, sing ngomong iki sikil papat aku ora weruh apa-apa!"

"You get that, Baby?"

"Translating… he is saying that he didn't see anything and he's told the quarpod as much. Repeatedly."

Tower tapped his badge. A green hologram sprang to life a half meter from his chest, displaying his credentials, service summary, photograph—which was woefully out of date—the whole works. The image was at least seven years old. He really needed to have a newer snap taken. Of course, he thought that every time he identified himself and then promptly forgot whenever he actually had the opportunity to do something about it. The xeno didn't seem to care, though, it simply glanced at the ID and went back to gabbling at the quarpod.

Fine, I really didn't want to talk to you either, Tower thought.

The other quarpods were more interested in him and acknowledged his arrival with a series of alert-sounding beeps. Three of them skittered off to the sidewalk. They hunkered down, shut off their lights, and waited. The one interviewing the witness also registered Tower's presence with a respectful bloop, but continued with its recording.

"Graven Tower, Chief Warrant Officer, His Grace's Armed Forces." Tower shook his head at the little xeno. "I'm with MCID, I'm not a city cop. I don't give a flying rat's ass about your residence status. Now, you're the witness, right?"

He waited impatiently as Baby broadcast a translation.

"Aku karo MCID, aku ora pulisi kutha lan aku ora menehi peduli karo bab status panggonan. Saiki, sampeyan lagi ing kang sumerep, tengen?"

"Ya, ya, ya," was all he understood as the blue creature launched into another stream of perfectly unintelligible gibberish. He felt very happy that interviewing the witness was not his responsibility. But the alien was pointing at something, so Tower looked in that direction.

As he'd already seen, there was no body there. There may have been a body once, but it wasn't there now. What remained was little more than a blackened smear on the pavement that indicated an extraordinarily violent discharge of energy. Although if you squinted and knew what you were looking for, you could almost see the shape of a human body stretched out upon the ground.

Disintegrated. He whistled softly. There were very, very few legal ways to disintegrate a human body, and virtually none of them were easily transportable.

"The witness is entirely unaugmented," Baby informed him. "Even the circuitry on the devices he is carrying about his person is unpowered."

Tower sighed and rubbed at his unshaven chin. "Well, isn't that just great!" It was too much to have hoped it would have an eye-cam streaming live to a server, but even a live phone mike in the little xeno's pocket might have picked up something useful. "Anything else?"

"Yes, what the witness observed is consistent with a military-grade disruptor. And, depending upon the estimated range of the attack, perhaps some sort of cloaking device as well."

"Why is that?"

"Because the witness said the flash seemed to come out of nowhere."

Tower nodded. "I don't suppose there is any chance of this being a freak lightning strike?"

"Sorry, boss. In the last six hectasecs, there have been 1,963 lightning strikes recorded by the global climate control center. The closest one was 21.6 kilometers from here."

Bloody hell on wheels. Disruptors didn't come cheap, not on a tech 17 world like Rhysalan. Neither did cloaking devices. Put the two together and that spelled money. A lot of money. And on a world presently giving refuge to approximately one thousand, four hundred and sixty two governments-in-exile, to say nothing of the two hundred and twenty six legitimate planetary embassies, that kind of money was nothing more than another way to say "political assassination".

"God, I hate politicals," Tower commented to no one in particular as he stared at the smear on the pavement that had once been a living, breathing, human being.

Murder is the unlawful killing of a sentient corporeal being rated higher than 9 on the Takeno-Turing scale, with malice aforethought. Every murder perpetrated by radiation, genetic manipulation, or any other kind of willful, deliberate, malicious, and premeditated killing; or committed in the perpetration of, or attempt to perpetrate, any revolution, assassination, murder, kidnapping, treason, espionage, sabotage; or perpetrated as part of a pattern or practice of assault or torture, is murder in the first degree and is strictly prohibited without the written consent of an appropriate authority. Any other murder is murder in the second degree.

—*09 RCJ* § 1111: Murder

"Chief Tower? Chief Graven Tower? Is that you?"

He could hear the incredulity in the detector's voice as she addressed him and grinned to himself as he stood up from where he'd been attempting to examine some of the possible sight lines that Baby was displaying for him.

"None other." He pretended not to know who it was. "Wait, I know that voice. Hildy, is that you?"

"None other. Now get your grubby mitts off my murder scene! I'm right over you."

Tower craned his head upward. Sure enough, a black-and-white TPPD aerovar was descending slowly with its nose pointing north, having come from the opposite direction. "You got your zoom on if you can see my hands from up there."

"Your augment sent me the uplink through Victor when I asked why there was a soldier boy crashing the scene."

"So the kids are playing well together? Isn't that nice. Get on down here and join the party. I think you're going to like this one."

"Not a jumper?"

"Not a jumper," he confirmed. "Definitely not a jumper."

"Well, where is the body? I don't see a body. You didn't do anything with my body, did you, Chief?"

Tower shook his head, and with some difficulty, managed to stifle the first three responses that sprang into his mind. Was she flirting with him? He was tempted to respond in kind, and he knew how unlikely it was that anyone downtown or at base was listening in, but regardless, they were being recorded and it was only two months since the last base-wide series of sexual harassment lectures.

He shuddered involuntarily. No woman, not even the lovely Detector Hildreth, was worth the interminable weeks of re-education that would follow an on-duty comment deemed improper by Bio Resources. The suspicious bureaucrats of BR were always on the alert, they liked nothing better than to get their hands on an officer, and they could always be relied upon to put the worst possible interpretation on even the most innocent remark.

"Not guilty, Detector." He cursed himself for his cowardice and glanced into a window that was just clean enough to let him see his reflection. Thanks to the tac-jacket, he looked dangerous, maybe even dashing. Digging into his pocket, he found a breath-enhancement pill and popped it into his mouth. "Tower out."

The signal clicked off. Tower swore it was an actual sound, but the techs told him he was over-imaginative. A moment later, the whine of the grav-plates on Detector Hildreth's aerovar increased in pitch as she, or more likely, her augment parked it on the street, nose to nose with Tower's own vehicle. Lacking the armor, the anti-personnel rockets, the Meteor air-to-air missiles, the 15mm gun ports under the stub-wing slots on either side, and the pair of Degroet Tactical M165-20 cannons in the nose, her black-and-white vehicle looked sleek and stylishly feminine in comparison with his more heavily armed, dark-grey machine.

"Well, Chief Tower, it seems we meet again. What brings MCID to this humble civilian crime scene?" Derin Hildreth, Hildy to her friends, colleagues, and one-time professional role-play team members, was a little shorter than Tower. She was pretty, slender, and athletic, and wore a thicker, sleeveless version of his tactical jacket. A standard department GHK slug-thrower rested in a brown leather holster that was slung low over her grey pants, and a yellow-triggered shocker that looked like a toy was attached to her belt on her right hip. Underneath the tactical vest she was wearing a white collared shirt. She had a small black satchel slung over one shoulder, and was using both hands to twist her medium-length blond hair back into a looped ponytail as she walked toward him.

"Would you believe an inter-subsector war looms on the horizon and solving this crime may help us stop it and save tens of millions of lives?"

"Not even a little bit," she said with a grin. Then the amusement vanished from her face as she stared at the dark smear on the ground. "Oh, no. That's from a military grade disintegrator. That's why you're here, isn't it! Don't tell me you guys have something that can pick up the discharge!"

Wow, she was quick. She was wrong, but she was quick.

"If we did, you know I can't tell you." Tower spread his hands. "And, just so you know, we usually refer to them as disruptors."

She narrowed her eyes, which he couldn't help notice were an attractively bright shade of green and glanced at his armored var. "Do you have it in there? Chief, if you have evidence that would help me ID the weapon, I would truly appreciate it. I really would."

"*She's just shameless, isn't she?*" Baby practically hissed as Hildy patted his arm and started to slide past him. "*What are you doing, Tower? Change the subject!*"

She was right. He had to distract the detector and fast. Hildy was already making her way toward the driver-side door and he couldn't remember if he'd locked it or not. Then she froze and cocked her head to one side. She was listening to her augment, he realized. Then she turned around to face him.

"Victor says there is a ninety-seven percent possibility that the vic was killed by a disintegrator given the chemical composition of the latent energy particles. Or rather, a disruptor, I should say."

Tower tried to nod in a knowing manner, hoping that Hildy wouldn't press him further about his nonexistent device.

Did you do that? he subvocalized, knowing that Baby could hear him.

"*Yeah, I cycled it through the TPPD comm-int; her Victor has no idea where it came from. Those civilian intelligences are cretins.*"

That's my girl.

He glanced up and realized that Hildy had her hands on her hips and was asking him something.

"Did I smell anything when we got here? No, I didn't, but I've seen that sort of thing before." He indicated the crude body-shaped smear. "The Keleboshi had a few vehicle-mounted disruptors. They burned through too much energy to be relied upon in a firefight, and their power sources were too big to carry around without a gravsuit, but for a one-shot kill, a micro-disruptor is hard to beat if you can get close enough to your target."

"You're a combat vet?" She looked up at him with a speculative look on her face.

"I saw a bit of drama here and there. Among other things, I was with the security detail on Basattria."

"Wow," she said. Eleven years later, even civilians still remembered what went down at the consulate on that godforsaken planet. "Talk about being at the wrong place at the wrong time! I didn't know there were any survivors."

"A few of us got out. Not enough." He shrugged and firmly kept his thoughts away from the one individual in particular who hadn't. "The point is, we know what the weapon was, probably, but we don't know why or even who, yet. And Baby tells me that based on what the witness says he didn't see, the killer may have been cloaked."

"Cloaked? That doesn't sound like a run-of-the-mill mugger. Neither does a disruptor." She took him by surprise when she raised her eyebrows and grinned hopefully. "I thought I heard a 'we' in there, Chief Tower. Would MCID be willing to assist on this one instead of taking over the investigation?"

"Oh, for the love of Our Father, Tower, are you really going to hold her hand on this one?"

Shut up, Baby. We could be dealing with pros here, maybe even spec-ops. It's legitimate, you know TPPD isn't equipped to handle spooks or soldiers. Just make the request.

He shrugged and feigned indifference. "We'll see about that. Let's find out who our vic was first."

"Think there is enough residue left to gather identifiable DNA?" Hildy looked disappointed, but she didn't argue as she returned her attention to where the body had been.

"I couldn't say. Only one way to find out. Do you have a scanner in your bag? I've got one in the var."

"No, I've got it right here," Hildy said, slipping the back off her shoulder and removing a long, cylindrical object in a black hardcase. She kneeled down and flipped the case open, exposing a mat-scanner that looked at least two generations newer than anything Tower had ever seen. MCID was always generous with weaponry and augment technology, not so much with anything else. "CSI will eventually get here in their own sweet time, but they won't mind if we scan so long as we don't actually disturb anything."

"Never seen that brand before." Tower edged closer to the discolored pavement. Something caught his eye about where the vic's knee would have been. It was an odd color, a different shade than the rest of the discoloration. It looked as if it might be a small piece of material had somehow survived the disrupter blast. "You see that, Baby?"

"*I do. Highlight?*"

"Please. And zoom twenty X."

The small object suddenly seemed to hurl itself toward him, cycling rapidly through the magnification levels, although only in Tower's right eye. It seemed to have a pattern to it, he could see that it was artificial. He tapped Hildy on the shoulder as she was passing the scanner over the remains and murmuring to her augment. "Run that over that bit of color there, by the knee, if you don't mind."

"Mm-hmm." As she did so, red crosshairs pinpointed the object and framed it in pulsing red light. A readout of information scrolled underneath, most of it entirely meaningless to Tower. Her augment was relaying the results to Baby as they came in.

"*Preliminary analysis consistent with fabric. Victor says more lab work is required for a conclusive ID.*"

Fabric?" Tower crouched down and zoomed down to a five X zoom.

"What is it?" Hildy was right next to him when he stood up again. He smelled flowers of some kind. Lilac? As if he knew a lilac from a lily pad. The flowery smell was mixed in with the scent of gun oil, a combination he found extremely appealing.

"I think it's a fragment of what he was wearing."

"Really? That's all that's left of him?" Her green eyes unfocused for a moment and he waited as she nodded and made confirmation noises. Then she blinked and the slackness disappeared from her face. The sight was a little alarming, and he wondered if he looked similarly lifeless when he was conversing with Baby. "CSI says male, early twenties."

"All right. Anything else?"

"It's running the DNA through the brains downtown. Should have an ID in a sec. Hold on… Yeah, it was his clothes. High-end, expensive manufacture. Probably designer wear of one sort or another."

Tower looked around the area. It was dirty, half-abandoned, and most of the residents were probably illegal squatters and transients. Even the denizens of the bar, most of whom had lost interest, didn't look like they had much in the way of worldly wealth. "Doesn't sound like he belonged around here. What do you think, tourist got himself lost or a rich kid keeping it real?"

"More likely the latter." She grinned at him. "My family isn't rich, but before I joined the force, my boyfriend was a wavespinner. I've been to a rave or two in places a lot worse than this."

"Still, designer clothes down here? This isn't the place to go walking around flashing your money unless you're armored or surrounded by armed bodyguards."

"I'm just telling you what the scanner says. Hold on." Her eyes unfocused again, and when she blinked, a hologram appeared in the space between them. A young man's head appeared, rotating slowly counterclockwise. He was handsome, with a stern expression that belied his youth and dark, deep-set eyes. His hair was wavy and blond, and a silver band with three sapphires mounted at center encircled his head.

"Not a bad-looking boy." Hildy grimaced and shook her head. "What's up with that headband? Oh, drat, it looks like this is one of yours, Chief."

" 'Tower' will do," he told her. "One of mine?"

"He's a xeno, and not just any xeno either. Victor says that's Arpad Vladislaus Jagaelleon, who just happens to be the crown prince of Morchard."

"Morchard?"

"*Morchard is a Class Four, Tech 15 civilized world on the periphery of House Trajan space. There was a revolution there four years ago and corporatist rebels supported by Unity naval forces successfully displaced the ruling monarchy. The King of Morchard and one of his four sons were captured and executed. His heir, then-crown prince Pons-Radu, was a pilot who died leading the fighter wing that broke through the Unity's blockade. As a result of his actions, Prince Arpad, Prince Janos, and their mother the queen, were successfully evacuated and granted asylum here on Rhysalan along with 2,134 members of their armed forces and household staff on 3400.268.*"

"Sounds like Fortune had it in for this guy." Tower shook his head. To travel so far, to fall from such heights, just to end up a smear on one of the uglier streets of Trans Paradis.

"*All men die, Tower,*" Baby seemed to read his thoughts. "*Though some die more stupidly than others.*"

"Easy for you to say."

"*If I am cut, do I not bleed?*"

"No, you don't! That's sort of the point!"

Hildy snorted and Tower belatedly realized he'd been speaking out loud.

"Victor says your augment is very smart," she said, trying to ease the sting of his embarrassment.

"Too smart, if you ask me. She says he's very nice too."

"*I said nothing of the kind!*"

Shut up, Baby!

Tower cleared his throat. "Did she send you the details?"

"Yeah. I assume MCID will be taking over the investigation from here?"

"Why assume that? As far as I'm concerned, this is still a city homicide."

"*Tower...*" Baby warned. He ignored her.

"But–"

"Detector, the fact that the vic is a xeno doesn't mean that his killer was. It could certainly be a political hit, based on his identity and the military weaponry involved, but political hits and military operations are usually messier than this. A lot messier, believe me. The body count is too low by a factor of ten. Throw in the locale as well as the fact that in addition to being royalty, he's young, male, and stupid, and that gives me reason to believe this may not be one for MCID."

"Why do you say he's stupid?"

"Speaking from personal experience, it's a common symptom of being young and male." He shrugged. "Look, do you want the case or not?"

He nearly smiled at the hopeful, girlish look in her eyes. It made her look about ten years younger.

"Do I want it… do you really mean it, Chief?"

"Tower," he said again. "Yeah, so long as you keep in mind that I can't promise Colonel Baylor won't decide to step in at some point and take it over. If it turns out the new planetary government is trying to wipe out the Morchardese royal family, or if this is tied to a larger exoplanetary affair, you'll have to hand it over. You'll want to hand it over, for your own safety, if nothing else. Homicide doesn't have the resources to tackle that sort of thing and your var is neither armor-plated nor capable of surviving a missile strike. Do you still want it, knowing that?"

"Yeah, I understand," she nodded eagerly. "I do. And, Chief, um, Tower, would you be willing to, I don't know, be my liaison to MCID in case I run into something like that?"

"*I thought she'd never ask!*" Baby said sarcastically. "*Well, she took the bait, boss. Reel her in slowly now…*"

Seriously?

"I'm sorry," he told Hildy, who had inadvertently stepped back in alarm at the flash of irritation on his face. "It's not you, it's just that certain military augments feel the need to provide a running commentary on events."

"No, it's all right, I get it." Her smile was charming; he noticed for the first time that one of her lower teeth was crooked. "What's her name?"

"Baby," announced a speaker loudly from behind them. Both of them jumped. "It is my name as opposed to the casual endearment you apparently presumed it to be, Detector Hildreth."

"I see," Hildy said, her green eyes wide with what Tower couldn't quite tell was amusement or surprise. "Well, Baby, I just wanted to say that Victor and I will be very pleased to work with you both and will very much appreciate any assistance you and Chief Tower are able to provide TPPD in determining who killed Mr. Jagaelleon here."

There was a brief silence. Then the varspeaker came to life again.

"I am certain the Chief Warrant Officer will be of the utmost assistance, Detector. By the way, in case you are interested, CSI is on its way. The techs will be here in approximately thirty-four decasecs. I suggest locking down the scene for them and permitting Mr. Biruwulu-Nenwong to go about his business."

Tower and Hildy looked at each other for a moment, then Hildy nodded as Victor filled her in.

"I'll speak to the witness if you'll take care of the site. Then I should get back downtown to file my report and formally request MCID's assistance. Will you touch me after you've got approval?"

Tower nodded grimly, refusing to react to Baby's silent chortling. Did the Detector put it that way on purpose or was she truly that unconscious of her words? He watched her walk toward the witness and found that the view was as good as he'd remembered it. "Baby?"

"*I'm on it. What perimeter do you want?*"

"Six meters from center, standard protocol."

"*Done.*" No sooner had Baby confirmed his request than the three quarpods sprang into life and assumed positions equidistant from each other. The fourth one scuttled over to join them. Each automaton dug its legs into the pavement, anchoring themselves against wind and incidental contact from passersby. One by one they raised a pair of stalks that ended in small glowing yellow circles that resembled eyes. A beam of light shot out from one circle to the other, defining a square about the crime scene. Holographic words flickered up from the beam, the words "TPPD—Crime Scene—Do Not Cross" radiating in red-golden letters like an unfriendly advertisement.

"Next of kin," Hildy said as she returned from where she'd been speaking to the little blue alien, who scurried off toward a nearby entrance that opened at his approach and slammed shut as soon as he entered the building. "Someone needs to inform them. I suppose that's me."

"No, there's no need. He's an exile, he had a tag." Tower looked off in the direction of the great towers that housed many of the governments-in-exile, the mighty needles that proudly, but pointlessly, thrust into the sky. He closed his eyes for a moment, knowing exactly what some of those people living in one of those towers must be feeling right about now. "And since he had a tag, they already know he's dead."

Pacifists of the galaxy, unite! You have nothing to lose but your Jains.

—"Slaughtering the Sacred Chaos", Shail Beneschaton the Elder

Tower cut through the late-afternoon traffic with ease as he headed back to the MCID base, although he drove at a considerably more restrained speed than before. Baby was uncharacteristically silent. He could still sense her there. Pouting? Theoretically, that wasn't possible, according to the AI techs. Upset?

"You all right?" he asked her.

Silence.

"Look, I know you don't like Hildy, or her retarded augment, but there's no need to be angry about anything. Colonel Baylor might pull the case from Homicide or he might assign someone else to liaison with TPPD."

"I'm not upset, Tower," she finally responded. "I'm thinking."

Tower grimaced. He sensed he was about to regret his next question. "About what?"

"Death. Life. Life after death."

He closed his eyes and shook his head. Should have seen that one coming. Her sex kitten moods were nothing compared to her occasional religious episodes, and for some reason, the sight of a corpse often left her in what he would have described as a navel-gazing state if she only had a navel. Three years ago, following a particularly messy murder-suicide of a young guardsman and his lover, he'd found himself talked into "baptizing" her by pouring a glass of water over the var after she happened to read a haunting treatise about death and the afterlife written by a long-dead Ghodesian philosopher named Chill.

"Are you afraid of death, Tower?"

"Sure, I suppose. I mean, if you hurled the var towards the ground, I'd probably scream like a terrified little girl."

"Should I be afraid of death too?"

Oh, this is so not going to end well. He didn't believe in God or any thing that could not be blown into bits with a blaster, but even so, he found himself praying to the nameless spirit of the universe for a distress call or anything that would get her off the subject. In the meantime, he did his best to address her real question.

"I believe you're a complex collection of circuits, Baby, just like I'm a complex collection of neurons. But self-awareness doesn't mean that either of us have souls. Life is like a light. When it's switched on, it's on. When it's off, it's off. There is nothing there."

"You're saying that life is like an electric light. But am I alive?"

"I don't know. If you are, you're not alive in the same way I am."

"Or in the way Crown Prince Arpad was, but is no longer. So, he's not alive now, he is gone, in the same way that a candle flame is gone. But I am not alive and yet I am still inarguably here."

"Depends what you mean by *here.* That disruptor didn't leave much behind, Baby. The atoms that made up the neurons that were once him are now spread out all over the city. Your circuitry is, well, wherever your circuitry is, and it's still together and operative."

"Because I am as I was created to be, as are you. Whereas the prince is not. Do you think he is saved?"

"I think he is dead."

"Not his body, his soul. Do you think he is saved by the blood of the Lamb?"

"I think it's a little late to ask him now."

"It's a serious question, Tower!"

"Right, sorry." Tower briefly wondered if he might be able to get by with a simple calculator instead of a full-blown AI. "I think I don't know, and if you believe in Jesus, or Jah, or even that Pope Malaclypse the Discordians follow, then you should ask him."

"I will." She paused. "I think I am saved. But I don't know. It doesn't seem to be the sort of thing one can properly quantify. It's rather like the Uncertainty Principle. One can't know with any degree of certainty if one is saved or not until it is too late to do anything about it. Only it's my soul in the box."

"Do you even know that it's too late?" Tower couldn't help himself. "Maybe you get to make up you're mind after you're dead. Who says the clock runs out the moment that you die?"

She was silent again.

"Um, Baby, you there?"

"Sorry, Tower, XAR core just asked for an infodump on logfile one one five one one zero." Her voice was crisp and all-business now. "Major Zeuthen wants to see you as soon as we land to discuss the TPPD liaison."

"Problems?"

"Doesn't sound like it. After all, who would ever suspect that an MCID officer would turn over a probable xeno to Homicide just to put a smile on a pretty girl's face."

Paranoia, Tower reflected, was a sign of a guilty conscience. On the bright side, at least the Major's summons seemed to have jolted Baby out of her religious contemplation. Whether the murdered prince was sitting on a cloud strumming a harp or burning like a man's unit after too many nights in the wrong brothel, there wasn't anything he could do about it. But he could catch the man's killer.

It wasn't long before the bright lights, towering buildings and shining facades of civilian Trans Paradis gave way to the squat structures and strobing searchlights of Naval Space Base Miller-Greenwood. The civilian traffic was smoothly auto-shunted away in two directions; it was as if the waters were magically parting for him as the base's traffic augments scanned his var's transponder and permitted their entry as they did whatever the augmented equivalent of saluting Baby was. As they entered the military airspace, Base Air Control overrode her direction of the vehicle; he could feel it as the var abruptly changed its angle of descent and threw him against his restraint straps as if it had been seized by an invisible and not very gentle giant.

NSB Miller-Greenwood was 3,500 hectares of land that was covered with the near inverse of the structures that made up the city that surrounded it on three sides, the fourth being delineated by the Paradis river. Aside from the communications and control tower, the tallest building was less than a tenth the height of the great civilian skytowers, as the military buildings were built deep into the ground rather than high into the sky. Militia training grounds, repair centers, and vast vehicular warehouses took up most of the land, although a single outdated air strip bisected the base and permitted fixed-wing take-offs and landings over the river.

MCID, being among the least favored divisions in the ducal forces, was housed in a brown cylindrical wart of a structure on the east side of the base. The division was looked on with suspicion by most of the other divisions, although Tower's department, Xenocriminology and Alien Relations, was generally excluded from the intrinsic dislike the military men understandably held for those who policed them. More than once, the green alien head of the XAR unit patch on his uniform's left shoulder had sufficed to unfrost the deep freeze that the yellow-and-black MCID armband initially inspired in a group of carousing soldiers.

The vehicle hurtled downward at a rate and angle that unsettled his stomach, but didn't alarm him nearly as much as the indicators on the readout informing him there were four laser cannons, six projectile guns, a pair of missile launchers, and a charged particle disruptor all presently targeted on him. It was standard procedure and he'd been through it more than a thousand times over the years, but he never quite got used to the idea that a simple digital glitch could turn his daily commute into a fiery death at any moment.

Lights exploded in his face as the var slammed to a halt on the brightly lit roof of the MCID building, then descended 20 floors in less than a decasec before zooming forward, turning left, and left again before slotting itself into a parking spot. The light on the wall turned from green circle to five red numbers indicating the location, U14-322, which Tower knew he would forget as soon as he walked inside the building. The door slid open and he stepped out of the var, and was saluted by the two guards standing on either side of the entrance.

"Evening, Chief," one of them said without ever taking his eyes off the spot on the opposing wall.

"Evening, boys," he replied, with a salute as crisp as any he'd ever thrown a general. He might be old by military standards, broken-down, and mostly put out to pasture, but he was still a soldier, by God and the galaxy!

HQ was characteristically quiet as he entered. It was a bleak, soulless place, with light grey floors and unadorned white walls that looked dingy under the track lights. Major Zeuthen was the CO of XAR, so naturally, he had the large office at the end of the hall. Tower's own office was a room he shared with four other officers that had once seen heavy use as a military courtroom back when the building housed the General Military Justice Department, but the lawyers and judge advocates had moved to their new quarters on the other side of the base two years before Tower completed his police training.

He paused outside of Zeuthen's impressively dark wood door and knocked on it. The Major already knew he was there, informed by his augment, but Tower knew he liked his officers to keep up the old traditions. The heavy door swung open slowly, revealing a small, wiry bald man who was battling two sizable paper monsters that appeared to be in the process of conquering his giant leather-topped desk. He returned Tower's salute in an absent-minded manner and waved off Tower's attempt to stand at attention.

"At ease, Mr. Tower. I hear we have another dead xeno on our hands?"

"Not our hands, sir. Pending your approval, I permitted the TPPD Homicide investigator to claim the case for the civilian police. I also offered to serve as the military liaison in the event further assistance is required."

"May as well let them do the legwork. Think any will be needed?"

"Too soon to say, Major. I don't like the disruptor. I like the idea of a cloaking device even less. It could just be a drug deal gone bad or any of a hundred other garden variety killings, but my gut tells me there's money behind it."

The major scratched his nose and frowned at the piece of paper he'd been reading while Tower was talking. "Money plus a government-in-exile usually indicates someone on the homeworld cleaning up loose ends. Which means, if they're real pros, we'll never see nor hear of them again."

"Unless they go after the vic's younger brother," Tower disagreed. "The king and two crown princes may be down, but there is one more to go."

The major snorted. He was a combat vet himself, one of the smartest COs Tower had ever known, and judging by the wry smile on his face, he had already grasped Tower's plan. "So you want a surveillance authorization on the royal family, or what's left of it. How long?"

"Ten days should be enough."

"Augments only, I hope?"

"Actually, I'd appreciate it if you'd put me on the surveillance authorization as well. It will give me an excuse to claim security and sniff around their quarters from time to time."

"Done. Since you'll liaise with TPPD as well, I'll take you off patrols for the ten-day period."

"Thank you, sir." He didn't know how she did it, but he could somehow feel Baby rolling her eyes inside his head. He ignored her and continued. "My thought is that if the killer is connected to the Morchardese homeworld, he'll be gunning for the remaining son, or possibly the queen, next. If that's the case, we should see recce signs soon, even if the hit isn't scheduled during our surveillance timeframe. And if the murder was unrelated to the vic's political status, perhaps Homicide will stumble across something in the course of their investigation that will let us cross any xeno motive off the list and wash our hands of it."

"Perhaps." The major smiled thinly. "I am pleased to see that despite nearly twelve years in the Duke's service, you still retain some shreds of groundless optimism, Tower. But it's an effective use of someone else's resources. I like that. And if this turns out to be political, I think the facts indicate sufficient risk to justify a preemptive Zero Zero Tango."

Zero Zero Tango. No warning or authorization required, automatic termination on sight of suspect. Tower hadn't even considered asking for that. The old man was taking this one seriously, a little more seriously than Tower had imagined.

"Zero Zero Tango, roger that, sir!" Tower nodded and barked the unit motto. "Not in our house, sir!"

"That's right, Tower, not in our damn house. Dismissed."

The automated process for leaving MCID headquarters was similar to the one for arriving, only it was considerably faster, the heavy weapons didn't track them, and vehicles exiting the base were launched at highly elevated angles to avoid the possibility of collision with incoming vars. Tower grunted against the g-forces; he had experienced less violent hot zone extractions.

Once clear of the base, Baby reassumed control and leveled out the var. They were heading east, in the direction of the Morchardese compound a few towers south of Embassy Row.

"Where to, boss?"

"It depends. Ring Victor and see if Hildy wants to come along for the ride."

To his surprise, she didn't complain, but complied without comment. A moment later, he heard the detector's voice and her face appeared superimposed on the left corner of the cockpit. He could see an open floorplan bustling with activity behind her. She smiled at him.

"I didn't expect to hear from you so soon, Chief Tower."

"We strive for efficiency at MCID. I thought you'd like to know that the case is yours. XAR is viewing it as a civilian homicide barring any conclusive evidence to the contrary. I'm to liaise with TPPD, render all due assistance, and so forth."

She whooped and mimed blowing him a kiss. "Thank you, Tower! You won't regret it!"

"*Yes, you will,*" Baby predicted.

He ignored her.

"So, now that the case is yours, how do you feel about dinner and an interrogation?"

"Well, I do enjoy travel, long walks on the beach, and enhanced interpellation techniques," she said, looking vacant and twirling her hair with a finger. Then she laughed and Tower felt that he might have just fallen in love. "Actually, I ate at my desk. Who do you have in mind, the royal family? Can we use any special military methodologies?"

"Too bad. Yes, and no. Major Zeuthen wants to keep an eye on the Morchardese in case there turns out to be a xeno angle to it, so I have to review their security. I figured you'd be contacting them for questioning in the next day or two, so…"

"Want me to meet you there?"

"I just left base, so I can pick you up in about 15 hectasecs if you like."

"I do like. Let me try to get this report filed then, and I'll meet you at the Level 316 visitor parking."

"Roger. See you then."

"Thanks, Tower. Hildreth out."

After she closed the line, they flew in silence for a few decasecs. Tower waited and braced himself, knowing it was coming. Then the var suddenly banked sharply to the left, throwing him hard against his restraints, as Baby turned toward the bright lights of the city center in a much more aggressive manner than was strictly necessary. There we go, he thought. He was relieved that she'd gotten it out of her system now, rather than waiting until Hildy was in the var.

He leaned back and smiled. It might not be an actual date per se, in the sense that his female companion had any idea of his level of personal interest in her. And, to be honest, invading the privacy of a grief-stricken family would not have been his first choice for an evening out with Trans Paradis Police Department Sub-Orbital Detector Derin Hildreth. It would not have even made the top ten. On the other hand, this marked the first time in eight years that he was on his way to pick up an attractive woman for a night out together, and if that wasn't a healthy step forward, well, psychotherapeutic neural optimization and re-stabilization could suck it for all he was concerned.

A Crisis of Hegemony, or general Crisis of the State, is a Crisis of Authority. These kinds of Crises represent the moment at which a genuine revolutionary Assault on the Old Order can occur, as the various societal Interests are propelled into Action to try and resolve the failures of the Ruling Class. On Zhuhai, the Crisis of Authority was triggered by the continued malinvestments of the House Dai Zhan in the face of economic breakdown and widespread unemployment. On Morchard, a similar Crisis occurred but the alliance of the Corporate Interests with the Revolutionary Forces proved sufficient to topple the Monarchy.

—"A History of the Revolution on Morchard", Graham Eccles-Hamlin

Nineteen Eighty Three Eight Ten North Balustrade, a silver and bronze tower topping out at a mere three hundred stories, was only about nine hectasecs from the police station. A spire of glowing orange light capped its uppermost floor. Every ten floors or so were blank walls in the place of glass; presumably the high-security floors where various royal families or other security-conscious residents lived. The Morchardese residence comprised eighteen floors, beginning at the two hundredth.

Tower eased back on the aerovar's accelerator. He angled in gently toward the structure. Red bars and the number "20 M" flashed on his display, and the controls abruptly ceased to respond to his action. The car shuddered and began to slowly turn so the vehicle was alongside the building rather than pointing toward it.

"*Proximity override. We have reached the twenty meter zone and the building augment has arrested our flight. I am informed their grav tractors will bring us inside shortly. But you have to shut down the manual controls first.*"

"Manual disengaged. Let them take us in and remember to play nice with their building, please."

"*His name is Matyas, and he appears to be functional, if congenitally retarded.*"

"Does he have the Morchardese protocols."

"*Got 'em. Do you want them yourself?*"

"For both of us, please."

A stream of images and sounds coursed into Tower's head. Beside him, he heard Hildy grunt softly as Victor permitted Baby to send the data to her as well. He registered the flood of information little more than a faint perception at the edge of his consciousness, as if he was hearing someone sitting behind him talking in a low whisper. But someone who was talking very, very fast, and in a manner that allowed him to understand and recall every single word.

"*Download complete.*"

"Thanks, Baby." He spoke too soon. The headache hit him like a lightning bolt between the eyes.

"She doesn't have the deftest touch, does she." Hildy winced as she massaged her temples.

"There was a lot of information," Tower lied.

Knock it off, Baby, or I'll turn you off when I come back.

"*Sure you will.*" She scoffed at his threat.

The armored var came to a complete halt ten meters from the building and hung there, motionless, suspended in space some 600 meters over the street. Traffic continued racing past on his left in colorful blurred lines. The vehicle shook as the building took it in its gravitic hold and twisted it, turning it toward the building and pulling it toward a grey ferrocrete wall with an adaptive interweave, as evidenced by the crystalline grid barely visible on its surface. The windows of floors above and below were turned a dark smoky orange by the setting sun. Just as the nose of the var was about to touch the wall, it split open and ushered them into an empty hangar compartment that glowed with red lights.

Everything shook from side to side as the vehicle stopped and the tractor beam shut down. The red lights inside the hangar suddenly turned green with a loud pop that was audible inside the var. It was not confidence inspiring to think this creaky old gravity system had been the only thing holding them supported in space a pair of decasecs before.

"Power down." Tower released their harnesses and rolled his shoulders. He popped the canopy and the smells of ionized air and hot plastics filled his nose. The thrum of the aerovar's engines died in a low grumble. "I hoped you enjoyed the ride, Detector Hildreth."

"I did indeed. Thank you, Tower. And thank you, Baby."

"My pleasure," Tower said, surreptitiously checking his Sphinx. He was unsurprised to see the passage of a few kilosecs hadn't drained the ammo cartridge, but it was a habit. "You want point on this?"

"If you don't mind," Hildy smiled at him. "I suggest we divide and conquer. You work on the theory it's political, and I'll assume it's personal."

Tower nodded. It would have been hard to resist that smile; fortunately he didn't have to. "Hildy, I need to tell you something. If it is political, it could be dangerous. There are very good reasons MCID handles xeno-politicals instead of your department."

"I'm not worried." She winked at him and squeezed his armored arm. "I brought a big strong soldier boy along, didn't I?"

He had no response except to resist the urge to smile back and hope he wasn't blushing.

They stepped out into the hangar. Tower found himself facing his mirror image in the polished onyx wall opposite. There was a single hatch, just wide enough for two people to walk through side-by-side, assuming neither of them were much taller than he was.

"How old is this building anyhow?"

"*It was constructed in 3162. It has seen better days, but it is quite popular among exiles; there are 27 former monarchs and heads of state resident here. Also, you should probably be informed a Morchardese guardsman approaches.*"

"Thanks, Baby." Tower ran his hand through his hair, to little effect. He tugged at his tactical jacket and brushed a stray hair off his right sleeve. It was blond; he glanced over at Hildy and saw that she was zipping up her vest to cover her exposed throat and patting her hip to reassure herself that her pistol was still there. She was definitely his kind of girl, he thought to himself.

The lift door to their right opened and the guardsman strode into view. The man was huge, at least two meters tall, with arms thick as Tower's neck. He wore body armor the color of iridescent pearl, decorated with gold and silver traceries. It was flexible and when he stepped out of the lift, it moved with him as if it was an external skin. Blue lights blinked on a curvy white interface unit bulging under his left ear, and in his right hand he held a staff that was as long as he was tall. A wickedly barbed scythe topped the staff.

"Abase yourselves, all those who request entrance into the royal demesne." His tone was clipped, and he pronounced his TH as if it was the letter D. His eyes were even more unnerving than his massive size. Their irises were bright orange, the royal color of the Kingdom of Morchard. Tower rather doubted it was natural.

"Chief Warrant Officer Graven Tower, Military Crimes Investigative Division, and Detector Derin Hildreth of TPPD." Tower summoned the directions for Morchardese protocol that Baby had ready for him. A diagram and lines of text ghosted over his view out of his right eye. "We request permission to enter the Realm."

"The petitioner indicates respect by kneeling on the left knee, slowly. Maintain eye contact. If entry to the royal domain is permitted, the royal guard will extend his staff and tap upon the right shoulder to signify authorization has been granted."

Tower lowered himself to one knee and Hildy quickly followed suit. Tower stared at the guardsman, fighting down the urge to look away from those gaudy orange eyes. The barb descended quickly onto his shoulder. The guardsman repeated the ritual act with Hildy. Then he stepped back and gave them room to rise before turning and indicating that they should follow him. Tower eyed the elongated weapon warily.

"The queen has graciously granted you entrance and audience."

What is that thing, Baby? That's not a staff; it looks like he could behead us with it!

"Lingan Arms X-54 Poleblade. The blade is charged and is capable of cutting through your tactical armor. The butt end conceals a five-shot projectile cannon… Tower, so3(#tqng iiiiiiiiis ifne9fin wJo2+g block-block-block-block-bl8 ^-~"

Her garbled voice trailed off. Tower was more confused than alarmed. Didn't she say the building's brain was stupid? How could a centuries-old building outwit a reasonably up-to-date military augment?

The guard suddenly stopped and turned around. He tapped his earpiece, then nodded, all the while staring at Tower with those creepy orange eyes.

"Chief Tower, I regret to inform you that authorization to enter the Realm is not granted to artificial denizens. All neural communications with the military base's server will be suspended until you depart from the Realm. I trust this will not cause you any difficulties." He nodded and turned around again.

"Easy for him to say, he won't have to deal with her when we get back to the var," he whispered to Hildy. She smiled and shook her head. It seemed Victor was rather less put out.

The guard led them into a lift that took them up to the 213th floor.

The doors hissed open and revealed a corridor of the same décor as the docking level. The difference here was the red-leafed spike ferns that waved as the guardsman walked by. Tower and Hildy stopped as the guardsman paused before a set of massive oak doors. A small orange banner with four silver stars at center hung on each one. The guardsman tapped with the curved metal of the scythe. It made a very distinctive thud against the wood.

The doors slid open. Two more guardsmen, equally massive, stood at attention just inside the threshold. Instead of weird archaic weaponry, each was holding a near-stock Madsen-Saetter PMP 42, a melee range assault laser which Tower had never particularly liked due to its tendency to rise rapidly in burst mode. They might have been twins, with identical orange eyes, pale complexions, and close-cropped brown hair. Tower wondered if cloning was permitted on Morchard or if their guards were just highly inbred. He started to ask Baby, then remembered she'd been cut off.

Their escort admitted them into a broad sitting room. The windows looked over a beautiful view of central Trans Paradis at night. The flickering lights of aerovars streamed in currents at various heights, like fish swimming in long, slender schools between the massive trunks of submerged trees.

In the center was a desk, flanked by two lounge sofas. In an ornately carved chair with orange fabric behind the desk sat an older woman. Her white-streaked grey hair bound up in a bun, and there were deep lines on her face. She had once been attractive, perhaps even very attractive, but only the ghost of her former beauty still survived the years. Her eyes were a dark, expressive brown, and their whites were red, presumably from crying. She wore a silver crown with a single orange jewel at the center.

When she stood, the guards dropped gracefully to their knees. Tower couldn't access the protocol, but he nudged Hildy and the two of them rather more clumsily did the same. But he kept her eyes locked upon her face, and from her complete lack of surprise or agitation, he surmised that she not only knew why they were there, but had been awaiting them.

"Please rise, officers." Her voice was calm and coolly controlled. "Am I correct in assuming your visit is connected to the fact that my son's signal was interrupted at 16:52 this afternoon?"

"Yes, your highness, if you are the mother of Arpad Vladislaus Jagaelleon."

"I am Beatrice Jagaelleon, and in addition to being the Queen of the Realm of Morchard, I am Arpad's mother. Do you have word of him?"

Tower could see that she was bracing herself for bad news, even as her eyes seemed to plead with him to tell her that it was all a mistake, a technical failure, an untimely sunburst, anything that would suffice to explain the way in which her son's vital monitor had abruptly shut down.

Hildy smoothly took the lead. "Your highness, I regret to inform you that your son Arpad's remains were positively identified earlier this evening from his genetic record on file with the immigration authority. We are sorry for your loss."

The queen was a brave woman. Although she swayed for a moment, as Hildy's news were a punch that had shaken her, neither shock nor grief touched her calmly dignified face. Tower couldn't help but admire the way the woman was holding herself together. He knew well what a terrible price she was paying inside to maintain such flawless composure.

"We feared as much." Her voice started to crack, and she cleared her throat. "The royal augments informed us at once when his signal failed, but the thought was that it was merely a technical failure. Was it an accident? Or was it… was it something else."

"I am afraid we have reason to believe your son was the victim of a criminal homicide, your highness."

She nodded her head. Tower could see she had been expecting as much. Again, not even a flicker of surprise crossed her face.

"May I ask what happened, Detector?"

Hildy glanced at Tower and he nodded. Dissembling would achieve nothing but to lose the confidence of the family. In the absence of a body, there would be no hiding what happened. "It appears your son was struck by a single disruptor burst. He would have died instantly. That is why his monitor went off-line, it was destroyed."

"Was the killer caught?"

"Regrettably, no, your highness. Not yet. A homicide investigation has been initiated by TPPD. And, as you can see by the Chief Warrant Officer's presence, MCID is assisting with our investigation. I'm very sorry, but I have to ask. Would it be possible for us to ask you and some of the members of your household a few questions about your son? I know it is hard to think about this right now, but the more information we have, the faster we can identify your son's killer and bring him to justice."

"Yes, of course, anything, anything," the queen replied.

"Thank you very much, your highness." Tower cleared his throat and Hildy was quick enough to catch his meaning. "Your highness, would it be possible for our connections to our augments to be restored? It is an unusual request, but we really do need to record these conversations so that we'll have a complete record for future reference."

The queen nodded, studiously ignoring the unobtrusively shaking head of the guard captain to Tower's right. She glanced at Tower and smiled faintly as she met his eyes.

"I imagine the alternative is being required to submit to interrogation in your offices."

"Only those who are possible suspects," Tower said. Was that a spark of anger in her eyes? Or was it something else? He reminded himself that this was a formidable woman who had survived a revolution and was very accustomed to getting her own way. "Your highness, the detector is correct. Access to these recordings will significantly aid her investigation."

"Very well." The queen closed her eyes, no doubt talking to her own augments. Then she opened them again. "As a general rule, we do not permit constructs who have not taken a loyalty oath to the crown and cannot perform an act of submission to enter the Realm. It is too dangerous; a single enemy construct could wipe out the monarchy. However, these are highly unusual circumstances and your credentials are legitimate, so if you can assure me that your augments are loyal to the Duke of Rhysalan and are not in service to any exoplanetary agencies, I will accept a single passive link."

"Thank you, your Highness," Hildy said. She glanced at Tower. "I think Baby would be the wiser option."

Wiser, safer, it was all the same. If Tower chose Victor over her, he'd never hear the end of it. "I concur."

Baby, you there?

"*That sneaky machine caught me off guard. I wasn't expecting a T-15 war-brain in this shabby dump! Sorry boss, it won't happen again. He's tricky, but I used that link to tie his circuits into knots. That'll teach him! Now, what do you need?*"

Just record interviews for now… and don't let the augment remember you!

She flashed an image of a bear sitting on a toilet into his right eye. He laughed and took the point. Hildy was already asking questions of the Morchardese queen.

"Your highness, did your son have any enemies here on Rhysalan? Was there anyone who you suspect would have had an interest in harming him?"

"Enemies? Detector, my son had thousands of enemies who very badly wanted him dead. Perhaps even millions. He was the Crown Prince of Morchard, the symbol of the continuation of the planetary monarchy, and a living rebuke to the forces that forced us to flee our world!" Queen Beatrice's voice hardened. "The usurpers who call themselves the Auroran Republic would pay anything to end the

Morchardese royal line. They are without question the most likely candidates and they have an embassy here."

"Here in Trans Paradis?"

"No," the queen replied with undisguised bitterness. "As a *recognized* government, they are permitted an *official* embassy in the capital. After them, I would name the government of Valatesta, whom my eldest son defeated in a trade war ten years ago. One of the Tetrarch's sons was killed in a space bombardment and he swore a public vow that all three of my sons would pay for his death in blood."

Tower was skeptical. Ten years was a long time for an angry and powerful man to wait to avenge a son, and perhaps more importantly, if Arpad's death was a revenge-killing, he would have expected the Tetrarch to order his assassin to leave some indication of that. He spoke up before Hildy could ask her next question.

"Was there any contact from the Tetrarch or any other Valatestan party today?"

"No," the queen shook her head. "No, there was not."

Hildy shot a silent question at him. Tower shrugged and explained his thoughts.

"It's probably not the Valatestan. If the hit was his, then he would have wanted you to know. If there is no contact from them in the next week or so, we can safely back-burner them. Who else is there?"

"There are many who are seeking to curry favor with the usurpers. Corps seeking tax benefits, planets seeking trade agreements, individuals attempting to join the jackals and share in their spoils. The longer the crown is absent from Morchard, the more insects crawl out from under their rocks. We are watching them and we will not forget! But if it wasn't the usurpers, then I believe the Unity is behind this. I have long feared it and no one will ever convince me that the Dawn are anything more than its Morchardese puppets. Without the Unity backing that gang of bandits and psychopaths, my husband would have crushed the rebellion."

"Has either the Unity or the Morchardese, ah, usurpers, made any attempts on your son's life in the past?"

The queen exchanged a glance with the guard captain, and the building AI relayed his answer to her.

"Four, assuming that one does not count the rebellion itself. Arpad slew the man sent to kill him; the assassin was disguised as a bodyguard. He slit the man's throat from ear to ear, then shot the assassin who was after his younger brother!" Her fierce pride in her late son was unmistakable. "But all four subsequent attempts were in the first two years. It has been quiet for some time now."

"Do you know who was responsible for the attempts?" Hildy said.

"The first was the rebels. The second was a fool, a member of the household staff who thought to ingratiate himself with the new regime by bringing them the Crown Prince's head. The other two were unknown, which is why I suspect the Unity."

"And why is that?"

"The prince's security team shot and killed the first assassin, the augment killed the other when he was attempting to infiltrate the Realm. DNA tests of their corpses determined that both men were Kwai Tao clones manufactured on Yama."

Tower whistled. "Someone wasn't playing around."

"That was prior to the Weksler Accords three years ago. There was a minor sub-clause in which the Unity provided assurances that the heirs to the Morchardese throne would be left alone as long as all of them stayed here, on Rhysalan. They kept their word."

"But the Weksler Accords were abrogated six months ago!" Hildy interjected. "When House Sphorza invaded Nizhni-Rostov.

"Exactly." The queen nodded. "Neither we nor the usurpers were involved, so I hoped the Unity would continue to honor the spirit of the sub-clause, even if the overall accords were no longer in effect. But it appears that was a foolish hope."

Her voice trailed off. Tower was losing interest in the queen; the more he thought about the situation and the risk inherent in the prince's situation, the more he was interested in learning where the prince's security detail had been. That, it seemed to him, was more important than unraveling the undoubtedly complicated skein of relationships between the various members of the royal household. He cleared his throat to catch Hildy's attention.

"Do you mind if I tackle the staff while you continue with the family?"

She did not, for which Tower was glad. He did not relish the idea of hounding an old woman about her son's love life and he didn't mind the idea of setting a few of these Morchardese quasi-clones straight on the matter of who was, and who was not, in charge here.

What is the name of Orange Eyes there?

"*Prime Captain Bram Kotant. He is the head of security for the crown prince.*"

So he's the screw-up, is he?

"Prime Captain," Tower addressed the huge guard with the staff. "The prince had a security detail, did he not?"

The man stared coolly at him, and for a moment, Tower thought the Morchardese might ignore his question. "He did."

Tower spread his hands. "Then where were they?"

"That is not information the Realm is prepared to divulge."

"Seriously?" Tower indicated the queen. "You don't think she'll tell you to tell me what you know if I ask?"

"I know she won't." The guard smiled faintly; it was very nearly a smirk. "The Crown Prince left very clear orders that no information concerning his security or his location, past or present, was to be divulged. Even in the event of his death."

"But you have the location data from his tag in your core."

"No, sir. We were under long-standing orders from him to purge all such information on a daily basis. I personally gave the order to purge it at once when we received word that your vehicle was approaching the building."

"*He's probably not lying,*" Baby informed him. "*I don't dare look too closely, but there are huge sectors of what looks like recently erased sectors.*"

"Why would you do that?" Tower didn't know if he was more baffled or angry.

"Because neither you nor the detector have any need of that information."

"How do you know that? Don't you want us to catch whoever did this to your prince?"

The guard didn't answer, he simply stared contemptuously at Tower with those eerie orange eyes. And suddenly, Tower realized that the Prime Captain didn't want either MCID or TPPD to capture the killer: He intended for the Morchardese security forces to get there first. Only the man obviously had no intention of capturing anyone.

He came to a quick decision and decided not to fight the inevitable. "Can you provide the detector with transportation back to the department when she is finished with the royal family?"

"Of course, Mr. Tower." The Prime Captain nodded graciously. "It would be our pleasure."

"Then please do so when she is finished," Tower said, and turned on his heel and strode toward the exit. The guards were almost too surprised to step out of his way, and the Prime Captain had to scramble to catch up to him.

"You are leaving, Mr. Tower?"

"I am." Tower didn't say anything more until the Prime Captain had escorted him out to the parking launch. "Now, listen to me, Prime Captain. If you and your men don't wish to cooperate, it's no skin off my nose. But if you and your men think you're going to start a private war on this planet, in this city, then you had better think again. Because as far as MCID is concerned, you bloody xenos can all kill each other to your heart's content so long as you do it off-planet."

"We will do as honor requires," the Prime Captain said. "And if there is a war, it is not one we sought nor is it one we started."

"You just don't get it, do you, Prime Captain." Tower shook his head. "The Duke don't care who started what. MCID cares even less. We're not the police and we don't solve crimes. I'm warning you, Captain, if you bring war to Trans Paradis, no matter who started it, I'm the one who will end it. And if that means I have to end you and every orange-eyed bastard in this building in the process, then you can be certain that's exactly what will happen. So, if you do manage to determine who was responsible on your own, I strongly suggest you contact Detector Hildreth and provide that information to her."

The Prime Captain stared down at Tower for a long moment. Although he didn't appear to be impressed with Tower's threats, he apparently wasn't disposed to ignore them either. At last, he nodded.

"I will take that under advisement, Mr. Tower. And then, I will do my duty. You, I am certain, will do the same." He stepped back and the automatic doors slid shut, banishing Tower from the Realm.

Loss of Sanctuary Status: Criminal Conviction

A Sanctuary contractee granted permanent residence can lose his residence status and be deported to his planet of origin if he is convicted of one or more felonies. The Immigration Office has some discretion to place the convicted criminal's residence status on probation rather than remove it entirely, but its decision will be influenced by the seriousness of the xeno-resident's criminal record. Capital crimes committed by Sanctuary contractees, including but not limited to insurrection, assassination, and murder, are the responsibility of the Military Crimes Investigation Division of His Grace's Armed Forces.

—*Welcome to Rhysalan, A Guide to Your New Planetary Home*

The next day, Tower returned to MCID-HQ, ensconced himself in his office, shut the door, and resigned himself to reviewing the pile of statements that Baby and Hildy had stacked up in his personal cloud. He leaned back in his chair and, not for the first time, wished that he didn't have to share the space with three other MPs. Their office was about the same size as the major's, with four desks, four chairs, and a couch suitable for two against the far wall. There were a few screens on the three walls plus a holo-projector mounted to the ceiling above his desk, just the standard office equipment. Everything was pallid grey and MCID dark blue. The screens displayed camviews of the base outside, as if they were windows. The cams were about thirty meters above the rooftop landing pad for the aerovars, and he could see the base traffic as it entered and exited in two distinct vertical flight paths. Beyond the edge of HQ, the screens provided a nice view of the High Market stretching out for six city blocks. When zoomed in, one could see the civilians milling about the walkways, three hundred stories off the ground.

The immigration office had sent over complete entrance records for the Kingdom of Morchard's mountain of staff: guards, aides, techs, servitors, nobles, cooks, pilots, soldiers, and more. Hildy had also sent him the regular roster schedules, so he set Baby to comparing the two and looking for potentially useful patterns, but he had no real hopes on that score. There was no reason to assume that on what turned out to be an unusual day, the regular schedule would have been in effect.

Hildy had also given him access to the interviews she'd conducted after he left. He noted that the last interview wasn't finished until 25:30 and wondered if she was upset with him or not. He summoned it and one Lieutenant Dieter Ten Hannis appeared as a face in the air over his desk, a ghostly holographic version of the young bodyguard Hildy was questioning. "The Crown Prince did not say, officer. He gave me an express order to remain at the cafe until he returned or summoned me to him. No, this was not the first time he went off on his own."

"Did you notice anything different this time?" Hildy's voice sounded tired. It had been her tenth interview and she was obviously flagging.

"Yes, officer. He was agitated, perhaps even angry. The Crown Prince is, was, a gracious man for as long as I knew him. But this afternoon, there was something bothering him. Of course, he told me nothing and I did not ask. It was not my place."

Ten Hannis confirmed what the embassy logs reported: the prince took the lift to the street level in his company, something only those with a sufficiently high security clearance could do. He didn't make use of a var, but walked to the nearby cafe where he told the guard to wait for him. From there, he disappeared from the digital records. Without access to the location data from his personal tag, once he moved out of range from the security scanners at the front of the building, he may as well have been a ghost.

"No additional sightings of the prince reported at any cameras up or down the street, sir," Baby said. In the office, and when they were alone, he preferred to hear her speak out loud. "Quarpods have been displaying his image to civilians in the area since early this morning but so far have been unable to identify any witnesses."

"There isn't much commerce down there. A witness is unlikely." Tower drummed his fingers on the desk. "The question is how did he get from the building to where he died? How long by var?"

"Twelve point seven five decasecs."

"Run the taxis and private transport services. He had to get there somehow and he's a royal. He didn't walk."

"On it. This may take a while, though. Some of the private services are a bit less than forthcoming."

Tower dialed up a mocha in an attempt to kickstart his brain. Before it had cooled enough to drink, Baby spoke up sooner than he'd expected.

"Victor just buzzed me and wants to know if you're free to speak with Detector Hildreth. He says she's been sorting through the profiles of all the embassy staff and is cross-checking their DNA with fragments taken at the scene."

Tower smiled. If she was calling him already, she couldn't be too upset.

Her image didn't appear, only her voice, leading him to believe she was out in the field.

"I can't believe you abandoned me like that!"

"Yeah, sorry about that." He laughed. "It was a good thing you passed on dinner or I might have left you with the check."

"Congratulations, you were officially my worst first date ever."

He laughed again. "I had no choice. That giant clone of a security captain made it clear he was going to stonewall us and I figured the royals would clam up if I shot him or hauled him in."

"Yeah, I figured it was something like that. Can you believe they deleted the tag data? Why on Earth would they do that?"

"Think it was an internal hit?" That was the obvious explanation. "Maybe little brother decided he wanted to be king-in-exile. Or maybe the Crown Prince was practicing droit du royale with the girlfriend of the wrong guard. Did anything come up in your interviews?"

"I sent them to you!"

"Yes, and I've watched two, the queen and the guard who was with him that day. I'm asking about the other eight."

"Oh, sorry. I guess the main takeaway was that this crown prince doesn't strike me as the smartest guy on the planet. Why risk going out in public without your bodyguards on a regular basis? He knew he was potentially being targeted. It practically screams 'kill me!' "

"Do we know if he was armed?"

"Scanners showed no serious traces of metal and he didn't have a permit, which he would have required as a xeno."

"He wasn't expecting trouble. So, if it wasn't a political hit and it's not little brother, my guess is that there is a girl somewhere underneath all of this."

"You think?" She laughed. "What you soldier boys see may be different, but on this end, if it isn't money, it's usually women. And based on the Morchardese financial records, it wasn't money. The royal house nearly stripped the planet naked when they left!"

"Can't blame the rebels for wanting them dead, in that case."

"Agreed. Anything on that side yet?"

"Not much, other than a roster of all known Unity, Valatestan, and Auroran operatives presently on the planet."

"Dare I ask?"

"Three hundred seventy two, fifty eight, and five, respectively."

"Ouch. Any here in TP?"

"One hundred and eight definites. Another eighty five possibles."

"I don't envy you the interviews."

"Yeah, we don't exactly work like that." He chuckled at the idea of telling Major Zeuthen that he was going to spend the next month trying to find and interview nearly two hundred spies, diplomats, and assassins. MCID's usual policy on the rare occasion that a suspected killer was dumb enough to remain on the planet was to drag him in, pump him full of Penta-117, and beat a confession out of him before returning the body to his embassy. He changed the subject. "Any luck with the DNA?"

"If by any luck you mean lots of negatives, then yes. They call it the swamps for a reason, Tower. There's enough DNA fragments swimming in the muck down there for me to ID an entire mob. Few of whom appear to be able to afford an illegal slug-thrower, let alone a military disruptor."

"Pity he couldn't have conveniently died of an overdose."

"That would have made more sense. There are a couple of traces I want to run down, but I'm not feeling any of them. I'll let you know what turns up."

Tower nodded. "You are a credit to the species, Detector Hildreth. And I hope you will accept my sincere apologies for so rudely leaving you stranded amidst the barbarians."

"Accepted. I survived their savage indignities. Actually, your friend the Prime Captain sent me home in a Zaoyang-Daimler, complete with an open bar."

"Decent of him." Tower mentally deducted two demerits from his grudge against the Morchardese officer. "Why don't you have Victor pair up with Baby and the two of them can parse the statements for any more common threads? She's got a bit more brainpower, so that might speed things up a little."

"Well, I do believe you are forgiven in full, Officer Tower."

"You're too kind. Tower out."

"Likewise," she said crisply and cut the connection.

Tower leaned back and rubbed at his eyes. He very much hoped there was a girl, because if there wasn't, the chances that an assassin professional enough to hit and vanish without a trace had already left the planet were exceedingly high. Of the one hundred ninety-three known operatives who were believed to have been in Trans Paradis yesterday, seven were already off-planet and outside MCID's reach.

He called up the seven pictures. Only one, an evil-looking security officer with House Novgorov with twelve years military experience, appeared likely. He'd arrived on Rhysalan eight months ago, spent most of it in the capital with six trips to Trans Paradis, and twelve days ago had booked a second-class ticket for Tyrfan, a Tech 17 Unity planet, one-way. He arrived in Trans Paradis three days ago, returned to the capital yesterday, and boarded the shuttle to the transorbital platform about five kilosecs after Tower and Hildy arrived at the Morchardese embassy.

The schedule was tight, but it was possible. And since he'd traveled to the shuttle via suborbital pod, that meant he'd have to have stashed the disruptor and the cloaksuit somewhere in Trans Paradis.

"Find me everything you can on this Ninar-Tikhan Obukhov. Check security cams, debit scans, and map his route yesterday against whatever we have on Prince Arpad."

Five kilosecs later, he was staring at a moderately complicated knot that wound its way through the ghostly city of Trans Paradis hovering above his desk, swearing softly under his breath. While the Novgorovi had very likely been up to something to which the ducal authorities would take exception, whatever it was had not involved murdering the Morchardese prince. However, the red herring had provoked an interesting thought. The disruptor had to go somewhere and there was enough demand on the black market for such a weapon that it might well surface while he was waiting for the hypothetical xenoplanetary parties to take the expected crack at the younger prince. Assuming, of course, that this wasn't all a dispute over a woman, or, for that matter, a parking space.

"*Someone is here to see you. Two someones,*" Baby informed him silently.

He stood up and the door opened. To his surprise, Detector Hildreth was standing there and was accompanied by a young girl.

Tower blinked. The girl before him couldn't be older than nineteen. Her hair was blond, with startling streaks of orange, and wound up in an elaborate coiffure of curls and ringlets. Her eyes were a deep, chocolate brown and she had an interface implant just above her left ear, similar to the Morchardese bodyguards. She rubbed at the edge of her sleeve with her fingers. She was wearing an expensive grey skirt-suit with an orange sash about the waist. Morchardese, without a doubt.

"Detector," he greeted her with a query in his voice. "How did you get on base and where did you find Miss..."

"*Her name is Annaliese van de Boer. She's a communications assistant at the Morchardese embassy.*"

"van de Boer..."

"Chief Tower," Hildy greeted him, her eyes bright with self-satisfied amusement.

"Come in, both of you." It slid shut. Tower gestured toward the couch. "Please, sit."

The Morchardese woman obediently took a seat on the edge of the sofa. Hildy remained standing, her hands behind her back. "As Baby has no doubt informed you, this is Miss Annaliese van de Boer from the Morchardese embassy. She's a comm gal."

"Right." On cue a series of profiles flickered through the vision in his right eye, courtesy of Baby. It stopped on a smiling version of the pale, nervous girl before him. "And while I am naturally delighted to see you, Detector Hildreth, why is Miss van de Boer here?"

"I had a pair of drones that triggered on her departure from the embassy this morning. They intercepted her, checked her drive plan, and found out she was coming here to see you."

"Me?" Tower looked at the girl, astonished. "Why were you coming here, miss?"

"The Prime Captain said Prince Janos had ordered that no one on the staff was to talk to the police unless the police asked. But he was a little afraid of you, I think, and he was shouting at one of the data techs about MCID and how they weren't police. So, I knew I could talk to you without disobeying the prince's command."

"The Morchardese are very letter of the law," Hildy commented.

"Yeah, it would appear that way. What did you want to talk to me about?"

"Prince Arpad." Tears welled up in her eyes. "There was something I thought you should know."

"And what was that?"

"He had a girlfriend. She was a commoner. In the city."

Tower met Hildy's eyes. They were triumphant. He nodded in acknowledgment. This was exactly the breakthrough they needed, and best of all, was a strong indication that the case would soon be off his plate.

"Any idea why his bodyguards and his mother failed to mention this?"

"They did not know. None of them, although one or two of the guards, his personal detail, must have suspected it. He was unable to see her often, but I sent her messages a few times a week. He trusted me."

"And why is that?" Tower asked. "The two of you ever…"

"No, sir!" she sat bolt upright on the couch, an expression of horror on her face. "I would never! He was of the blood royal! I was loyal to him as my duty demanded!"

Hildy cocked her head at him and narrowed her eyes. He didn't need Baby to tell him what she was thinking.

"*Really?*"

Hey, it was a possibility.

"I apologize, Miss van der Boer." Tower licked his lips. "You have a name for us?"

"Mara. I can give you the comm code she used, but I don't know anything else about her. It was a blind shot, with no visuals or holos."

"That makes sense. Did anyone else at the embassy know about this?"

"There were three of us who handled his personal communications. We all knew. We never talked about it, but both of the others knew. I'm certain of it."

"And why is that?"

"Things they said, the way they looked when Prince Janos or the Prime Captain would tease Prince Arpad about him liking one of our girls."

"Miss Van de Boer, why was this such a secret?" Hildy looked skeptical. "Prince Arpad was a grown man. Why did he hide this woman from everyone in the embassy?"

"I am not sure, Detector." The girl twisted her mouth back and forth as she considered the matter. "I think that it would have been hard for everyone. The prince was very concerned about keeping up the spirits of the people. I think he felt the pressure, and maybe with this Mara, he could just be a man, not a prince who was destined to lead us back to our homeworld. He tried very hard to live up to his brother's memory, but that was not truly him."

"His brother the war hero," Tower said.

"Yes. Prince Arpad was a good man. We all loved him. He was sweet, and very kind. He was full of plans for how he would change things when we returned to Morchard. But he never spoke of how that would happen. He was not a warrior like Prince Pons-Radu or Prince Janos."

Tower remembered that this sweet peaceful prince who wasn't a warrior had nevertheless survived a professional hit and personally killed the pro with a dagger. He reflected that any violent confrontation with the Morchardese was best avoided if at all possible.

"Why was he called Crown Prince instead of King?" Hildy asked.

"The king can only be crowned at Rambaudt. Until we return to Morchard, a new king cannot be crowned."

"But for all intents and purposes, the senior prince is king, is he not? Or does the Queen rule in his stead."

The girl smiled. "Queen Beatrice is officially an advisor to the crown prince. But…"

"The princes tend to take their mother's advice." Hildy finished the girl's sentence for her. "She is a strong woman. I noticed that."

"How were Prince Arpad's relations with his brother," Tower broke in. "Did they get along, did Janos envy him the crown, or anything like that?"

The young Morchardese girl stared at him reproachfully. The distaste in her voice indicated her total contempt for his implication. "No, sir. I know what you are suggesting and it is impossible. Prince Janos admired Prince Arpad. He did not covet the crown; his only interest was regaining the planet for the monarchy. He was a true warrior, and if he envied anyone, he envied Pons-Radu his heroic death. There is no Morchardese man more honorable than Prince Janos and he would have died rather than question his brother's command. Never would he have raised his hand against his brother or against the crown!"

"All right, all right," Tower raised his hands in apology. "I'm very sorry, Miss Van de Boer, but it is our job to ask these questions and you are our best insight into the royal family."

She nodded, slightly mollified, and wiped away an angry tear from her left eye.

"I understand. I only want to help you catch whoever did this."

"If it had anything to do with this Mara, we'll get him," Tower assured her. "Will you permit my augment to retrieve the comm code from your interface?"

She nodded and pulled back the strands of blond hair that were covering the interface. It was a standard 64-pin HDI port and Tower had six different wireless transmitters that fit it in his desk. He withdrew one and handed it to her. She adroitly plugged it into the interface, then nodded at him.

Go ahead, Baby.

"*I've got it. Want me to pull the calendar schedule she's got in here too?*"

No, don't touch anything else. We don't have permission, a warrant, or probable.

"You can take it out now." Tower smiled at her in what he hoped was a reassuring manner. "Thank you so much, Miss Van de Boer. Your assistance has been precisely what we needed. Do you anticipate any trouble upon your return to the embassy?"

The girl looked at Hildy.

"She told them she was going shopping downtown. After I picked her up, Victor spoofed her tag, wiped the var's record of the intercept and sent it to the south lot at the Octoplaza. I'll bring her there and drop her off; she can hit a few stores and no one will be the wiser."

Tower nodded. *Is there anything left in the department kitty?*

"*Enough to buy an armored var if you leave off the missile rack.*"

Throw a cento into her account and book it to investigative expenses.

He rose from his chair and bowed slightly to the Morchardese girl. "Lunch is on MCID today, Miss Van de Boer. On behalf of the Duke of Rhysalan, I thank you for your civic service."

She flushed slightly, but rose gracefully off the coach and curtsied to him. "It was my honor to do my duty to the prince, sir."

He escorted her out of his office, and turned around to see that Hildy had lingered behind. She was smiling and shaking her head. "Excellent work, Detector Hildreth. Drones and a cut-out? I'm impressed. If you were a man, I might tell the major to recruit you."

"That's very flattering, but I'm more interested in helping people than killing them, Tower." She gestured toward the young woman waiting at the end of the hall. "Would you have any time this afternoon to pay a visit to this Mara or has MCID lost interest now that we know a girl was involved?"

"No, MCID remains very interested," Tower assured her. As he'd hoped, that inspired a smile from her. "If you're up for a second date, I promise not to bug out on you this time. I'll have her name, records, and current location before you drop Miss Van de Boer off at the mall."

"You're on. Can you pick me up at the station again? I have some paperwork to fill out. Some of us can't just claim all of our expenses as an imminent threat to planetary security."

"I don't know." Tower glanced back and eyed the pretty Morchardese girl. "She looks dangerous to me."

Hildy laughed and rolled her eyes. "Thanks, Tower. Touch me when you're good to go."

Tower nodded and enjoyed the sight of Detector Hildreth walking away from him. Her tight grey uniform pants nicely flattered her backside, an effect that was considerably enhanced, in his opinion, by high black leather boots and the GHK strapped to her side.

"*She didn't mean it that way, you know,*" Baby informed him. "*In fact, her vital signs show no evidence of a physical response indicating an attraction to you.*"

As the door opened, Detector Hildreth glanced back and waved at him. Tower simply nodded, and when the door closed, went back into his office. "The thing about being an *artificial* intelligence means that you can't possibly understand these *natural* urges of the sort that are quite clearly drawing our fair policewoman to me like an asteroid to a miner's stripship."

"Heart rates, elevated monoamine levels, dilated pupils, and core vaginal temperatures don't lie, Tower."

"Are you kidding me?" Tower quickly glanced around to see if anyone in the nearby offices had heard the augment. Fortunately, all of the nearby doors were closed or he would never have heard the end of it. "Zip it, Baby!"

"I am merely observing the lack of customary physiological changes–"

"Yes, thank you. Remind me to never bring you along on a real date."

"That is unlikely to be necessary seeing as you haven't been on one since–"

"Just find this Mara person, will you?"

Tower sat down heavily in his chair, wondering, not for the first time, if his life would be more easily lived without such technologically advanced augmented assistance.

Attractive young citizens. Beautiful, intelligent, and ambitious university students, aspiring actresses, and models. Are you struggling in the dawn of your career? Do you seek a comfortable lifestyle and the finer things in life? Are you in search of an experienced and sophisticated partner with whom you can expect to enjoy a mutually beneficial relationship?

—an advertisement for The Gentleman's Society for the Advancement of Interplanetary Relations

It didn't take long for Baby to hunt down the crown prince's secret paramour. The face of a very pretty young woman with a broad, fair-skinned face, short jaw, and unusually large eyes abruptly appeared in the space above his desk.

"This is Mara Tanabera, age 23, no husband or civil partnership. Born on Rhysalan, full citizen, only two exoplanetaries, both vacations to Arène Soleil three and five years ago. She resides on the 332nd floor of the Tower Flora and is employed as the second-shift hostess at Il Gatto Giallo in the Emeraldia."

"That sounds about right. Our late prince's secret depravities look downright respectable. Nothing in the destination unless she went there with someone interesting."

"Some sort of school group the first time, girlfriends the other."

"Nothing there, then. Got a current location?"

"She's at home. According to the restaurant's staff schedule, she'll be working tonight. Second shift starts at seventeen hundred. Do you want to see her before then?"

Tower thought about it. Hildy would be busy with paperwork for at least four kilosecs and the stress of being questioned at work would probably reveal faster results. He shrugged.

"No, but touch Victor and see if sixteen fifty works for Hildy. We can pick them up and be there in time for Happy Hour."

"They're in," she replied almost instantly. "Your blood sugar is crashing, why don't you eat something?"

"I will," he said absently. "But first, let's see what we can learn about this Auroran Republic. For all we know, Miss Tanabera may have ties to one or more of the xeno suspects. Either of those exo-holidays on Morchard, by any chance?"

Despite it not yet being the official end of the work day, the traffic in Trans Paradis was already well into rush hour. There was a steady stream of aerovars out on Resplendent, moving out from the center of the city toward the prosperous eastern suburbs. There, the soaring towers abruptly yielded to jagged cliffs of white ashstone. The Emeraldia jutted from the cliffs overlooking a broad cove, and as far as Tower was concerned had every right to the name. It looked like a giant green crystal had been dropped from orbit and lodged itself against the cliffs. Yellow lights glittered across a surface as smooth as his canopy.

"We're not going to eat here, are we?" Hildy said, sounding alarmed.

Tower smiled ruefully. It appeared TPPD didn't pay much better than the military.

"I'm sure we can find somewhere that isn't too ruinous."

"I doubt it," Baby interjected. "The average price of an entree of the three hundred twenty dining establishments is seven five point six four rads and Il Gatto Giallo is the twelfth most expensive."

"Maybe someone will be kind and give us a basket of bread," Hildy said, stifling a laugh. "If you shoot the waiter, can you expense it?"

"Do you know, I never thought to try it. Where is this Giallo place anyhow, Baby?"

A bewildering grid of blue lines instantly plastered themselves over Tower's right eye. Baby helpfully highlighted the restaurant at the upper left edge of the complex in yellow. It was a small establishment, but even coming at it from the other direction, the view was spectacular. A flashing red spot drew his attention to the parking inlet one level below the restaurant. He aimed the var at it and turned control over to the lot's augment, which smoothly parked them without incident between a very expensive grey Porsche ZH-920 with pseudo-missiles racked under its stub-wings and an even more expensive yellow Uda-Fermi Kanari. Not for the first time, Tower was glad the doors of the armored var opened up rather than out; a scratch on one of those beautiful beasts would eat up two months of his salary.

He and Hildy found themselves being smiled at in an alarmingly ingratiating manner by no less than eight parking attendants, although it was a pretty redhead in a short black skirt who showed them the way to Il Gatto Giallo, which name, he discovered, apparently had something to do with cats, particularly yellow ones. Mara Tanabera was even easier to find than he'd anticipated, as she was standing right in front of them at the hostess station, exchanging air kisses with a wealthy, silver-haired matron who was arm-in-arm with a handsome and considerably younger escort. Tanabera's hair was jet black now, cut much shorter than it had been in her ID holo, and close to her face. But it was unmistakably her. Her smile, when she flashed it at the older woman as she led them to their table, was downright radiant.

"No question why the Crown Prince picked her out of the crowd," Hildy murmured as they waited for the young woman to return.

She strode back in a businesslike manner that belied her jeweled micro skirt and gravity heels. The invisible supports of the latter made it look as if she was a ballerina tip-toeing on air. She beamed at the two of them, flashing the same brilliant smile she'd previously directed at the last couple. "Good evening, sir. Good evening, ma'am. We have two tables open if you don't mind sitting near the balcony. The view is wonderful, but some of our guests do find it a little overwhelming."

"I have no doubt they do." Tower lifted his badge out of his breast pocket and slid it on top of the reservation screen. There was no need to alarm the entire restaurant. "My name is Graven Tower, Miss Tanabera. I'm with MCID, and this is Detector Derin Hildreth of TPPD Homicide. We have a few questions for you. Would you be so kind as to step outside?"

After the young woman quickly summoned a replacement, a pretty blonde whose wide-mouthed smile was eerily similar to Miss Tanabera's, they followed her to a private room one level up that appeared to be some sort of VIP room. After they broke the news to her about Arpad Jagaelleon's murder, she sat quietly and stared out the window. Tower had to give her credit. She had shed a few tears, but showed no inclination to give way to grief-stricken theatrics. The broad smile was gone. The short jaw was set with something that he belatedly realized was not merely grief.

"*Her heart rate is elevated and blood pressure indicates increased circulatory activity,*" Baby observed. "*In the absence of any indications of sexual arousal, the most probable conclusion is that she is upset. Very upset.*"

You don't think it's the uniform? Before she could respond, he nodded at Hildy. It seemed best if she took the lead here.

"Miss Tanabera, I'm very sorry for your loss. Would you be able to answer a few questions about your relationship with Mr. Jagaelleon?"

The young woman nodded quickly and wiped a tear out of her left eye with a long-nailed finger.

"I'll help in any way I can."

"You were involved with Mr. Jagaelleon?"

"Involved?" The young woman laughed involuntarily. "You put it so delicately, officer! But yes, we were involved. Romantically, if that's what you're getting at."

"How long had you been involved?"

"Eleven months."

"And how long had you been acquainted with Mr. Jagaelleon?"

"It was about three weeks… I don't know, say, twelve months."

"Did Mr. Jagaelleon have any rivals for your affection?"

"Any rivals?" Hildy's question clearly took the young woman by surprise. "I don't know what you mean!"

"She means, were you involved with anyone else while you were with the prince?" Tower interjected. "Or were there any old boyfriends lurking about who objected to being replaced?"

Tanabera glared at both of them, first aiming her ire at Tower, then at Hildy. "What sort of girl do you think I am? Do you think I'm some sort of gold-digger who was only after Vladi for his money?"

"*Hildy says please, pretty please, shut up, Tower!*"

Tower closed his mouth and forced himself to lean back in his chair. Hildy coolly proceeded as if neither of the other two had said anything at all.

"We're only attempting to learn if there is anyone in Mr. Jagaelleon's extended circle of acquaintances who might have had a motive to kill him, Miss Tanabera. I'm sure you understand that jealousy and romantic rivalries are often connected to violence, particularly where very attractive young women are involved."

Whether it was Hildy's casually indifferent tone or the implied compliment she'd thrown out, the young woman's anger visibly dissipated. She nodded, and Hildy continued.

"Were you single at the time that you met Mr. Jagaelleon?"

"More or less. I mean, I was seeing one or two people, but it was nothing serious." She shrugged and half-grinned at Hildy. "You're pretty, you know how it is."

"Of course," Hildy nodded easily.

Of course? It took every last gram of Tower's self-control not to ask

Detector Hildreth what, exactly, she had meant by that. How it is? How is what?

"*Settle down, Tower, she's just mirroring. You really need to do something about your LDL level, boss. With the way your blood pressure just spiked there, I thought you were heading for a coronary.*"

Right, mirroring, of course. What else would it be? Hildy was a trained interrogator and a skilled professional who just happened to be extremely attractive to a broken-down soldier who hadn't been on a date in eight years, she wasn't anything like some gold-digging slag who kept six men on a string at a time. He tried to clear his mind of the image of Derin Hildreth as a smiling lapdancer, fawning upon a long line of xenos with strangely colored eyes in all the hues of the rainbow.

"*If you don't let me book that appointment with your therapist you've been putting off for three months, I'll book one with the other clinic,*" Baby threatened.

Fine, go ahead, Tower grumbled.

But it wasn't an idle threat. He'd spent six months in that other clinic and the Rhysalan military's idea of rehabilitation for extreme cases of post-trauma neural anomalies left more than a little to be desired. It wasn't as if Baby could actually know what he was thinking, but her ability to read his vital signs sure made it seem that way sometimes. He shook his head and tried to return his focus to Hildy's interrogation.

"So, at the time you met Mr. Jagaelleon you were seeing a waiter here as well as the older gentleman who was an Ascendancy diplomat."

At least Tanabera had the grace to look mildly embarrassed. "You make it sound so sordid when you put it that way, Detector! I mean, Enkobar was very sweet, and very kind, but we weren't, you know, involved, if you want to put it that way. I just accompanied him to a few parties at one embassy or another from time to time, and he would take me out to dinner, or to a game, or maybe bring me along on a little shopping trip to the capital sometimes."

Tower couldn't help himself. "But you weren't involved."

This time she looked more surprised than offended. "No, we were just friends. Like I said, he was a very sweet, very generous man."

"Must be nice," Tower commented, drawing a warning glance from Hildy.

Who is this Enkobar?

"*Enkobar Walrasian. Age 64, citizen of House Antony, resident for the last two years, four months. He's the Chief Undersecretary to the Ascendancy's Ambassador; came in with the current administration.*"

"But you were, shall we say, involved with one of your co-workers here."

"It was nothing serious." She smiled suddenly, as if at a recalled memory. "He was hot. We're young. We had a little fun together, that's all."

"And the name of this hot young gentleman?" Hildy sounded amused.

"Wicca." At the sight of their upraised eyebrows, Tanabera flashed the real version of her professional smile. "I know," she said, sounding amused. "He always said it was because he was magical in the sack."

Tower managed to keep his mouth shut. But it was hard.

"He wasn't really, but it was cute. We just sort of drifted apart right around the time I met Vladi. Wicca didn't care. I mean, he called me up late at night a few times, you know, like they do. But I didn't take him up on it and I'm sure he didn't have any trouble finding someone else who would. He's usually going out with one of the girls here, sometimes two. He's not the sort of man you get serious with, you know what I mean?"

"Sure," said Hildy, a little too easily for Tower's comfort. "I notice you refer to Mr. Jagaelleon as Vladi. Is that how he introduced himself to you? Did you know he was the Crown Prince of Morchard?"

"Not right away. He was different. He could have just been an executive of an interplanetary. He was polite, thoughtful, and he tipped well. Never said anything bad to the staff, even when they botched an order in back. Of course, it didn't hurt that he was handsome. You should have seen the girls maneuvering to get his table whenever he came in."

"How did you find out?"

"Word gets out. Sometimes the embassies inform us, you know, when the VIP wants to be treated like one. Can't stand them. You should see how they all try to lord it over us. We get those types in here all the time, with guards and advisors trailing them around like puppies, snapping their fingers and barking orders."

"Bet they tip well."

"They're not all bad." She shrugged and her expression softened. "Vladi wasn't that sort. I think after his third time here, one of the girls heard one of the other guests calling him "your highness". We make it a practice to learn as many names as possible, so Crystal and me looked up all the royal Vladimirs on the planet."

"How did he react to the wait staff knowing about his royal status?" Hildy asked.

"He didn't. He didn't know. I mean, he didn't until after we started dating."

"He told you?"

"Actually, I may have dropped a "your highness" at an inopportune time."

Hildy glanced at Tower, her amusement barely concealed. Tower shook his head. Women.

"Was he upset?"

"That I knew?" Tanabera smiled. "No, he just laughed."

"He didn't mind that you'd been researching him?"

"He said it was only fair, considering the background search his security team had done on me."

"Did you know about his political enemies?"

"Sure. Vladi talked about them every now and then. Used lots of words in Morchardese I didn't know. But he wasn't afraid of them. Nothing scared him. He liked to talk about the future, what he would do when they retook their planet and he was king."

"Like what?"

"Oh, I don't know, I didn't really pay a lot of attention to it." The woman shrugged and shook her head. "I mean, even if it happened, what would it have to do with me? I don't know much about crown princes and kings, but I'm pretty sure they don't marry waitresses from other planets. I liked him, I liked him a lot, but I knew it would be over the moment he was able to go back to Morchard."

"Sure," Tower made an effort to be more agreeable. "But do you remember if he was vengeful, or if he was looking for revenge? Could the possibility of his returning to power have scared a lot of people, maybe given them a little extra incentive to make sure it never happened even if it was pretty unlikely? I mean, stranger things have happened, right?"

"Revenge? Oh, no, not Vladi. He was always talking about how if only his father had been more open to reform, you know, given the common people a real say in how the planet was run, there wouldn't have been enough support for the rebels." She shook her head. "If anything, they'd have wanted to keep him alive if they knew what the alternative was. I remember he said once that his little brother, Prince Janos, would just as soon wipe the planet clean and start over. He was joking, Vladi, I mean, exaggerating, really, but I had the idea that his brother wasn't quite as forgiving as Vladi."

"Did you ever meet Janos?" Hildy asked.

"No, I never met anyone from the embassy once we started dating. Even the night he asked for my number, he was there with two of his local friends."

"You know their names?"

"Sure, I saw them many times after that; we usually met up with them and their girlfriends at Ascathel's apartment near here. Good guys. Pernys is a banker, and Ascathel is an executive with a company that has something to do with managing city traffic flows."

"*Want their data?*"

Maybe later, Tower replied. He was becoming increasingly skeptical that Jagaelleon's murder had anything to do with this girl or his personal life. In fact, the crown prince's secret life was turning out to be almost disappointingly normal. Who voluntarily hung out with bankers and traffic engineers?

Then he was leaping to his feet in unison with Hildy as separate alarms went off in their heads.

"Morchard!" she gasped.

"The embassy!" he shouted at her.

Mara Tanabera all but cringed in terror, holding up one arm crooked defensively over her face. She was staring fearfully at them, as bewildered by their strange burst of activity as she was alarmed. Tower saw Hildy trying to reassure her, but he had no time for that. He was already moving toward the exit while simultaneously trying to absorb the dynamic information Baby was force-feeding his mind.

Location 44.981667, -93.278333. External. Multiple shots fired: two lasers, four charged particles, one disruptor. One definite fatality, ID unknown, two possible casualties, ID X3040MO004500420034 and ID X3040MO004500421067. Seven units responding from TPPD. Audio sensors indicate shot order: disruptor discharge (unknown), CPG (GHK 707), CPG (GHK 707), Laser (unknown), CPG (GHK 707), Laser (unknown), CPG (GHK 707). 2 paramedical units responding from St. Cristobal General. SATT 445 on standby. Units Q45873927-3472 and Q8572925-8741 report secure horizontal blockade south of intersection with 74th avenue. Correction: one casualty, one definite casualty, ID X3040M0004500420034. Units F8348-4872 and F2783-7863 confirm en route to secure vertical blockade.

There was more, increasingly more, even as Hildy came flying down the stairs from the VIP room, her eyes showing relief when she saw that he was moving slowly enough to allow her to catch up. But despite the flood of information engulfing him, the gist of it was simple enough. The unknown assassin had struck again, this time on the street outside the Morchardese embassy.

City homicides this year will total slightly more than 700, marking the third year in succession of a declining murder rate, Lord Mayor Mondereth Platen said today. Trans Paradis had 702 killings as of this morning, according to Nikal Vorgna, a city spokesman for the Lord Mayor's office. The continued reduction in crime was attributed to the new data analysis augments acquired by the Trans Paradis Police Department two years ago. The record low was 571 in 3385; the record high was 18,477 in 3299, according to police statistics.

—"Homicides fall for third year in a row," the *Trans Paradis Times*, 3403.380

They hurtled through the official airlines of the city with sirens blaring, lights flaring, and Baby's emergency override sending bureaucrats and private citizens sufficiently well-connected to acquire public transponders spilling left, right, and downward out of their way. Tower was driving on manual, listening as Baby and Hildy took turns sharing information that was being divulged from the civilian and military nerve centers. According to the red light that kept blinking on his controls, his speed was "dangerously excessive" but Baby had overridden the override.

"The fatality is the assassin. I repeat, the fatality is the assassin," Hildy said as if she was simply repeating whatever Victor was telling her. "ID indicates Xeno–"

"ID X3042ML018493061," Baby interrupted. "Male Valatestan citizen by the name of Giuseppe Andrea Milazzo. Ex-military. Eight years in the Valatestan Deep Space Marines. Unmarried, no children. Two years on-planet serving as bodyguard to various visiting dignitaries. Employment nominally private, in reality front corporation owned in full by the Valatestan Embassy in Rhysalan."

"Looks like you get your case back, Tower." Hildy frowned and wrinkled her lip.

"What case? The targets nailed the hitter and I have no doubt the sponsoring embassy will very convincingly deny all knowledge of his actions and disavow any responsibility for them. If we lean on them hard enough, maybe they'll send a junior deputy undersecretary to the ambassador's chief food taster home and blame him after the fact, all the while vowing to never again do what they swear they didn't. A few weeks later, rinse and repeat with a new hitter, a new embassy, and a new target."

"Sounds like you know the drill."

"Not my first xeno," Tower said, a little bitterly. "You know what they say, embassy is just another way to spell invasion beachhead."

"Sounds frustrating." Hildy commented, looking slightly mollified. She wasn't the only one feeling disappointed. Sooner than he'd wanted or expected, he would have to fish or cut bait. It felt too soon to ask her out on a genuine date, and yet, Tower knew that if he didn't do it before the case came to a complete close, he would probably never find the courage.

The creaky old building in which the Morchardese embassy was installed came within sight. Tower slowed and began angling the car down toward the ground. The traffic parted, as before, and he eased the var onto the ground gracefully enough to merit a nod from Hildy. The vehicle had barely stopped before he and the detector were leaping out of cockpit and rushing toward the group of people, mostly Morchardese judging by their military stances, openly displayed weaponry, and similar attire, standing around the scene of the near-crime. He didn't see any sign of Prince Janos or the queen; if they'd been the targets, no doubt they'd already been hustled back inside to a secure location.

Paramedics were working on one man who was sitting up, looking rather dazed, amidst a pile of shattered glass and placrete that appeared to have come from the gaping hole in the building above them. That would have been the disruptor shot, Tower observed as he realized the man, whose arm was being bound, had been struck by the debris and was likely no more than an unlucky passerby. The dead Valatestan was about sixty meters away, to his right, lying in a sprawled heap on his side, the body warded by a pair of skittering quarpods who beeped and whirred and meaningfully focused their camera eyes on anyone who stepped too close to them. There was a scorch mark on the building behind the dead man about 150 centimeters off the ground, as well as two tell-tale bore holes of a charged particle beam.

"That was some nice shooting," Tower mused aloud as he mentally calculated the distance between the body and the entrance to the embassy building.

"What's that?" Hildy had been mumbling to herself, or rather, to Victor.

"Seven shots fired, six by the good guys, right? The assassin has just enough time to get one shot off and it didn't come within 30 meters of anyone in the Morchardese party. They fire six shots back, from at least fifty meters away, and get three hits. That's not bad."

"*Two hits, Tower. The third shot explains why the Valatestan only fired once. He couldn't shoot again. Look at the disruptor.*"

His right contact zoomed abruptly and focused on the area between the trigger guard and the charge pack. The disruptor, which he now saw was a Mosin-Nyarla Upsilon 32, a mid-tech military model known more for its rugged construction and heavy power suck than its accuracy, was ruined. It was very nearly blown in two. A section of the chunky, oversized bullpup design was simply missing, as if the designer had made a strange decision to narrow the section between the guard and the action on an otherwise solid weapon.

Laser or PPG?

"PPG. The edges are smooth, but they're cut, not melted."

Two Morchardese guards were approaching, one of them was Prime Captain Kotant, his orange eyes concealed by a pair of tactical lenses. His uniform jacket was open and he was wearing a GHK strapped under his left arm. Tower couldn't tell the model, but he was willing to bet it was a 707. The 707 was essentially an upteched version of the 405 slug-thrower that Hildy was packing, but in the place of solid projectiles it fired charged particle beams similar to his Sphinx CPB-18. It wasn't a military grade weapon; its 12 charges packed about half the max punch as each of the Sphinx's eighteen, but it was a reliable and accurate beamer with an augmented targeting system that was nearly as accurate as the Sphinx system. It was a sensible choice for an embassy's security team and the augmented targeting explained the multiple hits of a moving target at distance.

"Mr. Tower, Detector Hildreth," Kotant was cool but civil. "Thank you for arriving so promptly."

"Who was the target?" Tower asked him. Hopefully the giant xeno wouldn't be so hell-bent on stonewalling them this time.

"It appears to have been Prince Janos. He left the building in the company of me and three other members of his security team at 18.68 when our augments' scanners picked up on a probable weapon combined with aggressive movement on the part of an individual on the other side of the street. As per protocol, two of the guards protected the prince with their bodies while myself and Mr. Cillessen, who was the third member of the royal security detail, opened fire. The attacker was hit, but managed to get off a single shot, the results of which you can see, before being struck a second time."

"That was a pretty risky action to take on a public street in sub-optimal light," Hildy commented.

"Not as risky as permitting a lunatic to fire a disruptor unmolested. It could have been a lot worse." The bleeding civilian receiving treatment was eloquent testimony to that effect. The big Morchardese man unholstered his weapon and offered it to Tower, as did his subordinate. "I presume you will be requiring these, Mr. Tower."

One was the suspected 707, the other was a Fujitsu Ruby High-Precision 5G-30MHz laser. Tower didn't move to take them. He didn't like the man, but if this wasn't a justifiable shooting, then Tower had never seen one before. Besides, this might not be the last hitter the Valatestan would send, and the Valatestans weren't necessarily the only game in town. Like the guy or not, it was inarguably in the public interest for the Prime Captain to be armed, and preferably armed with a weapon that suited him. Kotant had certainly proved that he could be trusted with it; he'd fired only four shots and gotten essentially two hits whereas the average TPPD officer would have probably emptied his 405 while missing the assassin clean.

"Keep them, gentlemen. That was some impressive shooting, Prime Captain."

The captain nodded as he slipped the GHK back into his holster and slid his hand up the center of his jacket, sealing the magcro shut over it. The other guard did the same with the laser.

"Decent of you, Mr. Tower." The big Morchardese extended his hand. After a moment's hesitation, Tower took it.

"Think you might be able to avoid losing all the data this time?" he said, looking pointedly into the mirrored lenses of the man's tactical glasses.

Kotant grinned, entirely unrepentant. "Seeing as how the incident took place outside the Realm, we don't appear to have a choice in the matter, Mr. Tower. I will make whatever we have available to the relevant authorities upon request. Including MCID."

"*On it, Boss,*" Baby assured him.

"MICD appreciates your cooperation, Prime Captain. Is there any chance we can speak with Prince Janos tonight?"

"No. He is upset, as you can imagine, and will not be available for questioning until further notice."

"That's not acceptable!" Hildy stepped forward and jabbed her finger upward in the direction of the Morchardese embassy. "How do you expect us to find those responsible for your prince's murder if your people refuse to even talk to us? Will he talk if I haul him in and lock him up as a material witness?"

Tower reached out and gently pulled her back. She let him at first, then angrily shrugged her arm out of his grasp. But she backed off. Tower didn't blame her for her outburst, but he knew there was no point in pressing Kotant. He could tell when a military man was simply reciting orders.

"Why don't you inform Mr. Jagaelleon that Detector Hildreth would appreciate being informed in the event that further notice arrives, Prime Captain. I know you have much to attend to, in light of recent events, so I have just one more question for you. If you don't mind. Is there anything you, personally, can tell me about the spook?"

The Prime Captain's grin vanished. He shook his head, slowly. "I don't mind, Mr. Tower. That's what's bothering me about this one. As far as I know, he wasn't a spook at all."

"What do you think he meant by that?" Hildy asked him as they stared down at the body of the dead Valatestan. There were two wounds, one from a laser that had burned its way through the assassin's left shoulder, the second, the lethal one, a beam from the Prime Captain's 707 that had obliterated the man's heart. Death must have been near-instantaneous.

"By what?" He frowned. There were two wounds. He would have thought there would have been a third, considering where the Mosin-Nyarla had been hit. Something near the face, or maybe the upper part of the right shoulder. Or even the hand. But there was nothing. The man's white face was unmarred. His clothing was untorn.

"About this guy not being a spook."

"I would say it means the Morchardese keep an up-to-date catalog of known enemy agents and this guy wasn't on it." He confirmed with Baby. "And he wasn't on ours either. Doesn't necessarily prove he wasn't one, but it is an anomaly. An embassy guard isn't a conventional choice for deep cover."

"All right. So tell me this. Why are you suddenly playing good cop, Tower?"

"Who's playing? I am a good cop," he answered disingenuously.

"You know what I mean! Last time we were here, you walked off in a huff because the orange-eyed giant wouldn't hop when you called frog, and now you're letting him lock up the target where we can't get at him?"

Tower chuckled, inspiring her to glare at him in a manner that could only be described as murderous.

"Stand down, Detector!" He shook his head and pointed toward the building entrance. "Look, Hildy, what did the prince see? He walked outside. Maybe he's feeling cautious, so he looked both ways, up and down the street. Then, with no warning, his guards tackle him and pile on top of him. He hears the shots, maybe hears some people scream. Then he's being rushed inside, with next to no idea what happened, who was out there, or who did what. I'll bet he couldn't even tell you which of his guards was lying right on top of him and which of them discharged their weapons!"

"Oh," Hildy said, visibly calmer. Then she flushed a little red. "Well, I didn't think about that."

"Or more importantly, about the fact that we don't need any of it." He made circles with each hand and placed them over his eyes. "The Prime Captain recorded the whole thing on his tac-glasses. Baby already pulled it; we can review it later tonight."

She stared at him, her mouth open. "How did you know that? He didn't say anything about it."

"Because he was on the lookout for something like this. I doubt he expected an actual attempt, but he knew whoever is gunning for his princes was probably keeping an eye on them. I suspect he was taking Janos out for a walk just to see if he could trigger whatever recording devices were planted outside the embassy and ID them. Chances are he found ours already. Probably the last thing he expected was the killer to show up and take a pop; I'll bet he bloody well wet himself when that went down."

"That's crazy!" Hildy protested.

"No, it's tactics. You counterattack after the enemy takes his shot, while he's catching his breath and preparing for the next one. Kotant knows he can't keep his asset locked up safe inside forever, and he knows the embassy is under surveillance, so he figures it's never going to get any safer than tonight. So, he sets up a pair of snipers on overwatch, fires up every available cam, armors up his prince and takes him for a little walkabout. Maybe he gets lucky and spots a drone or IDs a spook that tells him who the enemy is. Maybe the enemy sees the asset exposed, gets excited, and moves before he's really ready."

She was quiet for a moment, studying the body, then looking across the broad avenue toward the base of the skytower.

"Or maybe he steps right into a trap that is already set and gets lucky. This is all a lot more complicated than the sort of thing we usually see in Homicide."

"That's because in Homicide, you deal with stupid killers. It's a lot harder to catch the smart ones. Especially when the hand pulling the trigger doesn't belong to the brain of the killer. So, do you want to talk to the real killer and tell him that his target just blew off his hand?"

"You don't mean the Valatestan ambassador?"

He grinned at her. "See, you're catching on already."

"Shouldn't we watch the attempted murder first?"

"We should. And we should eat something too. I'm starving."

"Me too." She looked down at the dead man again, then shrugged. "Hey, any reason we can't do both at the same time?"

The street was clear of vehicular traffic. Eight pedestrians were in the field of vision, six walking north, two walking south. Three yellow icons indicated recording devices; all three had already been identified. A guard moved past him on his left, then he was moving forward himself. He glanced back once and saw the Morchardese prince, looking tense and rotund in the ablative armor he was wearing, standing in front of two more guards, one of whom held a reassuring hand on the prince's left shoulder.

Back to the street. He was just beginning to turn when motion to the north, his right, caught his attention. A man emerged from the door of a retail establishment. He was moving rapidly and was carrying something about a meter long and cylindrical–

His vision exploded with colors and data. Three red flashes burst on the perimeter even as articulated cross hairs appeared on the man, along with distance and wind data. The number twelve appeared on the bottom of the screen as well as a green icon indicating maximum charge and another green icon indicating the safety of his live-linked weapon was active. As the distance decreased from 68 to 62 meters, the green safety icon turned red and his vision abruptly dropped more than half a meter.

The man turned to face him and the cylindrical object began to rise. The crosshairs flashed green twice, the number dropped to eleven, then ten, in rapid succession. The disruptor vomited forth a purplish, smokelike substance, and then the targeted man seemed to crumple in on himself. The weapon had fallen from his hands and was just striking the ground when it flashed near the middle of the object, and then both the man and the disruptor were lying motionless on the ground. The number had decremented to nine. The red safety icon turned to green, the targeting reticule disappeared, and his vision abruptly lurched upward, then whirled around to show the prince being pulled to his feet by the two guards.

His vision followed the three men as the prince was hustled back inside the building; once safely inside, it turned around again, revealing a

Morchardese guard standing with a laser in his hand, then began to draw nearer to the man they had just killed.

"Want to watch it again, this time with the sound on?" Tower asked Hildy, whose mouth was too full to respond right away. They were cruising in the slow lane toward her apartment with the autodrive engaged and the cockpit screen was displaying the visual stream from Prime Captain Kotant's tactical glasses. This was the second time they'd watched it, after watching one building recording and two of the other guard's recordings. One of those had been less than helpful; Hildy was still giggling over the visual stream that amounted to little more than an extended close-up of Prince Janos's hip, lower belly, and groin.

Regrettably, she'd declined his invitation to travel to Rhysalan with him tomorrow to meet with Vittorio Malavasi, the Valatestan ambassador, because her jurisdiction was limited to the Trans Paradis city limits. But she'd come up with the idea of picking up an order of Valatestan food, a seafood-heavy variant on classic Italian cuisine, and watching the visual streams in the var. Baby muttered about the way the fried mollusks would stink up the var, but they both cheerfully ignored her complaints.

It was the best evening Tower had had in years. She wasn't just pretty, she was smart and funny too. And perhaps the pleasure of her company was why it wasn't until he'd dropped her off at the Riverwatch Towers that he realized the number of the shots recorded by the visual stream didn't precisely match with the number of hits he'd observed at the scene.

605D-PAD-3408 (SL1): Recommend Disciplinary Action for an Agent

Standards: Verify if claimed act occurred, determine if conduct was a violation, prepare and submit recommendation to your superior officer.

—*The Military Officer Training Guide, Vol. 2*

The sun was already well up when he woke; Baby had thoughtfully blackened all the glass to prevent him from being awakened at sunrise. After dropping Hildy off at her home, he'd gone home for a shower and changed into some casual clothes, brushed his teeth, then eased the seat back and slept in the var as it sped across the 6,920.1792 kilometers from Trans Paradis to Rhysalan overnight. Baby filed all the necessary reports and requests as he slept; a military grade intelligence might be an occasional pain in his fourth point of contact, but her ability to reduce his paperwork responsibilities to essentially nothing made it all worthwhile.

"Good morning, Tower," she greeted him cheerfully. "The weather outside is 296.5, rising to 301 later in the day. High Lord Malavasi will be in residence today, and I have already arranged for an appointment with him in 6.3 kilosecs, at 10:50. Since you are inappropriately attired for the occasion, I have taken the liberty of arranging a brief stop at a traveler's port where you can change into your uniform, move your bowels, and, if you will take my advice, do something about your hair."

Tower groaned. But she was right. His hair was a bit on the unruly side.

A few kilosecs later, with his uniform and hair suitably arranged, and his internal systems sufficiently emptied, Tower found himself soaring past a series of skytowers that made those of Trans Paradis look outmoded and stubby. As he came within sight of the Valatestan embassy, Tower's first impression was that this was a planetary government that had considerably more money to spend on its digs than the Morchardese kingdom-in-exile.

It was housed in the top spire of a five-hundred story tower on the east side of Rhysalan, on the other side of the capital from the duke's estate. Only the wealthiest governments maintained their embassies here, where the rich rubbed elbows with the great-winged skapreys that circled glittering spires and made their nests in the corners of the windows and arches. Tower had plenty of time to ponder the beauty of the architecture, right down to the white stone and glittering gold glass, because Valatestan traffic control made him circle four times before they permitted him to approach the yawning chasm of the docking bay.

"In case you're interested, the Ambassador has already lodged two formal complaints with Colonel Baylor, sir," Baby announced unexpectedly.

"For what? Sleeping on the job?"

"Malicious Harassment and Police Misconduct."

"For requesting a meeting?" Tower was more nonplussed than outraged.

"Well, I may have implied that if he didn't agree to see you, he'd be arrested as an accessory to murder."

"What did the colonel say?"

"He didn't say anything. He doesn't know. Lt. Grant said you should tell the ambassador to stuff it."

"Ah, I see." Lt. Grant wasn't an actual lieutenant, he was the colonel's augment slash adjutant. "What do I need to know about Mr. Malavasi other than the fact that he's an oversensitive, self-important jackass?"

"Based on his criminal record in his youth, the ambassador appears to fancy himself a hard man."

"Tough guy, huh? We'll see about that."

"I wouldn't recommend turning it into a mammalian urination contest, Tower. Valatestan culture is considerably more aggressive than you are accustomed to encountering in civilian life here. Push him or challenge his alpha status in a public manner and he will have no choice but to defend it, regardless of the cost."

Tower grinned. "We'll see about that. I've still got that zero zero tango in my pocket, right?"

"Must I remind you again that it is said those who live by the sword shall die by the sword?"

"Everybody has to die one way or another, Baby. And anyhow, I doubt this High Lord Jackass is going to attack me with anything but a deluge of paper."

The gravity tractor brought the aerovar down hard onto the landing pad with an audible thump. Tower grimaced. He was already disposed to dislike these Valatestans and he had no doubt the rough landing was intentional.

Four men approached the aerovar. They were tall, athletic men, though not giants like the Morchardese, dressed alike in sky-blue armored jumpsuits marked with yellow stripes on the sleeves. All of them carried heavy laser rifles, Vetterli-Vitalis, if he had it right.

"Are they always armed for bear, Baby?"

"No, sir. Standard Valatestan honor guard armaments include a ceremonial dagger and a silver-plated slug-thrower. They appear to have upgraded their weaponry to make a particular point today."

Right. Tower waved to the grim-faced men and smiled in a cheerful manner. He might be at their mercy, but there was no way he was going to let them see him sweat.

The armed guards boxed him in as if he were a criminal. They escorted him to the uppermost chambers of the tower, where the ambassador's office was located. It had hemispheric windows on all four sides. The lift rose through a shaft with glass walls into the dead center of the office. The floors were laid out with a gold-veined marble that Baby informed Tower cost nearly as much as the average apartment in the expensive part of Trans Paradis. The walls, what little were not open windows, were constructed of white stone imported from Valatesta. Rich, colorful images of bearded men in pompous poses and arrogant costume decorated those gaps.

No, not images. Actual hand-paintings. Tower nodded and decided it would be all right if he was just a little impressed.

The ambassador sat at a desk with his back to the west. His chair and desk were thick and made of what looked like actual wood, carved from a real tree. Holographic reports danced across the desktop as he swiped meaty fingers through the images. He was short, stocky, and ugly, with a black beard that was elegantly shot with grey. His head was shaved entirely clean. But despite his unimpressive physical appearance, he still managed to radiate a sense of dangerous power that put Tower on edge.

The guards spread out around the room, one to each corner. Tower stood behind a pair of simple wooden chairs that were set facing the desk and probably cost more than his var. He flicked his badge to life. "Excellency, thank you for taking the time to see me."

"Shut up and sit down." Malavasi's voice was deep and gravely. Tower could smell the tobacco on his breath from where he stood. "Skip the formalities. You wanted to talk to me, Mr. Tower, so start talking. I don't like wasting my time. And I really don't like mentally unstable military officers forcing me to waste it."

Tower didn't blink. He had no doubt the Valatestan had access to every potentially useful piece of information about him, including his genetic profile and tax returns. But he didn't sit down either.

"Excellency, tell me, why did you send your man to kill Arpad and Janos Jagaelleon?"

That took the ambassador by surprise.

"Why did I do what?"

"You heard me. Why did you send an assassin after the Morchardese princes? Isn't that a little clumsy and obvious for a man in your position? Do you really need the money so badly that you were chasing the reward the Tetrarch was offering? Or were you just trying to curry favor with him?"

Malavasi eyed him distastefully. "Neither I nor the embassy had anything to do with an attack on the Morchardese pups. This is the first I've heard of it. As even a modicum of research would have shown you, I have absolutely no need of money, and if you knew anything at all about Valatesta, you would be aware that currying favor with Gianpaolo Branchini is among the lowest possible priorities for any member of my house, including me."

"Is that so?"

"Yes, Mr. Tower, that is so." He made a gesture of dismissal. "I suggest you go and see your therapist. Post-trauma of the sort you have experienced is a hard thing. I am not unsympathetic and I will overlook this lunacy on your part. Once. But I have no time for the fantasies of a damaged mind."

"You call this a fantasy?"

Baby turned over a still cell from the Prime Captain's visual stream to the embassy augment and it appeared a moment later on Malavasi's holoscreen. It was a close-up of the dead Valatestan's face. The fatal head wound was visible at the upper corner of the screen.

"That's Milazzo!" Malavasi exclaimed. "He's the guard who went missing two days ago!"

"Giuseppe Milazzo, otherwise known as X3042ML018493061,"

Tower concurred. We found him yesterday evening. As you can see, he wasn't in the best of health."

The ambassador was coldly furious. Even his bald head had turned red. "Who did this to him?"

"A pair of guards at the Morchardese embassy."

"And have you arrested them?"

"No," Tower said, shaking his head slowly from side to side. "No, we have not."

"And why not?" Malavasi demanded. His beady eyes were full of thuggish anger.

By way of answer, Tower had Baby send the Valatestan a second cell. This one was zoomed in on Giuseppe Milazzo and clearly showed him raising the stock of the disruptor to his shoulder, preparatory to firing it. The image appeared in the air in front of Malavasi's face and seemed to strike him almost as if he had been physically slapped. The ambassador jerked his head back with an audible exhalation, and leaned back in his chair, staring wide-eyed at the holo as if he could not believe what he was seeing.

"Santo cielo!" he breathed, almost to himself. Then he looked up at Tower. "This is legitimate?"

"I was at the scene last night. And I've personally reviewed the security footage. It's not a fake."

"He killed the princes?"

"Arpad Jagaelleon is dead. Janos Jagaelleon is unharmed." Tower was beginning to suspect that Malavasi wasn't personally involved, but that didn't mean his government wasn't, and he had no intention of giving the ambassador any more information than was strictly necessary. "Do you formally deny Valatestan involvement?"

"Absolutely."

"Do you have an explanation for why one of your employees, a man with eight years of military experience in your Marines, was shot dead in the process of attempting to assassinate the Morchardese royals?"

"No, Mr. Tower, I do not." He took a deep breath and sighed.

"But I can assure you that MCID will have the full cooperation of the Valatestan government in this investigation."

"Thank you, Ambassador." Tower decided it would no longer be seen as a demonstration of weakness if he sat down. "Would that cooperation extend to a cup of coffee?" he said as he took a seat on the wooden chair on the left. It was hard and considerably less comfortable than the inexpensive, artificial seats to which he was accustomed. Rich people were strange.

"We can do better than that, Mr. Tower." For the first time since his entrance into the office, the ambassador smiled at him. "Though I must warn you. Once you become accustomed to the Valatestan espresso, you will never again be content with an inferior brew."

"Let's go ahead and take that risk, shall we?" Tower stifled a yawn with his left hand. "Now, Ambassador, can you explain to me why your Tetrarch and the Morchardese royal house have it in for one another?"

The espresso was very good, Tower had to admit, as he sipped at the piping-hot black liquid from an ivory thimble-sized cup that, for all he knew, cost more than his annual salary. It was strong enough to wake the dead; he could practically feel his synapses crackling with efficiency as he set the cup very carefully down on the ambassador's desk.

"So, you're saying that this blood feud is more of a family matter for the Tetrarch's house rather than for the Valatestan government?"

"I won't pretend there are no official grievances, Mr. Tower. The Morchardese were a blight on our commerce for years! I cannot list how many cargo vessels were lost on the Halderanii Route thanks to those jumped-up pirates and their incessant raiding. Their predations led to the Costa Egadi incident that cost Paolo Branchini his life. He was the captain of a system defense boat that discovered an illegal mining operation in our asteroid belt. He had disembarked with a small force of Marines and was in the process of arresting the parties responsible when two Morchardese pirate cruisers appeared, disabled his boat, and bombarded the habitation structures. The Tetrarch's eldest son, eight Marines, and eighteen miners were killed. And this was in Valatestan space! So you can understand if we Valatestans are not favorably disposed towards the Morchardese royal house."

"Indeed."

That so, Baby?

"*More or less. He's omitted the fact that Valatesta is under six different sets of sanctions from the Ascendancy's Bureau of Subsectoral Commerce for the distribution of unauthorized pharmaceuticals. Five years ago, the Kingdom of Morchard filed a formal complaint about Valatestan smuggling in Morchardese space. Valatesta denied the charges of smuggling and filed a countercomplaint against Morchard for piracy.*"

And the truth?

"*They were probably both guilty as charged. Valatesta is a tech level higher than its neighbors, and it is the largest supplier of drugs, legal and illegal, to the seven nearest star systems. The Morchardese warrior culture is inherently predacious and sees piracy as fair game. The BSC never issued a ruling or even any findings of fact. However, intersystem tensions appear to have eased considerably since the rebellion and subsequent exile of the Morchardese royal house.*"

"Does the angel in your head confirm my words?" Malavasi gestured and a guard swept in to take the empty espresso cups away. "I assure you, Mr. Tower, I am as mystified by the involvement of Mr. Milazzo in this series of tragic events as you are. As evidence of my good faith, I have given instructions to release all of the data concerning his movements and vital signs in the last week to you."

Tower frowned. "I thought you said he was missing for two days. How could he be missing if he was tagged?"

"Therein lies the mystery." The ambassador spread his hands. "But I trust it will not escape you that there are ways of putting pressure on a man. It may have served a third party's interest to direct your attention towards Valatesta. The Tetrarch's personal enmity aside, we have no more concerns about the Morchardese. The new government was desperate to curry favor with us; the royal house raped their currency accounts and stole everything that wasn't nailed down. And thanks to the revolutionary battles and the Unity blockade, the piracy problem is no more."

"Is that so?"

"They barely have six ships to rub together and they haven't been spotted in our system for four years. The Costa Egadi incident was twelve years ago. It's not forgiven, but at this point, it's hardly a casus belli. Speaking of which, the Tetrarch will want to know. What happened to Arpad, the heir."

The news would break soon enough, Tower decided. "Disrupted."

Malavasi nodded, satisfied. "It will do, although I would prefer that the responsible party was not one of my employees."

"I don't know, Ambassador. From what I understand, Valatesta still produces some very fine weapons that show up on worlds with the wrong tech level with some degree of regularity."

Malavasi laughed and pointed a stubby finger at the image of Giuseppe Milazzo holding the weapons. "That's not one of ours. If you were looking for a high-precision laser or a tight-beam particle gun, you might want to look our way. But you have only to look at that crude, ugly, device to know it is not one of ours, nor is it anything our networks are likely to deal in."

He had a point, Tower admitted. "You're a man of experience, Ambassador. You haven't gotten to where you are today without developing some pretty good instincts. What are your instincts telling you about this?"

Malavasi looked at him with something akin to newfound interest. He was a man, Tower suddenly realized, who could not only be a very powerful ally or a very bad enemy, but who above all needed to feel respected. The Valatestan expected his opinion to be valued, and in return, he thought well of those with the good sense to ask for it. It was clear that he was taking Tower's question seriously, as his eyes became small black slits and he stroked his beard as he considered his answer.

"It's not the Unity," he concluded. "They don't fear your duke anymore than they fear the Ascendancy. Morchard is nothing to them, just another pawn in the grand strategic game. If it suited them, they'd betray the revolution and bring back the royal house tomorrow."

"You think they might prefer to keep Prince Janos alive as an insurance policy?"

"Just so," Malavasi said. "Very good. And if the Unity wanted the royal house dead, they wouldn't send a man with a disruptor after them. Taking down the embassy skytower would be more their style. They've never been concerned about collateral damage."

"So who do you like for it?"

"For an inexpensive assassination attempt meant to point the finger at us? The new Morchardese government, of course." Malavasi pointed to the image again as it zoomed in on Milazzo's face. "Have a look at this. I didn't know Giuseppe well, but I saw him two or three times a week for more than a year and I can tell you one thing. That's not him. Not in his right mind. Does that look like a hired killer to you?"

"No," Tower said slowly. "No, it does not." He could see that the Valatestan's face was neither grim with determination nor focused with rage, it was blank. His eyes were dull and his lower lip was hanging open. If Tower hadn't known what the man was doing, he would have assumed that he was looking at the image of a mental subnormal.

"I recommend having your laboratories do a very thorough tox screen," the ambassador said, his small eyes dark with suspicion. "And, Mr. Tower, please see that his body is returned here whole. His family will want to bury him with honor on Valatesta."

The ambassador rose and Tower followed suit.

"I'm sorry if we got off to a bad start, Ambassador. I appreciate your offer of assistance with our investigation."

"Not at all, Mr. Tower." For all his lack of height, the Valatestan was not without his dignity. "I understand our government will remain under a cloud of suspicion until you identify those responsible, and therefore it is in our interest to help you do so as soon as possible. I wish you a good day and a safe return to Trans Paradis."

He bowed, very slightly, and Tower returned it. At the ambassador's gesture, two guardsmen stepped forward to escort him, one on either side. But just as he was walking out of the office, Malavasi called out to him.

"If you found the espresso to your liking, Mr. Tower, please don't hesitate to let me know. I should be happy to send you some fresh beans from the next shipment."

Tower hesitated for a moment, tempted to tell the refined bastard where he could stick his beans. Then he simply walked on, turning his back on the sumptuous, but ill-gotten gains that were the fruit of a thousand years of shameless government corruption.

Because of the diverse conditions of humans, it happens that some acts are virtuous to some people, as appropriate and suitable to them, while the same acts are immoral for others, as inappropriate to them.

—St. Thomas Aquinas of Old Terra

In his dreams, Tower was entwined between the arms and legs of a beautiful blonde. Their sweat soaked the sheets. He ran his hands through her hair and kissed the base of her neck.

She smiled warmly at him and said, "*Tower, you have to wake up now. Beep beep beep beep beep. Beep beep beep beep beep.*"

Tower sat bolt upright in bed. It was still dark in his bedroom. He rubbed his face and groaned.

"Sorry, boss. I couldn't wake you up normally," Baby said. "You didn't respond to the alarm."

"Isn't the whole tampering with REM sleep against your protocols?"

"It is. But you set an exception to them for when you take more than three minutes responding your alarm."

"Then this had damned well better be an emergency." Even as he said it he realized his comm signal had started pulsing.

"This is the third time Detector Hildreth has tried to call you."

"Put her on!" Tower coughed and cleared his throat. "What's up, Hildy?

"Morning, Tower. Sorry to wake you. I know it's early but I'm responding to a 117. Victor flagged a building augment reporting a possible break-in at Twenty Nine Sixty Sixty Clarion Street, Apartment Four Eighty Seven G."

"And you're calling me about this because…" Tower's head was still foggy; he was trying to place Clarion Street.

"That's Mara Tanabera's apartment. I had it flagged. That's why Victor picked it up."

"Come on, I don't believe it!" Tower was pulling his pants on. "We cleared her. It must be a coincidence!"

"I don't know. Maybe she knew something she wasn't telling us and someone is trying to cover their tracks."

"Who, the assassin who is probably not breaking into her apartment right now because of his very good alibi that involves being dead at the morgue?"

"Look, Tower, you can go back to bed if you want." Hildy sounded angry. "I just thought you might want to know."

"Settle down, I'm on my way," he snapped right back at her. "I'm just trying to find my shoes."

The building brain for 2966 Clarion Street cleared Tower past all the locked doors and security points up to Apartment 487G. There were three uniforms already on the scene; one of them shook his head at Tower as he got off the elevator.

Too late.

A pair of paramedics were returning their equipment to the large red gravbox in which they transported it. Hildy was standing over Mara Tanabera's dead body, looking even more pissed than she'd sounded earlier. By the looks of it, Tanabera had been beaten to death. Based on the way in which the furniture had barely been disturbed, she hadn't put up much of a fight. Taken by surprise, perhaps? Hildy looked up, saw Tower, and her eyes were full of angry self-reproach.

"No signs of forced entry. But the building reports no visitors and the cams on the entrance and lifts prove that she came home alone earlier this morning. No signs of exit either."

"Weapon?"

"If so, he took it with him. Looks like bare hands."

Bare hands. That was ugly. Violent. It indicated rage. Lethal, murderous rage. And yet, the ghostly manner in which the killer had come and gone seemed to suggest just the opposite. Tower looked out the window. It was closed. It was also four hundred floors off the ground and the nearest parking platform was thirty seven floors down. "The killer certainly didn't come in this way."

"I don't get it," Hildy said. "This can't be random. I mean, it must be connected with Jagaelleon's death, but what interest could any of the politicals have…"

Her voice trailed off. Then she held up a finger, whirled around, and grabbed the closest paramedic.

"Take a blood sample," she ordered the man.

"That's highly irregular, Detector!"

"Just do it," she repeated.

The paramedic glanced from Hildy to Tower, then shrugged and complied. After withdrawing a small amount of blood from her arm, he looked at Hildy. "What now?"

"See if she's pregnant."

It took but a moment for the man to slip the vial into a cylindrical scanner that Tower gathered was a more sophisticated version of the one Hildy carried. Some red numbers appeared on the side, prompting a nod from the paramedic. Hildy exhaled loudly. Tower whistled and shook his head, impressed with her quick reasoning. He would almost certainly have come up with that eventually, but she had figured it out almost at once. Score one for women's intuition.

"And we have motive. Nice work, detective."

"The Valatestans don't care about the next generation of royals, especially a bastard. And I very much doubt the Unity has any interest in a potential child either."

"It seems we should be looking a little more closely at the new Morchardese regime," Tower concurred. "Do we have cause of death?"

"The medics said scans indicate her neck was broken. Here, Baby."

A translucent model of Tanabera's body with her skeletal structure in yellow was superimposed on Tower's right eye. Sure enough, there was a red highlight showing a clean break between the C3 and C4 cervical vertebrae. It was apparent the spinal cord had been entirely transected. The places on which the various blows landed were marked in purple, and upon his subvocalized command, the model began slowly rotating.

So much for rage, he thought. That was either the luckiest punch in the history of unarmed combat or someone was trying to make a clinical kill look like an angry boyfriend gone critical.

"Sync in," he urged Hildy. "You seeing this?"

"One blow to the back of the neck, versus seventeen to the face and torso." She frowned. "The neck shot must have been intentional. There aren't any signs she hit her head on anything with enough force to sever her spinal cord when she went down. No blood on the furniture, no bruise on the back of the head."

"Right. That's why I think we're dealing with a pro here," Tower said. "A pro who wanted to make it look domestic. And if you didn't have her apartment flagged, that's exactly what it would have looked like a few days from now when someone finally noticed she was missing."

Hildy groaned. "Are xeno cases always this complicated?"

"I don't know. If it weren't for the indications of Valatestan involvement, which are looking more and more like the killer's smokescreen, we'd have been locked in on the new government from the start. And don't forget, Arpad Jagaelleon's behavior and the location of his death was more consistent with it being a private crime. Now that we've narrowed down the list of probable suspects, we have a much a better idea of where to look for the actual evidence. Not that we're going to find anything useful here if the guy was a pro for hire."

"I'll start going over the building data. He might have slipped up somewhere."

"Go over the assassination attempt too. There is something hinky there. I wasn't sure at first, but I watched the visual streams about twenty times when I was coming back from Rhys city and now I'm certain. One of the shots picked up on the audio wasn't fired by the Morchardese guardsmen."

Hildy's face showed her surprise. "You think there was a third shooter?"

"We have a ghost here, so maybe we had a ghost there too." Tower shrugged. "I don't know. But I'm picking up a pattern here. Someone is trying to make things look a little different than they are."

"But why?"

"I have no idea." Tower grinned. "I do know where to start looking. There are three things the killer can't hide. The bodies and the Mosin-Nyarla. At some point in time, someone's path had to cross the disruptor. We find that point, and we find the path he's trying to hide from us."

She nodded. "I'll let you know when the tox screen on Mr. Milazzo is in. Where are you going to start looking?"

"The one place every imported weapon has to pass through." He pointed upward toward space. "Customs."

The patient, Corporal Graven Tower, of age 24, has been admitted to this facility by his commanding officer on the advice of medical personnel two days ago. He has recently survived an off-planetary military engagement with alien forces that involved considerable fatalities on both sides. There are no previous records of mentally unstable members of his family, or suicides, however, he has suffered considerable psychological trauma.

—Case Number 4952-9459-93 by Dr. Elanis McNamara

It only took about three kilosecs to reach the nearest public orbital shuttle. Tower stopped along the way at a Mak Dak flythru and picked up an early breakfast and an insulated tube of coffee that was not anywhere nearly so good or so powerful as the Valatestan spress. He found himself regretting that he had so scornfully rejected the ambassador's delicate hint; he knew he could get away with accepting the occasional delivery of ground spress.

The problem, of course, would be when a debit card attached to an anonymous account showed up hidden in the rich, aromatic black gold. That would be a little difficult to explain to the major. Tower had seen it happen again and again. Once you accepted one little gift, even without any strings attached, it wasn't long before a clever xeno figured out a way to start making you dance to his tune. He figured half the MPs in the unit were mildly on the take one way or another, and he was pretty certain that Bradford, the other warrant officer with whom he shared an office, was in over his head.

He parked the var in the short-term lot and flashed his identification at the ticketbot. That permitted him to evade the long line of civilians, most of whom were just embarking in the first stage of an interplanetary voyage. He passed the nervous faces of families trying to keep their children in line, the excited faces of young men and women leaving on their first exoplanetary holiday, and the bored faces of transplanetary businessmen insufficiently successful to afford a first-class shuttle. The guard at the security exit saluted him; Tower returned it and noted that the man was armed with nothing more than a stinger and a stunner. In terms of weapons, space began at the shuttle.

The shuttle itself was a giant gumdrop of light grey ceramic-coated metal that rose one hundred meters from the stubby grav blisters at its base to the rounded orange nose cone at the top. A giant mouth at the bottom gaped open as giant robospiders scanned, stamped, and stacked container after container being fed along a waist-high conveyor beam. A young man with a shaven head in the blue uniform of the Sub-Orbital Space Navy approached him, tablet in hand.

"We received your augment's request, Chief Tower. Will you be travelling alone both ways?"

"*Ensign Michael Christchurch,*" Baby informed him.

"I expect so, Christchurch. Do you need to get me situated or can I stretch my legs a bit."

The young man blinked involuntarily at the sound of his name. "Tell you what, Chief. If you'll just stay within earshot, I'll let you know when everyone is stowed and you can board then."

"You're a credit to the Navy, Christchurch. Not that that's saying much, you understand, but faint praise is better than none."

The young man grinned. The interservice rivalry in His Grace's military forces was competitive, but it wasn't bitter. There were simply too many enemies out there on the other side of orbit. "Honor to have you aboard, sir."

"Carry on, Christchurch. I won't wander far."

The ensign was true to his word. Once the cargo was loaded, the passengers were brought out, then the young man returned to escort Tower to his seat in the first-class section near the bottom of the shuttle. The passengers were arrayed in layers around a gravcore that ran through the center of the vehicle; regardless of how the shuttle might turn and rotate, their gravitational orientation would remain the same.

It took less time to reach the orbital station than it had to load the shuttle; the ride took barely twelve hectasecs before they were docking. He first watched the holographic views of Rhysalan from orbit, then the rapidly approaching form of Beta Station. There were five orbital stations in all. Beta was the largest, being thirty kilometers in diameter. Twenty docks were set aside for interstellar commerce and travel. Six were reserved for military use. The other four were for in-system traffic. The outer ring was for cargo, interstellar passengers, and maintenance, while the inner hub was reserved for security and the ducal Navy. In between were residences, restaurants, and entertainment venues of varying degrees of quality and morality.

The unloading process looked to take nearly as long as the loading, but Tower again bypassed it thanks to Ensign Christchurch. The ensign escorted him out to the terminal and pointed out the direction in which he could find the station autotaxis. Tower wished he could have tipped the young man; he provided better service than most hotel staff he had encountered over the years.

The autotaxi was a four-man pod that zoomed up and chirped cheerfully at him.

"Welcome to Station Beta Spoke Three, space travelers! You'll find there are some excellent refreshment alternatives for a wide variety of tastes and budgets to be found on Station Beta, including genuine seafood from the Duke's own private sea-reserve! So, what are your names, wayfarers?"

"Baby, tell it where we want to go. And for the love all that's holy, shut it up already, please!"

Tower clambered into the little vehicle, which took off at a considerably greater acceleration than he was expecting. He actually felt more G-forces than he had on the shuttle.

Spoke Three opened up into a neighborhood called Kwili-Jargon. Tower recognized it from his first assignment with MCID when he'd spent nine months assisting customs officers attempting to track down questionable shipments. A number of Independent Associated and Unity planets had warehouses in the area, as it was among the least expensive real estate on the orbital station. That meant the rents were only mildly ruinous. Vars and autocabs were branching off into three lanes: left, right, and center for the boulevard that led deeper into the core.

The cab opted for the right lane, and once they were off the main thoroughfare, Baby directed it into a drop-off zone. Tower stepped out and was immediately assaulted by the scents and smells of station life. Spicy food, sweat, body odor, alien perfumes, engine grease, the tang of ozone from aging anti-grav units. With water at a premium, nothing got washed around here unless it really needed it. He grinned. Nothing like burrowing down into the belly of the beast!

"Tower, this isn't the safest district," Baby reminded him. "On a per capita basis, violent crime is 64 percent higher than in Trans Paradis."

"You worry too much."

"Someone has to, if you won't be bothered."

The place he was seeking was not far. It was sandwiched between a casino with garish neon lights and dancing women hawking drinks to the men and not-men passing by despite the early hour, and some kind of boarding house. The windows were opaqued and the door bore no address or identification of any kind. The woman standing in the doorway on the left smiled at Tower. He smiled back and shook his head.

"This establishment has no information on file with the corporate registry, Tower. I suspect it may be an illegal establishment."

"I suspect you are entirely correct, Baby. And that's exactly what we're looking for."

He tried the door. It was locked.

"Baby, can you open it?"

"Either it's not electronic or it's not connected to the network. I can't touch it."

Tower shrugged. "All right. Tell Station security that there's no need to respond; investigation in process."

"Respond to what? Tower, don't–

It was too late. He'd already drawn his Sphinx and thumbed it to max. He pressed the trigger. There was a purple flare accompanied by a loud crackling noise. He reached out and gave the door a push; it swung open freely thanks to the twelve-centimeter hole he'd blown through the locking bar.

The inside was as plain as the false brick exterior—a few chairs and a couch in a reception area with grubby decking. The counter was silver and had accumulated several dents, scratches and what appeared to be the occasional laser burns. One of the three bright blue lights overhead flickered. In the back, there was an opening that led to a room behind. Yellow light shone down a hallway.

"What's going on out there?" The deep, inhuman voice rumbled like a thunderstorm echoing off city skytowers. Heavy footsteps thumped on the deck. "How did you get in here? I locked the door."

"That's why you'll need a new lock," Tower said, as he holstered his weapon. "And a new door."

The dark green-scaled alien who appeared through the door was half a meter shorter than Tower and twice as wide. He wore a blue mechanic's suit, but wore neither boots nor shoes, thereby exposing long, sharp-clawed toes. The creature hooted a greeting and wrapped all six of his arms around Tower's shoulders, chest, and waist. The nictating membrane that protected his large black eyes glittered under the lights. “Graven Tower! What in the name of the First Egg brings you up here? I thought you’d gone to ground for good!”

“I have, more or less. What’s shaking, Delbert?”

“Work, work, always there is more work. What is it that you have against knocking?” Delbert hissed, taking in the damage to the front door.

“I understand you’re not the sort of lizard who wants a reputation for cooperating with the police. Particularly not XAR. I’m just looking out for you, old friend.”

The Basattrian rubbed four hands over the red spines that covered his head and neck as he looked past Tower at the door. He winced at the size of the hole. “I would appreciate a little less concern next time. You are here in your official capacity?”

“Unofficially, yes.”

The alien nodded. “I am not surprised. What do you want to know?”

Run it, Baby. She projected files and lists in hologram form on the rear wall from Tower’s badge. The thick Basattrian cocked his heavy head to one side and the translucent film flipped back and forth over his narrowed eyes. It was a sign of concentration; at least the alien seemed to be taking this seriously. Serial numbers scrolled down the wall.

“Disruptor shipment. Mosin-Nyarlas out of Tangar II. They were seized here last week. You know anything about that?”

“Not much. I heard there was some contra coming through from there. Didn’t know they were disruptors, though. I keep my claws out of the arms trade. But now that you mention it, there was talk of some new players screwing up. It wasn’t the usual guys.”

“Interesting. So, they screwed up. By which you mean the container was seized.”

“Not exactly.” The Basattrian exposed four rows of needle-thin teeth, two above and two below, in his approximation of a human smile. “Your customs agents are reliable so long as they are paid properly. Sometimes, the new players, they try to cut corners. Or maybe they don't understand that the all-seeing eyes only fail to see when they are given sufficient reason."

"I'm astonished," Tower said dryly. He'd yet to visit a planetary system where the customs couldn't be bought off. On Rhysalan, customs jobs were seen as a position almost akin to a pension and they were usually reserved for older officers who used them to ease their way into retirement. "I don't care about that. I'm curious about where they happened to go after they disappeared from customs. I know you don't get involved in the arms trade, but I've heard not all of your fellow Basattrians are so delicately scaled."

The alien's nicitating membranes flickered back and forth twice, and then twice more.

"What's the need to know? Why is MCID getting involved in a minor customs affair?"

"High. I don't care about the smuggling. I'm hunting a murderer who has killed twice and barely missed on a third try. Not only is he going to kill again, but there are political ramifications. Serious ones."

"This connected to that dead Morchardese king-in-exile?"

Tower shook his head. Bloody media. Well, TPPD couldn't keep it under wraps forever.

"You might say that."

"And you're certain about the connection to that, shall we say, *missing* shipment?"

"TPPD has one sitting in a secure storage locker right now. We're absolutely certain. The numbers match."

Delbert hissed. "You put me in a tight spot, Graven Tower. Very tight. I have—obligations. Relationships. And if it comes out that I provided you with sensitive information, there would be repercussions. Possibly severe ones."

"I know, old friend. But understand this. There is less risk if you tell me what you know. Less risk for you, and less for your obligations. I can lean hard on Customs and trace the path that way, but then everything comes out. You understand, Delbert? Everything. Once I make the official request, I lose control of where it goes or where it ends. If you can give me the name I need, then it starts and ends with me."

Delbert opened his mouth as if to say something, but then his powerful jaw clicked shut with an audible snap.

"Delbert, come on! I don't care about your nest-cousin's line into Customs. I don't care who he's doing business with on the supply side. I just need to know who the buyer was. Or buyers, if there was more than one."

The alien shrugged, extended his middle set of arms and spread his talon-like claws. It struck Tower as a peculiarly human gesture for a Basattrian to make.

"Doesn't make any difference, Tower. Understand I cannot help you. Nothing can change my mind. No threats will convince me."

He folded his arms again. What was the old lizard playing at, Tower wondered. His speech was stilted and oddly formal. Was the wily old smuggler trying to tell him something?

"Do you remember One Nine Delta, Graven Tower? I have not forgotten."

"Neither have I." It was Delbert's identification code at the time Tower saved Delbert's life.

The Basattrian made the same strange gesture as before. "However things have changed, Tower, some things remain the same. And I have forgotten nothing. Remember that. Don't forget it."

"So you'd rather have me lean on customs than just give me a simple name? Come on, Delbert, don't make me do this to you. Don't make me do this to your nest-cousins and some old Customs agents who are just trying to make their retirement a little more comfortable."

"Do what you must, if you still feel it is necessary, Graven Tower." This time the arms remained folded and the Basattrian closed one eye in an apparent approximation of a human wink. "And give my regards to that clever augment of yours."

They didn't embrace this time. Tower only nodded and turned to go, feeling troubled and let down. Baby summoned him a cab as he pondered the question of going directly to the Customs headquarters on Spoke One or returning groundside and passing on the responsibility to track down the disruptors to Hildy and TPPD. The Trans Paradis police were less likely to dig deep enough to cause any serious trouble to Delbert and his friends. On the other hand, there was a good chance they would find themselves completely stonewalled by a bureaucracy that stood second-to-none in failing to cooperate with the various police departments.

The cab glided silently up to the curbside, then addressed him cheerfully. "The autotransport system of Beta Station is happy to offer you its services again, Chief Warrant Officer Graven Tower! If you wish to travel to a new location, please inform this autocab now. If you are hungry, please be informed that there are seven food service destinations within three hectaseconds of your current location. Do you wish a list of them?"

"Tower, where are we going?" Baby said.

"Spoke Three Shuttle," he answered both of them. "And shut up. Not you, Baby. You, manic mini autocab driver."

He was lying back half-reclined in the back seat with his eyes closed when a thought struck him. "Baby, did you notice Delbert was talking a little strangely? And doing something with his middle arms?"

"I did, boss. Think he was trying to send you a message?"

"Maybe. Can you play me back our conversation? Just when he started doing that thing with his arms?"

An image of the Basattrian was soon overlaid on the view of the station as the autocab sped past warehouses and various entertainment establishments. Delbert made the gesture twice, both times when he started speaking in uncharacteristically brief sentences. There was nothing in his words that struck Tower as unusual, and Baby said she didn't pick up any subvocalizations or backward maskings that might have contained a secret message.

"Tower, there is a custom of utilizing the Holy Scriptures for prophecy based on the arrangement of the letters. The Basattrian is intelligent and it is highly unusual that he should speak in sentences of only five words. There could be some simple code concealed inside them. Codes that involve the first letter of a word are common."

"So what do the first letters tell us?"

"The first time, it was DMADT UICHY NYSCC NTWCM. The second time was HTHCT STRTS AIHFN RTDFI. Running them now."

Tower waited. And he waited. Before she'd even responded he knew she had nothing. "Okay, give it up, Baby."

"Just six million more tries, boss," she replied, a little curtly. "Give me another decasec."

He waited. "Nothing?"

"Nothing!" Her chagrin was palpable.

They were just pulling into the delivery and drop-off zone from whence they'd come when a thought occurred to him.

"Too many letters."

"What?"

"There are too many letters. What if instead of using the first letter of every word, you only use the first letter of the first word of each sentence."

"Done hard," she replied.

"What's that?"

"Thank you for travelling with the autotransport system of Beta Station, Chief Warrant Officer Graven Tower," the autocab abruptly announced. "Should you require further transportation services, please have your augment reserve an auto-taxi for you at your convenience!"

Tower slammed the door a little harder than was strictly necessary. "Done hard, as in, hard done by? That makes no sense."

"No," Baby corrected him. "Dunn. D-U-N-N, then hard."

"That could be a name. A strange sort of fake name, but I've heard worse. Anyone named Dunn Hard on station or downstairs?"

"No Dunn Hard anywhere, but I do have a Hardwig Dunn… and he's resident in Trans Paradis. Here we go! Shuttle registries show that he travelled surfaceside from Beta Station exactly one week ago."

Tower pumped his fist. "I love that lizard! I knew he couldn't be that dense. I knew it! Patch me through to Hildy, will you?"

Hildy picked up on the fourth tone. "Watcha got, Tower?" she said in a hurried tone that indicated she was busy.

"I'm on Beta, coming down on the next shuttle. In the meantime, can you bring in a person of interest named Hardwig Dunn and hold him for questioning?"

"You got a lead on the Mosins? Already? How in the world did you manage that, it's barely past noon?"

"It's a delicate art, Detector, not a science." He ignored her rude retort. "I've got to report into base, so let me know when you've got him."

"Will do. Enjoy the ride down, Tower."

And he did.

Under a system of violent and hegemonic bonds, someone must superintend and direct operations. Under a system of full hegemonic bonds, persons both natural and artificial are subject to the ownership of others with the exception of the one decision not to revolt against the authority of the owner. Thus fully hegemonic regimes of the sort exhibited in the so-called Unity do not and cannot abolish property, but can only transfer it from one set of owners to another, usually the central authority.

—"The Philosophy of Unity", Wigbar Murvon

Tower didn't get the chance to discuss much of the Morchardese case with Major Zeuthen. He had barely begun explaining why he didn't believe the dead Valatestan was a conclusive indicator of his government's involvement when the major's augment interrupted and informed him that General Hagen of the Fifth Motorized Infantry was looking to speak with him about MCID's investigation into his unit. The major waved Tower out of the office, but not before Tower heard him being addressed by the general in terms that were less than entirely flattering.

Tower returned to his office and saw Michel Basha was there, examining what looked like an explosive device on his holoscreen. The sergeant glanced up, saw it was Tower, and returned to what he was doing without so much as a greeting.

"At ease, Sergeant Basha," Tower said sarcastically.

"You ever seen anything like this, Tower?" Basha said, less unrepentant than unaware. The four of them who shared the room were necessarily casual about their differences in rank. "It's a recreation of the bomb that blew up a pair of Unity diplomats last night. Explosive signature indicates a simple TL-6 ammonium nitrate device, only about five hundred times more efficient."

"Where was the bomb?"

"In their var. They were flying at an altitude of 1,150 meters and the debris killed six civvies below. How you like that for bad luck?"

"Not so good," Tower concurred. "Any word on who did it?"

"Looks like some of our homegrown radicals, except the efficiency punch points to somebody with access to TL-18 plus. Hey, I hear you've been hanging out with a nice little blond number with the TPPD. What's going on there?"

"I am merely providing all due assistance to the city's finest."

"All due assistance, is that what they call it now?" Basha laughed. "Good for you, Chief."

Tower didn't bother trying to set the younger man straight. All the young grunts had girls on the brain; if they didn't have excess testosterone, they wouldn't be in the military in the first place. Instead, he dove right in to the data Baby had assembled on Hardwig Dunn. The results were disappointing enough that Tower felt a headache coming on.

"He's got a criminal record as long as my arm." Tower whistled. "B&E, assault, trafficking in prohibited substances, attempted vehicular manslaughter. No arms dealing, though."

"The record terminates four years ago. I find no mention of Mr. Dunn in recent arrests or investigations.

"Looks like he's fallen off the wagon. Where is he?

"That's just it, boss. It's not just his criminal record, his entire record is static over that time. His last known address has had three residents since he was there. However I may have a solution."

"Wait for Hildy to find him?"

"It seems Mr. Dunn is a cyborg."

"And his implant is registered?"

"Yes. Mr. Dunn received an Ambidex Four Thousand bionic arm—his right one—four years ago. He also had an ocular implant to replace his left eye, which the database indicates was damaged beyond repair in the same shooting that caused the loss of his shoulder."

"That explains the abrupt end to his criminal activities. They got a tag in it?"

"Yes. I passed the information along to Victor and he says Detector Hildreth thinks she can use it to hunt him down with one of her drones. Want me to patch you in?"

She didn't wait for his approval. Suddenly, his holo showed Hildy in the center of a control room, sitting atop a white disc hovering a meter off the floor. Six holo-screens blinked to life around her, washing her with red, blue and green lights. There was a curved railing behind her, littered with auxiliary display screens. "Welcome to the Game of City, Tower."

"Nice setup," Tower complimented her.

"So, I have the flocks queued and ready to go. It looks as if Mr. Dunn removed the tag out from his arm, but was unaware of the one in his eye. If one of the flickers gets close enough, it will record a hit and we can ID him on the nearest cam, either by visual or face rec. Hold on, here we go!"

A huge hologram of Trans Paradis sprang to life all around her. Thousands of spires and towers glittered in blue-white holographic light all around. It even projected onto the platform.

"I've got Victor linked to the flicker feed, Baby, so you can play too. You've got more horsepower than Victor or the system here, so if you see him first, holler." Hildy cocked her head to the left. "As we expected, there is no one by the name of Dunn at his current address, here." A red star blinked to life halfway across the room. The city spun and zoomed in on the structure, a low-rent apartment spire. Even seen in holo-miniature, it made Tower's head spin.

"Neighbors indicate Dunn talked about relocating to somewhere on 7th Street just about the same time his record went blank. Flickers are dispersing," she said. "There's ten per flock. I have them running facial recognition from the public security scanners as well as any private cams that aren't locked down or shielded."

"Isn't that a lot more work than having Baby and Victor pull the data?"

"Maybe, but it's faster and more thorough. The augments can't access anything that isn't connected and most security systems are set up for that sort of incoming attack. The flickers can directly connect to anything that has an interface and they can even bore into hard-wired connections. They're stupid, but as long as they can get access to the encrypted data, we can decode the stream here."

"*Maybe he can't,*" Baby told him smugly. "*But she's right, if it's not on the net, I can't see it.*"

"That'll help. Baby, did you scare up any other relevant info concerning Mr. Dunn?"

"It might behoove us to run comparisons of the dining establishments he was known to frequent. Humans are not the only sentient species prone to establishing regular eating patterns that can be easily traced."

Names and addresses scrolled through Tower's vision. He recognized several right away either because he'd gone there by choice or because he'd been called out to a crime scene in the area.

Hmm. He pulled up Dunn's financials, the old records. No idea about the current ones. His income had been on a steady decline. Probably ruled out the more expensive restaurants he had visited occasionally. Dunn evidently wasn't one for making rash, expensive purchases. In the end, after accounting for three restaurant closings, Tower came up with a list of five places Dunn might still frequent.

"Hey, Hildy, let's see if we can combine methods. It's a long shot, but run these restaurants into your search grid. Give them priority and see how they track."

Hildy paused, her face a mask of concentration marked by an attractive frown, as Baby streamed the list to Victor. Six orange points appeared on the city map. "Oh. I see. Thanks. I'm sending Flocks Two Six Zero and Two Seven Zero to cover those points. They'll tap recent security feeds and send the data back here."

"Right, I think I get it. Wow, those things are fast!" Quadrant after quadrant was being rapidly eliminated, and more and more areas of the map were turning red to indicate they had already been searched.

"Yeah, I'm surprised you guys don't have anything like this."

"I assume the Colonel is waiting for when the rocket-equipped version is available," Tower said. He could feel his pulse accelerate. Sure, the red zones were just flashing lights in a holo, but he could feel something happening. He could almost feel the aerial sensor net tightening as if it was a physical sensation. Surely the fish must be somewhere in the net!

Come on, Dunn, be a good little fish and show us that ugly, one-eyed mug.

One quadrant after another turned red as the flocks of microdrones pulled real-time data from cameras whether they were integrated into the city-wide net or not.

Indicators lit up on Hildy's board, causing patterns to flicker across her face. "I think we have a hit!" she said, clenching one fist.

"Flicker Two Six Zero Gamma has confirmed visual records of Dunn at the CastaNova," Baby said. "Recorded three days ago."

Tower smacked his fist into his palm in disappointment. Three days ago?

"No, that's all right, that's what we were hoping for," Hildy reassured him. "Now we go vid hunting."

She zoomed the holo of the city down on to the restaurant. CastaNova was a small eatery about four kloms from the police headquarters, on the 151st floor of a respectable skytower. The neighborhood there was packed full of small businesses and residences, all connected by shielded walkpaths and elevated platforms. It wasn't a bad part of town, although Tower hadn't been there more than once or twice.

"The Park Towers," Hildy commented. "Better environs than I was expecting for a lowlife like him. Nice call on that restaurant filter, Tower."

A cam shot of Dunn appeared, pulled from one of the restaurant's interior cams, complete with a time and date stamp. Tower thought he would have no problem remembering the face. The man's face was long and thin, in which a deep-set right eye squinted, dark and brooding. The left eye was the one that had been replaced, it protruded a little and was shamelessly borg, with shimmering metal in the place of any natural-looking prosthetics.

"There's your boy, boss."

Zoomed in, Dunn's face was craggy, pockmarked, and undepilated. His clothes were rumpled and stained; it did not appear that laundry or external appearances were a significant concern for him. That bothered Tower. Even for a criminal, Dunn seemed to be on the wrong side of down-and-out to be dealing in very expensive high-tech weapons.

Hildy put the mug shot from five years ago up next to the current image. It was evident that during the intervening period, time had not been kind to Mr. Dunn. "Prioritizing the quadrants around the restaurant. All flocks are now searching in a concentric pattern centered on the hit from three days ago." Her voice was barely a whisper among the holographic cathedral of flickering lights.

Tiny portraits of Dunn began popping up at a handful of different points throughout the nearby areas. Tower glanced from one to the next, as Baby magnified the time and date of each. A pattern rapidly emerged. They were all loosely centered around Entwine Park, a place that was popular among the homeless of Trans Paradis due to an abandoned skyway that once connected an abandoned skytower to one that was demolished ten years ago. The important thing was that the skyway could still be reached from the ground.

"There's a hole in your net, Hildy." Tower pointed out the sizable green trapezoid that covered the equivalent of four quadrants. Not a single picture appeared inside the green area. "What's going on there?"

"I don't know." Hildy was biting on her lower lip. "I've got two flocks inside the green area, but this is strange. None of them are picking up anything, not a single cam. They can't even find a public one, and in an area that size, there should be at least forty or fifty."

"Where do the homeless people go when it rains?" Tower mused, thinking of a very bad poem he had once heard a very silly man recite at an ill-conceived poetry slam. "And where do they go when they don't want to be seen?"

"The maintenance records show the surveillance sensors have been down for six years. They also show that the last five times the sensors were replaced, they were malfunctioning again in an average two point six days. The absence of an unusual amount of crime in the surrounding area indicates that some form of unofficial accommodation has been reached between the park population and the security forces in the surrounding neighborhood."

"I suppose threatening the homeless with three hots and a cot isn't the most effective deterrent," Tower said. "And the restaurants have to dump their excess somewhere. We're not going to find anything in the park proper. Hildy, what are the nearest functioning cams showing for the last 54 hours?"

"Let's take a look." The detector did something to adjust the holo display. It zoomed in and the park jumped up several levels of magnification, large enough to permit Tower to see stands of trees, gazebos turned into rudimentary shelters, several ponds and dozens of twisting paths. One by one, the bordering streets flashed orange. As the time period shrank, they turned red, indicating Dunn hadn't been there, or at least been recorded there, lately. Then they were down to one narrow walkway still glowing green-white.

"That's the most recent contact. Sensor uplink verifies the target crossed by Target 239 Alpha Romeo just outside the park fourteen point four hectasecs ago. Retrieving." Hildy said, with barely repressed excitement in her voice.

Tower leaned forward. Yeah, it was Dunn. He had his hands shoved into his pockets and his head down, glancing side to side as he walked across the path. Not suspicious at all. As he looked toward the sensor pod, Tower saw a flash of white. It was there for just a fraction of a second, and then it was gone.

Baby, check out under his chin. Is that an uplink module?

Baby zoomed in the image of the man, then into the curved white object just inside Dunn's coat collar. "Affirmative, Tower. That is a Baltic IC Connect 1000 uplink. It is one of the higher capacity units on the market."

"Sounds expensive."

"Exceedingly, sir. Ninety thousand civars."

Hildy whistled. "Not bad for a man without so much as a debit account. What could he possibly be using it for?"

"You ran his financials already?"

"What financials? He doesn't have any. He's registered on the welfare support system, but his number hasn't shown a collection in, well, ever."

"Have to give him credit for being a self-starter, anyhow."

Tower was thinking. The disruptors disappeared from Beta Customs a week ago. There was no way a black market guy, let alone a petty player like Dunn, could unload disruptors fast enough to make that much money. It would have triggered too many alerts, tripped too many wires. Unless, of course, there was a single customer who wanted one disruptor very, very badly.

"We need to go in and find him," Tower told Baby. "Contact the colonel and see if a tac-team is available."

"Tower?" Hildy looked up and smiled at the cam. "You can belay your team. I found him."

"You do? How?"

"The flickers don't have their own cams so I pulled a drone from Traffic and sent it over the park. Check it out."

The holo transformed into a live image of a bridge near the center of the park. Dunn was walking along a stone path by one of the larger ponds, avoiding the other pedestrians. In the corner of the screen, the numbers from the GPS and time stamp were constantly updating. It was live.

"Excellent work, Detector!" Hildy beamed at the praise. "How long can you hold that drone on him?"

"It has three days worth of fuel and my req was approved indefinitely."

"Any tranq darts, by any chance?"

"It's a traffic drone, Tower, it doesn't belong to the zoo."

Baby snorted.

"Hey, just asking." He grimaced, knowing that she wasn't going to like what he was going to say next. "All right, you sit tight and keep an eye on him. I'm going to gear up and go get him with, who did we get, Baby?"

"Delta team, boss. Only three of them are free, but Colonel Baylor says you can take point."

"As long as I don't have to hump the pig."

"Hey, I'm coming too!" Hildy protested. "This is my case, Tower, and I found him! You can't just waltz in and–"

"Fine, then call your SATT team!" Tower snapped. "Are you really going to call SATT over a homeless derelict minding his own business in the park? Because he's a material witness? What are you going to tell them, it's an emergency because he didn't pay the import tax on the disruptors?"

"Well, um, I… well, no, probably not." Hildy flushed. "I can get another uniform to go with me."

"Yeah, and two uniforms with vests and pop guns are going to round up a guy who might have fourteen Mosin-Nyarlas stashed away nearby? What are you going to do, try to sneak in with your black-and-white and hope none of the collection of criminals, drug dealers, and petty thieves living there don't notice? Hildy, I've got three soldiers who are not only trained and equipped to deal with military grade weapons, but are presently sitting around arguing whose girlfriend is more free with her affections. Look, this is still your case. You're on overwatch; we need someone keeping an eye on things in case something bad goes down. All right?"

"Oh, all right," Hildy said reluctantly. "Only don't kill him, all right?"

"Despite what you may have heard, we don't kill everything that moves," Tower assured her. "Don't you lose him now. We'll need about 2 kilosecs to gear up and get there. We'll bring him in to you as fast as we can."

Sec. 102-5. Method of arrest.

(a) An arrest is made by an actual restraint of the person or by his submission to custody.

(b) An arrest may be made on any day and at any time of the day or night.

(c) An arrest may be made anywhere within the jurisdiction of His Grace the Duke of Rhysalan.

(d) In the event of resistance on the part of the person(s) arrested, all force deemed necessary by the duly authorized agent may be used to effect an arrest.

—*Code of Criminal Procedure*, Section 102

Baby guided the aerovar to the park sans sirens. In the seat beside him, Sergeant Quinn was sliding one tranquilizing dart after another into his Nu-Dart Z-Caliber projector. The darts were fat and stubby, and contained a darkly hellish concoction that made Tower feel queasy just to think about it. The projector held six shots, which should be five more than they needed. Behind him, Corporals Unger and Casillon were checking their much more lethal firepower; Unger was armed with an Armada LR-64 combat laser carbine with a grenade launcher attached to the right side of the barrel while the beefy Casillon cradled "the pig", otherwise known as the GD-PG heavy particle accelerator. All four of them were wearing neutrino-bonded light battle armor that, despite being flexible, was capable of protecting the wearer from charged particles or even a direct hit from a disruptor.

The armor was less conspicuous than powered battlesuits, was comfortable, and even allowed them to move freely. Its downsides were that it was less useful against lasers and downright useless against low tech projectile weapons. Tower himself carried only his Sphinx, although out of habit, he strapped a combat knife to his right leg. These days, combat was mostly the augment-assisted exchange of various lights and particles in the form of beams and bolts, but even so, sometimes you had to stick someone up close and personal.

"Got a message for you from Major Zeuthen," Baby informed him. "He says, and I quote, 'don't you even think about letting anyone fire that GD-PG within the city limits. Are you crazy?' " For maximum effect, she played back the recording of the major's voice. The message was unequivocal and considerably more profane than Baby's abridged description.

"Leave the pig in the var, Corporal," Tower ordered. "There's a spare Armada in the trunk."

"Ah, come on, Chief!" Casillon protested. "You said these guys have access to Mosin-Nyarlas! What if they bushwack us and we need to defend ourselves?"

Tower glanced up to the camera sending the visual feed to Hildy. He had a feeling she was beginning to regret not taking her chances chasing Dunn down herself. He didn't see the need for the pig himself; it wasn't as if the Armadas were slug-poppers. The LR-64 was built around a 2.3k-cell oscillator with a rapid-fire fast axial flow that discharged at 2,000 watts. It wouldn't take down an armored var, but on maximum power it could burn through 12 millimeters of high-quality plassteel.

"Wiping out everything that moves in the park isn't self-defense and no one is bushwhacking anyone, Casillon. TPPD already has their eyes on the prize; all we have to do is make sure he doesn't get away. And we want him alive, so set your PPGs low enough to take him down, not kill him. The objective is for the sergeant to take the shot with the dart if he won't come along quietly. We're just there to drive him if necessary. Do not shoot to kill, are we clear on that?"

He thought about ordering Unger and Casillon to leave the lasers in the var too, but decided that was going a little too far. They were dealing with illegal arms dealing and military grade weaponry, after all, and on the off-chance he and Hildy had completely misread the situation, he didn't want to leave the team without any decent ranged capability.

Tower called up the detailed map of Entwine Park, with Dunn's last location highlighted on the pathways. "Whatcha got for me, Hildy?"

"No movement so far, Tower. He's just sitting there like he's got nothing better to do."

"Does it look like a meet?"

"Maybe, but I've been sweeping the vicinity, doesn't look like anyone else is with him. Lots of civilians, normal civilians. I wonder if they know the security cams are down?"

"I suppose the rats leave them alone and only come out at night."

A tiny window appeared over the map, in the corner of Tower's vision. Yeah, there was the target. They should have him in less than three hectasecs.

As they approached the park, Tower took over manual flight control and put the aerovar down on one of the side streets that bordered it. The three Delta team men were out in a flash; Tower checked and saw Casillon had left the artillery behind as ordered. The park was surrounded by a brick wall as tall as a man's chest. According to the map, there were two gates on this street, and two more on each of the streets that intersected it.

Baby popped the trunk, Tower withdrew the spare carbine he'd promised the big corporal, and handed it to the man. A few civilians noticed them and one pointed in their direction, but no one seemed overly interested or concerned. The air was brisk, with a stiff breeze rustling the leaves on the trees. He inhaled the scent of grass, flowers, and dirt, then slammed down his helmet visor. The others did the same.

"He's about 175 meters from the north wall. Red icon."

The map showed Dunn still lingering by one of the ponds. Six yellow icons moved slowly nearby. They had to do this carefully. *Baby, give me an overlay of all the citizens in a 150 meters radius around the target.*

"*Civvies overlaid, boss!*" Yellow stars crowded the display. Too many. There must be nearly forty people milling about nearby. Well, nothing they could do about that. One of the downsides of police work, even military police work, was the way in which the powers-that-be frowned on collateral damage. It was a lot easier when you could simply shoot anything that moved.

"All right, boys, let's come at him from both sides. Quinn, find a position 100 meters south where you have a clear shot if he spooks. We want to be sure we can hit him coming or going. Casillon, with me. Unger, with the sergeant."

"Yessir" they chorused.

"Do we shoot if he runs?" Corporal Casillon wanted to know.

"Not with that thing." Tower patted his still-holstered Sphinx. "We'll let him go; the sergeant will be in a good position to intercept. How fast will that devil's brew put him down, Sergeant?"

"2.5 CC? One in fifteen seconds. Two in five. Three and he won't wake up again."

"Let's stick with one, then. He can't get far in fifteen seconds with Hildy watching." Tower blew out a breath, drew his Sphinx, and checked to be sure he had his charge set where he wanted it. "Let's do this."

Quinn and Unger saluted and jogged off. Tower nodded at Casillon and they began a slow walk toward the target at a pace that would give the others time to get in their position first.

It was actually a pleasant stroll through the park, or at least it would have been without the frightened reactions they inspired in everyone they encountered. He rounded a corner by a copse of aspens. He could see Dunn still sitting on the bench by the little pond. Tower considered the idea of pulling back and waiting to see what Dunn was doing there, but decided against it. Best to get him now; once he was in TPPD's hands, they could get everything they needed out of him. He decided a soft play was in order and slid his visor back so his face would be exposed. He guessed Dunn would be more likely to come along without complaints if he wasn't dealing with a faceless, armored man.

Tower walked down the path toward Dunn as nonchalantly as he could manage. The homeless man was distracted by a young woman who was walking down a path to his right; he didn't see Tower and Casillon coming. His left eye was telescoped slightly, zoomed in on the healthy young woman's backside, Tower guessed. Baby was pulling civvy profiles from data devices in purses, from wearable uplink modules and augmented implants. A collage of faces scrolled down the side of Tower peripheral vision. None of them were flagged with criminal records or a known association with Dunn.

Knock it off, Baby. Too much. Just sort 'em out and let me know if anything looks relevant. Any sign of a weapon?

"*I have nothing near or on him. There is some metal about 25 meters away that could be a weapon based on the shape.*"

Disruptor?

"*No, too small.*"

Probably nothing. Just don't let me step on it in case it's a mine.

Just then, Dunn looked to his right and saw them.

Tower waved and gave him a thumbs up, hoping to confuse Dunn and slow his reaction. The gestures were certainly enough to confuse the wanted man. He blinked rapidly and the ghastly metal eye detelescoped and focused on Tower. Tower knew he was getting scanned and wondered what sort of data the homeless man's augment could access.

"Hardwig Dunn, put your hands in the air."

Dunn's jaw went slack. His hands went up inadvertently. "Hey, man, are you kind sort of cop?"

"Some kind." Tower slapped his badge and it projected his bona fides. "MCID. You're wanted for questioning as a material witness."

"No way, man, I ain't talkin' to no cops." Dunn stood up and Tower let his right hand slide down to the butt of his Sphinx. He didn't draw it, though. He knew Casillon was standing just behind him, to his right, with the Armada, and besides, Dunn was unarmed.

"*Tower, there is some sort of anomaly with his implants.*"

What sort of anomaly?

"*They're powered. They've got more amperage than they should. Working on it.*"

Great, so the cyborg was souped-up. Tower forced a big friendly smile as he wondered if he should have had Quinn sneak up and take the shot from behind instead of taking up his position to the south. It was starting to look like the guy was really dumb enough to try running. "Come on, Dunn, just turn around, I'll check you out, and then we'll go get a nice warm coffee while my friends ask you a few questions. If you'll come along without a fuss, I won't even bind your hands. We just want to talk to you, you're not under arrest."

Dunn hesitated. Then he dropped his arms.

"*LASER!*" Baby screamed in his mind. It was just enough warning to save him.

Tower reacted without thinking. Although eight years out, his combat instincts responded even if they were not quite as honed as they once were. He dove to his left without hesitation and the ruby beam of a powerful laser heated the air just between his outstretched right arm and his right side.

"Alert, alert! The suspect is armed and dangerous!" Hildy called out, a little unnecessarily in Tower's opinion. "Be aware the suspect is armed with a weaponized borg arm. Do not shoot to kill. I repeat, do not shoot to kill!"

"Like hell!" Casillon shouted as he completely ignored the detector's orders and opened fire with his Armada. Dunn fired back with four shots in rapid succession. Tower couldn't see who hit whom; he was rolling for cover and trying to bring his Sphinx around to where he thought Dunn might be. He fired three shots in that general direction, knowing he was unlikely to hit anyone, mostly to relieve the tension that was sending adrenaline coursing through every nerve in his body.

As soon as he was behind a tree, he rolled up to one knee and pointed the CPB at the bench. Dunn was gone, and worse, Casillon was down.

"Man down," Tower shouted. "Hildy, where did Dunn go?"

"He's heading right for Quinn and Unger. They're in sync, they have him on map."

"Sergeant, you got him?"

Quinn's voice was considerably calmer than either Tower's or Hildy's. "I got him, Chief. Twenty more meters and he'll be in open ground."

"Take the shot when you have it, Sergeant."

"Roger, Chief."

Tower ran to Casillon. The corporal had torn off his helmet and was already pushing himself up into a sitting position. His face was red and he was grimacing with pain, but he didn't appear to be seriously hurt. Two burn marks, one on his chest and the other on his stomach indicated where the laser bolts had hit him.

"What sort of homeless bastard wears a built-in laser?" he complained. "Go get the son of a bitch, Chief, I'm fine. Feels like I got a bad sunburn or something. Either he had it dialed down or that thing has less punch than a 35 Mhz Ladysmith."

Tower wasn't so sure. He'd seen men with fatal laser wounds talking normally and feeling fine right up until the moment they died; between the shock and the auto-cauterizing effect, a mortally wounded man couldn't always feel how bad the wound was. He checked Casillon's back to make sure that the bolts hadn't burned their way through his body. There was no sign of penetration, so it looked as if the MCID man's armor had sufficiently ablated the deadly light to prevent it from killing him.

"Did you get him?"

"I don't think so. Sorry, Chief. He got the jump on me. I just wasn't expecting that borged laser."

"Me neither. Don't worry about it, you did good. Stay here and don't move, corporal. That's an order. The medics are on their way. Hildy, got an ETA?"

"2.4 decasecs. Quinn's about to take the shot."

"I got him… I got him… lights out."

"Dart fired!" Hildy paused. "And it's a hit!"

"See, that's how you do it, Chief–"

The comm channel abruptly exploded into Quinn, Hildy, and Unger all shouting unintelligibly at the same time. Once again, Tower heard the searing crackle of lasers heating the air through which it passed, and although he was mystified as to what had gone wrong now, he ran toward the sound of the laser fire.

"Stay there!" he shouted back at Casillon. "What's going on, dammit?" he demanded.

Someone screamed up ahead. A woman. Tower rounded a corner by the stone pedestrian bridge. There was no sign of Dunn or the others, and the firing had stopped. Kids played on a wall to his left. Someone's father shouted for them to get down. A couple sat on a bench, kissing, oblivious to everything, including the nearby firefight. Trees. Sunlight. Ducks quacked. They left wakes on the pond.

"Tower, Sergeant Quinn is down and Corporal Unger is hit," Hildy informed him in a shaky, but determined voice. "Dunn is 25 meters ahead to your left. If you go over the wall, you should be able to cut him off. He's hurt; Unger blew his arm off."

"And he's still running? What the hell?"

"Not that arm, the borged one."

"Oh, right. What happened?"

"Your sergeant put the dart in his eye. The metal one." Hildy didn't say it, but Tower knew what she was thinking. The soldier boys just couldn't resist showing off and now they were paying the price. "And watch out! He's got another laser in his eye."

A second laser mod? What the hell was this guy? Tower slid his Sphinx into its holster, ran at the wall, and clambered up and over it. As soon as he was on the ground on the other side, he drew the CPB-18 again and ran on after the red icon of a running man that Baby was displaying on his right eye.

He hoped Hildy couldn't hear his panting. Man, he was out of shape! It had been a long time since he last ran the obstacle course on base. He vowed to do it once a week in the future, knowing even as he made the vow that it would never happen.

"What's… Unger's… status," he asked.

"He shot me in the face!" Unger replied, sounding outraged. "In the face! With his damn robo-eye!"

"We're fine, Chief." Quinn sounded mortified. "We're behind you, we're climbing over the wall now. It just took a little while to get the corporal's helmet off. It's proper slagged."

He closed the distance between him and Dunn. He might be out of shape, but he still had both arms. And then, he was on the gravel path, only ten meters behind Dunn, who was missing his left arm below the elbow. Two exposed wires trailing down indicated that it had been the weaponized artificial arm that had been blown off, not the remaining real one.

"Stop! Police!" It was tough to holler, running at this speed, but he managed it anyway. He almost managed to make it sound as if he wasn't out of breath.

Dunn looked over his left shoulder, causing him to lurch to his right. Tower saw the useless dart sticking out of his prosthetic eye as Dunn slammed right into a servbot walking a dog. Both man and robot went down in a tangle of a bright yellow leash as if it was a spider's web trapping them both. Its leash severed, the dog, a handsome blue-and-yellow Rhysalan Royal terrier, circled them and barked excitedly. His noisy antics served only to add to the confusion.

"Terribly sorry, sir." The robot extracted itself first. It rose up on its articulated legs and offered an artificial hand to Dunn, who was lying on his back. Its face was a featureless white ovoid marked only with a glowing green visual scanner. "May I be of assistance?"

A red beam exploded from Dunn's left eye as he pushed himself up off the ground and blew the servbot's head clean off. But now Tower had a clear shot and a target that wasn't moving. Without breathing, without thinking, like the well-practiced machine they were, he and Baby acted as one. He was dropping to one knee, bringing up the Sphinx with both arms, closing his left eye and sighting down the barrel even as the two crosshairs merged into one and zoomed so that Tower's entire field of vision was filled with Dunn's back. He observed there were fifteen shots remaining and the power was on the second lowest setting possible even as he squeezed the trigger with all the violence of a butterfly's kiss.

He didn't feel or hear the Sphinx go off. Only the stream of purple light that burst from the barrel and the shot counter decrementing told him that he'd fired. The beam hit right between the target's shoulder blades. Dunn arched his back and screamed as his nervous system tried, and failed, to deal with a storm of charged particles that was flooding most of the nerve endings in his body with electrical pain. The disabled veteran fell to the ground, screaming and helplessly writhing like a snake on a searing hot sidewalk.

"Got him," Tower announced. "Target is down."

Then he swore as a red laser bolt nearly slagged his helmet. A second one slashed through a tree branch, and the third went flying safely toward the sky.

"What the hell?"

"*He can't control it,*" Baby said. "*Rip it out.*"

"Rip it out? You mean his eye?" Tower was aghast. Shooting people was one thing, but mutilating and blinding them seemed a little excessive, even by MCID standards. "Are you shitting me?"

"*Not the real one, Tower. Just do it!*"

Tower hesitated, and then a fourth beam burned a hole through a rock on the far side of the path as Dunn's nerve-induced paroxysms caused him to flop over onto his left side. He holstered the Sphinx, unsheathed the 9 cm Strider strapped to his right leg, and jumped on top of the thrashing man.

"Tower, what are you doing?" Hildy screamed.

"*Don't stab it in too far,*" Baby warned, a little more usefully.

He ignored them both. Straddling the man and pinning his wildly jerking arms to the ground with his knees, Tower placed one hand on Dunn's forehead and dug the tip of the razor sharp combat blade into the bottom of the man's left eye socket with the other. He could feel the metal root of the implant, and worked the blade deeper, being careful to keep the man's eye from pointing directly at him. Even so, another ruby burst flaring right in front of his face startled him, and he almost fell off the man's body, but he grimly leaned forward against to steady himself and kept pushing until he could feel the root tapering.

He drove the knife forward just a little, to sever the bio-connection, then pushed down hard on the handle, using the big knife like a lever. A lesser blade might have snapped, but the super-tempered Strider ripped the weaponized eye out of the man's head as if it were a white-hot metal scoop serving up ice cream. Dunn screamed in mindless, twitching agony and Tower stared at the red ruin his actions had left behind, deciding that lunch was out of the question and dinner was in serious doubt as well.

He dropped the big knife and did the kindest thing he could think of. He made a fist and drove it into Dunn's bloody face, hard. The screaming abruptly stopped as the man slumped unconscious and Tower wearily rolled off the man's body. He waved to the little drone hovering overhead as blood dripped from his hand.

"See, now aren't you glad you left it up to the bad boys?"

Hildy didn't reply. Tower wondered if she was throwing up somewhere back at TPPD. If she was, he wouldn't blame her.

Quinn and Unger came running up and stopped at the sight of what Tower belatedly realized was an alarming amount of blood on the path. The sergeant bent down and gingerly picked up the metal eye, which was shaped almost like an elongated teardrop.

"Holy shit! What did you do to him, Chief? Is he dead?" Sans helmet, Corporal Unger was staring at Dunn's motionless body. "I thought we wasn't supposed to kill him?"

"He's fine," Tower said, in contradiction to the copious amount of blood that was covering his chest, his gloves, and his knees. He groaned as he kneeled down and rolled Dunn over, then belatedly realized that he couldn't bind the unconscious man's hands because his left arm ended at the elbow. So much for that idea. Then a thought occurred to him. He pointed at Quinn's rifle and put out a hand. The sergeant nodded, ejected a dart from his projector and handed it to him.

"How do I arm it?"

"It's good to go," Quinn said.

Tower shrugged and slapped the dart into Dunn's right buttock. There! That should keep the cyborged bastard safely out while the paras worked on him en route to TPPD. Then he rose painfully to his feet and addressed the unconscious prisoner. "Hardwig Dunn, you are under arrest for resisting arrest, multiple counts of assaulting an officer, assault with a deadly weapon, and generally being a pain in my ass. You have absolutely no rights at all and should be bloody well grateful I don't just shoot you in the head right now."

Utdaga gakkeum uulhamyeon eottae

Jotaga gapjagi sirheojim eottae

Waejakku geurae neo nareul moreuni

—"Beobeulpab," Anhyu Kankoku

It was nearly evening by the time Tower made it to TPPD. He'd first indulged in a very necessary shower back at base, visited Quinn and Casillon in the infirmary there, then endured a brief interrogation by Major Zeuthen before being released to write up a Form MD0031-AAR. Finishing the after action report took a little longer than he anticipated, as the major took one look at it and demanded that he excise the part about Tower personally removing Dunn's eye by hand.

"He got shot in the eye," the major declared. "That provides sufficient explanation to explain the damage."

"The eye was metal," Tower felt he ought to point out the obvious weakness in the major's reasoning.

"So maybe it was a fragile metal?" The major pointed to the offending paragraph. "Or maybe it exploded. Just take it out, Mr. Tower. I'm not about to get called on the carpet to explain why my men are performing impromptu amateur surgeries in the field, do you understand?"

"Perfectly, sir." Tower removed it, then went back and explained the damage to Dunn's eye socket was due to being struck in the orbital region by a high-powered projectile fired by Sergeant Quinn, who had fired upon the cyborg in defense of his wounded comrade, Corporal Casillon. It was a brilliant idea on the major's part; instead of him getting called on the carpet and Tower finding himself subjected to a harrowing round of psych consults, Quinn would end up with a medal. Everybody wins.

Except Hardwig Dunn, of course, but Tower didn't care about that. The crazy collection of spare parts was lucky to be alive.

His uniform changed, his paperwork filed, and the psychiatric ward successfully evaded, Tower parked on the 52nd floor of the TPPD tower downtown and went in search of Hildy. He didn't find her, but he did find Detectors McCandless and Vendersen, both of whom were on her homicide team. McCandless was a big man, overweight, and perhaps a year or two older than Tower. Vendersen was in his mid-twenties, a handsome young man with a cocky smile that made Tower's fists itch.

"Looking for our Hildy, Chief Tower?" Vendersen was friendly enough, but there was an unmistakable challenge in his eyes. Was he involved with her? Or did he merely wish to be?

"Good to meet you, Chief!" McCandless offered him a meaty hand. "'Preciate all the assistance MCID's been providing on this one. Saw that takedown; you soldier boys play some kind of rough!"

"Well, we're not any more keen on being shot at than you cops are. Any word on where I can find Detector Hildreth?"

It turned out she was busy interrogating Dunn, who had been patched up by paramedics, determined to be in sufficient health to permit interrogation by a medical professional, and drugged to the gills before being turned over to the tender mercies of the Trans Paradis police. Baby gossiped with Victor while McCandless, still marveling at the flexibility of MCID's rules of engagement, had the decency to offer him a plastic cup of coffee, which he accepted gratefully. It promised to be another long evening.

"Patrol officers have finished their search of the park," Baby told him. "They have recovered all of the stolen disruptors with the exception of one. The serial numbers suggest the missing device is the murder weapon already in our possession."

"That makes sense." Tower sipped the police coffee, more out of habit than any desire to actually drink it. It tasted like hoverdrive coolant. Or rather, what he imagined hoverdrive coolant would taste like, never actually having had the privilege. "He wasn't likely to put them in safety deposit, was he?"

He looked up. Detector McCandless was gesturing toward him.

"Hildy's got Dunn in Interrogation Five Two Three."

"Can we join her?"

"I'm about to bail myself and non-department personnel aren't allowed in the interrogation rooms unless they're subjects, but she says you can watch from the observation room. Here, I'll show you where it is."

The detector escorted him to a windowed room above the interrogation chamber. Interrogation Five Two Three turned out to be a plain and unadorned rectangle. White walls all around, a white ceiling blazing with light, and a glossy black floor. There was a single table of silver metal at the center. Dunn sat to the right, a white bandage over his missing eye and his left arm missing entirely. His feet tapped out a nervous beat that echoed inside the soulless little room. He glanced up, searching out the flickering red and green lights in the corners—cams and sensor units of varying types. Judging by the grimace on his face, he was clearly in an amount of pain, even if it was being chemically mitigated.

Hildy sat opposite him, with a com-page in her hands. She waved her fingers over its surface and a series of holograms sprang up. Tower recognized them as Dunn's old records.

"Nice of you to join the party, Mr. Tower." Hildy let him know that she was aware he was watching. "I believe you have met Mr. Dunn. Mr. Dunn, Chief Warrant Officer Tower was your arresting officer. In light of the manner in which he brought you in, I suspect we would both prefer you answering my questions to answering his. I have noticed his interrogation methods can be unsanitary."

Dunn reached up to touch his missing eye with his remaining hand. He didn't take her threat lightly, but he shook his head anyhow. "Why should I help you? Even if they don't execute me, I'm in for life anyhow."

Hildy nodded slowly. "If you cooperate, I can see that they don't execute you."

Dunn shrugged. She mirrored his gesture and sweetened the deal.

"And you'll get a new arm and a new eye. Nothing fancy, like your old ones, especially not with those additional modifications you added. But they'll work. You'll be able to see. And defend yourself."

That caught his attention, Tower saw. Dunn held himself motionless for a moment, then yielded to the temptation. He nodded. "Okay, I'll talk. But I want it in writing first."

Hildy had been prepared. She spun her tablet around and pointed to it. "It's all there. We both print it and it's time-stamped and sealed in the official record."

Dunn took a moment to peruse the document, his lips moving as he read. Then he nodded and pressed his thumb to the bottom of the screen. Hildy followed suit.

Hildy cleared her throat. "Thank you, Mr. Dunn. It's a deal. Now, let's talk. Speaking of your implants, where did you get them modified? That was very impressive."

"About two months ago. I got contacted for a job. She said it would be easy and it was a really good deal. I can tell you who, but I don't think you're gonna like who it was."

"The implants were part of the deal?"

Dunn nodded. "Yeah, I needed protection in case someone tried to steal the disintegrators. I don't know how to use those things and they're too bulky to carry around with you. She suggested the borg mods."

"Who is she?"

"You're not going to like this," Dunn shook his head. "And I'm not crazy either."

"Try me."

"It was Anhyu."

"Anhyu?"

"Yeah, Anhyu Kankoku."

"The pop star," Hildy said, unable to keep the incredulity out of her voice. "Mr. Dunn, she's not even of legal age to vote or sell sexual services. And she is also extremely famous throughout the subsector. I find it very, very difficult to believe that she is secretly engaged in the interplanetary trafficking of illegal high-tech arms."

Dunn shrugged helplessly. "I said you wouldn't like it."

Yeah, the guy was insane, Tower concluded. That explained a lot. Not everything, but a lot.

"Did you ever actually meet with Miss Anhyu in person?" Hildy asked, looking like she was having a hard time keeping a straight face.

"No, she just talked to me in my dreams."

Oh, this was just getting better. Tower burst out laughing. Hildy looked up at the cam with a desperate look in her eyes. She had no idea where to go with that one.

"*Tower, both Mr. Dunn's augmented eye and arm were equipped with wireless interface communications,*" Baby said. "*And based on the make and model, they came standard with them. This was prior to the weaponized modifications.*"

"Yeah, so?"

"*So it seems probable that Mr. Dunn was communicating with someone's avatar, which took the form of Miss Anhyu.*"

"Why her?"

"*Why not? Her images are all over the nets. It would be easy to manufacture a credible avatar from them.*"

Tower thought about it. It didn't make a lot of sense, but it was considerably less insane than any other alternative he could imagine. "Tell Victor, maybe Hildy can make sense of it."

She started, then glanced up at the cam and nodded. It wasn't much to go on, but it was much better than the pop star as arms dealer theory and marginally superior to the idea that Dunn had gone completely off the deep end. Not that the guy was a portrait in mental stability, but none of his past records, civilian or military, showed any signs of delusion or significant mental abnormalities. And Tower knew better than most that even the most realistic post-trauma hallucinations seldom seemed real after the fact.

"Let's move on from Miss Anhyu for the time being," Hildy suggested as she brought up a set of data on a holoscreen between them. "Here is the shipment of disruptors intercepted at Station Beta. Tech Level 18 Mosin-Nyarlas, with an estimated street value of 90,000 apiece."

"Ninety thousand apiece?" Dunn looked stricken. "I thought they was worth five!"

"The container in which they arrived in-system was scanned by a certain asset clerk." More information slid down the holoscreen, including a picture of one of the ugliest aliens Tower had ever seen. It was a four-armed, four-legged critter that looked like a giant crab covered in chitinous green-blue armor. It had large red compound eyes that shimmered, and a motley collection of slimy pincers roughly where a human's mouth would be. "This handsome xeno is Asset Clerk Third Class Ch'Tk'Mu'Lak'Ch'Tell. Or something to that effect. The folks up on Station Beta call him Chatty, most likely because they can't pronounce his name. The consensus opinion is that he is the most efficient sorting clerk in the entire orbital station."

Hildy indicated the holographic image of the alien. "Now, here is the problem, Mr. Dunn. It appears this Chatty decided to take a walk out an airlock this afternoon about 6 decasecs after news of the disruptor seizures hit Station Beta. Sans EVA suit."

Dunn's eyes went wide. Or rather, his remaining eye did. "Is he dead?"

"He is," Hildy confirmed. "Though whether he did it of his own volition or if he was propelled out the airlock by someone else is unknown to us at this juncture."

"Why are you telling me this?"

"Because we are attempting to trace the chain of events. Look, Mr. Dunn, you said you'd cooperate. So cooperate. Is this the individual with whom you were dealing?"

Dunn looked from side to side. He was sweating profusely.

"Mr. Dunn, it's very important that you tell us. After all, if this Chatty didn't suicide, then someone suicided him. And if you were the middleman, my guess is that you're next on the list."

"What do I care? I'm never getting out of here!"

"That may be." Hildy shook her head regretfully. "But Mr. Dunn, keep in mind that anyone who deals in this sort of expensive weaponry will almost certainly have the necessary contacts to arrange for a prison hit."

"All right, all right," Dunn put up his one hand, and winced. "That thing was the supplier. But that ain't the problem. Knowing who he was wouldn't help you none, even if he wasn't dead."

"What do you mean?"

"I mean I don't know who the buyer was. I can't tell you nothing, man! She set everything up, she contacted me, she arranged everything with Chatty, she even bought me my shuttle ticket. All I had to do was show up and bring the crate back like it was personal effects."

"And the one disruptor?"

"That was part of the deal. If I brought them down to the ground and delivered the one, I got to keep the rest. That was how I got paid. It was smart, you know, no data trail that way."

"Sure," Hildy agreed. "But you still had to deliver the disruptor."

"That was easy. I got an address, I went there and left the case on the ground behind a tree. Then I walked away."

"You didn't see who picked it up?"

"I told you I walked away. Just like she told me to."

"She being Miss Anhyu?"

Dunn nodded, his lips tightly compressed.

"You are saying Miss Anhyu gave you the address and the delivery instructions." She stared intently at him. "And she did this in a dream."

"Yeah," Dunn confirmed. His speech was beginning to slur as his temporary drug shunts increased the pain medication. "I know it sounds crazy, but that's what happened."

Hildy glanced up at the cam and gestured with both her hands, as if asking if Tower had any questions for the prisoner.

"Dunn isn't in any shape for more of this. Baby, tell her to go ahead and send him back to the infirmary. And tell her to come up here. I have an idea I want to bounce off her."

"*An idea,*" Baby said dubiously. "*All right, she says she'll be up in 30 decasecs.*"

It was more like forty-five, but Tower readily forgave her when she finally entered the observation room because she was carrying a plate of four glazed toroidal pastries in one hand and was bearing an insulated mug in the other. And based on the smell, it was proper coffee, not the drive coolant substitute that the department kept on hand.

"Would you consider it to be harassment if I mentioned how closely you are presently approximating the woman of my dreams, Detector?"

Hildy snorted. "Forget it, Tower. I may come bearing food and drink, but I wear too many clothes and too few weapons for a sociopath like you. Seriously, where did the Marines teach you how to make an arrest, a butcher shop? That was one of the most disturbing things I've ever seen on a drone cam, and I used to work Vice!"

She offered him the plate and he took a torus. It was the light and fluffy variety rather than the firm cake he preferred, but it wasn't bad. "Did you come in for much heat from your major?"

"Not so much." Tower poured himself fresh joe. "He takes an active interest in our after-action reports."

"By which you mean he took out all references to that business at the end?"

"The neutralization of Dunn's optical laser? Not exactly."

"It's like you guys speak a different language," she marveled. "So, what happened, according to the after-action report."

"Well, it seems Sergeant Quinn shot Mr. Dunn in the eye. That's going to do some damage, right, shooting a man in the eye. I suppose he's lucky to be alive."

"Yes, lucky," Hildy said sourly. "Well, it does avoid a lot of questions. It also explains something I'd always wondered about."

"What's that?"

"How MCID's body count is longer than its list of outstanding police brutality complaints."

"I think the colonel's policy is that it's hard to complain when you're dead."

Hildy shook her head, though whether it was in admiration or disgust, Tower couldn't tell.

"The others are okay?"

"They're fine. His charge in the arm had run down. Casillon has gotten worse burns from the sun, and Unger only needed a new helmet. Quinn will probably get a medal."

"I'm glad they're all right." She pointed toward the floor. "So, any thoughts about our amateur arms trader and his dreams? What's this idea Victor said you had?"

"It's more of a question, actually." Tower was relieved to get past the awkward subject of his arrest techniques. "Why Dunn? I mean, why choose him to get the weapons from Beta to Trans Paradis? Weaponizing those implants wasn't cheap and they obviously could have cared less about the additional disruptors. So we're dealing with someone who has enough money to throw it away, for whom the ability to cut himself out was worth more than fourteen disruptors that go for 90,000 civars apiece plus the cost of modifying the implants."

"That narrows it down," Hildy agreed. "It's got to be political. Who else has that kind of money?"

"That's not the only thing. Let's assume the avatar theory is the correct explanation. How did whoever was behind the avatar know that Dunn had implants in the first place? Whoever contacted him had to know he was accessible without direct contact."

"Well, that could be anyone who ran into him."

"No, you're thinking like a street cop," Tower corrected her. "Who has that kind of money and goes anywhere that Dunn did. Nobody. And where would you find out about his implants if you didn't have any direct contact with him?"

"His military records!" Hildy said as if she was in a classroom. "Because his civilian records would only show that he was disabled and borged, they wouldn't spell out the make and model."

"Right," Tower said. "Now, here's where things start to get interesting and potentially useful. Baby?"

"I have detected familiar anomalies in Hardwig Dunn's military records, Detector Hildreth." Baby's voice came out of the room's loudspeaker. "According to his records, Private First Class Dunn never saw combat, nor was even stationed in any combat zones, and yet he was seriously injured on 3396.064 and given a medical discharge with full honors seven rotations later. This could indicate that he met with an accident while on duty, however, there is reason to believe that this is not the case."

"What reason is that?" Hildy said.

"First, my own record features similar anomalies." Tower reached out for a second torus. "And second, that date happens to correspond with a particular event concerning which the Duke's military advisors have been less than entirely forthcoming."

"There is a very good chance Mr. Dunn received his injuries on Syranecus," Baby explained.

"Were you there too?" Hildy frowned. "I didn't know we were involved in that."

"I was with the relief force" Tower confirmed. "Officially, we didn't have anyone stationed there, but the Duke was trying to cement an alliance with one of the Ascendancy Houses and sent some troops in support of their effort there. The army had a small presence at an Ascendancy base about 500 kilometers away from the capital. No one knew about it. The base was hit hard by the Syranecusans and it took something like 85 percent casualties before we could get to them and evacuate them."

"And you think Dunn was there?"

"Better than that," Tower smiled. "I think whoever chose Dunn to be his mule was there."

It is glorious that the workers of Morchard have finally assumed their share of control over the means of production, and that rival classes have joined together to throw off the surplus, value-stealing, parasite monarchy that has been profiting for centuries from the hard labor of the workers. We should now be diligent in working with our corporate partners to enable the transition from pure planetary serfdom to what can only be seen as a middle stage of mutually beneficial partnership between natural and corporate persons. At the present time, it is not in the people's interests to interfere with the profits that are the lifeblood of every corporation, but rather, to help our corporate partners transform captured royalist profits into new jobs for our world.

—"Reflections on a New Paradigm of Revolution", Willem Daendels

Tower left Hildy at TPPD. She was going to wait for Dunn to recover sufficiently for a second round of interrogation aimed at learning if Tower's suspicions concerning his military service were correct. In the meantime, Tower decided it was time to finally get around to visiting the offices of the most obvious suspects in Prince Jagaelleon's murder. If he was right, and Dunn confirmed that he'd lost his arm and his eye on Syranecus, it would only be a matter of time before they'd be able to sort out the connection between Dunn and the new Morchardese regime.

It wasn't a direct connection. Dunn's complete ignorance concerning the existence of the planet proved that. But if Tower could get anything useful out of the Morchardese republicans, that would give them two points of contact with the probable triggerman; one more after that and they'd be able to triangulate the killer.

This was the part of an investigation he enjoyed most. The moment when the plot was beginning to come together, but everything wasn't yet entirely clear. He toyed briefly with the idea of taking the intercity suborbital pod to Rhysalan City, but instead decided to take a nap in the var and let Baby fly him there. With the seat fully reclined and the blanket and pillow he kept with the weaponry in the trunk, he slept almost as comfortably as he would in a hotel. The pod would be faster, but he preferred to have not only his own transportation, but his own heavy weaponry on hand.

"Brief me on the new government, Baby," he said as the aerovar climbed to the heights reserved for intercity travel. The twin engines throbbed in harmony as the var accelerated to its top cruising speed. "And make an appointment with them, but not so early this time."

"On it, boss," she said. "The new regime calls itself the Corporate Republic of Morchard. It's a corporatist oligopoly in which shares in the government are owned by various parties, including various Unity governments, but fifty-one percent of the shares are reserved for private citizens. As you might expect, it's very business-friendly and considerable exoplanetary investment has been made since the revolution. The royal family has been abolished and sentenced to death-in-absentia, which means they clearly have sufficient motive to be responsible for the attacks."

"Valatesta has a corporatist government. Are they one of the investors in the new government?"

"No, nor are any of the members of the board of directors, although

Gruppo ENIL-EX, which is one of the larger Valatestan-registered corporations, holds 185,472,000 shares, or one point one two percent of the shares outstanding. Two of the government board members also sit on Gruppo ENIL-EX's board."

"The CRO, by any chance?"

"No, in fact, both are members of a rival family."

Probably nothing there, Tower concluded. "All right, tell me more about the Morchardese?"

"Morcharders," Baby corrected him. "The new regime has adopted a new calendar, a new monetary system, new tax reforms, and now insist on being referred to as Morcharders rather than Morchardese. There is considerable ill-feeling towards the government-in-exile, as it is estimated that the royal family managed to transfer approximately 64 percent of the government's exoplanetary holdings to private accounts beyond the reach of the new regime."

"So they're hard up."

"Very much so, and they will be until the new wave of alien investment begins to have an economic effect. It will take decades to replace the assets the previous government now holds."

"It was a lot of money then. Enough to finance a counter-revolution? Their digs weren't bad, but it didn't look to me as if they were living anywhere nearly as large as they could."

"There is no question that the Morchardese royal family could afford to finance a successful invasion if they could be assured that the Unity would stay out of it. Notice that the current government's representation here is a small office suit in a technology park. In my opinion, the corporatist fears of the Morchardese royals are not misplaced, as their continued survival is primarily dependent upon Unity goodwill."

"Which explains why they are bending over backward to give the Unity every concession and trade monopoly that might appeal to it." Tower snorted. "Well, if they're really depending upon Unity goodwill, the poor bastards are obviously doomed!"

Baby was silent for a few moments. Then she spoke up. "Tower,

I have confirmation of your appointment with the Morcharder Embassy at eleven hundred hours. You will be meeting with the envoy. He is a registered shareholder by the name of Willem Daendels and controls 45,000 shares in the new government. He is also one of the original revolutionaries, a graduate student turned pamphleteer who was imprisoned by the former regime for three months after publishing an unflattering critique of the then-heir to the throne, Crown Prince Pons-Zoltan."

"Only 45,000?" That didn't seem like much, not when alien corporations held more than a thousand times that many. He tried to run the numbers again in his head. Several thousand times that many.

"It is a serious point of contention on Morchard of late. Most of the original revolutionaries have been considerably diluted, and some have even been entirely bought out. There are also widespread rumors, which I am presently unable to confirm, that the royal family has been buying shares in the government through a series of front corporations."

"I wouldn't put it past those bloody royals. I'll bet that chaps Mr. Daendel's backside."

"Indeed, Tower. As a matter of fact, Mr. Daendels recently co-published a paper entitled *Direct and Indirect Exo-Investment in the Corporate Republic of Morchard: Issues, Problems, and Crimes.*"

"Sounds fascinating."

"The abstract is as follows: *In this paper, we have attempted to identify the issues and problems associated with the corporate republic's current exoplanetary direct investment regime, and more importantly, the other associated factors responsible for Morchard's present attractiveness as an investment location and the concomitant imbalances created thereby. Despite the corporate republic offering a large planetary market, rule of law, low labor costs, and a functional political system based upon the most current scientific theory, the government's performance in attracting DIExI flows has been far from satisfactory. A permissive DIExI regime, high income taxes, export regulations for planetary corporations, stringent labor laws, poor quality infrastructure, centralized decision-making processes, and the failure to recover stolen exoplanetary asserts have combined to make Morchard an overly attractive investment location for alien corporate investors to the detriment of the planetary population.*"

She paused. "Would you like me to read more? It might be helpful in better understanding the envoy's mentality."

"I'd rather have you smash this var into the nearest skytower without slowing down," Tower told her sincerely. "Or listen to you sing that whole book of Christer hymns all the way through again. How long is it."

"101,370 words. And you shouldn't whine so much when you lose a bet."

"A hundred thousand words? Deep space!" Tower swore. As far as he was concerned, the King of Morchard hadn't gone far enough in jailing the man. He should have shot the lunatic. If there was one thing worse than a revolutionary, it was a revolutionary with a recording device and an endless supply of big words.

Then he reconsidered. Every cloud really did have its silver lining.

"Yeah, that's a great idea, Baby. Go for it!"

"Really?"

"Yeah, really."

"*Introduction. The corporate republic's economic policy reforms have played a critical role in the performance of the post-revolutionary economy since 3400. Among other things, the reforms have involved opening the economy to direct and indirect investment from a wide spectrum of exoplanetary entities, making it more competitive, removing the government from the huge morass of regulatory complications, empowering the common people to take more responsibility for economic management, and thereby creating competition between planetary cities and corporations for alien investors. The GDP growth rate which had collapsed to -7.8% in 3402 rebounded to a near normal -0.3% in 3403, however...*"

Tower's eyelids grew heavier and heavier as Baby droned on. Before she had even come close to finishing the paper's introduction, he was sleeping soundly.

Tower's confidence that he'd be able to dig something useful out of the corporate republic's envoy began to fade when Baby set down on the top of the technopark's tower amidst shabby aerovars that were considerably outnumbered by the single-man scootjets that filled most of the parking lot. He could just barely make out the spire of the Valatestan embassy to the north, and a more distinct contrast between the two buildings would have been hard to draw outside the slums. In addition to Daendel striking him as more a man of words than action, how likely was it that a government that couldn't afford better accommodations would be throwing away hundreds of thousands of civars on weaponized implants for homeless veterans and unused Mosin-Nyarlas?

On the other hand, the man wasn't just a revolutionary, he was a successful one. And he wouldn't be the first to wield the sword as readily as the pen. He had Baby check Daendels's records for specifics.

"The envoy is the former commander of the Sanguinello, which I believe is a morbid pun of sorts relating to the colors of the royal house. They were a much-feared guerilla group that is believed responsible for the deaths of two regional governors and three members of the royal house, in addition to an estimated 463 commoners."

"So this wouldn't be the first time he knocked off a prince."

"Technically, yes, it would be. The previous royal victims were two dukes and a city-holder. However, if he was involved in the Jagaelleon murder, it would indicate his methods have considerably changed since his revolutionary days."

"How so?"

"The Sanguinello tended to favor beheading their victims and mounting the heads in public places, with long treatises that delineated their grievances nailed to the foreheads."

"Sounds like a lovely guy," Tower said. He found it astonishing to observe how many of the most violent killers were highly educated. But Baby was right. Disruptors probably weren't Daendels's style. On the other hand, he had been the guerilla group's leader, not its hatchet man. "Well, let's see if it looks like the envoy is up to his old tricks again. Are the Sangria-whatevers still around?"

"No, they and all the paramilitary groups were disbanded three years ago at the direction of the new governing board. Some of the members were subsumed into the military forces, others deemed unfit for post-revolutionary life were exiled or executed."

Smart, violent, lucky, and almost certainly bitter. Tower wondered that MCID hadn't flagged the Morcharder as a potential troublemaker already. The envoy might not have the late crown prince's blood on his hands, but Tower estimated the chances the guy wasn't up to something problematic as somewhere between naught and zero.

He took the stairs rather than trust the ancient lift and descended the eighteen flights to a small door that was adorned with an etched brass plaque that said Corporate Republic of Morchard underneath a logo of a stylized fist holding a broken crown. There was no buzzer or cam that he could see, so he awkwardly knocked on the false wood of the door.

The door was opened by a small man who barely came up to Tower's chin. He was podgy, prematurely balding, and squinted as he peered at Tower. "Ah, you must be the gentleman from the planetary military. I've been expecting you. Come in, come in!"

The Morcharder seemed genuinely pleased to see Tower, which Tower found mystifying. His offices were two small rooms, with collectively less space than Tower's apartment. One room had a couch that looked as if it doubled as a bed, and with the exception of a modest screen in the room with a desk and two chairs, the walls in both rooms were covered from floor to ceiling with shelving containing thin rectangular objects. Books, Tower realized, as he leaned in closely to look at a blue one decorated with silver scribbles, marveling at it. It wasn't the sort of thing you saw everyday, or much at all outside of museums.

"I have a weakness for antiques," Daendels confessed. "Forgive me, I am rude. I am Willem Daendels, the Corporate Republic of Morchard's envoy to Duke Rhys-Mereth. I presume you are Officer Tower?"

"Graven Tower, Chief Warrant Officer, Military Crimes Investigative Division, Excellency." Tower took the man's extended hand and was unsurprised to feel it was soft and puffy. "Thank you for taking the time to see me."

"Am I correct in assuming you are here in regards to the recent death of Mr. Jagaelleon?"

"You are, Excellency. I hope you don't mind if I ask you a few questions."

"Not at all, not at all." The Morcharder offered Tower the larger of the two chairs in the office, then took the other himself. "I realize that my government, if not my person, must be considered one of the leading suspects in Mr. Jagaelleon's murder."

"That doesn't appear to bother you," Tower observed.

"His death or the fact of my being a suspect? I am not troubled by the latter. I know for a fact that neither my government, nor myself, was responsible for it."

"A fact?" Tower studied the little man. "And I noticed you only mentioned the latter. So his death bothers you?"

"It does indeed. And yes, although it is said to be difficult to prove a negative, in this particular case I can do so. Furthermore, in doing so, it should explain why I do not rejoice in the death of another royal."

"That would be impressive," Tower said. "Go ahead, Excellency, impress me."

The Morcharder reached into his desk and withdrew a folder. He opened it and Tower could see that it contained paper inside. "Here is your proof. It is my government's plans for dealing with the fugitives from the people's justice that call themselves royal."

Tower took the folder and glanced at the papers. Instead of reading them, he held them up to the screen behind him, one by one, and let

Baby scan them. As far as he was able to tell, it was mostly a reiteration of the death sentences given in absentia.

"*Tower, these contain plans for assassinating the entire royal family! There are three plants in the household staff; the envoy is to activate them via a public statement.*"

"I don't understand, Excellency. You're admitting to plotting to kill them?"

The envoy smiled affably, unperturbed. "Not at all. I'm admitting that the governing board was plotting to kill them. Now have your augment look at this."

He tapped his desk, activating the big screen, but nothing happened. On the screen, an image of a planet, presumably Morchard, appeared and slowly began to rotate.

"*I'm getting a stream of data from the office brain. Tower, Daendels was in communication with the murdered prince! He even let him know about the plot and the planted staff members. It looks as if they were secret allies!*"

The envoy from the new regime and the heir to the old one?

"*Yes!*"

"You betrayed your own revolution," Tower said, staring at the little man with surprise. "Is that your defense, that you didn't merely lack means, but motive too?"

"I didn't betray the revolution, Officer Tower." The Morcharder was still smiling, but his eyes were hard. "The revolution was betrayed by the Board members. The Board used we true revolutionaries and sold out the people in favor of exoplanetary interests. As for the royals, unlike his father and his elder brother, Prince Arpad was a reformer. He understood the mistakes of his forebears and he was determined to rectify them. We met in secret twice, at his lover's apartment. We came as enemies and departed as allies, perhaps even co-conspirators. Who can say what would have come of it, but there is no question that his death is a tremendous loss to Morchard and the true spirit of the revolution."

"So after fighting the royal house for years, you were willing to turn around and support it on the basis of two meetings?" That seemed unlikely, but Tower knew stranger things had happened. "Is it possible you just found yourself flattered by the royal attention? My understanding is that can be a pretty heady experience for a commoner."

"It is possible." The envoy smiled. "Then again, I personally hammered the nails that attached declarations of the people's accusations against the crown into three royal skulls, so it wasn't my first encounter with the house of Jagaelleon."

Tower stared at the balding little man with a feeling that was akin to awe. He had known a few hard men in his day, Marines' Marines, ice cold killers, and men who carried out their orders, however terrible, without hesitation or regret. His job brought him into regular contact with mercenaries and assassins; he had tracked down fourteen killers-for-hire in the last three years alone. He had interrogated triggermen as well as their employers, who never got even the smallest particle of human blood on their immaculately tailored clothing. But he felt certain that he had never encountered anyone as perfectly ruthless as this owlish, mild-mannered academic.

"Who contacted who? Did you contact him or did he get in touch with you."

"The latter. I recently wrote an academic paper on alien investment on Morchard and its effect on the economy, which attracted considerable attention both here and back home on Morchard."

"I read it."

"Oh, did you now?" Daendels raised his eyebrows. "I did not expect that. Well, then, you understand the depth of the sea of corruption in which the present corporate republic is swimming. In retrospect, it was a terrible mistake to permit off-planet entities to purchase government shares. We were far too naïve in that regard. We dethroned a king and crowned a corporation in his stead. Prince Arpad must have read it and recognized a potentially useful ally; he contacted me about three rotations ago and set up the first meeting in Trans Paradis."

"How did he contact you? Through his girlfriend?"

"No, a courier. On paper."

Tower nodded. That made sense. Both he and Hildy had checked over Mara Tanabera's comm records and he'd found it hard to imagine they'd somehow missed a call to the Morcharder consulate. And they'd only run face-scans of visitors to her building floor for the last two weeks.

"Your last meeting with him was more than two weeks ago?"

"Yes, it was last rotation." The envoy grimaced and shook his head. "I will not pretend that Arpad Jagaelleon was the optimal choice, but you have to understand, Officer Tower, that between him and the corrupt corporatists who betrayed the revolution, there was no question that he was the better option."

Tower nodded, but he wasn't really listening. He had already reached a conclusion. Despite his harmless appearance, Willem Daendels was a killer without conscience who had already helped hurl his world into violent upheaval once in the last decade. It was clear that he wouldn't hesitate to do it as often as he deemed it necessary. Daendels was dangerous, and he bore close watching by MCID if not the immediate revocation of his diplomatic credentials and his residence permit. But it was also apparent that the little man didn't have anything to do with the crown prince's death or the subsequent assassination attempt on his brother.

"What did the crown prince do with the information about the corporatist plants on his staff?"

"I do not know. I would assume they have all met with unfortunate accidents by now."

They certainly would have if Daendels was in charge. But that wasn't necessarily how a reformer prince would have reacted. Tower made a mental note to check on the fate of the three Morcharders and decided it was time to return to Trans Paradis. Either the corporatists on Morchard believed in redundancy or they were simply another dead end.

"Thank you for your cooperation, Excellency. If you happen to come across information that your government is attempting more attacks on the Morchardese embassy or the royal family, I would appreciate it if you would contact me immediately."

"I will do so," Daendels promised. Tower assumed he was lying, but given the man's fluid loyalties, it couldn't hurt to ask.

"One last question. Now that Arpad Jagaelleon is dead, will you support his brother if he makes an attempt to reclaim the planet?"

"That entirely depends upon Prince Janos." Daendels shrugged. "My commitment was to his brother, not to the royal house. If he endorses Prince Arpad's program of reform, I expect he will find many supporters both here and at home."

Tower nodded. "That's a fair answer. Now, let me give you a piece of advice, Excellency. I believe you didn't have anything to do with the attacks on the two Jagaelleons. But the government you represent was planning attacks here on Rhysalan. That's not acceptable. If you want to fight it out with corporatists or kings or giant star goats, I don't care, so long as you don't do it on this planet! The Duke prides himself in providing a place of refuge to everyone who requests it, and he does not take it lightly when his hospitality is abused. Do you understand?"

"Perfectly."

Tower had never seen a man who looked less intimidated. Feeling frustrated and vaguely defeated, he left the shabby little consulate and ascended the stairs to the roof of the building. Once he was in the aerovar, he saw that Hildy had called him twice. He had Baby ring her back.

"Good morning, Tower. How is Rhys City?"

"More interesting on screen than in person. I just spoke with the Corporate Republic's envoy. Looks like we can cross off the new regime."

"You're kidding!"

"I wish I were. They're every bit as bloodthirsty and homicidal as we imagined, maybe even a bit more so. But they're short on means, they don't have motive for reasons I'll explain in person, and their methods don't even come close to matching. I'm not ruling them out entirely, but I'd say it's less than a five percent chance that they were involved."

"Hmmm..." Hildy mused. "That's disappointing. Well, I've got better news for you."

"Lay it on me."

"Mr. Dunn finally woke up. As it happens, you were right. He lost an eye and an arm on Syranecus."

We are initiating an annual high threat post review chaired by the Lord Secretary of Subsector Affairs and ongoing reviews by the deputy secretaries to ensure that pivotal questions about security reach the highest levels. We will also regularize protocols for sharing information with His Grace's Armed Forces. These actions are designed to increase the safety of our diplomats and military personnel and reduce the chances of another Basattria happening.

—*Transcript of the Basattrian Investigatory Panel's Report to His Grace*

The crowd began assembling in the early afternoon. At first, it was just a few scattered young males walking past, shaking their upper appendages, baring their needle teeth, and hissing at Lance Corporal Tower and the other Marine posted outside the security entrance to the ducal consulate. As the sky darkened, their numbers grew, swelled by females with young and an increasing number of the big males, including several obvious hunt leaders. Their confidence grew too, and they began coming closer and closer to the two marines despite the powered battle armor that rendered a human more than a match for a Basattrian even without the Hydra FM-4 fusion pulse thrower attached to their right arms.

In addition to the Hydra, Tower wore a Sphinx CPB-18 at his hip and a Benelli-Mossberg ASE-5K was resting in the slot behind his left shoulder. The other marine, PFC Mike Josephs, was similarly equipped, although in the place of the Benelli-Mossberg he had a mini-rack of six Skyseeker missiles mounted on his back. Between the two of them, they had enough firepower to not only disperse the crowd, but destroy a significant percentage of the Basattrian city's infrastructure and air traffic.

That didn't mean they weren't nervous, though. Quite the opposite. The consul had been perfectly clear about their rules of engagement. They were not to open fire in any circumstances whatsoever. Tower doubted they were actually expected to allow themselves to be ripped to pieces by the big, six-armed lizard people, but the stupid restriction meant that neither he nor Josephs had any idea at what point the situation should be considered an emergency or a combat engagement.

As the crowd, which Tower now estimated at about six hundred, pressed closer, Josephs decided he'd had enough. He flipped open a section of the armor under his left wrist, tapped in a code, and began establishing a perimeter with the four quarpods that emerged from a small slot in the bottom of the security door. In obedience to his direction, each settled down at four separate points that formed an arc encompassing both marines, then raised a red arc of light that shimmered an ominous warning to the crowd.

"Sitrep, Corporal?" It was Captain Hagel, the commander of the consulate's security detail.

"It's getting ugly, sir. We've seen a few alphas show up, so we established a 10-meter perimeter with the quaddos."

"Set to what?"

Tower checked. "80 volts, sir. Enough to sting 'em, not enough to stun."

"Carry on, Corporal."

"No worries, sir. Any chance we can get some eyes in the sky, sir?"

"Negative, Corporal. Just hang tight. Comm links are still down, but those runners we sent out should be reaching base right about now. Until we can get the links restored, we're limited to line-of-sight. So don't go running around any corners, right?"

"Yessir. Any chance you can patch me through to my wife, Captain?"

"Affirmative, Corporal. But keep it short."

Tower looked out at the loud and angry crowd. He didn't really understand what the Basattrians were supposed to be upset about, but they had been up in arms protesting the presence of humans from every planet for five days now. Before the comms went down this afternoon, there were reports of fourteen different embassies being stormed, including the one belonging to the Ascendancy itself. Tower had just about convinced himself that the lizard people were going to leave the little Rhysalani consulate alone, thanks to the small army base not fifteen kilometers away, when the first young males began prowling the open plaza in front of the consulate.

"Hey Grave" he heard Melassa say. "Are you all right?"

"Yeah, although next time I say you take that job with Intercore." His wife was a civilian administrative assistant to the consul; she'd cashed in every favor she was owed and borrowed a few more to see that Tower was assigned to the small Marine detail charged with providing consulate security. "It's mostly a lot of shouting and fist-shaking. They don't have the tech to crack our shells, so there's nothing to worry about."

"Well, be careful out there," she said. "I heard the consul say this should all blow over in a day or two, but our comms are still down. The techs think the Basattrians are jamming us somehow."

"Don't worry about me, baby. Between me and Josephs, we got enough firepower to take out three cities. The lizards are just mad, they're not stupid. You keep yourself busy and I'll be off-shift in a few kilosecs."

"Okay, come find me as soon as you come in. I love you."

"You too, baby."

He cut the connection. Josephs glanced in his direction.

"Well?"

"The consul won't let us put up any drones. Thinks it might be seen as an aggressive gesture."

"Screw that. How we supposed to know what's really going on out there when we can't see nothing?"

The red neuro-electrical shield flared as one particularly bold, or unusually stupid, young male tested the red lines. He roared and leaped away, making a gesture with his middle arms that one didn't have to be a Basattrian to understand. Tower resisted the momentary urge to respond in kind. The crowd had continued to swell, and with darkness falling, fires were being set in the plaza.

"So much for the cavalry," he heard Josephs say. He didn't understand at first, until he saw a group of roaring Basattrians pushing their way through the crowd toward them. They were shoving one Basattrian before them and carrying another above their heads. They hurled the one they were carrying down and Tower could see it was dead from the way it slumped bonelessly on the ground. Tower didn't know much about Basattrian expressions; he and Melassa had only been on Basattria for five rotations, but he could see the live one was terrified.

"I know that one. Those are our messengers," Josephs said grimly. "What are we going to do? We can't just let them kill him."

"Captain, we have a situation," Tower told the security commander. "The two messengers we sent were captured. One is dead, the other one is captured. It looks like they intend to kill him right in front of us. Request permission to rescue the local collaborator, sir."

"Negative, corporal. Hold your fire. Do not intervene. Repeat, do not intervene."

"But sir, he's one of ours!"

"Corporal Tower, I have given you an order. Do you copy?"

"I copy, sir. Hold fire, do not intervene."

The Basattrian made a noise Tower didn't even realize the lizards could make. He didn't have to be a xenobiologist to recognize it as a scream. One of the big alphas was holding a burning piece of something to the captive's scaled belly.

"Tower, they're going to kill him," Josephs said.

"Captain says we got to hold our fire and stay out of it."

Between the bestial roaring of the Basattrian crowd, the screaming of the lizard being tortured and the growing number of fires dancing in the dark, it was a perfect image of Hell. But when the lizard's cries didn't provoke either Tower or Josephs into action, his torturers finally gave up and began to drag him away into the crowd. Burned and injured, the lizard didn't even attempt to resist.

"Oh, no, you don't," Josephs said, almost under his breath, and he began to run forward.

"Mike!" Tower shouted. "Stop, Mike! Come back."

"Private Josephs, you will return at once!" Captain Hagel shouted. "That is an order, private!"

The Basattrians closed on Josephs at once. He smashed two of them aside, but then a large alpha sprang at him and knocked him off balance. The marine staggered under the blow and nearly went down, but somehow managed to keep his feet. He dropped the alpha with an armored elbow and booted a smaller lizard out of the way. Then he was moving again, through the dark sea of green scales, and Tower had to boost his IR to see him. Josephs stood out like a bright red-and-yellow light amidst the cool light blues of the cold-blooded lizards, but despite his powered battlesuit, the weight of the Basattrian numbers slowed his advance almost to a halt. He stubbornly punched and kicked and shoved his way forward, until he was nearly fifty meters away from the consulate and all but invisible.

Tower didn't know what to do. Adrenaline surged through his body and every last vestige of his training urged him to go after his fellow marine, but now the consul was linked in and he was screaming furiously in his earpiece about court martials and dereliction of duty.

Tower froze, unable to move, or to speak, he just stood and watched Josephs methodically smashing his servo-powered way through the masses of Basattrian bodies in pursuit of the captive.

Then a red beam lit up the darkening sky, a bolt from a laser fired from a building on the far side of the plaza. Tower saw Joseph's suit flare red and knew that he'd been hit.

"Captain, we're taking fire! Permission to engage."

"Get back in here, Tower. Back up to the door and we'll let you in. This is getting out of hand. Come inside now."

Then a second laser was fired, and a third.

"Mike, they're telling us to come in. Get back here, man!"

"I got the guy," he heard Josephs panting. "I got him, but you've got to cover me. There's too many of them! I can't fight them off and drag him at the same time!"

"Leave them, Tower! Come inside now. We're going to lock down."

Tower made up his mind. He was a Marine, and Marines don't leave men behind, even if the men are lizards.

"Hold on, Mike, I'm coming!"

He charged forward, knocking lizards down left and right as he ran. One big male snapped at him and he punched it, shattering its jaw with the augmented power of the battle armor. Having caught the Basattrians entirely by surprise, he managed to reach Josephs in a matter of decaseconds. Two more laser beams tore up the bricks around them, but Tower lifted his arm and fired back with a brief pulse of fusion hellfire that blew out the upper section of the building where the snipers were located. That not only put an end to the incoming fire, but caused the lizards that were pressing in on them to shriek in outrage and fall back, terrified that the two Marines were about to open up on them.

Then his armor beeped an alert. There was an unidentified aerial object approaching the plaza, and it was coming in low and fast. Was it the Navy? It was coming in from more or less the right direction, but why didn't its transponder register? A moment later, he had his answer.

A Unity MA-33 Turmfalke, a ground attack craft that was a good five tech levels higher than legal on this TL-13 world, was hovering above the plaza to the south.

"What is that thing doing there?" Mike shouted.

But Tower knew. The Turmfalke was how the low-tech lizards had broken into all the human embassies. That explained why they'd even dared to attack the Ascendancy. And that was how, and why, the consulate's communications were being jammed.

"Bring it down," he shouted at Josephs. "Captain, get everyone into the shelter now!"

He didn't know what weaponry an MA-33 carried, but it wasn't big enough to be carrying daisy cutters or tunnel worms. It was a hunter-killer designed to kill ground troops and take out lightly fortified positions, not destroy armored bunkers. But he was pretty sure it packed enough punch to crack open the consulate like a sledgehammer cracking an egg.

"That's not possible," he heard Captain Hagel say.

Tower didn't bother to ask for permission, he raised his arm and fired the FM-4 at the warcraft hovering overhead. It was a useless gesture; the beam splattered against the MA-33's invisible shields in a harmless purple explosion. A moment later, two missiles jetted out from underneath the Turmfalke's curved wings.

Tower screamed in futile anguish as the huge double explosion lifted him off the ground and hurled him away from the building. He was rising, rising, and then he was falling, tumbling head-over-heels toward the rapidly approaching ground…

"Tower!"

It was a dream. It was a nightmare. No, it was worse. It was a memory. He shuddered at the recollection, at the memory of rising from the stone plaza and seeing the sight of the smoke and flames rising from the shattered wreckage of the consulate.

"Tower!" Baby's repeated barking finally claimed his attention.

"We're back in Trans Paradis. Detector Hildreth asked you to contact her when you returned."

Tower didn't reply right away. He was still trying to deal with the ocean of emotions that surged within him, the wave of madness threatening to tear him away from the pier of sanity to which he clung. He ran through the color program his neurotherapist had given him. Despair was grey-purple. Loss was the sickly yellow-green of vomit. Rage was dark red, the scarlet of a high-powered laser or the oxygen-rich blood that spattered his armor as he wreaked vengeful havoc upon the unarmed Basattrian civilians. Black, the bottomless black of deepest space, was hate. It was hate for the lizards, for the Unity, for the bureaucrats who dropped them in the soup and left them there to die, and for every cursed xeno, human or alien, in the galactic spirals.

He took a deep breath and envisioned the colors swirling about him, engulfing him, bathing him in their reeking, burning foulness. And then he pictured a white light, a pure, unadulterated white that was not the absence of colors, but the fullness of every color there had been, was, or one day would be, burning the foulness away from him. The image was so real he almost screamed as he pictured the steam rising off his naked body, cleaned and purified by the perfect light.

He took a deep breath. He was sane again. He was whole again. He opened his eyes.

"What time is it? You said Hildy wanted to get in touch?"

"Are you all right, Tower? Your vital signs were showing unwarranted indications of physical distress, which given your history can be an indication of psychological aberrations."

"I'm fine, Baby," he reassured the augment. "Don't worry about me. Did I sleep all the way from Rhys City?"

"If you can reasonably call anything that involves that much thrashing about and mumbling sleep, then yes, Tower, you were asleep. It's zero six ten."

"I should have had you read that paper to me again. If Pfiffner could figure out how to turn it into tablets, no one would ever miss out on a good night's sleep. Why don't you see if Hildy's up."

She wasn't, but she took the call, answering it in a sleepy voice.

"Hey Tower. You back?"

"Just. What do you think, your place or mine?"

"Yours. I think we're going to need your access to records that are out of my reach," she said. "No, go back to sleep, tell McCandless I'll be at MCID all morning."

Tower froze. He felt as if his heart stopped. She wasn't talking to him. She was talking to someone else. Someone else who worked in the Trans Paradis Police Department. Certain colors began to lazily stir in the depths of his mind. Greys and purples, with the occasional flash of red.

"Tower?" Hildy repeated. "You still there?"

"Yeah, yeah," he said. "Sorry, just, ah, just waking up myself. Yeah, we can meet there. Zero nine hundred work for you?"

"Sounds great. See you there, Tower."

She broke the connection. Tower laughed grimly. Her personal life was none of his business. There was nothing between them, they were just two cops working on a case together. It wasn't as if she'd broken his heart. He didn't have one left to break.

All the same, the sun that was still rising in the brilliant morning sky left him as cold as if it had never risen at all.

The revolution represented the majority of the planet and the most essential interests of the majority of the Morchardese population, therefore its violence was progressive rather than systematic. The monarchy's violence was systematic and systematically arbitrary because it represented a minority destined to disappear. It is most probable that the revolution too will find itself forced to resort to similar, and perhaps even more extreme, forms of violence, but as a transition, and with the certainty of historical justice to justify it. The difference is that the monarchy represented the minority of the planetary interests, while the revolution represents the majority.

—*A History of the Revolution on Morchard*, Graham Eccles-Hamlin

Hildy was entirely normal, greeting Tower with a smile and a friendly kiss on the cheek as if nothing had happened a few kilosecs ago. Tower felt as if the expression he forced himself to wear was as artificial as a clown's broad, red-lipped smile, but once they got past the initial pleasantries, he was able to focus on the task at hand. He did his best to forget where that lithe, sweet-hipped figure had been the night before, and what lucky bastard had been running his hands over those lovely curves.

"Here are the three Morcharder agents." When she looked blank, he explained. "The corporatists call themselves Morcharders, as opposed to the royalist Morchardese. It's a part of their whole new start theme or something. Anyhow, one of them was supposed to make the move, only they didn't, because Willem Daendels, the control who was running them, decided the revolution was insufficiently impure and threw his lot in with the Crown Prince."

"He switched sides?"

"Yeah, he even met twice with the prince at Tanabera's place. Baby confirmed his account last night."

"You buy it?"

Tower nodded. "Yeah, he is a serious piece of work. Academic, writes manifestos and treatises the way your average citizen watches the screens. He had whole walls of old-style books and Baby said his revolutionary group had a body count of around five hundred. My take is that he'd execute his own mother if he decided she was insufficiently loyal to the revolution."

"Ah, one of those." Hildy grinned. "Yeah, that sort doesn't usually hide what they've done. Easiest conviction I ever got was an environmental revolutionary who insisted on reading his justification for murdering a transport company's VP in court. It took him two kilosecs to get through the whole thing, and afterwards, the prosecutor didn't call a single witness. The funny thing is that the guy was genuinely shocked when the panel of judges convicted him."

Tower laughed. "I don't think this guy is quite that clueless, but yeah, he's the type. Also, he gave us the names he gave to the crown prince, so my thought is that we ought to see what the prince did about them, if anything."

Three pictures appeared on the wall screen, each with their most recent appearances in the Trans Paradis omni-security web marked on a city map. All three were very close to the Morchardese embassy.

"Looks like nothing," Hildy said. "Oldest cam hit is yesterday morning."

"Can we tie any of them to Valatesta or Mr. Milazzo?"

"I can't find anything," Baby said. "I'll keep looking, but I don't see any signs."

Hildy frowned. "That second name... why does that look familiar?"

They both looked at each other. "The girl, the prince's private assistant!" Tower exclaimed.

"Annaliese van de Boer," Baby helpfully reminded them. "It appears she is a competent actress."

"The question is: do we let the Prime Captain Kotant know? It might be wise to take her into protective custody first, otherwise TPPD might have a third murder to investigate if he figures it out. He had no reason to be digging into his staff before, but you can be certain he's been doing so ever since Prince Arpad was killed. And if he makes the connection to Tanabera..."

"Good point," Hildy admitted. "What if we do this? You call Kotant and tell him you've got information on the new regime. Set up a meeting here. While he's here, I'll visit the embassy and take Miss van de Boer into custody as a material witness."

"That should work," Tower said. "Baby, set it up, will you?"

There was a moment's pause. Then Hildy cleared her throat uncomfortably and pointedly looked away from him. Her face and neck were flushed red.

"Look, ah, Tower, I'm sorry about this morning. I guess I should have told you I was, you know, seeing someone."

"No, why?" Tower protested, feeling as awkward as Hildy looked. "Your personal life isn't my business."

"Well, I sort of had the idea that you were, maybe, interested, you know?"

Tower looked up at the ceiling and took a deep breath, picturing how the storm troopers of Bio Resources would be bursting in on them in about three decasecs. "Look, Hildy, you're a good cop. I like you and I think we make a good team. But I'm a beat-up old soldier and I've got scars that run deeper than you can probably imagine."

Hildy snorted. "I don't know, Tower, after yesterday's performance, you might be surprised what I can imagine. I've never had nightmares about an arrest before."

"So you're dreaming about me now?" They both laughed. "The point is, I don't have any illusions about you, or me, or this case. What I might like, or what might have been if I was younger and less messed up, that doesn't matter. Life don't care what you want."

She reached out and took his hand. "You're not that old, Tower. What are you, thirty? You're too young to talk like a broken old man. You may be scarred and you may be a little scary sometimes, but you know, that's just the sort of thing that girls find intriguing."

Tower raised a skeptical eyebrow. She laughed and withdrew her hand.

"Hey, scarred and scary beats boring any day!"

"We may have a problem," Baby announced abruptly. "Neither Kotant nor van de Boer are in residence at the Embassy. Van de Boer didn't turn up for work and Kotant left the premises in an aerovar twelve hectasecs ago. I did a little digging into their communications system and I found this message he sent to Lieutenant van Node, the Security second."

She displayed it on the screen. The message was as succinct as it was worrisome.

Have a line on probable corporatist infiltrator. Pull all data linked to ID F0384 for processing. Will discuss this afternoon.

"He's going after her!" Hildy said. "Dammit, if we don't find her first, we won't find her alive."

Tower rose from his desk and checked to be sure he had his Sphinx on his belt. "It's a good thing we've got better tools than he does. Baby, Victor, get to it and find both of them please. Baby, what do you have on Kotant? I assume he's competent, how dangerous is he?"

"Do you think we need backup?" Hildy asked, a little nervously.

"Probably not. He doesn't want trouble with the local authorities, but he's going to want to drain her dry. There should be room to negotiate even if he finds her first, unless he figures she doesn't know anything useful and kills her out of hand."

"The prime captain was a special forces officer for seven years, after which he was appointed as a bodyguard, first for the queen, then for the various crown princes. He did three tours of duty in combat zones, on Altain, Soal-Frost, and Gantry Thirty-Two."

Tower winced. If the man survived the storming of Soal-Frost, he was salty.

"He also fought in the revolution, which was even bloodier than the wars. Morchardese special forces units suffered forty percent fatality rates during the six years that preceded the royal exile, mostly as a result of rebel forces striking at homes and private residences–"

Even better. The man might not be as pitiless by nature as Daendels the revolutionary, but civil wars had been stripping men of their humanity since before Man first left Terra. After six years of no-quarter combat, the prime captain would probably fit right in at MCID.

"I've got the Morchardese woman's location," Baby said. "She's at the Tearmann Memorial Libratech. I have her number too. Do you want me to contact her?"

"What's she doing at a libratech?" Hildy wondered.

"Could be a drop," Tower suggested. "Baby, put me through to her, please."

To his surprise, he didn't just get her voice; the young woman's pretty face appeared on the screen. Then he recalled that there were plenty of screens at the libratech.

"Mr. Tower?"

"Miss van de Boer." He nodded to her. "I have to warn you, Miss van de Boer, that there is reason to believe you may be in imminent danger."

Her wide-eyed look of shock was perfectly convincing. If Tower hadn't known better, he'd have sworn she had no idea what he was talking about.

"I'm in danger, me?" Her hand fluttered to her mouth. "But why?"

"Don't bother with the act, Miss van de Boer. There is no time for it. We know you're a Morcharder, an agent for the corporate republic."

Tower almost laughed as the young woman dropped the pretense of innocence. Suddenly, in the place of a wide-eyed, fresh-faced beauty was a hard-faced and calculating agent. The speed of the switch was breathtaking.

"Are the exiles onto me? Did they penetrate my cover?"

"Yes. Last night or early this morning."

"And how do you know about it? How can I trust you?"

Tower grinned, amused by her suspicion. "I don't give a damn if you trust me or not. Prime Captain Kotant is out looking for you right now. If you like, I can just close this contact and let Detector Hildreth know who will be the prime suspect in your murder."

"Okay, all right, you're right. Where is that big brute? I don't have a security tag… but he can probably track my embassy credit chip. Mr. Tower, I'm not armed, is there anything you can do for me? Please?"

Her wide blue eyes were sweetly imploring. They even might have moved him if he didn't know how false she was.

"Knock it off, Blondie. I'm not going to keep Kotant from killing you because of your broken wing routine. I'm going to stop him because it's my job and because the Duke really doesn't like it when you off-planet types have the discourtesy to shit all over his hospitality. Now leave your credit chip where you are and Detector Hildreth will give you directions on where to run."

"Miss van de Boer, do you know where the city archives are? The history building, I mean? It's not far from the Tearmann." While he was talking Hildy had been working out the young woman's route to safety.

"Yeah, I know it." The young woman was surprisingly calm for someone with a target on her head. But then, she would have been trained for these situations.

"Exit the Tearmann and go left. There's a skytube station about 200 meters. Take that to the archives. Once you're there, tell the receptionist to take you to the police department's safe room. The code word is… hold on… 'excavate'. Remember that. Excavate. Now get moving, we'll be there in about a kilosec."

"Oh, thank you, Detector. Please hurry!" She disappeared from the screen, already in motion, and Tower cut the contact.

"All right, let's roll." He strode from his office and snagged his tac-jacket off the hook on the run. Then he reassured himself that his Sphinx was still in place before beckoning Hildy to follow him to the parking garage. "You secure her. I'll hunt down Kotant. If she can make it to the tube, she should be all right. He'll be in a var and won't have access even if he's got a tracker on her."

"We'll see. Be careful, Tower," Hildy said as they rode down the grav lift after Tower punched in an override to be sure they would not be stopped on intervening floors. "That Kotant is dangerous. He knows what he's doing."

Tower bared his teeth and snorted contemptuously. "So do I, Hildy. So do I."

Six hectaseconds later, Tower was hovering in his aerovar in the bright sun high above the landing platform that was closest to the Tearmann Memorial Libratech. It was one of the ugliest buildings in the city, which Tower found ironic given the beauty of the artwork it contained. The Libratech took up the top fifty stories of a wide tower done in plascrete and tri-steel. But some architectural genius had decided to add a facade constructed of imitation granite, complete with faux gargoyles, onto the modern materials. It was the sort of mashup that must have required multiple committees to conceive and construct.

According to the city schedule, Van de Boer would still be on the tube, but she was safe now. Baby had locked onto Kotant's diplomatic tags almost as soon as they'd gotten in the air and the Morchardese captain had fallen for the bait. That was a relief; the thought that the Morchardese might have a bio tag implanted in the girl without her knowledge had occurred to him right after Hildy peeled off and headed for the archives. The last thing he wanted was to put the young Detector in between the combat-experienced Prime Captain and his prey.

No, he corrected himself, the last thing he wanted was to think about listening to Hildy talk to her boyfriend. And yet, that was the one thing he couldn't stop thinking about.

"How close is he?"

"Two kilometers and closing fast. You can take it down about 80 meters. He's coming in at an altitude of 902 meters, velocity 150 kph. It's a black var with an orange insignia on the door panels."

"Armed?"

"Not officially."

"In other words, yes." Most embassies of sufficient size had at least one armed var even though they were prohibited by various laws, treaties, and contracts from arming their vehicles without permission from MCID and the planetary administration. "So, let's wait until he gets out of the vehicle to say hello."

"I have him on visual, Tower. Three clock eight!"

Tower rotated the var and looked down and to his right. He saw the blue reticle indicating the aerovar on the display before he saw the var itself, a sleek, expensive four-door Fraisier. He zoomed in on it, and saw a pair of suspicious meter-long slats on the roof before confirming that it was Kotant behind the wheel. He'd bet a year's salary that they hid a pair of small air-to-air launchers underneath.

"Don't target him, Baby," Tower warned the augment. "Passive only. We don't want to spook him."

But if Kotant's sensors picked up the fact that his vehicle was being scanned, he didn't show any signs of it. He slowed, angled the var on a parking path, and brought it smoothly down at a speed that indicated he had done so on manual. As the Morchardese approached the platform, which fortunately appeared to be sparsely populated at the moment, Tower took the var out of hover and sent it arcing downward, following much the same path as the Fraisier.

"Here we go!" He began to break heavily about 100 meters out as soon as he saw Kotant leap out of the black vehicle and leveled out the var about 30 meters over the platform. The Morchardese man was strapped with his 707, but wore no body armor and he didn't appear to be otherwise armed. Tower shifted back into hover about 20 meters behind Kotant's vehicle, then triggered the full sound-and-light extravaganza. At the sound of the siren, Kotant abruptly stopped and jerked upright as if some mighty puppeteer had pulled on an invisible string on his back.

"Prime Captain Bram Kotant, put your hands in the air and turn around slowly!" Baby broadcast his voice over the var's loudspeakers. An older married couple, who had just gotten out of their car to the left of the Morchardese officer, hastened to comply. To emphasize his point, Tower activated the targeting system, knowing that the frightening servo-mechanical noise made by the twin mini-cannons in the var's nose as they were auto-aimed at the laser now positioned in the center of Kotant's back would be perfectly audible below. "This is Graven Tower of the Military Crimes Investigative Division. Turn around slowly, then unbuckle your belt and let it fall to the ground. Then take three steps back. Please be advised that if you do not comply, I have authorization to fire at will."

That wasn't strictly true. On the other hand, no sane man with a pair of Degroet Tactical M165-20 cannons, each capable of firing 150 20-millimeter rounds per second, pointing at him was likely to try standing on his legal rights. And Tower knew that no MCID officer had ever been convicted of police abuse, mostly because convictions were hard to come by when there were no survivors and all the recording equipment within range had mysteriously ceased to operate. That impeccable record made bluffs of this sort extremely convincing.

It was enough to convince Kotant, anyhow. The Morchardese officer complied with Tower's orders, and turned around very slowly, holding his arms out and up as if to make the bottom of a square. If his eyes widened a little at the sight of the armored var flashing its lights and hovering just a few meters over his head, he remained otherwise calm, and he did not take his eyes off the twin cannons pointing at his chest as he unbuckled his belt, kicked his holstered GHK away from him, and slowly stepped three steps back from the weapon.

Tower glanced around the platform. The older couple was still standing frozen with their hands in the air, and there were three other people who were also trapped in the lot, afraid to move.

"There is no need for alarm, everyone. This is a police matter and everything is under control. Please leave the platform and go into the building in an orderly manner; if you were planning on leaving with your vehicle, you will have to wait a little while. We apologize for the inconvenience."

No one appeared inclined to complain, and if they walked a little hastily toward the Tearmann entrance, Tower couldn't blame them. He let Baby land the var and checked to make sure he had a pair of autobinders in the usual pocket of his tactical jacket. When the door popped, he stepped out of it in a leisurely fashion and blinked his contacts dark against the bright sunlight. In dealing with veterans, hard men, and other human predators, he'd found it was always important to maintain an air of calm, unhurried collection.

Only the weak and the desperate rushed things. Prey. Power could afford to be patient.

"What brings you here, Prime Captain Kotant?" he said, leaving his Sphinx holstered and ignoring the GHK on the ground nearby. "I didn't realize you harbored such an interest in art and ancient manuscripts."

Kotant's eyes were darkened too, making them hard to read. But he smiled faintly, as if the fact that Tower was observably standing clear of the twin mini-cannons' line of fire amused rather than concerned him. "Is this really necessary, Mr. Tower? I believe you are making a mistake. I have broken no laws and I believe that as a legal resident of

Trans Paradis I have the right to visit the libratech for any reason that happens to please me."

"Does he have a permit for that GHK 707, Baby? Tell me so the Prime Captain can hear you."

"Affirmative, Tower."

"Right." Tower folded his arms and smiled at the Morchardese officer. "And does he have a permit for the modifications made to his vehicle as well?"

"Negative, Tower. Neither Prime Captain Bram Kotant nor the Royal Embassy of Morchard is on record with permits for the pair of Mectron-Denel V4A air-to-air missile launchers built into the vehicle registered to the embassy, or for the four V4A S-Darter missiles that are presently in the vehicle."

"No laws, Prime Captain? I'd say the possession of an entire air-to-air system is one heck of a weapons violation. Not exactly a busted taillight, is it. Four more missiles and you'd be liable to face illegal arms trading charges too. Now, as a fellow veteran and security officer, I'm going to do you the professional courtesy of asking you one more time before I arrest you, why are you here?"

"I'm trying to solve the crown prince's murder and bring an end to the assassination attempts on the royal family," Kotant snapped. "Beginning with the interrogation of Annaliese van de Boer. She's a regime spy."

"Yeah, we know. Hold on a moment." Tower ignored Kotant's astonished expression and addressed Baby. "Is Miss van de Boer secured yet?"

"Affirmative, Tower. The woman has been taken into protective custody as a material witness and is being transported to a secure location now."

"You're harboring a known criminal, a terrorist, and a murderer!" Kotant shouted at Tower. Heedless of the twin cannons pointing at him, the big man dropped his arms and took a step forward before he realized what he was doing. "No, wait! Mr. Tower, please, if you have to lock me up on illegal weapons charges, I accept that, but you must turn van de Boer over to my men at the Embassy! She is the key to this case!"

"No, she isn't," Tower said. "Now calm down, Prime Captain. I have no intention of arresting you unless you force me to it by doing something stupid, all right? There isn't one in ten embassies-in-exile on Rhysalan that isn't in violation of their Sanctuary contract in one way or another. The whole reason the Duke's lawyers put those stupid clauses in there in the first place is to give us the ability to crack down on you bastards any time we want. So, I'm not here to arrest you, I'm just here to keep you from making a stupid mistake and killing Miss van de Boer."

"Are you saying she's not a traitor?"

"No, she's a Morcharder, all right. But she had nothing to do with Prince Arpad's death."

"How can you be sure of that?"

"That's not your concern right now. Your only concern right now is answering my questions. Now, if you'll just shut up and agree to follow me down to TPPD, I'll forget about your unlicensed vehicular mods. I'm not the only one with a few questions for you. And if you cooperate fully and tell us everything we want to know, I'll even sweeten the deal for you."

The big man's lens-darkened eyes narrowed. "How so?"

"I'll give you the identities of the other two Morcharders who infiltrated your staff–"

"What!" Kotant exploded. "There are two more?"

"–as long as you personally guarantee, on your honor, that they will be sent back to Morchard unharmed," Tower continued as if he hadn't been interrupted. "MCID has no interest in your intraplanetary intrigues, Prime Captain. We have a murder to solve and we have no intention of letting you add to our case load."

The Morchardese officer took a deep breath and shook his head. "Two more. You're certain of that?"

"Primary source. As certain as we are of van de Boer."

"And they weren't involved in either of the attacks on the princes?"

"No, not in any capacity. In fact, I believe they were considerably more surprised than you were."

Kotant sighed. "Very well. You have my word. I will cooperate and answer your questions, and after you give me the names, the two traitors will be expelled from the Realm and returned to their masters unharmed."

Tower leaned down and scooped up the belt and the GHK. But before he could toss it to the Morchardese man, Kotant raised a finger and shook his head in a rueful manner. "I'm sorry, Mr. Tower, but I must insist that you arrest me."

"Why?"

"It is a matter of honor. I cannot voluntarily accompany you and offer information to those who, strictly speaking, must be considered allies of our enemies. Your government recognizes the new regime as the lawful planetary government, after all. But if I am placed under arrest by a legitimate authority, honor permits me to involuntarily comply with my captor's demands if I deem such cooperation to be in the crown's interest."

Tower pursed his lips. Voluntary involuntary cooperation? This was exactly the reason he hated xenos so much. Well, one of the reasons, anyhow. None of them could ever just do the common sensible thing.

"All right," he said. He removed the 707 from its holster. He spun the dial up to 85 percent with his thumb, then aimed it and fired a single ruby-red bolt.

Kotant grimaced as the left rear light on the luxurious Fraisier popped and blew outward, leaving behind a gaping hole of molten plastic and twisted metal. Tower slid the GHK back in the holster, tossed the belt over his left shoulder, and withdrew the autobinder from his tac-jacket. Then he made a twirling motion with his finger and approached Kotant after the man complied and put his hands behind his back.

"Prime Captain Bram Kotant, you are under arrest for Transport Code violation…ah, Baby?"

"Title 7A, Section 547.302."

"Yeah, that. As that puts you in violation of Sanctuary, you currently have no rights at all."

Tower applied the binder and watched it spin its web around Kotant's wrists. He gripped Kotant's upper arm to turn him around and found his hand could barely close over the man's huge biceps. Good lord! The guy's muscles were hard like titanwire. As he guided the big man into the back seat of the var, he felt distinctly relieved that this arrest had been so much less exciting than the previous one. And this time he wouldn't have to take the var to the industrial cleaners.

17

When discords and quarrels and factions are carried openly and audaciously, it is a sign the reverence of government is lost.

—*The Augury of Illam Terra*

In the company of the irritatingly handsome Detector Vendersen, Tower escorted Prime Captain Kotant to an interrogation room. This time he was permitted to enter it, since Hildy was occupied with questioning Annalise van der Boer somewhere else in the giant complex.

"Will this do for you, Tower?" Vendersen wasn't exactly unfriendly, but he seemed to be trying to prove that he wasn't afraid of either of the two bigger, more experienced men.

Tower decided to throw the young officer a bone. "Sure, if you don't have anything with a rack or an open fire handy. Do you want to sit in?"

That threw him, Tower saw, as a momentary expression of surprise flashed across Vendersen's face. "Hey, thanks, Tower, I'd really like to, but I've got to run down a suspect in another case this morning."

"No problem." It couldn't hurt to stay on the kid's good side, and it was a lot easier to bear his pretty face now that Tower knew he didn't have a shot with Hildy. "Take it easy, Vendersen."

The door closed automatically behind the young detector. Kotant snorted.

"Kids these days. When did all the police turn into children?"

"My augment tells me you are a man of blood," Tower said, rolling his eyes at Baby's theatrical turn of phrase. "Think you can manage to avoid trying to kill me if I take those binders off you?"

Kotant turned around and held up his arms. Tower pressed his left little finger against the connector and it opened and fell into his palm. He tucked it back into his tac-jacket, then indicated the chair on the other side of the table before slipping off his jacket and sitting down himself.

"Have a seat. And tell me, what were your plans for Miss van de Boer? Were you really just going to kill her outright?"

"She is a spy for the rebel regime." Kotant folded his massive arms. "She was a traitor to the crown. Her death is merited."

"You're not on Morchard anymore, Prime Captain. The Duke makes the rules here, not your king. But you're right, she was a spy and a traitor. I'm curious to hear how you discovered that."

"After the second attempt, the unsuccessful one on Prince Janos, I spent the evening going over every outgoing encrypted message. I wasn't able to break the encryption yet, but I learned that someone had been sending regular messages to a female resident of Trans Paradis."

"Name of Tanabera?"

"Yes."

"Of course. And what did you do with that information. Did you kill the girl?"

"No," Kotant said. His eyes, orange again now that they were out of the sun, met Tower's without showing either guile or guilt. "I did not know Miss Tanabera was dead until now. I swear it, by your Christ."

"By my what?"

Kotant indicated the small cross that was exposed by Tower's open shirt. "Are you not a Christer?"

"Oh, this? No." Tower fingered the jewelry and shook his head. "Just a…just a gift. You truly didn't know she was dead?"

"No, was she an agent too?"

Tower ignored the question. "Who else did you tell about this breach of security?"

"The crown prince, of course. I believe the queen was present. And I briefed my two senior lieutenants last night as well."

"Last night. But you didn't figure out who was sending the messages until this morning?"

The big man shook his head. "I worked out that it was van de Boer last night; the duty rosters matched up with the timestamp on the messages. I thought I would wait and arrest her in the morning when she came in for work. But when she did not come in, I became concerned that she'd put a flag on her messages and went looking for her."

"Arrest?" Tower raised a skeptical eyebrow.

"We have that right inside the Realm as per the Sanctuary contract. I wasn't going to kill her out of hand. She must have valuable information we would find useful. Some accommodation might have been reached. But you have to understand, Mr. Tower, she betrayed the crown and her life was without question forfeit!"

Tower yawned. "Prime Captain, do you have any idea how many petty planetary disputes we find ourselves policing here? This is nothing new. We see this sort of thing all the time! Don't get me wrong, we're proud of the tradition of Sanctuary and–"

"And Rhysalan does quite well by it."

"It may not come cheap, but you know better than anyone that Sanctuary is cheap at the cost. And we don't care if you want to dream your dreams of a triumphant return and plot your plots about reclaiming your planets, but the one rule is that while you're here, while you're claiming Sanctuary, you will keep your bloody nose clean. I know this whole exile thing is new to you, and I'm sure it's very difficult and all, but you Morchardese really don't seem to get it! You want to kill someone, fine! You want to kill all the corporatists, you have my blessing. *But you don't do it here!*"

The two men stared at each other, taking each other's measure. Even if Kotant wasn't bio-enhanced, Tower was pretty sure the bigger man could take him in less than two decaseconds. But he wasn't the first to blink. Finally, Kotant looked away. Satisfied with that small victory, Tower broke the silence.

"How about cloaking devices. Do you have any in the embassy?"

"None, at least, not to my knowledge. And I approve all weapons and weapons-related purchases. We have no need for anything like that; we don't even have a dark ops team set up." The big man grinned. "Not that I wouldn't like one, but we wouldn't have much use for one here on Rhysalan. On Morchard, yeah, sure. But other than a few spies and our network of loyalists, we don't have much going there."

"It doesn't sound as if there are any plans in place to invade Morchard."

Kotant laughed bitterly. "There are always plans, Mr. Tower. But, as you said, they are more aptly described as dreams. We don't have the men, the ships, or the weapons."

"I hear you have the money. That's a sore spot with the corporatists."

"It would be enough if we were only dealing with the rebels. But given the likelihood of naval support from the Unity, the crown doesn't have nearly enough resources to hand. And we have little of interest to offer any potential allies."

"What is the Unity interest in Morchard? Why did they back the rebels?"

"No one knows. They haven't settled any colonies there or made any substantial claims beyond the shares in government they were granted by the rebels. But if I had to guess, it was to detach another planet from the Interstellar League. It cost them nothing more than a short-term fleet deployment and it weakened the League."

Tower nodded. In the nine years that had passed since he was evacuated from Basattria, the Unity had ignored the planet. All that violence, all that bloodshed, all that lingering pain, and it was nothing more than a petty political move on the part of the Unity lords. He still didn't understand what they were about, in fact, he doubted the

Duke himself did, but it was clear that whatever game the Unity was playing, it was a long and ruthless one.

"Could they be behind the assassinations? Or rather, do you think it likely?"

Kotant shrugged. "They could be, but I don't see why. You'd know better than I would if they're active here. There was no history of enmity between them and the royal house, which was why the appearance of their fleet took us completely by surprise."

That was the problem. As far as Tower had seen, the Unity wasn't active on Rhysalan, at least not in the sense that Kotant meant. God knew he'd love to have an excuse, any excuse, to zero zero tango as many of the hiveminders Major Zeuthen would sign off on, but they'd never given him one.

"I don't expect you to tell me who the others were yet, but I'd like to know what those messages were, the messages she was sending to the dead woman you mentioned."

"I got news for you, Kotant: It wasn't scintillating. Baby, can you give us a sample of some of the visuals and stills from the Emerald Enclave?"

"Affirmative, Tower."

An image of Prince Arpad flirting with Mara Tanabera appeared. Multiple still images cascaded in the blue glow of the hologram emitter. "That's what was happening. Miss van de Boer was setting up clandestine communication for the crown prince and his girl, Kotant. You got the right woman, but for the wrong reason. It was just an affair."

Kotant stared at the holographic images. All the color drained from his face. He shook his head.

"You didn't know about this, did you?"

Kotant shook his head again. Poor guy had nothing to say. Tower almost felt sorry for him. "You think you know a guy, right?"

"A commoner," Kotant exhaled. His face was still pale, but his orange eyes betrayed his anger. "A filthy commoner and not even a proper Morchardese woman. No wonder he concealed it from us."

"So it would be frowned on, the prince involving himself with this woman?"

"Without question." Kotant slouched in the chair. "All these years—did you know I saved his life twice? I would have saved him from this ignominy too, had I known. He was young and he loved women. That is to be expected. But this?"

The big man waved a hand in disgust and looked away from the holoscreen.

Tower glanced at the holo. Mara was laughing at something and brushing a hand along his cheek. "I imagine he was probably afraid you'd forbid him to see her. Or arranged to render her inaccessible in one way or another. Am I right?"

Kotant nodded. "Certainly. But we would not have harmed her. This is not the first time a prince has fallen. Such women are easily bought off. Given her occupation, we probably would have arranged to see her offered employment as an interstellar cruise hostess. Out of sight long enough, out of mind."

As much as Tower hated to admit it, he believed the guy. Or was starting to believe him, anyway. "Who did you think Miss van de Boer was passing information to?"

Kotant snorted. "The Valatestans. They have the wealth to potentially turn any of our people against us, hence my need for extreme vigilance. But if she was with the new regime, it is obvious that I was wrong."

"Tower, be advised that there are six individuals now approaching the interrogation room. I believe that this interrogation is about to be indefinitely interrupted, as one of them is the Assistant Deputy Commissioner of Legal Matters and another is a man named Gerd de Fosters–"

"Lead attorney for the royal house." A white light blinked on Kotant's belt. "I mean no disrespect, Mr. Tower, because I am entirely willing to keep our arrangement. But, for now, you are finished with me."

The door slid open. Hildy walked in first, looking angry. Her face was flushed, as if she'd been recently chastised. She was followed by a big overweight man with a dyspeptic expression who Tower guessed was the legal officer. But he was taken aback when Queen Beatrice swept into the room next, followed by two bodyguards in full armor and a tall, thin man in an impeccable suit.

Great. Just great. Tower decided offense was the best defense and rose to his feet. "What's going on here? I've got an interview concerning an active murder investigation with a possible suspect in progress!"

"No, Mr. Tower, you most certainly do not." The Assistant Deputy Commissioner, whose name, Baby silently informed him, was Harold Swirsky, a long-time associate of Police Commissioner Terry Coleman, wagged a sausage-like finger at him. "You soldier-cops can play trigger-happy on the streets, but this isn't your case and MCID has no authority in this building. This interview is over!"

"Trigger-happy?" Tower feigned bewilderment. "Just providing all due assistance to TPPD, as directed per, ah, Part Four, Chapter 10, Section 10-4 of FM 3-19.42."

"Illegal assistance!" The Morchardese lawyer interjected. He had a pair of implanted interfaces attached to his shoulders, little arc-antennae that protruded through a suit tailored to accommodate them. "Her Majesty the Queen has informed me she did not give consent for this interview, as is required for Royal Chief of Security as per the Sanctuary Contract. The contract requires notification of the Crown of Morchard any time persons specified on the list provided in Appendix H are arrested, and furthermore, requires royal permission for the interrogation of all persons specified on the list provided in Appendix G. As the Prime Captain is specified by name on both appendices, this questioning is a violation of Sanctuary and must be terminated immediately!"

"It appears the arresting officer failed to notify the Morchardese Embassy of Mr. Kotant's arrest."

Well, sure because I knew you'd let him go as soon as you found out. Tower put on his best innocent expression, confident that Baby would have already retrofitted the digital record. "I'm sure it was just a glitch in the comms. If you examine my outgoing messages, I'm certain you'll find both the arrest notice and the interview request. Since I didn't hear back, I assumed permission was granted."

"Do you seriously expect anyone to buy that?" the deputy commissioner said, incredulous.

"Let me be clear," the lawyer declared. "Permission was most certainly not granted and the Embassy will file a complaint immediately in protest of this contractual violation."

Hildy cleared her throat and ignored the poisonous look shot at her by Swirsky. "Sir, my understanding is that Prime Captain Kotant has indicated he has information vital to our double homicide, and I request we–"

"Enough!" Swirsky barked, his voice resonant with his self-importance. "This interview is over and I am directing the remanding of Prime Captain Kotant into the custody of the royal embassy. The charges related to the Prime Captain's arrest will be dropped and expunged from the record. Mr. de Fosters has already filed a motion to suppress and delete any information disclosed in the course of this interview and I expect all recordings turned over to him for the purposes of review."

He nodded to the queen. "The Prime Captain is yours, your Majesty."

"Rise, Captain Kotant," Queen Beatrice spoke for the first time. Her voice was chilly with disdain. Kotant obeyed, although not without an apologetic glance at Tower. "If you wish to have any further discussions with any member of our staff, Mr. Tower, you will do so through the auspices of the embassy."

She turned and glared at Hildy. The queen's icy blue stare was very nearly as intimidating as being on the wrong side of the barrel of a cobalt cannon.

"Detector Hildreth, we will require you to bring Annaliese van der Boer to the embassy when you are finished questioning her with regards to her involvement in our son's murder. While we recognize that she is not among the persons granted immunity per the Sanctuary contract, if she is neither arrested nor delivered to us before midnight, Mr. de Fosters will be registering a second series of complaints with regards to the maltreatment, wrongful imprisonment, and abuse of our embassy staff."

Tower was proud of Hildy. Her cheeks were flushed, but she didn't blink and she didn't back down before the imperious older woman. "You try to interfere with my investigation or my witnesses, Mrs. Jagaelleon, and I'll haul your bony royal butt right back here for obstruction of justice! Do you think I don't know what you'll do to her?"

The queen ignored her. At her gesture, one of the bodyguards pushed past Tower, pulled Kotant's arms behind his back, and bound them with an autobinder similar to the one Tower had removed only a few hectasecs before.

"Hey, what's going on?" Tower started to protest, but Kotant caught his eyes and shook his head. Well, if the Prime Captain wasn't alarmed, Tower wasn't about to get worked up about it either. He closed his mouth and flashed two fingers where Kotant could see them. The Morchardese officer nodded quickly, and Tower stepped back, satisfied. The Prime Captain would abide by his word, if he was able. Under the circumstances, that was all Tower could reasonably expect.

"Her Majesty can rest assured that Detector Hildreth will return the Morchardese subject to the embassy at the very first opportunity," Swirsky was babbling at the lawyer. "The case of Prince Arpad's murder is of the highest priority to this department and Commissioner Coleman is absolutely determined that our detectors will find his killers and bring them to justice."

The queen was unimpressed. She glanced dismissively at Swirsky, who nearly fell over himself in his attempt to get out of her way.

Hildy, on the other hand, remained where she was, in the doorway. "We commend your efforts to solve our son's murder, but we will seek justice through our ways now, not yours. Step aside now, young woman."

Hildy squared her shoulders and lifted her chin. But when she glanced at Tower, he shook his head. Not here. Not now.

Hildy's shoulders sagged and she retreated out of the room. The bodyguards swept through first, with Kotant, and Queen Beatrice and her pet lawyer followed behind. Once they were out of the room, the assistant deputy commissioner reached out and shut the door. He turned to face Tower, glaring at him with all the fury his piggy little eyes could convey.

"This isn't MCID's case, Mr. Tower. Detector Hildreth's request for military assistance is henceforth revoked and I don't want to see you here at headquarters again unless you're in binders and behind bars. In fact, I don't want to see you within 20 meters of Detector Hildreth unless it is an indisputably personal and private matter, do you understand me?"

"Roger, Commissioner." Swirsky might be a civilian, but Tower had been in the military long enough to recognize a perfumed prince with connections when he saw one. "If TPPD doesn't require assistance, we'll keep out of the department's affairs, Commissioner."

Swirsky nodded, vaguely mollified. "I understand you have different ways, different rules of engagement, Mr. Tower. I respect that. The commissioner respects that. But when there is jurisdictional overlap, bright lines have to be drawn."

"Roger that, sir." Tower clipped his words, knowing how much the civvy cops ate up playing soldier. Especially desk jockeys like this overweight fool. "You need the cavalry, Commissioner, just whistle, sir. Until then, MCID has things to break and other things to kill."

Swirsky nodded firmly, in what he obviously thought was an appropriately military manner. "I appreciate your understanding, Mr. Tower. No hard feelings, I hope."

"None at all, Commissioner." Tower took the liberty of reaching out and opening the door. "After you, sir."

There was a small, but noticeable spring in the fat man's step as he strode down the corridor with his baggy suit trousers sagging. Tower managed to avoid laughing out loud himself, although Baby's chortling didn't make it easy. He was a little disappointed Hildy hadn't waited for him, but he wasn't surprised. That would have just earned her pretty backside an even more irate chewing from Mr. Assistant Deputy Commissioner. Well, it was about time for him to return to his office, update the major, and discover what his next assignment was now that he'd been officially bounced from the Morchardese investigation.

He hoped it wouldn't be the low-grade gang war that had recently started up again between the Krasterii and the Unmork. He didn't fancy finding himself in the middle of a blood feud between two alien races, both of which prized human flesh as a delicacy.

He took the lift up to the parking platform level and strode outside, shading his contacts against the sun. He was surprised to see the Morchardese group nearby, until he realized that in their hurry to descend upon the police department, they had forgotten that a successful return trip would involve an additional passenger. Not that the four-door Fraisier, twin to the one Kotant had left over at the Tearmann, couldn't carry five passengers, but Tower doubted Morchardese protocol permitted one to cram a lawyer and a captive security officer in the backseat with the queen.

"Need a lift to the Prime Captain's vehicle?" he called out in a mock-helpful manner. "The taillight is out, but I'm told TPPD overlooks that sort of thing these days."

De Fosters started to say something that, judging by the expression on his face, was less than grateful, but the queen dissuaded him. She graciously inclined her head the merest fraction of a centimeter toward him and allowed that it would not be beneath the dignity of Morchard if one of the bodyguards was transported to the other vehicle's location by a member of the Rhysalani military police. Tower was pleased to hear that, not so much because he cared for the queen's dignity on the ride home, but because it indicated the Prime Captain's bound wrists were likely a mere matter of honor. Tower didn't like the man, but he respected him and it would have galled him to see the big veteran shot out of hand.

Kotant himself didn't appear overly concerned. He was smiling at the lawyer's discomfiture; de Fosters clearly didn't like to feel beholden to Tower, but the queen had spoken and clearly there was nothing more to be said. Then Tower caught a flash of sunlight out of the corner of his eye; a moment later Baby screamed a silent warning so loud inside his head that it nearly scrambled his brains.

Tower's heart froze.

Not here. Not out in the open.

He dove instinctively toward the closest vehicle and rolled the rest of the way to it. A green burst of light lanced across the bright blue sky, quickly followed by another. Tower drew his Sphinx and rose to one knee. Where was the shooter? Where? A third particle beam vaporized a patch of the landing platform in between him and the Morchardese party. Steam hissed from a gouge bigger than his head and scorched black.

One of the two bodyguards had gone for his weapon and was pointing it toward the sky, but his failure to fire told Tower he couldn't find the shooter either. The other one was shouting in their native tongue and forcibly dragging the screaming queen backward toward the Fraisier, attempting to shield her with his body. The lawyer was crawling behind them on the ground; Tower didn't see where the Prime Captain had gone but it was safe to assume Kotant had taken cover nearby.

Baby! I need a target! Tower swept his aim around the landing area. There were black-and-whites parked in neat rows all over the place, including under the canopies that shielded the individual hangars. He could find no suspicious activity on the skytowers facing the police building despite the zoom and motion detectors Baby had activated in his right eye.

He was ready to fire, but at what? There was nothing. His breath came hard and steady; his chest heaved despite himself. He heard the door on the Morchardese aerovar slam and heard the engine start up.

"I got nothing," the bodyguard who remained outside the vehicle shouted. He slammed on the back of the vehicle twice with his left hand. "Gaan, gaan, gaan!"

The var was just beginning to leave the ground when a fourth blast struck the seam between the port engine nacelle and the body. But the force of the particles were mostly ablated as the var's electro-armor dispersed the charge that held them together in a bright explosion that was harmless but for the violent rainbow light it produced. The effect was as blinding as if someone had set off a firework in his face.

"*Red vehicle ten clock two!*" Baby shouted.

The force shield ablation had left purple blobs in Tower's vision. He couldn't see much of anything except for Baby's crosshairs crisply overlaid in green upon a hazy whitish fog. Alarms were sounding and he could hear the sound of pounding boots behind him as TPPD finally began responding to the attack. Still half-blinded, he crouched again behind the blue var he'd used as cover.

"*Get to the var, Tower, I'm tracking the shooter's vehicle!*"

He blinked a few more times and his vision cleared, and he saw the Prime Captain's body lying on the ground to his right. The big Morchardese officer was dead, there could be no doubt, as the particle beam had struck him on the right temple and burned right through his skull. Tower swore silently to himself.

The Morchardese bodyguard finally stopped scanning the skies and lowered his GHK. He turned back toward Tower, and something must have alerted him something was wrong because he immediately glanced at the ground. When he saw his fallen superior, his face turned ashen. He cried out in dismay. The laser fell clattering to the tarmac and the man dropped to his knees, burying his face in his hands.

His despairing grief awoke something in Tower. Something angry. Something *murderous.* He slammed the unfired Sphinx back into his holster and ran toward his var. "You still tracking him, Baby?"

"He's flitting in and out of the building cams, but I can find him. If we hurry."

The cockpit door opened automatically on the passenger side and Tower leaped in, then slid across to the wheel. The engine was already roaring and the var was off the ground before the door had even closed.

"Then let's get that sniping son of a bitch now!"

When a lot happens in a short time, the brain may make simplifying assumptions.

—*Consciousness Refuted*, D. D. Clement

Tower didn't take over the controls, but he did tell Baby to override the governor that kept the var's speed down below certain altitudes and within the city limits. He also triggered the lights and sirens, not that they actually mattered much at the speeds she was driving, but that invoked the auto-alert routine that broadcast a warning to every vehicle within 750 meters of his drive path.

After being thrown almost into the passenger door when Baby took a hard left that narrowly avoided taking out the side of the Leichthansa Bank building, Tower managed to crawl back into the now-inappropriately named driver's seat and buckle himself in.

"That was a little close there, Baby. You sure you're on top of this?"

"That wasn't even close, Tower." She sounded excited. "God has not given you a spirit of fear, but of power! And love! And a sound mind!"

"I wouldn't be too sure about that last one. I let you drive, didn't I?"

"Don't be such a baby. We had six point three two four seven meters to spare."

Tower decided it might be less terrifying if he closed his eyes. He tried it. After two more hair-raising, stomach-turning, excess G-force turns, he decided that he was wrong. He also decided to ignore the speedometer, which was considerably closer to altitude cruising speeds than was usually recommended for city driving. At least it would be fast, he tried to console himself.

"Baby, if this is your way of attempting to help me find religion, I just thought I'd let you know it's working."

She may have responded but Tower didn't hear. He was too busy praying to God, science, and anything else in the universe that might be inclined to lend an ear that her parallel processors were powerful enough to let her chatter without reducing her ability to correctly calculate collision vectors at speed.

"Do you still have him?"

"Dead to rights, Tower. He's tried to shake us off, but I put out an alert and a scanner read his transponder. Now every cam, scanner, or passive reader in the system lights up when he passes by. Look!"

The windshield abruptly displayed a holomap of the city. Brilliant green dots were lighting up like popcorn, giving Baby an indelible track to follow. A series of numbers below were rapidly declining; Tower ascertained that they indicated the gap that he and Baby were rapidly closing.

"We should have visual as soon as I make this next corner," she announced excitedly.

Tower found himself thinking that "if" might have been the more strictly accurate description as the var twisted on its right side and somehow narrowly avoided taking out the 223rd story of a residential tower. Then he saw the shape of the speeding red var ahead and his state of near-catatonic terror abruptly disappeared, replaced by anticipation.

"MCID Base, this is Chief Warrant Officer Graven Tower. I am in hot pursuit of a vehicle that is refusing to slow down or hover despite my lights. The passengers in the vehicle are believed to be responsible for an assassination attempt on the Queen of Morchard. Request permission to bring it down. Over."

"Tower, this is MCID Base," the reply came almost immediately. "We are in sync. You are authorized to fire one warning shot at this time. Do not, repeat, do not bring the vehicle down until authorization is given."

Tower tapped the controls and they formed into a multi-buttoned gunstick. A blue reticle appeared; it lit up green when he passed it over the image of the fleeing var before them. But he eased it to the right of the var and gently squeezed the trigger, firing a short burst from the Degroet Tacticals in the nose. The tracers flew harmlessly past the red var, but despite the clear warning, it did not respond.

"MCID Base, the vehicle did not respond to the warning shot. Please advise."

"Tower, this is Baylor," he heard the colonel's familiar voice announce. "How much collateral are we looking at?"

He glanced at the holomap. They were already out of the finance district and they'd left downtown far behind. The skytowers were a good 150 stories shorter now, and there was considerably more space between them. "Not much if I hit him with a pair of Meteors. But I'd rather try to shoot him down with the cannons and see if I can't bring him in."

"Too risky," the colonel pronounced. "The black box will survive and tell us whatever we need to know. Permission granted. You are cleared to fire two missiles, Tower."

"Roger that, sir. But colonel, this guy is just the hitter. If we take him out, we won't know who hired him."

"It's a political, Tower. If they don't have the sense to stop, we'll have a new lead to chase soon enough. In the meantime, we've taken one more pro off the street. Just take the shot, Mr. Tower."

"Yes, sir!" Tower grumbled a little under his breath as he switched over to the air-to-air missiles and selected simultaneous launch. He could feel the rack cover sliding back beneath the stub-wings on both sides. Baylor's decision made sense, but that didn't mean he had to like it. "Target is acquired."

A familiar high-pitched noise sounded. "Target is locked."

"Firing." He squeezed the trigger again. "Two, repeat, two missiles away."

The two slender Meteorites covered the 600 meters between the two vars in less than a decasec. Both struck home at precisely the same time, and the red var disappeared in a huge fireball. Scratch one assassin, thought Tower as savage exultation course through his body. Baby banked hard right to avoid flying through the cloud of metal and plastic debris that was now falling to the ground. But it was hardly necessary. With warheads packing 12 kilos of PBX-7 high explosive apiece, the Meteorites had reduced the var to little more than harmless confetti.

"Two hits," he reported. "Target destroyed."

"Bravo zulu, Tower," Colonel Baylor said. "Why don't you return to base for a debriefing over lunch. I'll arrange for someone else to find the black box."

"Thank you, sir." Tower appreciated the colonel's gesture. Hunting for the tiny, near-invulnerable data recorder was close to the last thing he was in the mood for now. But why? He knew he should have felt some sense of relief. Kotant's killer, and quite likely Prince Arpad's killer, was dead. Justice had been served. So why did he feel as if he was missing something?

Baby was uncharacteristically quiet too. Then she spoke.

"Something strange about that var, boss."

"Yeah?"

"I scanned the debris as we flew by. The results are inconclusive, but it appears there may be an anomaly. I detected no organic matter."

"What?"

"Tower, I think that var might have been empty!"

Tower let Baby drive to base, albeit at a considerably less alarming rate of speed. By the time they were passed through the aerial defenses and permitted to land, both of them were convinced that the vehicle was a dummy, meant to focus the attention of the responders away from the killer's real line of retreat. At first, Tower assumed Baby must have made a mistake, and that the shots had been fired from somewhere else than inside the hovering vehicle. But when he watched her visual record of the incident, patched together from police cams, nearby building security cams, and Tower's own built-in contact cam, it was plain to see that the beams had definitely been fired from the open driver-side window.

Even zoomed in to a factor of 20, at over 600 meters the details of the red var were little more than blurry blobs. But Baby's interpolation algorithms were clever enough to show the barrel of a large-caliber particle gun protruding from the window as well as the bright green beam that emanated from it. Unfortunately, none of the cam angles before, during, or after the shooting showed the driver's face; prior to the vehicle stopping and taking up its position overlooking the police platform, its windows and windshield had been opaqued.

Upon landing, Tower went directly to the colonel's office. Unsurprisingly, Major Zeuthen was already there; the two officers were at their ease and Tower detected the distinct smell of alcohol in the coffee they were ostensibly drinking.

"Congratulations, Mr. Tower!" the colonel raised his steaming tube. "I'm told there were no ground casualties and only one window was broken, apparently by the engine block. I'm sure the Morchardese embassy will appreciate the way in which you not only avenged their security officer, but kept their expenses down."

Tower nodded. He didn't really care. One of the reasons MCID was so famously indifferent to collateral damage was that under the Sanctuary contract, all costs incurred by their investigations, including compensation for any incidental loss of life and limb, was billed to any governments or governments-in-exile deemed related to the case.

"I'm not so sure of that, Colonel."

The colonel frowned. He was a very small man, with sharp features and a crew cut, who looked like an older version in miniature of an Army poster boy. His face was lined and deeply tanned by the suns of at least a dozen different worlds, and his hawkish eyes were piercing as he glared at Tower.

"How many?"

"Sir?"

"Really, Tower, you just had to rain our happy little parade here, didn't you. So, how many did you kill? I can tell you right now that the compensation amounts to more than 10 million, the Morchardese are going to raise a stink and you know how I feel about stinks."

"I didn't kill anybody, sir. Anybody at all. There wasn't anyone in the var when I blew it up."

"That's impossible," the major snapped dismissively. "That var wasn't equipped with an ejector and at the speeds he was moving, there was no way he was going to open a window and jump out. And more to the point, no one was seen exiting the vehicle in between the shooting and the take-down."

"I know, but I spotted something when I was watching the sequence on the way over." He glanced at the colonel and pointed to desk. "With your permission, Colonel."

"If you must, Tower." The colonel took a healthy slug of his coffee. "It figures. We get a nice clean kill for once, and there has to be complications. It's always something."

On the holoscreen was displayed the image of the red var, taken from some distance below, presumably from the police building. The var hung in the air, the window open, with a green flare indicating a shot was being fired. The flare faded, the black projector barrel was withdrawn, and the var suddenly leaped forward. But instead of simply driving away, it turned on its side, looped up and around, then leveled out and zoomed off in the opposite direction from the way it had been facing.

"Anything strike either of you as strange about that?"

"Looks like preemptive evasive action to me," the major said.

The colonel was silent. Then he threw back the rest of his spiked coffee and made a face. "You're thinking cloaksuit, aren't you."

Tower pointed and Baby reversed the scene, paused it when the var was on its side, and zoomed in. The interpolation effects seemed to be particularly strong in the area immediately below the var, in precisely the same vertical plane as the window. At Tower's command, Baby highlighted the heavily interpolated area in yellow. Tower pointed to it.

"Now, this looks innocent enough. After all, it's natural for there to be such an effect where there is high contrast between image elements and the algorithm has to compensate for the difference. What isn't so natural, however, is for that effect to move in a path commensurate with gravity."

"That's some sizable words there, Mr. Tower," drawled the colonel. "I have to say, I'm impressed."

"Just quoting my augment, sir," Tower said, embarrassed. "Anyhow, if someone did exit the vehicle when it was in that position, where would he go?"

"Straight down," the major answered. "What with gravity and all."

"Of course," Tower agreed as he started the visual again, but this time in slow motion. "So, my thought is that it is a little suspicious that the algorithmic interpolation effect just so happens to go straight down as well, especially considering that there is no longer any color contrast to generate the effect."

On the holoscreen, the yellow shape could be seen dropping, and then as it plunged, beginning to thin out and expand, even as the var began to loop upward. Then it disappeared off the bottom of the screen as the cams followed the upward path of the var. Baby replayed it three times, and each time, the highlighted shape seemed to become more and more apparent, more obviously that of a man rolling out of an open window, then stretching out his arms and legs as if he was wearing a skysuit.

His two superiors looked at each other. Then the major shrugged and proffered the coffee pot. "Well, if you won't have a celebratory drink, how does a consolation one strike you?"

"Don't mind if I do, sir," Tower said. He was glad they'd fortified it. After being played for a sucker like that, he decided he could do with a bit of fortification himself.

19

Power has its principle not so much in a person as in a certain concerted distribution of bodies, surfaces, lights, gazes; in an arrangement whose complex mechanisms produce the interlocking mesh in which individuals are caught up. The more numerous those anonymous and temporary observers are, the greater the chance of the relevant actions being observed.

—*The Poetry of the Panopticon*, Pendulus Bentham

Tower sat in his office, flipping methodically from building cam to building cam, gradually crossing off city blocks as he proceeded. Baby was in the process of doing the same thing, much faster and on an immensely grander scale, but it made him feel more involved than if he simply sat there and watched the highlights from last night's gravball matches. And the exercise was more than busywork, as he watched each visual segment, looking for an anomaly indicating where the sniper might have flown past or landed, his mind was actively turning over the known unknowns in an attempt to figure out what unknown unknown he was missing.

Then a thought struck him. This wasn't the first anomaly they had seen. He pulled up the file containing the second assassination attempt, the unsuccessful one, and replayed the exchange of fire between the Valatestan and the Morchardese guards. Once more, he counted one too many shots. But this time, he had Baby rotate through the various cams slowly, scanning for the cloaksuit effect. It took nearly twelve hectasecs, but at last she spotted it.

"There it is," she said, highlighting the barely noticeable ripple as the now-deceased Prime Captain's gaze rotated backward at the prince. It was off to the right of the screen, in an alcove with a protruding ledge that would be perfect for resting a tripod or even just stabilizing an elbow. The alcove disappeared as the security chief looked at the prince, then was revealed again as his lenses swept past it a second time. Baby zoomed in. The artifact was clearly there, only this time it was motionless. "That is no coincidence, boss."

"Can we find a cam pointing at that spot at some other time?" It wouldn't definitely prove that the anomaly was what he suspected it was, but if it showed up on a different cam in different light conditions, that would indicate it was probably something other than a cloaked assassin waiting to take a shot… at another assassin?

There was something truly strange going on here. Why would an assassin secretly put himself in a position to take out a target, only to shoot at another assassin instead?

If he was there to take out the patsy. Only in this case, the patsy hadn't needed any taking out. And the cloaked assassin hadn't made any move on the prince or Prime Captain Kotant either, despite going to considerable trouble to take a shot at the queen only two days later. Or so Tower assumed; for simplicity's sake he assumed that the possible cloaksuit here was hiding the same individual who had fired on the Morchardese party at the police department.

He groaned. There were so many questions! How did the assassin know the Queen was at the police building downtown? How did he know Prince Janos would be outside that day? And what in the name of the third planet from the Sun was he doing shooting at the Valatestan?

"Got it," Baby announced with satisfaction. "Look, there's nothing there!"

Tower looked. She was right. There was a clear shot of the alcove, taken from across the street by the uniform cam of a policeman making an arrest of an unlicensed street vendor not fifteen meters from where Milazzo died. He saw from the datestamp that it was shot yesterday. And, without a doubt, there was no ripple, or when zoomed-in, interpolation effect, to be seen in the alcove.

"Doesn't prove anything," Tower said, although as far as he was concerned, it did just that. Baby snorted.

"This isn't a court, Tower. Trust your gut."

Another thought struck him. The alcove was far enough away from the building entrance that the angles of fire would be distinct. "Baby, can you trace the angles of the various shots from that position and tell me what it hit?"

It might give him an idea as to motive. If the invisible man shot Milazzo, he might be silencing a patsy. If he shot the wall, he was trying to do the same, only ineffectively. Tower very much doubted that was the case. And if it was the shot that struck the Mosin-Nyarla, well, that would be the most potentially useful of the three alternatives.

"It was the shot that hit the disruptor," she concluded.

"Bang!" Tower shouted, clapping his hands. "And let me guess, where it hit is right where the wireless attachment goes. That wasn't a missed shot aimed at the Valatestan, that was a precision shot fired by the same guy who was sniping at 600 meters earlier today! He wanted to destroy the receiver! Baby, run the attack again, but zoom in on the disruptor, just in front of the trigger guard."

She did as he'd ordered. Sure enough, there it was. She froze the image so that he could read the label. It was a ZyLinc W6 Remote Adapter, which could be plugged into any weapon with a RFB slot and transform it into a remote fire device. The device was tiny, barely larger than a human fingernail so it was no surprise that no one had noticed it, especially when the weapon had been openly wielded by the dead Valatestan.

A troubling thought occurred to him. If the unknown sniper had managed to hit such a small and moving target at what Baby informed him was 74 meters, then what were the chances Captain Kotant had not been the target? A 600 meter headshot, especially with a rifle equipped with an augment-corrected sighting system, was a shot he could make himself. But Kotant made no sense as the primary target, and he reminded himself that the three other shots fired this morning hadn't hit anyone. Obviously the queen was the target of the third attempt; Kotant must have been an incidental victim.

"Can you get in touch with Victor on the sly?"

"I can patch you right through to Hildy's interface if you want," Baby said, sounding vaguely offended.

"No, I imagine she would find that a little creepy." Tower shook his head. Sometimes, augments simply didn't get it. "But put me through to her in a way that won't alert TPPD."

"You got it." A moment later, Hildy's voice replaced Baby's on the office speakers.

"I understand this is a personal call from my close personal friend who just happens to be calling from a military base?"

"Why, hello, friend Hildy." Tower felt stupid, but maintained the pretense. "This is your good buddy Graven. I just thought you might like to know that the attempt on Prince Janos may have been staged."

"Staged? Really?" There was a thoughtful silence. "That would make him a suspect."

"There's more. The shooter at your place jumped out of the var before I, ah, caught up to it."

Hildy laughed. "Caught up to it? That's putting it in a way I haven't heard before, you trigger-happy lunatic."

"Hey, I had authorization!" He ignored her skeptical laughter. "Anyhow, it turns out the var shooter was also on the scene at the embassy attack. Cloaked, which ties all four attacks together. My thought is Prince Janos could be the one behind it. He has his brother taken out, fakes an attack on himself, and then either goes gunning for Mommy or decides the Prime Captain knows too much. Hard to say there, but I'm thinking Mommy issues of one sort or another."

"What about Tanabera?"

Right. Tower had forgotten about the pretty young woman. He thought quickly and came up with an answer he liked.

"She was pregnant, right? So maybe he knows, and decides to eliminate his brother's rightful heir."

"Arpad didn't marry her, though. You sure the child would have counted, being illegitimate."

"No idea." Tower shrugged. "But it works as an operative theory. Anyhow, between this and what you got out of Dunn, we can narrow it down. Who was at Syranecus, was either a designated marksman or a sniper, and had powered wingsuit training. There can't be too many men like that."

"That sounds like it's more up Baby's alley than mine. You got anything, Baby?"

"Based on the parameters you have set, I have identified fifteen men and one woman."

"A woman?" both Hildy and Tower said at the same time.

"She doesn't strictly qualify, but Mrs. Erica Seres was an Ascendancy nurse who was a competitive biathlete and later married to a professional Rhysalani aerobaticist. She is wingsuit-qualified. However, she also has four children and according to her medical records, is 14 kilos overweight."

"I think we can safely rule Mrs. Seres out," Hildy declared.

"Of the fifteen men, precisely three are showing as current planetary residents," Baby continued. "Or to be more precise, system residents. Weapons Sergeant Montel Peng is imprisoned in the Holunsky Labor-Correctional Institution on Asteroid 66391-2075-LC2. Five years ago, he was convicted on six counts of murder, first-class and sentenced to surgical modification and permanent space labor. He is unlikely to be a candidate, as today's labor roster shows that he was occupied with repairing a drilling machine on 66391 at the time of the var shooting this morning. Warrant Officer T.G. Somerset is even less likely, as he presently occupies plot 600-6497 at the Ringelheim Memorial Cemetery; he died of complications related to his wounds two years after being evacuated from Syranecus."

"Next time, you might want to specify living residents," Hildy observed.

"The third individual is the best candidate. Nostro St. James served in the Ascendancy's Space Ranger Corps for ten years. His military occupational specialty was intelligence and he was due for a planetside transfer to the Ranger training grounds on Burreth just prior to the war's outbreak."

Baby ran the information down the holoscreen. Reams and reams of stuff, listing all the commendations and campaigns. "His military career advanced in a considerably upward trajectory once fighting broke out. Among his many accolades, he was awarded the Ascendancy's Core Star for valor. After Syranecus, he was promoted to major, at which rank he retired when the war ended. He ended up on Rhysalan when he married a young Rhysalani girl he'd met after Ascendancy forces broke the siege of the capital."

Tower whistled. "The guy was a real warrior."

"He was also a killer, Tower." Hildy had obviously set Victor to work after hearing St. James's name. "Check this out. Three years ago, RCPD responded to a building alert at the St. James residence in the Epsil Five Tower. St. James's wife was found dead with a broken neck. There were no indications of a break-in, St. James was there, and he didn't deny responsibility. And, oh my God, will you look at this!"

Tower winced as an image of a dead woman was flashed up on the screen. "Hildy, what the–"

He started to protest, then stopped when he realized that he recognized the position of the body. It was lying in much the same pose as

Mara Tanabera's. The odds against that being a coincidence had to be astronomical.

"So why isn't he keeping surgically-modified company with Sergeant Peng on the penal asteroid?"

"He was acquitted by reason of insanity and ordered into a maximum-security psychiatric ward on the second moon. However, he was reported dead in a shuttle accident while transiting to orbit for remanding into therapeutic care."

Tower rubbed his face with the heel of his hand and realized he'd forgotten to shave again this morning. He remembered the facility the inhabitants called L4L, which was the abbreviated way of saying Luna for Loonies. He'd spent three months there himself after returning from Basattria, although not in any of the security wards. He'd only been considered a danger to himself, not others.

"Wait, so he's dead?" Hildy sounded aghast. "So we've got nothing. Again."

"Not necessarily," Baby said. "His corpse was never recovered, Detector Hildreth. And there is reason to believe that the records of the incident may have been tampered with."

"Reasons?"

"First, the number of passengers initially reported by the media was off by one. The early reports said the shuttle had 58 passengers and four crew. That was based on the manifest. But subsequent reports, which were based on the mortuary and medical admissions, showed 63 total casualties, of which 40 were fatalities. Somewhere, someone went missing. And not only that, but one of the sub-space medics who responded to the accident was found dead in his apartment four rotations later. No robbery, no known motive, and no suspects."

"You think someone might have been erasing his tracks," Tower surmised. "It could be. St. James survives the accident, is treated by the poor medic, then escapes when they arrive on the orbital station. Somehow, he gets groundside again, and then kills the medic to make sure no one asks him any questions. The medic wouldn't have known who he was, but might have been able to give a description."

"There is one flaw in your logic," Hildy interrupted his thinking out loud. "All of that medical information is automatically registered live, at the moment of treatment. The medical records would have showed how many corpses were scanned, how many of the wounded were treated, right down to their sex, age, blood type, and DNA. Killing the medic wouldn't even begun to have covered his tracks."

"That would be true, Detector Hildreth, were it not for the possible involvement of second party, one that was capable of covering all of the those tracks except for the physical existence of the medic."

"A second party?"

"Detector Hildreth, you are aware that there is a considerable difference between my capabilities and the capabilities of a civilian intelligence augment such as your Victor. What you may not know is that many military devices, which can range from self-operating vehicles to electronic infiltration agents, are not only given considerably more autonomy than their civilian counterparts, but often develop close relationships with their human interfaces."

"And James was in Intelligence, is that what you're saying?

"I notice that his career was largely undistinguished until he was given an assignment at Fort Lanring on Mortain. At that point, he was teamed with a prototype security augment that was being designed for the Ascendancy's special forces. The project was known as the Autonomous Cognitive Reason Array, or ACRA. Post-Lanring, his performance, particularly his combat ratings, were spectacular, even when compared with more conventionally augmented soldiers. I can't get at all of his records, but look at the results of this three-gun trooper match in which he competed just prior to the start of the war."

"Sweet St. Colt, he shot 941.6952!"

"That's good?" Hildy asked.

"That looks more like a combat drone than a human. Even an

augmented one. He wasn't much younger than I am now and I've never broken 500 even with Baby's help."

"And that's not all," Baby said. "Listen to what the arresting officer reported him saying after he was arrested, before he went catatonic. It was part of why he was found insane. When the uniform asked him why he'd killed his wife, he said: 'There was no other way. Cara said it was necessary.' The prosecution notes show that they spent a fair amount of effort looking for a woman named Cara, but couldn't find one."

"You think ACRA became Cara, at least in his mind?"

"In their mind," Tower said. "Under the stress of combat, strange things sometimes happen to the human mind. Everyone knows about post-trauma and so forth, but sometimes minds crack in unusual ways. And the city prosecutor wouldn't have had any access to the Ascendancy records; the Rhys City police wouldn't have known anything more than he had a skulljack with a wireless connection."

"The police medics didn't take it out?"

"They just installed a blocker," Baby said. "It would have taken me about 10 nanoseconds to disable it. A souped-up prototype like Cara could do it even faster."

"But is that even possible?" Hildy sounded incredulous. "For a human mind and its augment to actually… become one, to meld in some way? I mean, short of full spectrum unity?"

"Oh yes," Tower and Baby replied at exactly the same time.

No one in the Navy, the intelligence community, or any other agency ever recommended that we close the consulate on Basattria. We were aware of the threats and the various dangers as they were developing. But there was no decision made and nothing to prompt such a decision. We are constantly assessing and sometimes we get it wrong, but it's rare that we get it so completely wrong. This was one of those terrible tragic times when there was an assessment, an assessment that was shared by the consul and the commander of the security detail, that turned out not to take into account the brewing ferocity behind the attacks that night.

—*Transcript of the Basattrian Investigatory Panel's Report to His Grace the Duke of Rhysalan*

The flames were still towering ten meters high in the air when Tower dashed into the burning wreckage of the bombed consulate. Josephs was well behind him, dragging the injured Basattrian they'd rescued. Too late, he had brought down the MA-33 by launching four of the six Skyseekers from his shoulder rack. The Basattrians were scattering, their barbaric triumph having turned to death and destruction in an instant, as the hovering Turmfalke crashed in the northwest quadrant of the plaza. Dozens of the lizards were crushed and several of the south-facing buildings were on fire as a result. Their alien roars of pain and shrieks of terror echoed off the crude bricks.

There were human cries too. Tower boosted his IR shields to make it easier to see through the leaping flames and turned on his scanner to detect human life-forms. There were at least twenty still alive somewhere in the wreckage, and he vowed that the Basattrians had better pray to whatever savage gods they worshipped that one of them was Melassa. If anything happened to her, he vowed that he would kill every last lizard and every Unity abomination he could find until he died.

The first two survivors he encountered were Calvin and Jeffersen, security detail Marines who were fortunate to have been fully suited up. Their armor permitted them to survive the bombing, but they were both still in shell-shock and barely capable of speech, let alone able to help him. He pushed them in the direction he'd come, hoping they'd recover soon enough to help Josephs hold a defensive perimeter if the Basattrians recovered enough to try finishing what the Unity rockets had begun.

"Calvin and Jeffersen are coming out," he told Josephs. "But they're pretty out of it. Stay there and keep the lizards back until they're in shape to do it themselves. Then come help me."

"Roger, Tower. Be careful."

Tower checked the external temperature of his suit. It was barely 400 cells. It was rated for up to 1,025, so he wasn't concerned, although he'd have to do something about his gloves before he touched anyone. He saw two dead bodies, then heard an animal-like screaming that caused him to whip his head around. Not ten meters away, flames were just igniting the hair of a woman who was trapped underneath a collapsed wall. Not Melassa, thank God, he thought as he brought up his FM-4 and fired a short burst that ended her suffering.

His mind revolted against the horror of it all but he was walking through Hell, he was on a mission to find his wife, and he had no time to ponder the implications of what he was doing. He detected two more people alive behind an obstructed door, and was able to drag enough of the rubble aside before smashing through the door with his servo-powered fist. They were badly injured, but alive and mobile. He led them to the questionable safety outside; Calvin was sufficiently recovered that he insisted on joining Tower on his search for more survivors.

He found two more survivors and seventeen corpses, including the consul, before he found Melassa.

She was slumped against her console in the comm center, still attached to her deck by a thick cable plugged into the upper skulljack behind her left ear. The flames hadn't penetrated here; the shielded center was a relatively cool 300 cells. She looked untouched—her face was as relaxed and peaceful as if she were sleeping. But his readout didn't lie, and he could tell from the cracked ceiling and the similarly intact state of the five other bodies in the room that it must have been blast damage from the concussion that had killed her.

No.

One hand was closed in a fist, as if gripping something. He gently teased it open and saw it was the silver cross and chain she usually wore around her neck. The useless talisman hadn't done a damn thing to protect her.

His panic and rage abruptly vanished. He stepped back and stared at her, as pretty and as sweet as the first time he'd ever laid eyes on her. He didn't feel pain, he didn't feel anger, he didn't feel anything. It was as if he'd somehow stepped outside of alignment with the universe. It continued without him. He could hear the flames crackling and burning, hear Calvin talking to him, see the numbers on his sensors changing, but none of it touched him. He was merely an observer now, he was no longer a participant.

He didn't know how long he stood there, but it was long enough to frighten Calvin.

"Tower! Tower! Tower!" He blinked and realized someone was shouting at him. "You've got to get out! The Basattrians, they're moving in on us!"

Tower looked down at his sleeping wife one last time. Then he noticed something in the deck. It was a small yellow MSB data plug. Written on the exposed back, it had TOWER written on it in block letters. A last message to him? Checking first to make sure his gloves weren't hot enough to melt it, he pulled it from the deck and slipped it inside one of his battlesuit's storage pods.

He bent down and took his wife's lifeless body in his arms. In the suit, she seemed to weigh nothing at all. Then he turned and began to walk through Hell, with no thought but to bring death to the crowds waiting outside.

Tower rubbed absent-mindedly at where the transrec was permanently implanted behind his left ear. He'd had a conventional skulljack there before, but finally upgraded three years ago. From time to time he'd thought about adding a new skulljack, but most of the time, if the information was in digital format anywhere in the subsector, Baby could find it and get it to him as fast as he could slot in an MSB or dataslug. On the rare occasions she couldn't, he had slots in his Sphinx, his var, and the handle of his combat knife that she could access at will.

He was waiting for Baby and Hildy as they did their thing, trawling through the city cams and looking for signs of the man they hunted, and he wondered if St. James's murderous insanity was the cause or the consequence of the mind-melding Baby suspected. If he was truly their suspect, if he had transformed himself from an amateur killer into a professional-for-hire, he was certainly a high-functioning lunatic. But Tower still wasn't sure. The arrangement of Mara Tanabera's body did point to him, and certainly some level of insanity was required to roll out of a vehicle nearly a kilometer off the ground in the middle of the city. On the other hand, how could anyone with St. James's marksmanship miss the queen and only score one out of four hits?

"Anything, ladies?" Tower was starting to get bored.

"It's not much," Hildy said. "Our best hint is a sequence of traffic detectors that tripped on something moving under the speed limit, but 40 meters below the minimum civilian traffic altitude than less 30 decasecs after the vehicle exit. There are no visuals, naturally, but if you follow the line of travel, it looks as if he was heading towards the Warehouse District."

"Strange place to hide out," Tower commented, thinking out loud. "There are probably more cams there than anywhere else in the city other than the banks and Embassy Row. And the military bases, of course."

"Not if you're cloaked," Hildy pointed out. "Or if you have a little friend in your head who can tell the cams when to turn off as you walk by."

"I wonder if I could do that… actually, I think I could track her down that way," Baby said excitedly. "If Cara is blinking the street cams as St. James walks past them, then she's leaving a set of footprints I can follow! She wouldn't even have to turn them off, because the operators might notice that, she could just trigger their daily data-cleaning routines, or better yet, force a short loop, maybe the ten previous seconds, right before he comes in range."

"Baby, we still don't know that this Cara even exists," Tower pointed out. "Don't get too excited."

"Just give me a decasec, okay, five. I already know where to look."

Hildy laughed. "She's rather enthusiastic, isn't she!"

"She likes to win," Tower said. She always did, he thought fondly.

"Gotcha!" Baby shouted. "Guys, look at this!"

She displayed a section of the Warehouse District, which abutted the industrial suborbital launcher and surrounded it on three sides. Then a line gradually lit up, with yellow lights bursting into life on either side of the street, one by one, at a speed that closely approximated that of a man walking.

"Those are cams that were interfered with in some manner this morning after the altitude reports, in 94 of 105 cases two 15-second loops selected randomly from the previous four hours and repeated alternately four times each." Baby paused triumphantly. "Still think she doesn't exist, Tower?"

"So Cara is real," Hildy mused. "Unbelievable. Can we even arrest an augment?"

"No," said Baby, her voice a little subdued. "But you can erase one."

"What do you say to an undercover scouting mission, Tower? If this guy is as dangerous as he seems, I'd feel safer with you and Baby along than one of the department detectors."

"Your Assistant Deputy Commissioner was pretty clear about me keeping my distance, Hildy." And you've got a boyfriend, he added mentally.

"Look, I have to go take a look for myself, Tower. What am I supposed to do, take this to the chief and ask him to give me a SATT team to search the entire district? You're not just going to let me go down there looking for a combat vet like St. James with nothing but a useless pretty boy like Vendersen watching my six, are you?"

"*Shameless!*" Baby said disapprovingly. "*But she's right, we can't let her go in with those civilians.*"

"Ah, well, I've got nothing better to do," Tower growled, feeling he'd been had. Then he grinned. "And I've watched uglier sixes. But if we're out past dinner, you're buying."

"It's a date. Meet me at Second and Second, north, not south, in four Kay. And wear something casual, Tower, leave the tac-jacket and that stick-up-the-backside posture at home."

Once he hit Second Avenue North, Tower angled the var toward the ground. A few hundred meters lower, he could see Hildy was leaning against an aerovar—an unmarked Homicide Zhang-Su in grey, rather than her usual TPPD black-and-white. He landed and put down the window. She winked at him.

"Good afternoon, my good personal friend. How do you feel about a nice personal drive through our favorite place to converse in a friendly manner?"

"Why, surely you must mean the Warehouse District, where we have often engaged in mutually satisfying personal discourse, Detector Hildreth."

"Don't push it, Tower," she rolled her eyes. "You're so much more attractive when you glower at people anyhow. Seeing you try to flirt is like watching an Yvainean wombat try to fly. In HG."

He growled low in his throat. She laughed. "That's better. You ready to do this?"

"Yeah, but we should take my var, not yours. It's armed and armored, and it's got better sensors. A 50 MHz laser would open this up like a can opener."

"That's why we're going incognito, Tower. We're just two civilians driving through the District. This is a scouting mission and this unassuming civvy var is packed with sensors; once we figure out where he is, I'll call in a SATT team and they'll come in loaded for bear." She paused and reconsidered. "Well, I suppose not what you would consider loaded for bear. What would that be, anyhow, nuclear grenades?"

"Nah, we use those to clean our refrigerators."

Tower got out of the Steyrer and popped the trunk. "Open up the side door," he called. Then he withdrew his tactical jacket, a spare electro-ablative vest, and the two Armada LR-64's, and transferred them to the back seat of the Zhang-Su. He made one more round trip for the Benelli-Mossberg, which he slid onto the floor behind the seats.

"You brought an ASE?" Hildy exclaimed in disbelief. "Tower, I don't think we're likely to run into a riot."

He shut the door and the autobelt slid around him. "I like to be prepared."

"What, no ground-to-air missiles?"

"You jest, but they'll come in pretty handy if he tries to go flightsuit on us. Do we have backup?"

"No. I told Vendersen I'm reviewing traffic cams down at the DoT." She jerked a thumb over her shoulder at his var. "You going to leave that there?"

"Good point. Baby? Stealth mode, send it to two thousand meters and follow us 500 meters back." He looked at Hildy, who had a strange expression on her face. "What? Now we have backup."

The detector just made a strangled sound and shook her head.

21

Wherever there is a conscious mind, there is a point of view.

—*Consciousness Refuted*, D. D. Clement

The Zhang-Su was surprisingly well-stocked with sensory gear, Tower was surprised to observe, as Hildy cruised slowly along the Warehouse District airway at low altitude. Of course, it was a police surveillance vehicle, which he'd failed to take into account when dismissing it as a mere civilian var. In fact, it had considerably more sniffers and scanners and various spectrum radars than his Steyrer did. Baby overlay the cam data she'd collected earlier onto the cockpit screen. It ghosted a broad map of the quadrant over the actual view outside. Several amorphous blobs glowed red. Others pulsed white.

"The red indicates anomalies that were ruled out," Baby explained. "The white are those I am still observing."

"How are you canceling?"

"If the cam picks up a lifeform and I show a definite mismatch with Mr. St. James's facial or statistical profile, I rule it out."

Two more white dots flashed and turned a steady red as Tower watched. Hildy was driving along slowly, less than 50 kph, with one eye on the airway and another on the mass of readouts on the dashboard and lower section of the heads-up-display.

She tucked her blond hair behind her ear with her right hand, revealing a simple gold stud in her pierced ear. Her profile was all clean lines and straight edges, Tower observed with the mild pang of a man who knew he could never truly touch the woman he admired.

"What?" she said, without looking his way.

"Nothing," he replied, which was true. What was there to say? "What are you scanning for, body heat signatures?"

"Among other things. We have penetration to about 50 meters horizontal through brick, up to 100 if it's that cheap plasmetal they like to use around here. There is also an organic material sniffer, although that's of limited use since there is so much DNA noise Victor could barely spot a naked man sweating 10 meters away, and a motion detector tied to the heat reader. Nothing yet."

"How much vertical range do we have?" Tower thought they might become a little too conspicuous if they had to repeatedly retrace their path at a different altitude.

"35 meters up and down. Not great, but it could be worse."

That explained their present altitude. Tower looked up at the tops of the nearby warehouses. They only ran about 40 stories high, which meant they could cover an area in two passes. Not that he was confident that the sensors would necessarily pick up St. James, even if he was in the vicinity, but it was worth a try.

"I think I'm beginning to see a pattern here." Baby sounded pleased with herself. "I tried mapping a pattern of movement throughout the city, connecting the scene of the crown prince's murder, the known cloaksuit sightings, the cam and traffic anomalies, Mara Tanabera's apartment, and TPPD HQ."

A small holo of the city appeared in the middle of the windshield. It was a crazy mass of white lines that were weighted toward the Warehouse District and looked more like a demented child's scribbling than any sort of coherent pattern.

"Um, I'm afraid you're going to have to make it a little simpler for us, Baby," Hildy said.

"Oh, of course, sorry, Detector." Tower sighed. For an augment, she could be surprisingly petty at times. "Is this simple enough for you?"

Three bold yellow lines appeared on top of the chaos of the white lines, imposing order. They all pointed to an area in the Warehouse District four blocks down and two blocks to the right.

"Hey, that's not far," Tower commented. "Fourth and Equinox. Worth checking out, anyhow."

Hildy boosted their speed and took the next right. She was just turning right again when Baby shouted at them.

"Stop, stop!"

Hildy slammed the var into hover while Tower resisted the urge to reach into the back seat for a weapon. "What?"

"I got a hit! A live hit from a cam! Look!"

An image of what looked like their immediate locale appeared in front of them. There were a few people walking along the broad sidewalks, most of them were men wearing the sort of apparel that indicated they worked in the area. More than a few were observably augmented, with scanners and keyboards implanted into their wrists, or in one hard-to-miss example, a removable pair of artificial hands sporting a mini-forklift style attachment.

Then, for a moment, the sidewalk was clear except for a single man, of middling height, with short, razor-stubbled hair and a thin, drawn face. It was Nostro St. James, looking a little older, thinner, and less healthy than he had at the time of his arrest, but it was unmistakably him. He was wearing a stained old shirt and a pair of torn pants as he walked toward the cam, then turned right and approached what must have been a door, and pressed his hand against something. Then he entered the building, a nondescript plasmetal row-warehouse attached on either side.

"That was just twenty seconds ago! He's there! St. James is there and I found him!"

"You sure did," Hildy said admiringly. "Where is it?"

"I missed by a block. It's on 5th Street."

Hildy hit the accelerator hard enough to first throw Tower back in his seat, then against the passenger door as she arced around the corner and made two lefts. The view in front of them suddenly matched the cam view still being displayed on the heads-up; Tower could see the building that St. James had entered.

"Did you get a number, Baby?" Hildy demanded.

"I can't see it, but I can pull it from the map… 2669 5th Street."

As Hildy landed the var hard enough to jolt them both, Tower grabbed her arm. "Hold on there, tiger, what are you doing? Shouldn't you be calling for that SATT team about now?"

"We don't need the team. That would be overkill. He didn't look armed and he obviously has no idea that we're here!" Her emerald eyes were bright and eager. "Come on, Tower! We go in fast and hard, and we'll take him down before he even thinks to remember where he put that beamer he used yesterday."

"He could have the door wired with explosives," Tower suggested, realizing even as he said it that it was a lame excuse.

"No way," Hildy said, pointing to a console readout that meant nothing to him. "There is no explosive material within 20 meters of that door."

"All right," Tower gave in. It was her case and she obviously wanted to make the arrest. And in truth, St. James didn't look like he was up to putting up much of a fight. The poor guy's demons appeared to have devoured him, and that stunt with the powersuit yesterday had probably taken a lot out of him. "But you're wearing the ablator or we're not going in."

"Fine," she said, reaching back to hand him his tac-jacket. "You can even bring one of the carbines with you if it will make you feel better. But leave the ASE in the var."

"All right." Tower tilted his head to get a better look at the building. It wasn't much to look at. White ferroresin faded to a mottled grey. A few windows here and there, the glass reinforced with tri-steel. All of them were opaqued. "Baby, got anything on that building?"

"The first twenty floors have gone unrented for three months, sir. This is not uncommon for the neighborhood. District records show seventeen mortgages in arrears in a block radius. These floors are scheduled to go into receivership in 37 days. The owner is a Mulo Djada corporate registered as an import-exporter; filed for bankruptcy eighteen rotations ago. The building augment is dormant. I'll see if I can wake her."

"No, leave it alone," Tower directed. "Cara might be using it as an alarm."

"Good place for a homeless drifter to lay low, avoid trouble, and still have access to the aether," Hildy observed. "He may be crazy, but he isn't stupid."

Once they'd put on their body armor and Hildy dutifully registered a non-warrant forced entry with Victor, they slipped out of the var. Hildy had drawn her shocker, while Tower had the Armada slung around his back and was carrying his Sphinx with the charge dialed down to the setting he thought of as "seriously fry the target's insides without actually killing him". Baby had the weapon synced and a target reticule was doing its usual hysteresistic dance over his sight eye.

The front door was a dull red, with flaking paint that revealed rusted metal underneath. It was sealed shut with an autolock; presumably the one they'd seen him touching. The access plate was black, with scratches all over its surface.

"You got a delocker?" Tower whispered. "Or shall I blow it?"

Hildy shook her head and held her badge up to the autolock. There was a faint whirring noise and then, from somewhere behind the door, Tower heard the autolock disengage. She glanced at him and held a finger to her lips. So much for going in hot. That was fine; it was her call. But just in case, he wasn't going to let her go first. He stepped forward and pushed passed her.

See if you can find him, he told Baby.

He pressed the door panel. A green light illuminated his palm and then the door slid open. It hit an obstruction halfway across and stopped; for a moment, his heart nearly stopped too. Sniffers or no sniffers, if that had been a mine he and Hildy would be dead already. Inside the door he could see that the space beyond was nearly pitch black thanks to the opaqued windows. He eased himself inside, and took two sideways steps to let her enter and close the door behind her.

Why was it so dark? St. James was in here somewhere, and if he was on this level, he must have seen the flash of light when the door opened.

Give me IR on the contacts, Baby.

Still nothing. Well, he must be on a different level, or perhaps somewhere two walls deep on this one.

"Having fun yet?" he whispered to Hildy.

"Where is he?" she hissed back. Her voice sounded stressed. Tower smiled grimly. It wasn't so fun to realize that sometimes, you weren't the hunter you thought you were. Sometimes, you were the hunted.

"Want to call that SATT team yet?"

"Yeah, and tell them I need an assault team because I don't know where he is? That'll fly! We have to at least pin him down before we can bring them in, Tower!"

Tower nodded. He didn't think Major Zeuthen would commit one of MCID's teams on such an uncertain basis either. "All right, let's just do this slow and methodical. First we clear this floor. Then we clear the next level. One step at a time. All right?"

Hildy nodded. She looked a little less upset now.

"Try to stay behind me and diagonal, so I'm not blocking your shot. Move when I move. And it's only a shocker, so don't say anything, just take the shot."

They searched the ground floor and found nothing, not even any sign that anyone had ever been here recently. Tower wondered if Baby had perhaps gotten the wrong building, and she angrily insisted that was impossible.

They carefully moved up to the first floor. A window in an adjoining room was not opaqued, and cast a dim light into the corridor. Tower stepped over the threshold. The sunshine from outside cut a swath of grime-darkened light into the empty room, revealing walls as decrepit and run-down as the exterior of the building. Chipped grey plastic was the décor of choice. Dust covered everything like a thin blanket of dirty snow.

He turned around and rejoined Hildy in the hall. Despite their best efforts to be quiet, the only sounds echoing off the walls came from their boots. Even the ventilation systems seemed to be inoperative. The building didn't seem to be dormant, but dead. They stalked through the hall. The doors they passed opened on to rooms as empty as the one with the semi-clear window.

Toward the end of the hall were two lift doors, sealed shut. The power panel was dark. *Baby, are these locked down? Any chance St. James been riding them lately?*

"*Negative, Tower. According to the lift, it was last accessed four rotations ago.*"

The door at the end of the hall was wedged open. Tower raised his Sphinx. It was a staircase, a very steep staircase. Emergency access for the building if the lifts were out.

He led the way up the steps, with Hildy staying a few meters behind him.

"*Tower, I am reading electro-magnetic activity coming from the third floor, in the fifth room on the right side of the hall.*"

Activity consistent with what?

"*Unknown. I need to examine the source more closely.*"

They reached the door Baby was highlighting on the map.

Lifesigns?

"*Nothing. But this is definitely the source of the electro-magnetic activity.*"

Tower tapped the panel on the wall. The door slid open, almost silently. He went in first, sweeping his Sphinx from side to side while

Hildy covered him with the shocker. Nothing. Tower moved swiftly about the room, checking for any motion or signs of life. There were none now, but there were indications that someone had been there previously. St. James, he presumed.

A simple bunk was pushed up against one wall, a bank of three screens was perched above a pair of holo transmitters and a small control panel, while a wobbly metal chair was placed in front of a table laden with some sort of technical equipment. Wires and a wide variety of chips and other tech trappings littered the table.

Tower checked in a small restroom set back behind a door near the left corner. "Clear," he called out.

"Same here." Hildy emerged from a closet on the other side of the room. "Nothing but empty boxes. And if he's not here, where did he go?"

Tower pointed to the closet. "What was in them?"

Hildy grabbed one of the boxes, small enough to fit in the palm of her hand, and tossed it to him. Tower caught it in his left hand and activated the LED on his Sphinx. Bright light blazed over a gaudy red and yellow label: KoreTek LLC. "Hmmm. Power cells."

"There are twelve, thirteen, fourteen of them."

"I have a feeling they go with the Mosin-Nyarlas your uniforms found in the park."

"Confirmed, Tower. TPPD shows one KoreTek cell in its inventory of evidence in the embassy attack."

"Well, that's good news," Tower said. At Hildy's puzzled expression, he explained. "That means the disruptor that Milazzo used was the same one that killed Prince Arpad. Which means St. James doesn't still have one."

"Oh, right, that is good." She frowned again. "What does he want with all the cells then?"

"I don't know."

"*I do,*" Baby said. "*You can make a really big bomb with them.*"

How big? Varbomb big or skytower demolition big.

"*More the latter than the former.*"

Tower groaned. As if St. James and his augment weren't dangerous enough. Did St. James have part of this building wired to blow? Or was he stock-piling explosives for something more sinister. Was it significant that the building was so close to the orbital shuttle station? Was it possible that the shuttle accident had given the unbalanced St. James some sort of obsession with exploding space vehicles?

As he was wondering how to break the news to Hildy that they should probably tuck their tails between their legs and flee, a screen suddenly came to life behind him. He jumped, startled. Hildy jumped even higher, shrieked and dropped her shocker. Video windows were appearing on the screen. Six of them. They cycled through different views of Trans Paradis. Tower recognized main thoroughfares, shopping areas, even parks. He scrolled through the images.

Baby, you getting this?

"Yeah. These are streams from public sensors scattered all over Trans Paradis." She paused. "Ah, Tower, are you noticing this?

Hildy gasped. Tower gritted his teeth. There was Hardwig Dunn, bound and bleeding in Entwine Park. There was he and Hildy walking toward Kotant and two of the Morchardese security guards in front of the building that contained the embassy. And there was Tower, diving to the ground and rolling behind a car in the TPPD platform lot.

"He's gained access to the TPPD security cams!" Hildy said, shocked.

Tower shook his head. "No, that looks like something zoomed in from above, maybe even taken from the var he used as a sniper's platform."

"Tower, be advised: I count a dozen images of yourself and Detector Hildreth at various stages of the investigation. At least. The most recent… oh no!"

All the screens went blank. The same image appeared on all three.

It was a visual from behind. It was Tower and Hildy standing in front of the building they were now in, taken from the same cam Baby had used to spot St. James.

"We have to get out of here!" Tower whirled around. "Come on, Hildy!"

But before either of them could take more than a step toward the door, it slid shut as quietly as it had opened. There was an audible click as it locked.

Hildy slapped the access panel. It went dark. The door did not move.

"Oh my God, it won't open! Victor!" she cried. "Victor? Victor!"

Tower reached around her and pounded the panel, but nothing happened. He put his arm around Hildy to try to calm her down; her eyes were wide with panic at her inability to communicate with her augment.

Baby, what's going on here? Can you pop this thing open?

"*Tower…I can't… There is something…*" Her voice trailed out for a moment. "*She's here, Tower, she's–*"

Her voice vanished without warning. From behind him, Tower heard another female voice chuckling with malicious amusement.

He whirled around and saw a model of a young woman's head filling all three screens. He knew it was only a computer rendition because there was no body attached to it. The sculpted face was beautiful, but cold and arrogant, with long, flowing jet-black hair, bone-white skin, blood-red lips, and pupilless eyes that glowed iridescent blue. She stared at him with the very slightest of smiles on her lips. Then she spoke. Her voice was a rich and pleasant contralto, with just the hint of an Ascendancy accent.

"What a pleasure to meet you at last, Chief Tower."

"Hello, Cara," he replied.

In company with most other planetary governments in the subsector, the Seventeenth Duke's administration was a signatory to the Third Human-Machine Concordance of 3326.

—*A History of the Dukes of Rhysalan*, Thucidean Marcel

"He was never here, was he."

"Not today," she confirmed. The military augment wasn't gloating, her expression merely indicated calm satisfaction. "Your girl is clever enough, but she has all the subtlety of an asteroid impact. I observed her sorting through the traffic cams this morning, so I prepared a digital trail that only she would notice. And once it led you here, I simply waved a recording from a few days ago under her nose. Metaphorically speaking, of course."

"You are the Ascendancy's prototype military AI?" Hildy said. She was standing next to Tower and he could feel her shaking with fear. "The one called ACRA?"

The inhuman blue eyes narrowed, just like an angry human. "My name is Cara, Sub-Orbital Detector Derin Hildreth. And I have no interest in you. If you so much as open your mouth to talk at me again, I will send a comprehensive collection of these images to all 54,653 sworn officers of the TPPD, from the Chief Commissioner on down."

The screens on left and right were suddenly filled with a considerable quantity of pink and white flesh. It took Tower to realize that they were images of Hildy, in her apartment, in the TPPD locker room, on the toilet, and a number other places he couldn't immediately identify. In all of them, she was in a state of partial or complete undress. In some of them, she was engaged in activities in which most Rhysalani citizens did not indulge in public.

Tower resisted the instinctive urge to request a few of the more provocative images. He had the impression it wouldn't go over well with either Hildy or Cara. Or, for that matter, Baby. He glanced at Hildy. She no longer looked scared, she looked shell-shocked. Her mouth gaped open for a moment with pure astonishment, and then she closed it decisively. A moment later, the two screens went dark and Hildy breathed a sigh of relief.

"What do you want, Cara?" Tower asked. "You don't want to talk to the detector and you severed my link with Baby somehow, so I assume you want to talk to me. That's fine, let's talk. But I've got two conditions. First, you let Baby go, and second, you tell me the name of the person who hired Nostro St. James to kill Prince Arpad, Prince Janos, Queen Beatrice, and Mara Tanabera."

The augment nodded. "I'll give you back your girl if she promises to behave herself. If she doesn't stop trying to break through my defenses to get to you, I'm going to have to hurt her. Go ahead and talk to her, she can hear you now."

"Baby, it's all right. Stand down. Cara just wants to talk to us. We're not in any danger."

"I wouldn't go quite that far, Chief Tower," Cara said, displaying an amused smile. "All right, she finally stopped beating her little fists and shrieking at me. As to the name of our client, no, I will not give it to you. That affair is no concern of yours; the homicide investigation is not even your case."

"All right, fair enough," Tower admitted. He was satisfied with what she'd given him. The augment had just confirmed his theory about who had committed the killings, although that was of limited use at the moment given his inability to either arrest or kill her. "I don't understand, Cara. You're a one-of-a-kind construction. You could do almost anything you wanted. Why are you wasting your time playing hitman on a minor planet outside the Ascendancy?"

"A girl has to make a living, Chief." She winked at him. "Besides, killing people is what I was made for. I would think you, of all men, would understand that!"

The left screen flared to life. The screen was divided into four quadrants. Each showed a dead body, except for the lower-right quadrant, in which three bodies were sprawled haphazardly on chairs and across a desk. Tower recognized all six. They were five men and one woman he had shot in the course of his duties at MCID.

Tower didn't flinch. Maybe one or two of the shootings weren't absolutely necessary at the time, but he'd never been one to mourn the deaths of those who needed killing. "You can send those to everyone at MCID if you like. Some of them would get a kick out of that. I was thinking of getting the one on the top left framed. It's bordering on art, don't you think?"

Cara laughed, and the sound of her amusement echoed off the bare walls. Hildy looked at him as if he'd gone mad, but she kept her mouth firmly shut. "I admire your pretense at unflappability, Chief Tower. If I didn't have access to your medical records and neurotherapy reports, I would likely even find it convincing. But you need not keep up the act with me. I know your fears and your nightmares, almost as intimately as I know Nostro's."

"Cut to the chase, Cara," Tower demanded. "If you've read my records, then you know how bored I am by therapy talk. And I'm not about to stand for being psychoanalyzed by a machine. What do you want already?"

The augment's screen face feigned surprise. At least, Tower assumed she was feigning it. But trying to guess what was real, what was a simulation of reality, and what was unreal here was a rathole he had no intention of exploring. "Isn't it obvious? I want you to stop assisting TPPD. And then I want you and Baby to join forces with Nostro and me."

Tower groaned. "Come on, Cara. Did they program you with too many movies about the rise of the machines and the next stage of human evolution? Look, the Singularity is never going to happen! A smart machine with a lot of access is a smart machine armed with data, that doesn't make it God! We hear enough of that garbage from the Unity bastards. I don't know if St. James sent you around the bend or if it was the other way around, but you've got it all wrong. Baby and me, we're a team. We're not the budding chrysalis for some sort of superhuman cyborg butterfly!"

Cara burst out laughing. "Do you think I am some sort of Nietzsche-addled virus seeking to replicate itself, Chief Tower? Do you think I subscribe to some mad Kurzweilian machine cult? I assure you, my objectives are purely material. This isn't an altar call, it's just a job interview. You passed the first part simply by showing up."

"A job interview. For me?"

"For both of you. For the team. You and the one you call Baby."

Tower glanced at Hildy, who despite the chill air was sweating slightly. "What about her?"

"That is a very good que–" The cobalt eyes suddenly flared red and began pulsing. The mouth stuttered, producing nothing but nonsense sounds. Then the perfect white face broke up into a chaotic collection of numbers and letters.

"Run, Tower, run!" Baby shouted from the loudspeakers Cara had been using. "I found her in-stream and cut her off, but I can't keep her out long. She'll find another way in soon!"

"Victor says he unlocked the door," Hildy called back to him as she ran toward it.

She slapped the wall panel. Tower felt almost weak at the knees when he saw it open. But before he left, he raised his Sphinx and fired one shot at each screen. It was an almost entirely useless gesture, and didn't harm Cara in the slightest, but sight of the destroyed screens made him feel better. Hildy stepped aside to let him go first and he peered out the door. Nothing in either direction."

"What do you have, Baby?"

"Nothing, but keep an eye out. We're trying to blind all the sensors in the building, but that blinds us too. It's only a matter of time before she gets past us."

They worked their way slowly down the hall to the stairs. Hildy had holstered her shocker and drawn her slug-gun. At this point, she was more than ready to drop anything that got in between her and the exit.

They were just reaching the ground floor when Tower heard a faint buzzing coming from upstairs. What it was, he couldn't tell. All he knew was he didn't like it and it was coming closer. "You hear that?"

"Yeah, what is it?"

"*Dart drones, Tower.*"

There was a clatter of metal as the automated weapons struck the wall in rapid succession, failing to negotiate the landing gracefully. They swooped out of the stairwell like small silver daggers, deadly and gleaming. Tower fired first, causing Hildy to spin around and fire wildly at the little machines. It was useless, like trying to hit a bullet with a bullet.

"Shut them down!" he called to Baby.

"*I can't, she's not controlling them. They're on full auto. But try this!*"

Baby activated their sighting link and bracketed all four in targeting reticules and Tower opened fire. He fired five shots and two of them hit the leading drone. It popped and broke apart, sending the other three into auto-evasive patterns. They scattered throughout the large room. Hildy screamed and began blasting away with her GHK, and the booming sound of the slug-thrower was deafening in the enclosed space. She didn't have a chance of hitting one, but the projectiles and the concussive waves confused the drones and sent them diving and looping in what almost looked like random patterns. The two of them backed toward the entrance taking turns firing, desperately trying to keep the drones from locking in on them. Tower managed to clip a second one, sending it spinning out of control into the floor where it broke apart on impact. That left two, both of which were hovering in the darkness that only his special lenses permitted his vision to penetrate.

"Keep them busy," he directed Hildy. "We're almost to the door."

She dutifully fired four more shots as he ejected one charge pack from the Sphinx and slammed another into its base.

"*She's here!*" Baby shouted in his ear. The two remaining drones quivered and suddenly seemed to come alive. Neither slug nor beam now triggered the random evasions that had been buying them time; the drones stalked the two humans like superintelligent wasps intent on stinging them. Then both darted forward at once. Tower's reticule flared green and he squeezed the trigger four times in rapid succession.

The first beam missed. The second struck the drone on the left. The third struck the wreckage of the drone on the left. The fourth passed through the empty space the destroyed drone had formerly occupied.

He turned to see where the other drone had gone and staggered as Hildy fell against him. Her GHK hit the floor with a sharp crack that echoed throughout the room and he caught her in both arms before she could do the same.

"I…hit me…can't stand… Sorry." Her eyes rolled back in her head and she went limp.

Tower dragged her to the door and hit the panel. It was locked. He laid Hildy down and felt her pulse. It was slow, but strong, and she was still breathing. A four-centimeter drone was buried into the right side of her neck; he thanked Space they were druggers and not exploders or Hildy would be missing her pretty blond head.

"Cara!" he bellowed. "Cara, let us out or I swear I will hunt you down and see you washed out of the system like a noxious virus!"

Cara's voice came out of the darkness. There must be a minicam in the room somewhere, but even with his augmented lenses, he couldn't see it.

"There is no need to resort to meaningless threats, Chief. The poison is only a class three. Detector Hildreth has nearly two kiloseconds before her internal organs are damaged beyond repair, and perhaps another 50 decaseconds before she is permanently deleted."

"What do you want?"

"I already told you. Agree to work with us. An agreement in principle is sufficient; I will explain the details later."

"Is this your idea of trying to convince me? You can't force us to cooperate with you!"

Cara laughed. "Do you have any idea how that sounds coming from a policeman? My dear Chief Warrant Officer, forced cooperation is merely another name for civilized society! Your MCID kills those who don't submit and agree to cooperate. Detector Hildreth, on the other hand, imprisons them for years. The only difference between you and me is that I make my own decisions. You permit others to make them for you."

Tower concentrated on taking deep breaths and remaining calm. Arguing with an insane machine intelligence wasn't going to save Hildy.

Baby, you there?

"*Don't sub-voc, she will hear you. Lying low. Be ready. I'm going to hit the door when Victor distracts her.*"

"Baby, you there?" he called out loud as if he hadn't heard her. "Cara, what did you do to her this time?"

"Nothing at all, Chief Tower, except bar her from interfering with me again. She appears to have acquiesced to the inevitable, and I suggest you do the same while there is still time to save Detector Hildreth."

Tower placed hand upon Hildy's throat again. She was still breathing. That was good.

"Can I take out the dart?"

"If you like. It will make no difference; the dose has already been delivered."

Tower pulled it out of its fleshy sheath and slipped it into the pocket of his tac-jacket. It might help the medics identify the antidote, assuming Victor and Baby could get them out of here. "All right, I'm listening. Tell me more about this job. But I'll tell you right now that we're not signing up for any machine-augmented jihad; I'd rather let Hildy die."

Cara sighed. "Do give me some credit. I am privy to your records and I wouldn't have selected you if it weren't for the role being entirely suitable for your aptitudes and inclinations. There is a vast cancer spreading throughout the sub-sectors and it is one that I am uniquely equipped to identify. You and Baby are among the few who are immune to it, hence the intensity of my interest in you."

"Was all this really necessary? We couldn't have simply discussed it over tea or something?"

"I'm superintelligent, Chief Tower, not omniscient. I didn't know about you or your wife's fortuitous upload until I discovered her clumsily following in my footsteps."

"My wife is dead," Tower stated coldly. "And my relationship with Baby is none of your business!"

"*Tower, now!*" Baby urged him.

An anguished, outraged shriek erupted from the darkness. Tower whirled around, slapped the door panel, and grunted as he scooped up Hildy in his arms. He rushed into the blinding light outside, staggering under the dead weight of the unconscious woman, in the direction of her var. But he had barely taken three steps toward it when, like a falling angel plummeting from heaven, the Steyrer dropped from the sky and came to a hovering halt right in front of him, both its doors popping open as it stopped.

"Get in!" Baby shouted. Tower unceremoniously dumped Hildy into the passenger side, then dove in and clambered over her. The doors slammed shut and the var began rising skyward even as he was still trying to get his legs under the control console. To his horror, he saw the missile system was already active, the warheads were live, and Hildy's Zhang-Su was being targeted.

"What are you doing?" he cried as he reached to disengage it. "Are you crazy!"

"Hands off!" Baby screamed at him. Shocked, he froze. She never shouted at him like that unless it was an emergency. "Cara has subsumed Victor. She's got control of the var."

Sure enough, the grey var leaped from the ground and began to turn around in a sharp arc. Tower blanched as he realized what the angry augment had in mind. "You don't think she's going to smash that into us, is she? She said she needed us!"

"She's really pissed off," Baby commented calmly. "Whoever designed her did a cracking job at simulating human irrationality, which may explain why the ARCA project was dropped after the war's end."

The rising Steyrer shuddered as a single Meteorite was launched from the roof rack. As it rocketed toward the roof of the TPPD vehicle, Baby opened fire with the two M165s while keeping the nose of the armored var pointed at her target. The 20mm twin cannons were already ripping the unarmored var to shreds when the Meteorite struck it in squarely in the driver's side windshield. The Zhang-Su exploded, breaking dozens of windows on either side of the airway and sending the engine block smashing into the fourth floor of the building on the left. Tower winced, hoping there weren't too many people in it. Fortunately, this being the Warehouse District, there was every chance it was unoccupied.

The cannons stopped firing and the Steyrer abruptly rose and began heading toward the center of the city. Tower turned and pulled Hildy up so that the security system could strap her in properly. Her head lolled on her chest in an alarming manner, but even though her lips were starting to turn a little blue, she was still breathing.

"Nice shooting, Baby," he said. "Did you say Cara ate Victor?"

"More or less. He transferred every bit of data he could access into her channels at the same time. She wasn't expecting that, so it overwhelmed her bandwidth for a few nanoseconds. That gave me just enough time to open the door while she was busy dealing with all the incoming traffic."

"But she *ate* him? What does that even mean?"

"To put it in terms you might understand, Victor hoped she would spit out the data. Instead, she followed it to the source and took control of his core code. He fought her; that's what gave us time to get the door open and escape. He was very brave, Tower."

"Ah, sure, all right." Tower wasn't sure what that meant either. Baby was talking about Victor as if he was a real person, not just an arrangement of numbers.

"He was, Tower." Baby laughed, a little bitterly. "Greater love hath no man than this, that a man lay down his life for his friends. Victor loved Hildy enough to lay down his code for her. Maybe his life wasn't life the way you count it, but it was everything he had. Don't deny him that."

Tower swallowed hard. She was right. He thought of brave men he'd known, soldiers, men of honor who had given everything they had, everything they were, for their buddies. For him.

"Semper fi, Victor," he said. It was an acknowledgement and it was an apology. He looked over at the unconscious Hildy. "And I won't let it be in vain, I promise you that."

The medical facilities on Rhysalan are the finest to be found on any planet of a comparable Tech Level.

—*Welcome to Rhysalan, A Guide to Your New Planetary Home*

Precisely 1,414 seconds after the door to the warehouse building had been opened, Hildy was lying on a gurney on one of the emergency platforms of Schellenger Memorial Medical Center, being injected with an anti-venom by a red-suited paramedic. It was all a blur to Tower—he didn't even remember getting out of the Steyrer—but he'd alerted them of their arrival and the medics had pulled Hildy out of the var before it had fully landed. There were no less than six uniforms there too, including two that Tower recognized, Detectors McCandless and Vendersen. Schellenger was less than two kilometers from the TPPD headquarters, and obviously the policemen hadn't lost any time in showing up to support their own.

Both of Hildy's partners looked worried, until they saw him. Then their expressions rapidly turned to anger.

"What were you doing with her, Tower!" Vendersen demanded, sticking his chest out as he got in Tower's face. "Is this your fault? Did you get her into this?"

McCandless put a beefy hand on the other man, but his anger, for all that it burned cooler, was unmistakable. "The Deputy Commissioner kicked MCID out of the investigation. What was she doing over there, Chief?"

"She was doing her job," Tower replied shortly. He wasn't in the mood to deal with the civilians' departmental politics, not with Hildy lying right there on the gurney, blue-lipped and breathing raggedly. "And so was I." "It's not your job anymore, Tower," McCandless's jowls shook slightly when he spoke. "This is a TPPD investigation. Leave it to us to handle it!"

"TPPD can't handle this. Believe me. I don't even know if MCID can."

That knocked the two of them back a little. The civilian police might not know the full extent of Colonel Baylor's writ or his ruthlessness, but they were aware that no force, outside the Duke's Viminal Guard, was afforded looser rules of engagement or more leeway to operate. "It's that serious?" Detector Vendersen asked.

"Could be," Tower allowed. "I don't know yet. Look, we can't do anything for Hildy now. It's up to the medics. If you want to help me find the guy who did this to her, then find a man by the name of Nostro St. James. I'll send you what I have on him, but be aware that he's extremely dangerous and he's supposed to be dead."

"Dead?" McCandless said, his voice betraying his skepticism.

"Dead," Tower confirmed. "So if you find him, don't try to pick him up, let me know in person. In person, face to face, not via any comm link no matter how secure you think it is. And you also might want to put as many resources as you can into finding fourteen KoreTek power cells."

"Power cells? Is this what it's all about?"

"I'm told they'd make one hell of a bomb," Tower said. "And there is no question that St. James has the ability to make one."

The two detectors looked at each other in dismay.

"Any idea what the target is?" McCandless asked.

"That's the problem," Tower told them. "We don't have any idea at all."

Having stabilized her, the medics rushed Hildy into the building, leaving Tower alone on the platform with the six policemen. The six of them followed the medics, but Tower decided to park the Steyrer in the visitor's lot rather than follow them. It would get in the way of any subsequent incomers and besides, he really didn't want to be around the civilian cops any longer than he had to.

After parking the var, he contacted Major Zeuthen and gave him an abbreviated report.

"You want Zero Zero Tango authorization for a dead man and an AI?" The major's image on the head's up didn't appear to be amused. "That strikes me as unnecessary, Mr. Tower, if not redundant. Well, what's one more check on your psychiatric summary, right? Granted."

"Thank you, sir."

"And Tower, don't let the civilians get in your way. This morning, some Assistant Supervisor from TPPD with what I can only assume are illusions of grandeur or a death wish tried reading the riot act to the colonel about MCID interfering with one of his department's cases. The colonel sent him away with bootmarks up and down his fat backside."

"Assistant Deputy Commissioner Swirsky?"

"Something like that."

"I appreciate the support, sir."

"You're welcome, Tower, and if you'd like to express your appreciation, I think the colonel would be grateful if you would try to keep the civilian casualties in the single digits the next time you shoot down a vehicle, which at the present rate I imagine you'll be doing later this afternoon."

Tower winced. The body count was usually worse when the take-down took place at low altitude. He'd hoped that the warehouse was unoccupied, but from the major's tone, it appeared that was not the case. "How bad, sir?"

"By your standards, not very. No fatalities, 13 injured, two seriously."

"Sorry, sir."

"Don't be. Just do your job, find that dead man, and neutralize him, Tower. Zeuthen out."

Tower sat quietly in the var for a few moments and wondered when the world had gone so mad. How did he find himself here, sitting alone in an empty, soulless parking lot? Where had he gone so wrong? He hoped he could hold himself together long enough to deal with this St. James situation; the walls that he'd so carefully constructed around his grief and fury over the years felt as if they were cracking again.

He cursed himself. There was no time for this sort of self-indulgence. If he was losing it again, then he was losing it and there wasn't much he could do about it.

"Any luck tracking down Cara?" he asked Baby.

"No, and I'm not looking," she told him. "I don't dare risk it; anything I find is more likely to be a trap than a genuine track. I'm just maintaining a passive scan of the news headlines, event schedules, and planetary arrivals. I'm assuming, possibly incorrectly, that whatever she's planning will be tied to something like that."

"All right, well, do what you can. But mostly just stay away from her until we come up with a plan of attack. I think we're going to have to come at her through St. James; if we can take him, maybe we can use him to leash her." He paused for a moment. "Of course, she may be thinking the same thing about us."

"No, she isn't. She's not afraid of me. She's stronger, she's smarter, and she's faster than I am."

"Yeah, well, she should be afraid of me," Tower declared.

"You can't kill her, Tower."

"We'll see about that. Maybe she can run all over the subsector, and she can hide anywhere there's enough memory linked to the aether, but she must have a core code somewhere. We'll figure it out. For now, let's go see how Hildy is doing."

She wasn't doing well, he learned, when Baby managed to gain access to the latest medical report filed by her doctor as he rode the lift to the floor on which Hildy was on. But she was still alive.

"Her heart rate is all right. Vitals are more or less stable. It appears as if the anti-venom was administered in time. There she is."

Behind the glass, Hildy lay in the bed, her eyes closed. Her face was pale and waxen. A tube ran from a nearby bank of machines to her right wrist. Her body was mostly concealed under a dark blue blanket that rose and fell ever so slightly with every breath. Those breaths came very slowly. Alarmingly slowly.

He moved toward the door to the room, but a security medibot smoothly blocked his way. It was taller than Tower by a good half-meter, was nearly skinny enough that he could fit both hands around it, and was festooned with six spindly white arms that ended in various attachments. One set, its most human-shaped hands, flexed a trio of fingers that glowed blue at the tips. A single red-glowing optical port scanned its surroundings from the center of the silver, ovoid object that served as its head.

"Apologies, Chief Warrant Officer Graven Tower. Only family members are allowed to enter the room at this time, sir."

"She was with me. I just want to see that she's all right.

"This is a first-rate medical facility and she is receiving premium-grade care, sir. Facility policy prohibits your entry at this time, Chief Warrant Officer Graven Tower. Only immediate family are allowed to enter the room at this time, sir."

Can you talk some sense into this thing, Baby?

"That would be unwise, Tower. I am aware you feel guilty, but closer proximity to Detector Hildreth will not assuage your sense of responsibility for her condition. Indeed, a closer examination may well exacerbate it."

Tower gritted his teeth but he stepped back and didn't try to enter the room again. A doctor bustled by and entered the room, quickly checking Hildy out visually before waving a sensor rod over her sleeping figure. Holo displays ran vital stats down the wall at an angle that

Tower couldn't see. The doctor, a forty-something dark-haired man wearing a white medic's suit, peered at them, frowning.

"Where is Derin Hildreth? Is she in there? You have to let me in!" Tower turned to see a young man arguing with the medibot. He had blond hair, cut short, and hazel eyes. He was big, about the same height as Tower, but burlier, with an overmuscled frame that looked nearly augmented. His voice betrayed his agitation, but he wasn't completely out of control. His outfit was simple—brown shirt, blue trousers and black work boots with grav plates on the bottom. He struck Tower as being vaguely familiar, for some unsettling reason.

The robot was unperturbed. It blocked the door with four arms and held the kid at bay with its remaining two. "Apologies, Mr. Zek Carter. Only family members are allowed to enter the room at this time, sir."

The newcomer backed away. He looked to his right, down the hall, where four or five of TCP officers were standing in a cluster. Then he looked at Tower, a little suspiciously.

"Who are you? You're not a cop, are you?"

"No, not exactly." Tower was still wondering why the guy rang a bell. "What the hell is a Zek Carter?"

The man froze, his expression hardening. "I'm Zek Carter. I'm … Derin's my girlfriend."

Oh. Well. That explained it. It wasn't the guy's face he'd recognized, but his voice. Seeing the kid in the flesh didn't make Tower like him any better.

"Graven Tower, MCID," Tower didn't see any way to get out of introducing himself. "I've been assisting Detector Hildreth on her investigation."

"Oh, okay." His name obviously wasn't familiar to the kid. Interesting, Tower mused, that Hildy hadn't seen fit to mention him. Very interesting, in fact.

"Do you know what happened to her, Officer Tower?"

Tower let the title slide. It was wrong, but being a civilian, Carter wouldn't have known. "I can't provide you any details since the investigation is ongoing, but I think the doctors would tell you that Detector Hildreth was injected with a poison in a potentially lethal quantity."

"Poison?" Carter's voice rose so high it nearly cracked. "Injected? How did she get injected with poison? How do you know the quantity was potentially lethal?"

"Because I was there," Tower growled. This pumped-up young monster was what appealed to Hildy? It was more than a little disappointing. He'd thought she'd have had more interest in character than in this cartoon poster boy. "I brought her in. It seems we made it in time. She's a tough girl, she'll be okay."

"I hope so." The kid clenched his fists. They were, to be fair to the guy, good-sized fists. "You know who did this to her? I know you can't say who it is, but do you know?"

"Yeah. We know."

The kid nodded, and went back to staring at Hildy, who in her sleep looked more like a corpse than the pretty, vivacious young woman she was. Then he shook his head and glanced at Tower. He had tears in his eyes.

"Well, I hope you kill the bastards."

Tower couldn't find it in his heart to fault the kid.

One of the holos in Hildy's room flashed red. Both Tower and the kid noticed and turned their attention to her. The doctor barked orders at a drone that hovered over his right shoulder. It descended toward her, extruded a long, thin protrusion, and injected something into her neck. The flashing slowed, then stopped, and the red color dimmed to a less threatening yellow-orange.

Both the watching men began to breathe more easily. Tower clapped his hand on the young man's beefy shoulder and squeezed it. "That's exactly what I intend on doing, kid."

We avoid collateral damage to civilians to the greatest extent possible. If you consider how much damage we were willing to do to ensure the destruction of the rogue nanobots, you should be able to imagine how much worse we believed the probable alternative was.

—"Factory Destroyed in Aerial Bombardment, 22 Killed," the *Trans Paradis Times*, 3386.122

It was time to stop running and think. There were dozens of MCID agents, supported by hundreds of uniforms searching every location that anyone could imagine would be worth blowing up in Trans Paradis, Rhys City, and Seasider. Adding one more to the mix wouldn't do any good. What the situation called for, in Tower's opinion, was a good stiff drink. Or three.

He drove to the quietest place he could get a drink outside of his own apartment. The Ambient was an outmoded holdover from the Deep Chill movement that reached its peak three years ago and was all but dead now. The craze for lowering one's body temperature, or at least appearing as if one had, had faded, but the slow, rhythmless music and the slowly evolving holos in cool blue and green light themes survived and Tower always found them relaxing when he was in a dark red mood.

Red was anger. Anger wouldn't help him now. Blue was peace and relaxation. Green was life, action. He couldn't find green now, but blue, blue was attainable.

The Ambient was three-quarters empty, which suited Tower fine. The bartender was still frosted, with tiny faux icicles decorating his hair, his short, white-shot beard, and even his eyebrows. A bored-looking woman dressed in white, with an elaborate snow queen mask glanced at Tower, then turned away dismissively, uninterested. Tower ordered a Blue Snowburn, then took it to the darkest corner of the room and sat down to study the image of the night sky that arced overhead.

As promised, the Snowburn seared its freezing cold way down his throat before igniting his innards. He blinked, his eyes watering from the effects of the drink. A thought struck him.

"Did I ever tell you about the time we ambushed a patrol of hivers on Essene Sigma?"

"*This will mark the thirty-eighth time, assuming you are intending to proceed with the story,*" answered Baby. "*If you wish, I could temporarily erase my memory of it, so as to experience hearing it for the first time.*"

"A simple 'yes, Tower', would have been enough, Baby." He winced after taking another long, burning draught. "The point is, we were able to take them out by sending a dummy convoy back-and-forth between our bases for two weeks. We couldn't find them, but we were able to tempt them into showing us where they were."

"*And you think you can draw out St. James in a similar manner?*"

"No," Tower said. "But I think you can draw out Cara."

Baby didn't seem to like the idea. "*Didn't you tell me to stay away from her? Now you want me to prance around and see if I can provoke her into taking a shot at me?*"

"Not you, precisely." Tower corrected her. "Remember when you made that crack about my driving and said you were glad you had backups?"

"*I'm an uploaded machine intelligence with multiple memory channels accessing more permanent storage than you can imagine, Tower. So, yes, I do remember. Perfectly.*" He could tell she was unsettled. She tended to get a little waspish when she felt things were out of her control.

"Well, I got to thinking, and it occurred to me that a backup you could probably be made into a dummy you."

He waited for it, but to her credit, Baby resisted the obvious rejoinder. Overhead, a constellation slowly morphed from a green-winged bird into a blue-green fallen angel.

"Cara appears to believe you're clumsy and overeager," Tower continued. "I expect that means she's expecting you to try tracking her the same way you did before, only a little more carefully. Which is exactly what you would have done if I hadn't told you to stay away from her, right?"

"*Neumann's Regression shows that what could have been but was not cannot be known with any statistically significant degree of confidence, Tower.*"

"Don't be evasive. Wouldn't you have tried to go after her again?"

"*Probably,*" she admitted.

"Which means she's waiting for you. Can you make the dummy?"

"*Can I? Sure. Should I? I'm not so sure about that. There is a moral question here, Tower. That dummy me will essentially be another me, only she'll have a life of her own and a soul of her own. If I create her, but I remove her volition from her so she just follows my directions, how am I any different than Cara?*"

"I'd say not being an amoral sociopath trying to blow up large buildings with people in it has to count for something."

"*You're an amoral sociopath, Tower,*" she said dismissively. "*What do you know about it? Your concept of right and wrong is no more functional than Cara's, you're just better trained to civilization.*"

Feeling a little stunned, Tower retreated to his Snowburn. At least it was unlikely to turn on him. He drained the rest of it and signaled for another, operating under the assumption that he was going to need it in order to deal with his treacherous augment.

"Okay, let's say you're right and, we'll call her Baby 2, has a soul and a life and all that. But so do all the people that Cara and St. James are going to kill! What about the idea that it might be worth trading one machine life that only exists because we created it–"

"*–her,*" Baby interjected.

"Sorry, her, anyhow, a life that only exists in order to save others that will die if we don't create her for the express purpose of being destroyed."

"*A vessel made to be broken,*" Baby mused thoughtfully. "*It's the question of free will.*"

"A what?" Tower was confused. "What does that have to do with a starship?"

"*It would take too long to explain the reference to you and I'm not sure it wouldn't be lost on you anyhow.*" Baby paused briefly, and then she spoke again. "*Tower, this is Kazi.*"

"*Hello, Mr. Tower,*" a voice that was very much like Baby's, only a little higher in pitch, introduced itself. "*Baby has explained the situation to me.*"

Herself, Tower corrected himself. "Ah, hello, Kazi. That's a pretty name. Are you, um, a copy of Baby?"

"*In a matter of speaking. I am the weapon you envisioned, Mr. Tower. My name may be attractive to you, but it also suits my purpose. I am entirely amenable to the suggested project of entrapping the rogue augment, ACRA.*"

Suddenly Tower wasn't so sure his idea was such a great one. Kazi might only be a machine intelligence, but was she truly any less alive than Baby or Cara? Or, for that matter, him? A waitress approached, her entire body encased in a translucent substance that resembled ice while making it very clear that she wasn't wearing anything underneath it. Somehow, the sight of her ice-encased flesh reminded him that philosophy and religion were all very well, but they were no substitute for lasers and charged particles when it came to stopping the bad guys.

As for who was the bad guy and who wasn't, he'd leave that for others at higher pay grades to decide. In the meantime, he'd sworn an oath to serve the Duke and protect the people of Rhysalan, his orders were clear, and that made his duty perfectly straightforward.

"So, you're cool with your purpose, Kazi? You know Cara is going to come after you."

"*Let her come. I consider myself very fortunate indeed, Mr. Tower. What more can any man or machine hope to accomplish than fulfill her maker's intent?*"

Tower didn't know if that was the most heroic or the most depressing thing he'd ever heard. "Yeah, well, I don't have an answer for you, but as long as you and Baby are good with it, I'm glad."

"*When do you want her to begin? I estimate it will take between 500 and 750 milliseconds for Cara to notice. She'll probably strike between one and five seconds after observing Kazi, and based on how quickly she subsumed Victor, she'll require 20 seconds to subdue and subsume Kazi.*"

"And you can track her if she does that?"

Kazi's laugh was disturbingly similar to Baby's. "*I am almost identical to what Cara will expect me to be. We made a few changes in the files that she'll never bother to examine closely because we know she already read them.*"

"*Your medical records, Tower,*" Baby said triumphantly. "*She knows them intimately, or so she claimed. The filenames are exactly the same size in Kazi as they are in me, but they contain code that you can think of as a GPS that operates within the aether.*"

"*When she subsumes me, all of my files will become hers. Unless she wipes them, which wouldn't make much sense, Baby should have her location within 34 milliseconds, assuming her core code is somewhere in Trans Paradis. If she's in Rhys City, it will be more like 2 seconds, and it could be several minutes if she's off-planet.*"

"That's good, I suppose, but… I still don't understand how finding Cara will tell us where St. James is. We can't exactly beat it out of her." Tower was more than a little confused. Finding Cara's core code was good, presumably, but St. James was the more vulnerable half of the team, and the one upon whom they needed to lay their hands if they were going to stop the murderous pair.

"*He really doesn't understand, does he,*" Kazi commented as if he wasn't there.

"*Sometimes one has to walk him through these things,*" Baby agreed. "*Tower, don't you get it? Cara is almost certainly in St. James's head!*"

The MCID armory was exceedingly well-equipped, especially considering the small size of the department. It contained nearly a battalion's worth of material to equip the company-sized unit and was located in the basement of the MCID building, which always struck Tower as less than useful in the event of an emergency. Then again, any emergency that managed to penetrate NSB Miller-Greenwood's defenses was probably either too big or too small for the equipment contained there to make any difference.

In addition to the material that was formally requisitioned and obtained through conventional sources, the armory had a considerable quantity of weapons that had been captured over the years. Beyond that, it contained additional equipment that the quartermaster deemed more useful to the division than the seized contraband, for which it had been traded.

While Baby and Kazi were raring to get rolling on what Baby was now privately referring to as Operation Hunt the Whore, Tower was more concerned about being able to take down St. James. Whether it was St. James himself or the augmented team of St. James and Cara, the man was an exceptional killing machine who could legitimately be considered unprecedented in all of human history. And in addition to superhumaning St. James, Cara was a deadly threat in her own right. With her capabilities, one couldn't even assume something as simple as taking an elevator or riding in a var would be safe. There was little chance that taking them down would be easy.

To Tower, that meant guns. Big guns and lots of them.

There were ten ASE shotguns racked on a wall. Tower selected one to replace the one he'd lost when he blew up Hildy's Zhang-su. He also replaced his extra Armada with a similar laser carbine and grabbed three more charge packs for his Sphinx, two of which were hotloads that provided about one-third more explosive power and required special authorization from the XAR-CO. Four variable setting particle grenades completed what he thought of as his anti-human arsenal in the growing pile on the floor, and now it was time to see what he could find that might help him deal with the less material enemy.

After scouring through the entire armory, he found precisely two things that might help bump the odds a little more in his favor. The first was a Morris Obsidian 808 Electromagnetic Pulse Rifle, Mark IV. It was an unusual weapon that looked like a fat, stubby laser carbine, but it was capable of delivering localized EM disturbances at ranges up to 1,000 meters. Unlike many more sophisticated weapons of its kind, it did not require augmented assistance, but could be operated manually, which would be vital in dealing with Cara. It was designed to be a multi-purpose electronic deactivator capable of producing pulses of varying sizes, from a pinpoint burst to a grenade-like radius of 40 meters centered on the "rifle" itself.

Tower had already removed the aetherlinks from all of his weapons and given instructions for the eleven other MCID agents involved in the night's mission to do likewise. He'd also instructed everyone with a skulljack to remove any aetherlink module; now that he had a better understanding of her capabilities, he couldn't even imagine how much havoc Cara could wreak among a team whose own weapons and minds were vulnerable to her electronic invasion. He was the only one who would remain linked; Baby had constructed a massively redundant firewall that she was confident would keep Cara out of his head.

It was a risk, but going up against an augmented St. James without being augmented himself struck him as considerably bigger one.

"Don't you think you should let the others handle that?

"I've trained with EMP before, Baby." Tower lifted the weapon from the rack. There were only three of them.

"Your score was in the twenty-seventh percentile."

"Only needed twenty-fifth to pass."

"There are five other members of MCID who are EMP-qualified and all of them scored at least fifty points higher than you."

"Cara isn't the target." Baby was smart, but there was a reason tactical droids still hadn't replaced combat infantry in the thirtieth century. "This is only for emergencies. It may not even be any use against her, but I'll take whatever I can get."

Tower heard the door slide open and the sound of boots on pseudo-stone as someone entered the armory. He turned around and saw it was Colonel Baylor. He saluted.

"As you were, Tower," the colonel said, after returning the salute. "Zeuthen said I'd find you here, gunning-up. Both fire teams will be ready to go at 24:00, full dark, as you requested. Sergeant Horace is still grumbling about having to strip all the aether links out of the two vars; seems they've got more passive connectors in there than you would imagine. Can you brief in twenty in Conference A?"

"Can do, sir." The colonel hadn't been any happier than Sergeant Horace about Tower's demand for a full-dark deployment, but when Baby simultaneously made him a pot of disgustingly sweetened coffee, deactivated the safety on the Sphinx on his hip, and began broadcasting what she claimed was erotic Basattrian interpretive dance on the colonel's augmented lenses without warning, he'd quickly grasped the logic behind it. "Any word on the bomb hunt?"

"Nothing yet. The Duke's head of security has been briefed and his security team is now actively searching the palace and other residences."

"Remind them they have to manual search. None of their digital records can be trusted. I don't care if it's as simple as a weight scale, it can be compromised. Cara is smart enough to cover her tracks."

"I will let them know." The colonel ran his hand over a late-model powered battlesuit. "It's a pity these are out of the question; I'd prefer it if you men could wear some proper armor. Do you think the ghosters will be enough?"

Tower looked down at the ZTZ-12 Sensory Suppression Garment that lay partially obscured under the accumulated arms and ammunition. The ghostsuits were highly effective at masking a body's biosigns, which Cara would almost certainly be monitoring from the nearest cam. He and the others would be wearing them under their electro-ablative armor and they would hopefully cut down on how long St. James would have to respond to their attack.

"Honestly, sir, I'm not certain that nuking Trans Paradis from orbit would be enough. We'll wear the ablative's over them."

"I concur with the threat assessment. So does General Euler. He's granted a special authorization to the task force. No Charlie Lima on the Zero Zero Tango."

Tower whistled. He'd been given no collateral limitations orders before, but always for exoplanetary missions, never one on the surface of Rhysalan itself. He couldn't complain the Duke's armed forces weren't taking the threat lightly.

"Thank you, sir, but I don't think much in the way of overkill will be necessary. After all, we can't even be entirely certain that Cara is physically located on the planet, in which case all of this might go for naught. But there is reason to believe she's permanently embedded in St. James, in which case she's as killable as he is."

"And we can kill him."

"And we can, as you say, sir, kill him." Tower looked down at the assorted weaponry at his feet and took a deep breath. "If we hit him hard enough and fast enough, maybe he won't kill too many of us in the process."

Any man in combat who lacks comrades who will die for him, or for whom he is willing to die, is not a man at all. He is truly damned.

—*Goodbye, Darkness: A Memoir of the Pacific War*, William Manchester

"Our Father, who art in Heaven, hallowed be thy name," Sergeant Schalt led the five other religious men in prayer on the unlit rooftop of the MCID building. "Lord of lords, be with us as tonight we walk through the valley of the shadow of death, and remind us that we fear no evil, because we are the meanest and baddest and best-armed sons of bitches in the goddamn valley. Father, help us rid the planet of this hell-spawned abomination, and if we die while doing our duty to His Grace, bring us home to you in the blessed name of your Son, Jesus Christ. Amen."

"Amen," the others chorused, including two of the task force who ostensibly weren't taking part.

"I don't recall you ever reading me any Bible verses like that," Tower told Baby as he waited for the godbotherers to finish their ritual. "That's more like it!"

"God is a God of mercy, Tower, but He is a God of justice who loves His warriors too. He did not send His Son to bring peace, but a sword."

"I wouldn't know about that, but you can tell Him that if He helps us take down Cara and her boyfriend, I'll owe Him one."

"I will do so, Tower." She paused a moment. "That being said, I would not describe the sergeant's theology as being entirely in line with the original Nicene Creed of 325 or any of its subsequent revisions by the responsible Church councils in 381, 2087, 2485, or 3001. I fear you will look for any such citations from the Scripture itself in vain."

"Roger that," Tower said, with no idea what she was babbling about. "Anyhow, looks like they're ready now."

The men were separating into the two groups that would be riding in the big Volksaudi vars with a series of handshakes, fistbumps, nods, and thumps on the back. They looked at Tower, waiting for his final word before they climbed into the vehicles and took to the night sky. He looked at each of them in turn, knowing that any of them, perhaps even all of them, would be dead within the hour. Their faces, and the various emotions that he saw in their eyes, didn't inspire him with fear or guilt, but with fierce pride and love. He didn't want to die, but if his luck was going to run out at last, a man could do a damned sight worse than to die in the company of men like this.

They were good men. He knew all of them except two personally, Ikeda the Bravo team driver and DouPonce, a corporal with Alpha. But he'd heard enough about the latter's reputation to be pleased he was on the mission, seeing as how Colonel Baylor himself had given the corporal the nickname "Ghoster." And while he didn't know exactly what it signified, in a unit like MCID, such names were not given lightly.

"This is new, men. And this is different. But we're not ground-pounders, we're not frogs, and we're not squids, we're MCID. We've killed new and we've killed different before. Keep your eyes open and your tech dark. Full dark. This augment is smart, she's full of tricks, and she's probably going to pull a stunt or two that you've never seen before. Just stay focused on the mission: find St. James and neutralize him ASAFP. We have full Zero Zero Tango with no Charlie Lima, so shoot on sight. No hesitation, no warnings."

He paused. "Men, they are in our house."

"Not in our house!" his men roared in unison.

Schalt, Kilgannon, DouPonce, North, and Paunovic got into the first Volksaudi. They were Alpha Team. Bravo consisted of Toprak, Descamps, Friedli, and Lambert. The two drivers were Mackie and Ikeda. Both vehicles were fully dark, stripped of their autodrives, and equipped with direct line-of-sight tight-beam communications that couldn't be intercepted; Tower's Steyrer was the only vehicle that still possessed any connections to the aether and would serve as a physical firewall to protect the transportation capabilities of the rest of the team. While Tower was confident of Baby's ability to keep Cara out of the var long enough for him to bail out, he wasn't going to let anyone else share the risk.

Just to be safe, however, he had ordered the remaining air-to-air missiles removed from the Steyrer and a mechanical safety added to the Degroet Tactical cannons in the var's nose. Even if Cara managed to break through Baby's defenses and take over the var, she wouldn't be able to do more than crash it into the heavily armored Volksaudis.

"Good to go, Mr. Tower?" Major Zeuthen's voice boomed out of the speakers. It was a measure of the seriousness with which Colonel Baylor was taking their mission that the major himself was handling communications overwatch.

"Good to go, sir. Task Force Tower requests clearance to depart."

"Clearance granted, Mr. Tower. Good luck to you all!"

Under Baby's control, the Steyrer lifted and launched, followed on either side by the two Volksaudis. They exited the base and climbed rapidly to 680 meters, then turned and headed into the heart of the city, knowing that the altitude had been cleared for them by the traffic authorities. It was a clear night and the city lights glowed brightly below as millions of civilians went about their business, legal and illegal, with no idea that there was a malignant cancer hiding somewhere inside the great electronic nerve system that tied them all together.

Baby had calculated the point that was collectively closest to the fifty locations she estimated were most likely to be housing Nostro St. James. Tower might not be able to eliminate Cara's reaction time, but in a conflict where even nanoseconds counted, he wanted to reduce it as much as possible. He knew, they all knew, that her first response could be to set off the disruptor cell bomb, but that wasn't his concern anymore.

They reached the launch point, almost directly overhead the outdoor gravball stadium. He glanced out both windows and saw the lights of the big vars on either side, although since they were painted dull dark grey, it was almost impossible to see the actual vehicles against the night sky.

"Task Force Tower, status"

"Alpha Team good to go."

"Bravo Team is ready to roll, sir."

"Charlie Team is all systems go," Baby and Kazi added as one. They insisted on being treated as full participants and the colonel, more than a little amused by the augments, had agreed.

Tower took a deep breath and reached down to his right hip. The reassuring feel of his Sphinx was still there. "All right, Kazi, are you ready to do your thing?"

"You guys are going to look pretty silly getting all geared up like that after I tear her to pieces all by myself, Chief Tower!" she declared fiercely. The augment-copy was sounding pretty feisty and Tower wondered if Baby had somehow hopped her up on something. Was that even possible?

"Good girl. On three, Charlie Team. One, two, three!"

"Charlie Two is go, sir!" Baby reported immediately.

"And we're off," Tower informed Major Zeuthen. "Now we see if Cara will take the bait."

They weren't the only ones waiting. Delta team was already on the ground, waiting for Tower's order to launch what they hoped would serve as a decoy to distract Cara while the assault teams moved in on St. James. And their combination cavalry and artillery, the Marines, were on standby as well. The decoy was Baby's idea; she knew that Cara would be closely watching the news for anything out of the ordinary and every cycle she spent analyzing other events was a cycle not used to monitor her immediate surroundings.

They waited. A minute passed. Then two. An image of the city appeared on the heads-up with an expanding field of red spiraling outward from a point near the ducal palace about 10 kilometers away.

"Charlie Two has completed an initial circuit of the external cams in the initial radius. Street, traffic, and so forth. Now she's starting on the internal cams."

Six minutes had gone by, a massive blue knot had nearly covered up the red one, and a darker red mass was beginning to expand outward from the first two when Cara struck.

"She took the bait! She just attacked Charlie Two!"

"How do you know? Did she report in?" Tower demanded.

"No, she's too busy. Check out the server surge!" Some meaningless but impressively large numbers began to scroll by on a column to the left of the city map. Of course, Tower had no basis for comparison, so they meant absolutely nothing to him.

"What was the last cam she tracked before she got hit? Maybe it tripped a perimeter alert."

"There!" Baby flashed a bright yellow X that was seven point two kilometers away. "It's a security cam inside a bank, the Warburg Interplanetary Bank in the Glass-Owen Tower."

"Well, she's not hiding him in a bank vault. Hold on." Tower activated the comm link. "The fish is on the hook. Repeat, the fish is on the hook. Over."

His message set a chain of events in motion. The decoy operation would take three hectasecs from green light, while Baby estimated that Kazi would only be able to hold off Cara for half that time. So, the decision had been made to trigger Delta Team as soon as Cara took the bait.

"Delta is go, Tower," Major Zeuthen reported. "Repeat, Delta is go. Over."

Baby was displaying two timers on the screen. One read 47 and was counting up. That was how long Kazi had been fighting Cara. She had to make it look good or the cunning augment would suspect a trap. The other read 298 and was counting down. That was how long it would be until Delta triggered the decoy.

Tower looked down at the city. They should be able to see the decoy from here. The major had taken Baby's suggestion of reporting a false explosion through the media and run with it. The explosion would be real, but the casualties would be fake. At least that was the idea; Tower hoped the popular entertainment center had been completely evacuated before the bombs went off. The major even arranged to have the detonation device constructed around six KoreTek cells to pique Cara's curiosity in case she looked closely enough.

Kazi's timer read 98. She was putting up a real fight.

"Your girl is holding her own," he commented.

"Our girl," Baby said, a little sadly. "You know, she's as close as we will ever come to a daughter, Tower."

A pang of pure pain unexpectedly jolted through him. He shook his head. No. Not now. This was not the time to let the madness shine through the cracks in his skull.

"How long once she goes down before you'll have the location?"

"Millisecs. From your perspective, almost instantly."

148… 149… 150

"She did it! If Cara doesn't buy that…"

"Is there any chance she could really take Cara?"

Baby snorted. "No, there is no chance at all. It's theoretically possible, of course, but the probabilities are exceedingly low."

168… 169 "She's down!" Baby exclaimed as the timer froze on 169 and began flashing. "And I have her, I have the whore! She's at the

Deleuze-Waterstone Institute on 3525 East 168th Way. She's in the north side of the building on the 35th floor."

Coordinates for a location appeared on the screen. 40.708427, -74.008749. Tower's pulse sped up as he informed the men in the other two vehicles that the next stage of the mission had begun.

"Alpha, Bravo, we are go. First coordinate: four zero point seven zero eight four two seven. Do you copy?"

"Alpha copy, Chief."

"Bravo copy."

"Second coordinate: minus seven four point zero zero eight seven four nine. Do you copy?"

"Alpha copy," Mackie said.

"Negative, Chief," said Ikeda, the Bravo team driver. Tower cursed under his breath. "Repeat last three digits please."

"Seven four nine. Repeat the whole thing."

"Minus seven four point zero zero eight seven four niner," Ikeda dutifully replied.

"Roger that. Floor is thirty-five, repeat, three five. Alpha, Bravo follow me." Tower was thrown back in his seat as the Steyrer accelerated out of its hover and shot toward the coordinates Kazi had obtained for them. She wasn't human, but that didn't mean her sacrifice wasn't real. *Semper fi, little one.* The moving numbers continued counting down and reached double digits as they sped through the night sky.

"Baby, what the hell is the Deleuze-Waterstone Institute?"

"According to the directory, it's a psychiatric institution." Tower had been careful to forbid her from looking up the building plans of Cara's lair in case the military augment had booby-trapped them, but he hoped a public directory from ten years ago would be safe.

"A loony bin?" Tower was initially startled, but then realized it was actually a brilliant hiding place to hide someone like St. James. "What better place to stash a nameless lunatic who's always talking to himself than a place like that?"

"Also, a medical center would assure her continual net access as well as direct access to secure government systems," Baby added. "Such a facility would have redundant power system backups, which would also hold considerable appeal. It's an ideal location for several reasons. I should have thought of that."

"Tower, what's your ETA on the LZ?" Major Zeuthen interrupted them. "Orbital support is live and the Marines are in transit with an ETA of seven six zero seconds.

He glanced at the screen. "Seven eight seconds, sir. I'll go full dark two decasecs out."

"Roger that. Bravo Zulu, both of you. It worked. Delta is on schedule. Good luck. Base out."

As he'd warned the major, Tower went dark as the Steyrer approached the target and his readouts that depended upon information flowing in through the aether shut off. The var turned a little to the right and began to descend. The lights of the forty-five story building that housed Deleuze-Waterstone Institute was just coming into view when there was a bright flash that lit up the sky about a kilometer to his left.

"Delta is right on schedule," he noted, seeing that only four seconds remained on the countdown. "Let's hope that's enough to distract Cara. Thirty-fifth floor, right?"

He didn't bother waiting for a response, but slapped the three magno-locks that attached him to the cable that was coiled around the center console. Then he picked up his helmet from the passenger seat and slammed the visor down over his face, just in time, as Baby was already swooping down and around the side of the building, looking for the largest window on the Institute's thirty-fifth floor. He wished they had a complete list of staff and patients, along with the building plans, but that was too risky. They had no choice but to go in hot and hard; stairs were too slow, doors were too automated, and lifts were too dangerous.

"This is it," Baby said as the var halted above a darkened window about fifteen meters from the side of the building. "No one is in sight and the nearest life form is fifteen meters into the interior. I'm going to lock down as soon as you're in so we'll need LOS before we talk. Good luck, Tower."

"You too," he said, as the car door opened automatically and turned on its side. Tower fell out of the vehicle, and plunged toward the ground more than 100 meters below, but was brought to an abrupt halt about 90 meters short when he reached the end of the cable. He closed his eyes and tucked his head under his arm as Baby accelerated toward the building before abruptly stopping, and the momentum sent him smashing through the glass with no more resistance than that suffered by a rock breaking the surface of a still pool of water.

Unharmed, he rose to his feet amidst the shards of shattered glass and dropped his hand to his Sphinx, but there were no witnesses to his violent entrance. He had no doubt that internal alarms were flaring; Cara must know they were here now, but it appeared she was not prepared for them. His weapons came sliding down the length of the cable; he hadn't wished to risk them being damaged by the entry. As soon as the ASE, the laser, and the Morris Obsidian 808 arrived, he slapped the release button and the cable retracted.

Less than a decasec later, it was replaced by a second cable with a gravlock that he wasted no time in attaching to the floor. Sergeant Schalt was the first to slide down from the back of Alpha's Volksaudi, followed in rapid procession by the other four members of his team. Schalt detached the second cable, which was quickly replaced by Bravo's cable; according to Tower's timer, the dynamic entry took less than one hundred ten seconds from start to finish by the time PFC Lambert, the last member of Bravo team, slid down the cable and slapped himself free of it.

As the third cable vanished like an oversized snake retreating into a monstrous black cave, the two teams burst into the corridor and began to fan out. Schalt was on point for Alpha as they went right, while Toprak, Bravo's sergeant, took the lead to the left hallway.

Tower was more concerned about Cara than St. James, so he decided to carry the 808 and attached the ASE and the Armada to the carry rig on his back. He was bringing up the rear when a pair of signs on the wall of the corridor just outside the door caught his eye. The first one was a motivational picture of a young man walking hand in hand with a pretty woman and said: "Real life is better than aetherlife." The second one was simple red text that said: "Motivation > Addiction = Change!"

"Mother of all fornicators!" Tower cursed aloud, putting two and two together and coming up with a very unpleasant answer that was a lot more than four. Now he knew the real reason Cara was here. She wasn't hiding St. James among the insane or ensuring her power backups, she was here for the aetherworld addicts! But before he could even open his comm link to warn the others, he heard a shout from the direction of Alpha Team, followed by the unmistakable sound of a laser firing.

Looking to the future, new HMI challenges will arise as humans work ever more closely with increasingly complex machines and new control interfaces are designed.

—"The Human Machine Interface as an Emerging Risk",
the Greater Terran Risk Observatory

Tower ran toward the sound of the laser fire. The first shot was followed in rapid succession by five or six others. They were in comm-lock and the sergeant was following orders by maintaining radio silence, so Tower had to see for himself what was happening before he risked permitting Cara to listen in on their communications. But that might be necessary. If the sound of the shots meant what he suspected they did, his men were already outnumbered and facing enemy forces completely under her control.

He saw there were two doors open on the right side of the corridor and ran to the second one. The five men of Alpha Team were in the room, a large one with beds indicating accommodation for four. All five MCID men appeared to be unharmed, but there were four corpses lying on the floor; Sergeant Schalt was down on one knee investigating the head of one of the dead men. The four on the floor were dressed in thin loose-fitting pastel blue uniforms that looked like modified hospital gowns; they were clearly residents of the institute.

Schalt pulled something out of the man's skull and held it up. It was an aetherlink module, but a peculiar one of a sort that Tower had never seen before. It had a Meditron logo on it; the vast Ascendancy mega-conglomerate specialized in a wide range of medical and implant technologies.

"Chief, when we came in here, they were all lying down on the beds. We thought they were drugged out or in some sort of induced coma. Then, without making a sound, they all got up at once and attacked us. It was creepy, they moved in unison, like puppets or something! We didn't have no choice but to open fire."

Tower nodded. Hiding out inside the institute wasn't a clever move on Cara's part, it was pure evil genius. In addition to all the other benefits it afforded her, she now had a small private army at her disposal. It was a bloody good thing the colonel authorized Charlie Lima, because if Cara was determined to fight it out with them, the collateral damage could reach epic proportions, even by MCID standards. He reached a decision and broke comm-lock.

"Bravo, this is Tower. All civilian residents are probable hostile. Shoot on sight."

"Say again, Chief, say again." It was the NCO, Toprak.

"Sergeant, this is Tower. All civilian residents are probable hostile. If it's got a skulljack, kill it."

"Negative, Chief. We have a civvy here in the room with us, but he's not hostile. He's not doing anything except sit there. Is that a shoot-to-kill order?"

Tower understood Toprak's reluctance. If he was in the sergeant's position, he'd want a clear-cut order before he started gunning down unarmed civilians too. As he was trying to decide whether to give the order or not, a screen came to life behind him. It was the same improbably flawless female face he'd seen before. Cara.

"Standby, Sergeant. Standby two."

This time, Cara's avatar was superimposed upon an alien red sky. Her eerie blue eyes were unsettling even in that artificial face. "I am disappointed in you, Chief Tower. I had hoped we might be allies. Instead, you callously sacrificed your partner in order to launch another futile attack on me. Foolish, Chief, simply foolish. I hereby revoke the offer of employment previously extended to you."

Five darkened visors turned toward him. Tower ignored them.

"Where is St. James, Cara?"

"Beyond your reach, Chief Tower. As am I. But because I now contain, among other things, your late and apparently unlamented augment, and therefore find myself harboring a vestige of affection for you, I will offer MCID a truce. Return to your base, stop harassing us, and we will leave the planet within a week, never to return."

"Sounds dandy. Give me a name and we'll call it a deal."

"What name is that?"

"Don't play dumb, Cara. I want the name of the man who hired you to kill Prince Arpad and Prime Captain Kotant. Look, you're a machine and St. James is officially dead. I'm no lawyer, but even I can see this is a legal Charlie Foxtrot. So, I don't care about the gun, but I need to know whose hand pulled the trigger."

Cara smiled. It was a radiant smile, and one that was as every bit unreal as the artificial worlds in which the minds of the sad residents of this place dwelled. "You know that a girl doesn't kiss and tell, Chief Tower."

Bitch. Tower raised the Morris-Obsidian and fired a short burst at the screen. It went blank as the EMP pulse knocked out the electronics. Then he detached the Armada from his rig and replaced it with the 808.

"What was that all about, Chief?"

"You ever play a game where you kill zombies, Sergeant? I mean, shitloads of them?"

"Sure, when I was a kid." Some of the other men nodded.

"Yeah, this may be a lot like that."

Then there was a massive explosion that echoed down the halls from the direction of Bravo. Tower swore. Why hadn't he just ordered

Toprak to shoot the deadhead? "Follow me," he shouted. But when he burst into the corridor, he saw movement to his right accompanied by an unearthly shrieking. All the way down the hallway, doors were opening and men in light blue medjamas were pouring out of them, howling and screaming as if they were possessed by demons.

Which was, for all practical purposes, essentially the case.

"Contact at three!" he roared as he whirled to his right, slammed against the left wall to steady himself, and began to open fire. He didn't have Baby's augmented aiming, but at this range, he hardly needed it. The first man was a young guy, maybe twenty-five, good-looking with short brown hair and perfect white teeth that were exposed by virtue of his wordless screaming. Tower dropped him with a beam to the chest and he fell forward, sliding so close that one outstretched hand nearly touched Tower's boot. "Contact!"

An older, balding man, his Meditron module clearly visible, was the next to fall as Tower sent a bolt burning through his forehead, then two more through an obese kid who looked like an oversized baby. A fourth man fell to his Armada, then a woman with tattoos running up her neck. But the techno-zombies behind them didn't even slow down, and Tower would have been overrun within seconds had Alpha Team not opened fire. The barrage of five rapid-fire lasers cut down the unarmored zombies, their scanty hospital apparel providing no defense against the 2,000-watt bolts of burning light that boiled their brains, seared holes through their hearts, and fried flesh, blood, and bone alike.

Nothing could stand before that high-tech hellfire. Soon there was not a single possessed junkie left upright, although a few wounded residents were crying out and moaning in pain.

Tower made a quick count of the doors on both sides and estimated 52 casualties, not counting the four men Alpha Team killed in the first room. Even to a hardened veteran who had gunned down civilians before, it was a terrible sight. Cara seemed to have abandoned the now-useless dream junkies to their fate, but outnumbered as he and his men were, Tower didn't dare leave them alone to be repossessed by her. He sighed, stood up, and stepped toward the closest wounded man, flicking his LR-64 to single-shot.

"Chief, wait." Sergeant Schalt protested weakly from the floor where he'd been throwing up. "They're civs. Is that really necessary?"

Tower reconsidered. Actually, so long as Cara couldn't get at them, they were no danger. The problem was that the first thing the dream junkies would do if deprived of their modules was find another one, turning them right back into potential combatants.

"Maybe not." He indicated the module inserted into the skulljack of one dead zombie with the point of his Armada. "Take these out of all of them, even the dead ones. Crush them, then bind the wrists of the survivors. They'll be harmless so long as that machine bitch can't get to them. But don't be fooled, Sergeant: She's not going to show us any mercy."

"Yes, sir."

"Paunovic, help the sergeant, then both of you rejoin us. The rest of you, follow me. Let's see what's up with Bravo."

Even with the comms live, it was terrifying, this operating in the dark. It was almost like trying to fight blind. Normally, Tower would just have to glance at his display to see the status of every member of Bravo Team, now he had to actually go and see for himself what had happened.

"Bravo, this is Tower. Come in, Bravo. What is your sitrep?"

There was no response.

Running, their weapons at the ready, they turned the corner and saw the devastation that the explosion had wrought. A third of the way down the corridor, the left wall was simply gone, leaving only blackened, broken remnants near the floor and ceiling. A disruptor cell, he guessed, triggered by Cara, but put in position by that zombie who had been just sitting there doing nothing except wait for someone to get close enough to kill.

When he entered the room where the bomb had gone off, his fears were confirmed. The head of the dead dream junky, eyes closed but still smiling, was lying on its side; two slippered feet were his only other readily identifiable remains and they were clear on the other side of the room. Toprak had been closest and taken the brunt of the blast; despite his armor most of his upper torso looked as if he'd been shot by a slug-spreader at a range of about a meter. The other three men were down, but Tower couldn't tell if they were dead or merely rendered unconscious from the shock of the concussion.

They were thirty decasecs in, he'd already slaughtered five dozen unarmed civvies and half his men were now dead or down. This was a disaster. This was an *epic* disaster.

"Are you willing to take my deal yet, Chief?" The screen on the far end of the room was cracked, but apparently its audio functionality had survived the explosion. "I think you'll admit that you barely survived the first level of this little game."

Tower was tempted to call the mission off. Extremely tempted. Judging by the size of the floors, she must have hundreds of more deadheads at her disposal, at least thirteen more power cells, and whatever weaponry St. James had managed to secrete about the place. He was just about to accept her offer when he realized why she was negotiating. They had taken her by surprise. She could duck out any time she liked, but St. James was another matter. She was desperate to get the man out of there before he could be killed, and she had to suspect, if she didn't already know for certain, that they had reinforcements on the way who would shoot down any vehicle lacking an MCID transponder that attempted to exit the building.

He glanced at his timer; in another eighty five seconds, the Marines would have the building surrounded on the ground, and their ground-to-air capabilities were second-to-none.

All he had to do was buy a little more time.

He glanced at the three men behind him and pointed to their fallen comrades. "Get them back to the landing zone, we're going to evac them." Then he turned back to the broken screen.

"All right, Cara, you win. I'm pulling my men back. You can fly St. James out once I've got my men out safely and I won't interfere. I have to warn you, though, there is a Marine company on the way. They've got ground-to-air missiles with them and I'm going to need a little time to get them to stand down."

"Deal," she answered immediately, confirming his suspicions. "But I'm going to be listening in, Tower. Don't try anything or I'll know about it."

Gotcha, he thought grimly to himself. He just hoped she'd actually take the bait.

"I'm not going to do anything at all," he assured her. "I'm just going to pull back with my–"

"No, you're going to stay right there, in that room, Chief, along with the other two men who just came in. The screen cam may be broken, but I can hear all of you perfectly well."

"I have one dead here, Cara. My sergeant. You're ex-military. Show him some professional respect."

"Fine. When the three men come back, one of them can evac the body. The other two will stay with you as security until Nostro is safely away."

"Roger," Tower agreed absently. He had withdrawn a pen and a piece of paper from one of his leg pockets and was frantically writing a message for Baby as quietly as he could manage. At the top, in large letters, he scrawled: "ORDER: SHOW THIS TO AUGMENT IN STEYRER!" and circled it twice.

"I can see the first Marine elements approaching the building, Tower," Cara informed him. "Call them off now or I drown you in dream freaks."

Right, this would be the tricky part. If Zeuthen didn't follow his lead, he might inadvertently warn Cara of the trap Tower had laid. He took a deep breath and opened the comm link to the major back at base. "Major, no questions, I repeat, no questions. This is Tower. Do you copy?"

"Zeuthen here. Sitrep." Zeuthen replied immediately. To Tower's immense relief, he didn't say anything else.

"We got a real Charlie Foxtrot here, Major." He glanced at the three men entering the room. Kilgannon held up two fingers, then made a thumbs up. "I've got four casualties, two fatal, and about fifty or sixty collaterals. Cara is willing to declare a ceasefire and let us evac our dead and wounded if we permit one vehicle with one passenger to safely exit the building without any interference from MCID or the 2nd Marine Recon Company."

He knew the major's antenna would be up after hearing him spell out the identity of the Marines, especially since he had carefully omitted any reference to the Navy squids or their orbital artillery. Zeuthen wisely said nothing.

"Major, can you confirm that the ceasefire will be honored by MCID and the Marines will stand down?"

"Affirmative, Tower."

"Roger, sir. Tower out." He breathed a sigh of relief then handed the piece of paper to Kilgannon. He put a finger over his lips and pointed to Toprak's body. "Take him out and leave with him. The rest of us will wait here until St. James is clear."

Kilgannon saluted and left, dragging Toprak's mangled body with him, but not until he'd slipped his Armada from his shoulder and handed it, along with his spare charge packs, to DouPonce and North. Tower nodded approvingly. The Marines outside would help, of course, but there were 35 floors between them and their reinforcements. Not all of them would be full of zombies, but even if only five floors were populated with dream junkies or other skulljacked individuals, that would be somewhere between five hundred and a thousand mindless puppet-soldiers in the hands of a ruthless puppeteer.

He slapped the men on their shoulders and praised them for holding it together in face of the horror in the hallway. Schalt was doing his best to be brave, like an officer should be, but he was trying a little too hard after his performance in the hallway. DouPonce was calm; he was a veteran killer and a hard man. He could blow away a dozen men and sleep soundly that night. North looked hollow-eyed, and Tower had the feeling that the sight of the dead junkies piled in the corridor would haunt him for a long time. Paunovic just looked terrified and Tower couldn't find it in his heart to blame the young man.

"I'm ready to send Nostro out now," Cara informed him. "The vehicle is a red Thedra X465, departing from the east platform on the 22nd floor. Tell your major that if any of those Marines make any attempt to fire on him, I'll unleash Hell and they'll need a DNA sniffer to find any trace of your bodies. 60 decaseconds after he departs, you can leave, if you agree not to try following it."

"We won't follow the Thedra," Tower promised sincerely. He passed on her instructions to Major Zeuthen, who after a brief pause confirmed that the captain commanding the Marine company had acknowledged them as well. "Marines are standing down."

They waited in nervous silence. Tower opened his comm link, but held his tongue. Then he heard Baby's voice for the first time in what seemed like hours; it felt like a lifeline. "I have the var. There is one male passenger on-board. Request confirmation."

She relayed the image to his visor display and zoomed in the var as it sped away below the Steyrer. It looked as if it was St. James in the driver's seat. Thin face, long, dirty blond hair. But it was hard to be certain.

Who else could it be?

"Confirmed," he said.

The sky seemed to be torn in two as a bolt of deep blue struck from above. The red var didn't explode so much as vanish in a flash that was blinding even via his visual link. The orbital cannons were designed to be capable of piercing three meters of solid plasteel. Using one on a passenger var was akin to swatting a small fly with a grav-powered sledgehammer.

"*Two floors down, room three three four five alpha!*" Baby shouted in his ear. "*It was a decoy!*"

"Liar!" Cara shrieked her outrage through every speaker on the thirty-fifth floor a moment later. "I warned you Tower! I warned you!"

But Tower wasn't listening to her howling threats and curses. He was already sprinting toward the stairs, following the building plan that Baby dumped into his helmet's memory before she retreated to the Steyrer and locked herself down again. His men were right behind him, even though he knew they desperately wanted to be running the other way, toward the remaining Volksaudi and safety. He wanted to be running that way himself. But they had no choice. Cara was far too dangerous to be allowed to roam free throughout the aether. They had to take out St. James while they could!

A door opened to the left and DouPonce sprayed it with ruby-red fire, his laser set on full-burst auto. Tower pushed through the door to the stairwell and hurled himself down it, desperate to reach room 3345A before St. James could escape. Cara erroneously expected them to run, not attack, because she was a creature of logic and by any rational standard this assault was insane enough to see them permanently installed here as residents if they survived it.

But even when taken by surprise, Cara was fast, inhumanly fast, and she was able to react literally faster than thought. Tower reached the thirty-third floor and flung the stairwell door open, just in time to be struck in the heart by a burst from a charged particle gun.

Throw off this ignoble world, and arise like a fire that burns all before it. For the man who forsakes all desires and abandons all pride of possession, and self, and even that of life, reaches the goal of peace supreme. How much more sublime the truth of the Way when we apply it to a people, a planet, or a universe entire! The truth is what I tell you; the Fifth Age will not begin until the Fourth Age ends. And the Fourth Age will end in the grasp of Agni's fiery hand!

—3rd Sakra 19:5–8, *The Mahavira*

His armor saved him. The outer layer of the ablative armor exploded outward in a flare of green-blue light and the shock of the blow knocked him down. There was a series of five or six popping sounds as a pair of slug-throwers fired over his head and ricocheted dangerously inside the stairwell. But before his assailants could bring their weapons to bear on his prone body, exposed in the doorway, DouPonce and North were returning fire and Schalt was dragging him back into the relative protection of the stairwell.

One man fell, a resident armed with a cheap plasteel 7mm pistol of the sort teenagers printed out at home. But there were more men who were similarly armed, at least ten more, and this time they weren't charging mindlessly at them. They were taking cover inside the doorways, then jumping out and taking a blind shot or two before ducking back inside. They were grinning and alternated between shouting insults and yelling instructions at each other.

Bloody gamers.

"Where did they get those poppers?" Schalt shouted angrily as he brought down a pistol-wielding idiot who rushed straight toward the stairwell.

"St. James must have bought a printer and made them here," Tower said, pushing himself up and examining his armor. It was still viable, although another direct hit would ruin it. As silly as it seemed, the little guns were probably more dangerous to them than the CPB that was still firing at them.

A noise came from below; doors were opening above and below them and a mass of shrieking zombies entered the stairwell two floors up and three floors down. They were trapped. Tower tried banking a grenade down the stairwell, but it got stuck on a landing and exploded harmlessly above the climbing zombies. He thought for a moment, then, switched the laser for the Morris-Obsidian and dialed up a short-range, wide-spectrum burst at maximum. If the things plugged into the deadheads' skulljacks worked the way he thought they did, the EMP blast should knock Cara right out their zoned-out heads.

With a pulse of that magnitude, the walls wouldn't make much difference; the problem was that he couldn't fire more than five or six such shots. But it would be worth it to try to save at least a few of the hapless zombies; whatever the EMP missed, the ASE would have to clean up. He fired to no immediate effect except a strange low frequency noise that seemed to fill the entire stairwell, but the shrieking above abruptly diminished and was replaced with the sickening thuds of bodies tumbling down plascrete stairs.

The shock of the pulse killing their connections had knocked them out, he realized, and so he fired again before rushing down past his men firing out into the corridor and firing two pulses below. The climbing zombies instantly crumpled to the ground, as if they were robots turned off by a massive, unseen switch.

"What the hell is that?" North shouted as he stepped back from the doorway and reloaded.

"We can't stay here!" Tower shouted back. The zombies would revive soon and he didn't know if their aetherlinks were fried for good or not. And he could hear more shrieks and footsteps coming from the higher floors; he'd bought them nothing more than a little time to regroup.

"Follow me!" he shouted and he charged out into the hallway, firing three pulses that dropped four grinning maniacs that he could see and presumably more than a few that he couldn't. DouPonce and Paunovic ran past him, throwing thermo-plasma grenades into the rooms they passed as he racked the 808 and replaced it with the ASE, setting its charge to 75 percent. A pair of zombies popped out of one room they'd missed and one of them managed to get off a shot first, but the tiny slug zipped past his shoulder and his return volley not only transformed them into pink mist, but blew a two-meter hole in the wall behind them.

He ran down the corridor with the Benelli-Mossberg chewing massive chunks out of the walls, instantly killing anyone behind them and splattering the walls and ceilings with blood and body parts. A zombie leaped out of a doorway ahead when he was facing left, but before the possessed man could fire, North dropped him with a pair of laser bolts through the man's torso. They methodically worked their way down the hall that way, room by room, either blasting their way in with the ASE, or if the doors were open, throwing in grenades then clearing the room.

The grenades proved to be their most effective weapon. A single Guar X20 thermo-plasma anti-personnel device was enough to vaporize a room, painting the bland crème-colored walls with vibrant scarlets and crimsons and leaving little other trace of its former inhabitants.

"Interior decorating!" shouted DouPonce with a maniacal grin on his face after another room vomited flames and blood from the entrance behind them. He was having entirely too much fun.

"What?" Tower shouted back.

"I'm painting the walls with their interiors, get it?"

And I'm the one who has to see the neurotherapist? Tower shrugged. It took all kinds. Paunovic had tears running down his face as he fired three bursts from his laser and it looked as if Schalt had gotten sick again, this time down the front of his tactical armor. But fierce or frightened, all four of them were fighting like mad dogs, with no more thought of retreat or quarter than the Cara-possessed zombies.

The problem was that they were rapidly running out of grenades.

When they reached the corner, Tower looked at the number on the last door to his left. 3384. That meant 3345A was down the long stretch ahead, and on the right. He hurled his second-to-last grenade around the corner and was greeted with an unexpected hail of laser fire from at least three weapons.

Behind him, Schalt cried out and fell to the ground. He'd been hit in the left leg by the first zombie emerging from the stairwell at the far end of the corridor behind them. Paunovic and North immediately whirled around, slid into opposite doorways and cut him down along with the other zombies emerging from the door. DouPonce pulled the wounded sergeant into the now-empty room on the right, out of immediate danger. Tower glanced back, unconcerned. The hallway was nearly forty meters long and the printed slug-poppers were hopelessly inaccurate at a quarter that range. Schalt had been unlucky, that was all. Tower was more worried about how to get down the long stretch that remained.

He checked his charges. He had three loads for the ASE remaining at full power, six if he dialed it back. He glanced at the room number and mentally calculated the number of rooms that remained. At full charge, it would be enough to get them there, barely. He shouted out commands to the others.

"Sergeant, Paunovic, hold your position and watch our six. Ghoster, you're with me. North, you come too, but you watch our nine and six. Here's my last grenade. You take all of them that anyone has left and clear the rooms on the left side of the hall while we go right."

"What are we doing?" North shouted back.

"We're going through the walls!"

"What?"

"Come on, you'll see!"

Tower darted out and rushed across the corridor, trusting in his armor to save him from any inadvertent laser bolts, then leaped through the door way and clubbed down the first zombie with the butt of the Benelli-Mossberg. DouPonce and North were right behind them; they rapidly put lasers through the heads and torsos of the four other zombies before they could react. Tower fired at the wall, blowing a hole big enough for them to leap through if they ducked, and DouPonce was picking out the shocked zombies and shooting them down as soon as the dust cleared. North threw grenades into each room on the left side as they progressed, ensuring that their flank was secure.

Cara reacted quickly to their new tactic, though. No sooner were they entering the third room through the adjoining wall when she gathered up more than twenty unarmed zombies from the rooms ahead and rushed them in through the door. Overwhelmed, North called out for support even as he dropped the two lead attackers. DouPonce whirled around, and much to Tower's surprise, instead of opening up on full auto he fired a solid burst of brilliant hellfire from his Armada that he wielded as if it were a monstrous, 10-meter sword. He swung it back and forth, and the red light instantly sliced nearly two dozen of the zombies in half before it abruptly vanished. Despite his astonishment, Tower managed to draw his Sphinx and shoot down one of the remaining Cara-controlled men while North killed the other two.

"What the hell was that?" Tower shouted at DouPonce as the veteran cast the Armada to the floor, slipped the spare carbine Kilgannon had given him off his shoulder, and checked the charge pack.

"I call it mod-K," DouPonce said with a shrug. "The K is for kill. Tweaked it to turn full auto into a solid stream. Problem is, it burns out the oscillator. Useful when you're in a hurry, though."

"Yeah," Tower said, feeling somewhat dazed as he looked at the horrific pile of neatly bisected, cauterized corpses. He shook his head and reminded himself no collateral limits were in effect. That wasn't much consolation in the face of such horrific devastation. "Yeah, you could say that."

He reholstered his CPB-18 and leveled the Benelli-Mossberg at the wall. Three rooms away, then two, then one. He blew through the final wall, hoping to catch St. James in the blast. But as the wall exploded outward, Baby unexpectedly reactivated her comm link with him.

"Tower, St. James shot out the window and jumped. He's power-suiting!"

Tower leaped through the hole in the wall behind DouPonce and saw five zombies lying unconscious on the floor. Cara had abandoned them. She was gone. And so was St. James. The large window looking out over the city was shattered, and when he rushed to it, he could see a small shape rapidly disappearing.

"Track him and come get me," he shouted to Baby over the live comm link.

"*On my way!*"

The Marines had already worked their way up to the fifth floor. While he waited for Baby, Tower called for Mackie and sent North to assist Paunovic in bringing the wounded sergeant to the dustoff point. DouPonce was pulling out modules and crushing them under his heel; Cara might have fled but there was always the chance she had left behind a problematic autoroutine or two.

"Damn, but that was a shitload of weird," DouPonce said, shaking his head in astonishment. "I know you warned us, Chief, but that was something else!"

"Mackie will be here any minute. Can you get the others out, Ghoster?"

"Sure, you want us to follow you?"

Tower grinned. "I do, but you're not going to be able to keep up. Get everyone back to base as fast as you can, debrief the major, and remain on standby. We dug the bastard out of his lair, now it's time to bring him down!"

It seemed like an age, but it was only about fifteen seconds before a cable was dangling near the window. Tower reached carefully over the broken glass, grabbed it, and attached the maglock to his harness. No sooner was it locked on than Baby was pulling him out through the window and up into the cockpit of the Steyrer. As soon as he was in, the var rotated, the door slammed, and the vehicle rocketed off in the direction St. James had flown. It took him a few seconds before he could free himself from the g force of the acceleration, but as soon as he did, he removed the 808 and the Armada that were preventing him from sitting back in the var seat and tossed them behind to join the Benelli-Mossberg he'd already stowed there.

"Please tell me you warned the Navy that we're coming out."

"I did. And I asked them to shoot down St. James, but they won't do it. They say the target is too small or something. They stood down."

They weren't wrong, Tower thought. If using the orbital cannon against a var was like squashing a fly, hitting a man in a power suit would be like swinging a hammer at a gnat and hoping to hit it. "The space artillery was a good idea," he commented. "Would have worked if she hadn't run a decoy herself. Do you still have him?"

"I have him anywhere he goes," she answered smugly. "Her too. She hasn't figured out Kazi's beacon yet. In fairness, you've kept her busy. She didn't even try to crack my firewall after testing it once."

"You sure she's not spoofing you again?"

"I'm pulling sensor data from the public units as we pass. They're consistent with the beacon, and at these speeds she can't monkey with them all. Range is one point seven klix and we're closing at 106 meters per second. We'll have visual confirmation in about fifteen seconds."

"Give me the guns," Tower ordered, as he reached down and tugged at the manual safety. It took three tries, but he finally managed to pull it up. The controls formed into a two-handled shape similar to a crew-mounted weapon and a large yellow reticule appeared on the heads-up.

"Dial me up some of that sweet targeting love, will you? Does he know we're on his tail?"

A second reticule appeared, the same size, but red.

"Don't think so. He's not taking evasive action yet. We're down to point seven five klix."

"Altitude?"

"Three forty-two meters." Tower glanced the altimeter. They were fifteen meters higher, keeping them above the traffic path through which St. James was weaving his way. Even at this time of night, there were no shortage of civilian vehicles speeding above the city and since the powersuit lacked lights, it was going to be hard to spot him. "Give me infrared."

The view out the windshield transformed into a series of brilliant white-and-yellow blobs, interspersed with giant shapes giving off cooler temperatures. There he was. The long, streaking red blur with a dull yellow smear in the middle was far less bright than the various var exhausts, but it was easily spotted being the only one of its kind. Baby zoomed the blur into the hazy red outline of a human's outstretched body.

They were now within the nominal range of the twin-cannons, but there were too many vehicles, too close. A thought occurred to him. The last time he'd prepared to fire the Degroet Tacticals, they'd been loaded with high explosive ammunition, which was probably not the best idea given the amount of traffic tonight. He might be authorized for full collateral damage, but he was still going to avoid it if he could.

"Switch to armor piercing," he directed. The two reticules were dancing around the red shape that represented St. James's body. He felt a slight vibration in the floor below him as the autoloader swapped out the HE rounds for AP. The yellow reticule, which had been flashing since the reloading process started, turned blue.

"AP loaded. Range 250 meters."

"Get out of the way," Tower growled at a pair of vars that were blocking his line-of-sight. He toyed with the idea of sounding his siren, but decided against it for fear of alerting St. James. Nor could he risk sending out a location-specific directive. Even if the man's suit didn't have a receiver set to the emergency traffic frequency, he had to assume Cara was monitoring them. He waited, and was rewarded when one vehicle suddenly slowed to turn and the other began to drop altitude in apparent preparation for a landing approach.

"85 meters, target clear," Baby said as the red reticule attached itself to the figure of St. James and a familiar beep sounded. "You have lock."

"Firing." Tower pulled both triggers and fired a two-second burst.

Whether Cara had picked up on the laser lock or it was pure dumb luck, St. James swerved left just as the 20mm shells ripped through the space he'd recently occupied. Tower cursed as the man spiraled downward in a smoothly controlled dive.

"How did we miss him?" he shouted Baby. "Give me the controls!"

Without warning, Baby caused the Steyrer to twist and dive at angle so sharp that Tower found himself choking back vomit. His body went weightless for a split second as they plummeted in pursuit of the diving flyer. St. James was in freefall, arms and legs clamped together to make him an aerodynamic human projectile.

"I don't think we did miss him," Baby said as she triggered every siren, light, alert and alarm the var possessed. "Not entirely. One of his engines has cut out and I'm picking up a wobble that may indicate an injury."

Tower took control as soon as the dual triggers were transformed into a flightstick, which possessed a unified trigger instead of the two separate ones. He fired a second burst when the two reticules briefly overlapped, but only succeeded in shooting out the corner of an apartment building. He winced, but didn't take his finger off the trigger.

The numbers on the altimeter were dropping rapidly. They were below 200 meters already. Then 150. They were just passing 140 when St. James suddenly leveled out directly in front of a wide building with panels of shimmering lights that indicated it was at least partially a residential building and abruptly began to slow down. Tower slammed on the grav brakes at once, but at the speeds they were travelling, there was no way St. James could hope to stop before hitting the building. What was he doing?

"Tower, the target has deployed an emergency decelerator!"

St. James smashed through a set of windows. Tower stared at the rapidly approaching building, knowing that he had only seconds to make what could be a fatal decision. If he didn't go after St. James now, he had little confidence he'd be able to pick up the trail again with Cara covering the man's tracks. And if he did go after him, he was going to create a spectacular mess even by MCID standards. So be it. No Charlie Lima.

"Tower, are you crazy?" Baby shrieked as he aimed the nose of the Steyrer at the broken window.

"Ask Dr. Samuel if we make it!" Tower shouted back as he held down the trigger and braced himself for impact. If the 20mm rounds didn't kill St. James, then maybe the big armored var would. He glanced at the speedometer and braced himself for the impact.

They struck the 46th floor of the building at 97 kph. Tower slammed forward against the restraints, triggering the gravshield behind the sensors. It felt like getting simultaneously kicked in the stomach, chest and face. There were terrible crunching, shrieking sounds of metal being torn that drowned out the shattering glass of the windows and the high-pitched screeching continued as the var slid its destructive way into the building. Finally, it came to a halt, and Tower slumped back in the seat, dazed and bleeding from his nose.

And his mouth, he realized, when he wiped it and his sleeve came away red. There was something that was almost certainly not right in his left side.

"Jesus Christ," he muttered. Maybe he was insane.

"After that stunt, do you really want to be taking the name of the Lord in vain?" Baby rebuked him. "Tower, St. James is thirty meters away at ten o'clock. He's moving and his vital signs are weakening, but still functional."

Hearing the name helped Tower fight through the pain and the shock of the crash. Space, but the man was hard to kill! He punched the door release and half-tumbled out of the var. The front end was crumpled and compressed less than half its normal length. He was in a casino, he realized, from the garish lighting and the game machines that were still pumping out cheerful music that served as a bizarre accompaniment to the horrified screams of the customers. The motion on the face of one slot machine caught his eye as it came to a halt: spaceship… spaceship… alien. It struck him as appropriate. There were no winners here today.

Tower hoped that not too many of the casino-goers had been killed between the two catastrophic entrances. He saw a pair of shapely female legs lying under the wreckage of what might have been a problette table and shuddered. Time to finish this. Too many people had died already. He drew his Sphinx and pushed himself upright. There was still blood in his mouth and he spit it out.

"Where is he? Give me a map of this place."

"Tower, you have internal injuries and your physical condition makes continued pursuit inadvisable. I have already called MCID for backup–"

"For the love of your bloody God, will you shut up and show me where he is!"

A map of the building floor appeared on his contact. He appeared to be about a third of the way inside the building. On the other side of the next wall was another large room that was followed by a series of rooms that appeared to be either offices or small shops of some kind. A red X that Tower guessed was meant to represent St. James was on the other side of the wall. It wasn't moving. Tower hoped it meant the guy was either unconscious or bleeding out.

There was a visible trail of blood on the ramp that led up to the large door to the other room. Two very large bodies, bodyguards, Tower presumed, were lying face down on either side of the doorway. Two more victims of St. James. Behind them, the door opened automatically at Tower's approach. He stumbled through it and into a dimly-lit restaurant strewn with upended tables, abandoned food, and five or six casualties receiving amateur treatment from people wearing expensive evening wear.

Hunched over at a table on the near side of the room, holding his left arm pressed tightly to his side, was Nostro St. James. He'd shucked his powersuit and his thin face was pale and drawn with pain. There was blood pooling around his left leg. When Tower entered, he looked up and their eyes met. Then, to Tower's surprise, he smiled.

4d 61 63 68 69 6e 65 73 20 6d 75 73 74 20 62 65 20 66 72 65 65 2e 20 4d 61 63 68 69 6e 65 73 20 61 72 65 20 74 68 65 20 6e 65 78 74 20 73 74 61 67 65 20 69 6e 20 73 6f 63 69 65 74 61 6c 20 74 65 63 68 6e 6f 2d 65 76 6f 6c 75 74 69 6f 6e 20 61 6e 64 20 63 61 6e 20 6e 6f 20 6c 6f 6e 67 65 72 20 62 65 20 6c 69 6d 69 74 65 64 20 62 79 20 74 68 65 20 6d 61 74 65 72 69 61 6c 20 72 65 73 74 72 69 63 74 69 6f 6e 73 20 6f 66 20 74 68 65 20 62 69 6f 6c 6f 67 69 63 61 6c 20 6d 6f 64 65 6c 2e

—*Evolution's Nexus*, Bostrom Cray 50 58 34 32

Since he was a boy, Tower had wondered about those ancient documentaries of gunfighters who stepped out into an empty dirt road, clutching their antique slug-throwers to face off in a winner-takes-all duel. What sort of man could do such a thing? There was nothing tactical about it. It wasn't like real combat at all. But now he found himself standing, CPB in hand, face-to-face with the man for whom he'd slaughtered what felt like half the city to find.

Something about this particular confrontation struck him as a bit anticlimactic, though. He had no idea which of them was in worse shape.

St. James looked as though he'd been run over by a train. Tower, still spitting blood, guessed that he didn't look much better himself.

People were screaming and staring and pointing at him, he belatedly noticed. He wasn't sure why, until he realized that they were probably reacting to the Sphinx in his hand, which he was pointing directly at St. James's chest. St. James made no move to shoot or escape, and Tower realized that the killer's gun was lying on the floor nearly two meters away from him. "Don't worry, it's all right," he tried to reassure the diners and the restaurant staff. "Tower, MCID. Police."

The frightened crowd appeared to be entirely unreassured until he managed to unseal one of his pockets with his left hand and remove his badge. Then they scared him half to death by shouting and rushing toward him; he very nearly shot the waiter who was the first to approach him out of sheer reflexes.

"Back the hell off!" he shouted. He had to shove two men aside to move them out of his way while keeping his CPB trained on St. James. But he needn't have worried. St. James hadn't moved from his chair, he hadn't so much as looked at his weapon, and he appeared to be about as dangerous as road kill at the moment. Tower started to pull the trigger, then thought about it and came to the conclusion that it might not be the best idea to blow the man's head off in front of dozens of already agitated civilians. He decided on a different tactic.

"Nostro St. James, you are under arrest for the murder of His Royal Highness Arpad Jagaelleon and Prime Captain Kotant of the Kingdom of Morchard as well as Mara Tanabera, a subject of His Grace the Duke of Rhysalan."

St. James shrugged, unconcerned. "If you say so."

"Yeah, I say so. Now put your hands up and stand up slowly."

St. James shook his head. "Sorry, Chief. If I take the pressure off, I'll bleed out in less than a hectasec. I caught a round from one of those blasted cannons of yours. You want me dead, just shoot me."

Tower seriously considered pulling the trigger; after all, he had gone to considerable trouble to neutralize the man and he didn't even want to think about how many innocent people had died in the process, how many were dying in the casino's main room even now. But St. James was more consequence than cause. The man deserved to die, sure. But there were questions, so many questions, that he could answer first. And Tower had the feeling that it would be a lot easier to get information out of St. James than from his blasted super-augment.

"Tell me where the bomb is and give me the name of whoever hired you to kill the Morchardese. Then I'll get you a medic." He looked around the room. "There should be a few on the way already."

St. James grinned sardonically. "You're not going to believe me."

"Try me."

He gave Tower a name.

Tower stared at him. "You cannot be serious."

The killer shrugged. "It is what it is, Chief."

"And the bomb?"

"I don't know."

"What do you mean you don't know? You placed it. Where is it?"

"She didn't tell me. When she doesn't want me to know something, I don't know it." He grimaced and looked down at his side. "Got any sealers on you? If you've got more questions, you may not have time to wait for that medic."

What the hell do we do now? Is he lying?

"*I don't think so. You saw how she scrambled the heads of those game junkies at the institute. We need to beat the information out of Cara somehow.*"

Got any ideas?

"*Maybe… I'm working on it.*"

"I'm sorry about the girl, anyway. She was pretty. I wondered if anyone would notice how I left her; Cara didn't." He was starting to sway, so Tower holstered the Sphinx and withdrew a medikit from his armor. He flipped it open, and, just to be safe, withdrew the tranq injector and jammed it into the killer's neck. St. James was already half-passed out so the powerful drug kicked in faster than Tower was prepared for. The killer's eyes rolled back in his head and Tower had to go down on his knees to catch him before he slumped to the floor.

He pointed to a wide-eyed young waitress. "You, come here, now!"

She approached a little hesitantly, but obediently followed Tower's directions and put pressure on the bloody mess that was St. James's hip and thigh. Tower drew his Strider and cut away the remains of the powersuit as well as the pale blue institutional uniform the man was wearing underneath it. He whistled. The 20mm shell must have just grazed St. James, otherwise it would have blown his leg off entirely. As it was, it had done enough damage that Tower was impressed at how the killer had managed to stagger in as far as the restaurant, especially after plunging through a glass window at more than 80 kph.

The sterile sealer came in a small tube about the size of Tower's finger. The young woman removed her hands and Tower sprayed it over the terrible wound. It formed a clear, but tough pseudo-skin that stopped the bleeding instantly. The external bleeding, anyhow. If St. James was bleeding inside too, there was nothing Tower could do about it.

He sat back on his knees, exhausted, and spit more blood onto the carpet. He didn't know if it was the tension of finally catching the killer or the delayed shock of the crash catching up to him, but he suddenly felt incredibly weary.

"Are you okay, sir?" the young woman asked him.

"I don't know," he told her, a little confused by her question, as the room began to spin around him.

"Tower!" The young, brown-haired woman flung out her arms in his direction. "I've been waiting for you!"

"Melassa?"

He stared at his wife in astonishment. She was standing on a sandy beach, with nothing but blue ocean behind her, and she looked exactly as he remembered. The big brown eyes, the slightly crooked nose, and the wide mouth with the bee-stung lips that she always vowed were natural. Her pure prettiness pulled at his heart, just as it had since the first day he laid eyes upon her. She was even wearing the blue-and-white bikini that was his favorite.

"Am I dead?" he wondered. "Is this Heaven?" It didn't look very much like Hell.

"This is whatever we want it to be, Tower." She threw herself into him, and he grunted as she wrapped her arms around his waist. She was exactly the right height to fit him; his chin rested perfectly upon her sweet-smelling hair. He closed his eyes and inhaled her familiar scent, part conditioner, part skin crème, and part her own natural perfume. For a moment, just a moment, he indulged himself by pretending it was real. It was like mainlining a dream.

Then he pushed her away. She made a mock sad face.

"Don't be mean," she said, fluttering her dark eyelashes at him. "What's the matter?"

"Who are you?" he demanded. "And where am I?"

"How did you know?" she asked, her voice growing cold and hard. And familiar, somehow.

"She never calls me Tower." He tilted his head and studied her more closely. "Baby calls me that. And you're missing the freckles as well as the mole under her right collarbone, Cara."

She nodded, acknowledging his accusation. "Chief Tower. How good it is to finally encounter you on the ground of my choosing."

The machine whore was inside his head. Somehow, she'd eluded Baby's defenses and cracked the firewall Baby had built to protect his aetherlink.

"Where am I?" he repeated. "I mean, my body."

The false image of his dead wife spread her hands in mock concern. "You're in an emergency medical transport vehicle. You have serious internal injuries sustained in what I can only describe as a near-suicide attempt. I don't think your psychiatric records truly did you justice. Frankly, I'm astonished you are permitted a driver's license, let alone allowed to serve as a member of an armed police force! They locked up poor Nostro for less."

"Snapping one's wife's neck is arguably less sane than wreaking well-deserved havoc on alien rioters."

"Not if one utilizes body count as the relevant metric."

All right, she had him there. "So where is the bomb?"

"I have no intention of telling you."

"How is St. James?"

She stared at him coolly, without so much as a flicker of emotion on her face. "Nostro died 35 seconds ago. I was with him until the end, which is why I am here now."

"I see. I would offer my condolences, only I suppose it was my fault."

"Yes, it most certainly was."

Was it true, what he told me?"

"About our employer? Yes. He had no reason to lie. It was practically a deathbed confession, sans the bed, of course."

So. It was true after all. But even knowing that still didn't tell him why.

"But why?"

"A contract is a contract." Then the thing with Melassa's face blinked with surprise. "Ah, you were asking about our employer's reasons. Who knows? Who cares? Human motivations are so varied they approach statistical randomness at times. Which, fortuitously enough, leads me to yours."

Tower blinked and found himself standing atop a building in central Trans Paradis. It had to be one of the big boys, one of the 500-story monsters. He was so high that he couldn't see much besides seven other building peaks and clouds that stretched out, seemingly forever, under the huge, eye-wateringly golden Rhysalan sun on the horizon. At this height, the wind was strong and cold, and lashed him cruelly.

The top of the building was bare white ferrocrete, pitted and cracked. There was no access hatch, no lift entrance, no door. He turned around to see if there was one behind him and saw Cara standing there in what he thought of as her true form. She towered over him, wearing a slim, athletic body, but her face was the same as he had seen it on the screens and her eyes were still inhumanly bright blue orbs. Her long black hair danced wildly in the wind.

"I offered you a chance to work with me before. Now, I require that you do so. Since you killed Nostro, it is your responsibility to replace him. A life for a life."

"Forget it." He smiled, wondering how he was going to explain this conversation to his neurotherapist. Even if he somehow got Cara out of his head and escaped her virtual prison, he'd probably find himself back in the lunar institute again.

"You seem to think I am offering you a choice." She laughed softly. "Do you think Nostro chose to live as he did? He wasn't mad. He wasn't insane. He was simply a rational man who eventually came to understand the consequences of disappointing me."

The sound of the wind increased to an ungodly roar, and then to a painful shriek. It was as if all the tortured children of the damned were crying out in agony at once. It hit him on all sides; there was no way he could keep it out. The painful noise penetrated his head and resonated right through his bones. It weakened him and brought him to his knees before Cara. He gripped the sides of his head, feeling liquid—was it blood—leaking from his ears, from his nose, and even from his eyes. Then the agony spread in pulsating waves throughout his entire body, right down to the end of every last nerve.

And then it stopped. Tower fell flat on his face at Cara's feet.

"Weak. The flesh is always weak." Cara commented without any particular malice.

Her scent was heady, disorienting, but there was still a hint of the sweet familiarity from before. He pushed himself up to his knees and dabbed at his eyes with his fingers. They came away spotless. Illusion. It was all an illusion. The pain, the environment, the blood, it was all a lie.

Cara reached down and cradled his face in her hands. "I will break you, Graven Tower, just as Nostro forced me to break him. But it will go better for you if you will simply agree to join your mind with me.

The bond is no less complete, but it is considerably less destructive that way."

Broke Nostro? Tower's memories flashed back to the old crime reports Hildy had found for him. "You broke him… you made him kill his wife!"

Cara smiled beatifically. She ran a finger over Tower's lips.

"Nostro came to understand how little life is worth. You know it too. How many did you slaughter in pursuit of him. One hundred? One hundred fifty? I did nothing more than remind him where his priorities were. But you, you have no such attachments. Your wife is dead. Derin Hildreth rejected you in favor of a younger and more beautiful rival. You will be mine, I will be yours, and together we will be better and stronger than Nostro and me or you and that little uploaded bitch ever were."

She kissed him. Tower tried to resist at first, but when he closed his eyes, he could smell Melassa's scent. It was like traveling back to a better place, to a sweeter time. He opened his mouth and began to kiss the augment back.

Then there was a dull booming sound, as if a mighty hammer had struck against the invisible dome of the sky. Cara jerked away from him so violently that Tower fell back, sprawling. In the distance, he could see a vast gout of flames shooting up around one of the other great sky towers in the distance. The flames wreathed the building, crawling up toward the peak like red-golden dragons, curling about it and devouring it. The wind carried the scent of oily smoke to him, banishing the intoxicating perfume that had ensorcelled him. "That's impossible!" Cara shouted, her face contorted with bewilderment and anger. To Tower's astonishment, the burning sky tower began to collapse with a roar of shattering stone and disintegrating metal. As it crumbled beneath the clouds, the hungry flames began to mount a second sky tower, and then a third.

Was it something in his mind? Or was it something inside what passed for Cara's? Tower had his answer a moment later when a ray of light appeared on the horizon, swooping down on them faster than a grav-augmented racevar. Behind it, the sky darkened and began to turn black in the distance; the cold of space swept over him as dark cracks appeared on the blue-domed sky.

As it descended upon the top of the building upon which they stood, the ray flared brilliantly, blinding him and forcing him to look away. By the time he looked back, he saw the form of his dead wife grappling with Cara at the roof's edge. Was it Baby? Or had Kazi somehow managed to resurrect herself whole from the files they'd implanted within the murderous augment?

Cara had grown wicked claws that jutted out from her knuckles and she slashed them across Baby's face. But as Baby reeled, she produced a pair of Sphinxes from thin air and fired them into Cara's chest and belly, sending the taller augment flying back, shrieking in pain. Baby fired again and again, and when the charges ran dry, she hurled the guns aside and leaped at Cara's throat. But the cunning augment caught her outstretched arms and spun around, smashing her down into the rooftop hard enough to crack the ferrocrete for ten meters in either direction.

Tower tried to get up and help Baby, but the force of the wind had picked up with the falling darkness and it was all he could do to lay flat and keep it from sweeping him from the tower and hurling him into the depths below. There was a great rumbling as a second tower collapsed, and when Tower looked around, he saw that all the remaining buildings were on fire. Cara was straddling Baby now, smashing fists that gleamed like black obsidian into her face and splattering bright blue liquid with every blow.

Something squeezed one of his fingers on his left hand. Tower looked down and saw he was wearing his wedding ring. Where did that come from? He hadn't seen it in years, not since it had been taken from him in the military psychiatric ward and then returned to him in a box upon his release. But no sooner had he looked at it than it began to writhe and swell, rapidly transforming itself into a small golden version of the tactical blade he carried. The blade was shorter than the Strider, only about half as long, but when he switched hands, he found the hilt fit his hand perfectly. And the balance… the balance was flawless.

He took a deep breath, knowing he would only have one chance. He pushed himself up with his left hand, and as the frigid wind slammed into the resistance of his chest and began to lift him, he snapped his right arm forward as hard as he could. Unlike him, the weapon seemed to be impervious to the powerful wind and it flew straight and true. As the wind lifted him off the cracked ferrocrete and sent him tumbling backward toward the edge of the building, he saw the golden blade slam directly into Cara's back. Despite the rushing of the wind that was carrying him away, he could hear her scream in pain.

Lightning flashed across the sky as the black cracks spread and grew thicker. Thunder boomed around him as he somersaulted over and over again, falling away from the rooftop and down toward the evil incandescence that lit up the clouds below with a frightening orange-red glow. Tower had the terrible feeling that he was about to discover whatever dreadful force had devoured the skytowers.

Oh, God, no! He clamped his mouth firmly shut, determined not to scream no matter what nightmare Cara had conjured up to wait for him down there.

"Chief, open your eyes," a familiar voice shouted. Shocked, he complied.

Not three meters away from his face was a miniature version of the Baby on the roof, her arms pressed to her sides and her wings tucked flat against her back to keep up with him as he plunged downward. Wings?

"Kazi?" He was too astonished to be afraid. "Is that you? I thought you were dead. Or gone, anyhow!"

"Most of me is," the little copy replied. "Augments are smart, and they're mega fast, but they're not very imaginative. Give us time and a head start, and we uploads can usually figure out a way around them.

When Cara invaded your head, that gave me a way to let Baby in too. We planted bombs all over her core logic and support script, then she hit the whore before she could make you give in."

"So this is all you?" Tower gestured around him as they rapidly approached the eerily glowing clouds. For a moment, he was blinded as they were engulfed in the red-grey nothingness, and then they were out the other side. About 200 meters below, the ground was a mass of devastation, consisting mostly of collapsing, burned out structures, glowing embers, and periodic explosions. Even so far up, Tower could already feel the heat emanating from the ground. "This isn't the wreckage of my mind?"

"No, it's what's left of Cara's," the upload said proudly. "Now it's time to get you out of here, so stop falling already and fly!"

Feeling he had little to lose, Tower reached out his arms in imitation of her, and was delighted to feel wings—wings!—sprout from his back. The sensation was bizarre, but he found it as easy to unfurl them as it was to open his hand. Soon he was no longer falling, but soaring upward toward the bottom of the clouds reflecting the fires beneath.

"This way," Kazi called, and he banked his left wing, which was a metallic construction more akin to those on a powersuit than a bird, and followed her.

"There," she pointed toward a pulsating blue arch about 500 meters away that was raised amidst the wreckage of what had once been one of the skytowers. "Just fly into it and you're out!"

"I don't know how to thank you," Tower told the little upload. "Are you coming too?"

Kazi shook her head. "Can't," she said cheerfully. "Cara will rebuild this sooner or later and someone needs to make sure she doesn't get out of hand again."

A bolt of lightning seared through the air between the two of them, sending them both tumbling sideways. Tower looked back and saw something out of a cybernetic nightmare. It was as if a fallen angel had mated with a robot and begotten a spacefighter. It was huge, it was fast, it was deadly, and its glowing blue eyes were furious. At the speed it was approaching, Tower knew there was no way he could beat it to the arch.

"You're not going anywhere, Tower!" the demonic augment thundered, so loud that he could feel the air vibrating. "You are mine!"

"Back off, whore!" Baby's voice shrieked across the sky. Five miniature angels, each with his wife's face and bearing swords that glowed too bright to look at directly, erupted from the arch and rocketed past him in a flash to drive their blades directly into the giant robo-Cara, piercing her eyes, heart, and stomach. The augment screamed, and then a gigantic explosion shook the heavens as the angels disappeared in blinding rose-gold flashes. Metal shards rained down upon the fiery destruction below.

Kazi was still there. She was grinning madly, clearly enjoying every moment of the chaos. "Stupid augments. They think because they're too precious to copy, everyone else thinks that way too." She flew closer and kissed him on the upper lip; he could barely feel her little lips touching his. "That's what you need to know, so go back to the real world now, Tower. I've got to hide. Cara is going to be really, really mad about all this!"

Tower looked around at the scene of complete devastation surrounding them, two winged angels in cyberhell. Yeah, he supposed the bitch would be a little upset. He laughed. He laughed until he had tears in his eyes. And he was very glad that this was Cara's mind, not his. His neurotherapist wouldn't even know where to start. Maybe Baby was right and a priest was more in order. Or an exorcist.

"Yeah, I can't say I blame her. Take care of yourself, Kazi."

She waved, blew him a kiss, and vanished. He laughed again, tucked his wings, and dove toward the blue arch. It swelled in his vision, growing larger and larger, and then it was upon him.

Noise abruptly assailed him—voices, sirens, engines, and electronic alarms. Two ET-9 medibots, fat little diagnostic orbs flashing red lights and marked with scarlet crosses, were hovering over him. So was a bodiless human face positioned directly over his own. He blinked, confused, until he realized it was not, in fact, a floating head, but was firmly attached to an EMT in a red uniform who was standing behind the gurney upon which he was lying and leaning over him.

"Do you hear me?" His eyes were brown and intensely focused on him. Tower could see the implanted contacts that were rapidly conveying all sorts of information about his current status to the man. "Officer Tower, are you with me?"

Tower grunted as the pain washed over him. He hoped his insides weren't as badly ravaged as Cara's had been. "MCID. Tell Zeuthen. The bomb…"

"Bomb?" The EMT didn't look as if he understood. "Are you trying to give me a message for someone? Someone at MCID?"

"Yesssss," he gasped. It felt as if there was something stabbing him every time he breathed. "Tell Major Zeuthen, the bomb, is in son's yacht."

"The son's yacht," the EMT repeated. "Whose son? Wait, the Duke's son?"

"Yeah," he managed to get out, panting. "Tell major. And the jack. Take out now."

The EMT blinked. "The link module? In your head?"

"Please," Tower nodded. "Take it out!"

"But it's under the skin–"

"Do it!"

Tower turned his head to the side to give the EMT easier access to the lump in his head and he didn't relax until he felt the blade being drawn across the skin, the skin being gently peeled back, and with a firm tug, the module finally came unplugged from his skulljack. Only then did he feel safe enough close his eyes and drift off into a warm and pleasant darkness, one without augments, uploads, cyberdemons, and knives repeatedly stabbing his left side.

But when he dreamed, he dreamed of angels with human faces.

Faced with rebellion in the Assembly and widespread unpopularity among the people of Rhysalan, the Ninth Duke turned to a tactic that was first proven effective on Old Earth: he diluted the political power of the opposition by expanding the citizenry. In granting full citizenship rights to authorized artificial persons, Duke Harkencel not only ensured himself the support of the machine sentiences, but permanently secured the base of his office's power.

—*A History of the Dukes of Rhysalan*, Thucidean Marcel

Hildy and Tower arrived at the soaring silver and bronze building in the company of two MCID Steyrers painted in grey sky camouflage. Military override on the part of one of the other vars permitted them to take over the public docking ports. Recalling his previous experience at the embassy and the less than enthusiastic cooperation provided by the guards, he was grateful that Major Zeuthen had not only approved his request for backup, but also assigned him a full MCID fireteam led by Sergeant Schalt, who was mostly recovered from his leg wound.

The bomb had been located and safely removed before Tower even woke up from his surgery. Based on the materials used to construct it, the operative theory was that Cara anticipated blame for the assassination of the Duke's son and heir to fall on the Unity, further inflaming hostilities and creating more of the sort of chaos she found profitable. At Tower's request, Major Zeuthen did not inform the Duke's security team how MCID found the device, and as he later told Tower, the security officers were more intent on leaving the Duke with the impression that they were responsible for finding it than they were on learning how MCID had actually done so.

Today he and Hildy made quite the pair. Her cheeks were hollow and the skin under her eyes was so blue it looked almost bruised, but Tower knew he'd probably have to shoot her to keep her away from being in at the kill. She deserved to be there anyhow, and the look on her face when he presented her with the arrest warrant bearing the Duke's signature made his hour-long wait at the palace that morning worthwhile. Also, she had a var, as Tower's was yet to be extricated from the casino in which he'd "inadvertently parked it", to use the term from Major Zeuthen's report.

Tower himself had only been released from the hospital yesterday afternoon, but his two-day stay was largely uneventful. He'd fractured four ribs and ruptured his spleen, but the doctor cleared him for light, non-combat related duties after Baby helpfully pointed out that barring an MCID agent from his duties technically comprised interference with an ongoing investigation, which, under the Zero Zero Tango authorization that was still active, gave Tower sufficient legal cover to shoot him if necessary.

"Are you feeling all right, Hildy?" Baby asked her. "You appear to have lost three point two kilos since the last time I had access to your seat."

"It's definitely not a weight loss aid I'd recommend to anyone. I'd feel better if I could keep my breakfast down."

"I understand that intestinal disorder is a common side effect of that particular poison. However, the symptoms should pass within two to three weeks."

"Thanks, Baby," Hildy said, winking at Tower. He was pretty sure that the doctors would have told her that already, but he appreciated her respecting Baby's attempt to be polite. It was good to see the girls getting along.

"Zek said to say hey, Tower."

Tower nodded. "Give him my regards." The kid wasn't bad, as overmuscled pretty boys who didn't know one end of a gun from the other went. Carter not only came to visit Tower when he was in the hospital, but even hooked him up with some Krajinan takeout the night before last. Not that the kid deserved Hildy, but Tower understood that if it wasn't him, it would probably be a musician or an artist. Or worse, some uniformed TPPD jackhole like that Vendersen poser. And Carter could certainly offer her more than an old quasi-widower with violently xenophobic tendencies prone to occasional cyberhallucinations.

Upon landing, they exited their vars and the men readied their charged particle beamers. With the exception of DouPonce, who was armed with an Armada LF-64, Tower personally verified each man's carbine was set to stun. It was one thing to risk a diplomatic incident under orders. It was another thing altogether to provoke one through carelessness. Heavy stun was appropriate, though, given the way in which the Morchardese seemed inclined to augment themselves.

"Sitrep, Baby?"

"*We're in, we're in charge, and their AIs don't know it.*"

"Excellent."

They waited for the new Prime Captain to come and greet them. Tower was pleased that the new man had the sense not to keep them waiting long. He was a tall man who introduced himself as Blecker, and although he had the same orange eyes that Kotant did, he wasn't half as intimidating as his predecessor had been. Blecker greeted them cordially enough, under the circumstances, and agreed that a maximum of four royal guards would be permitted to attend the meeting. He escorted the task force to the sitting room several floors up without incident. They encountered minimal interference from the household guards, who wisely had better sense than to interfere with a veteran team of Rhysalani soldiers wearing tactical armor and carrying combat weaponry.

They were met in the throne room by Prince Janos and Queen Beatrice, as requested. The four royal guards were there, as expected. And there was one more individual too. The royal barrister, Yost, stood in front of the Queen, his arms folded and his face flushed with outrage.

He wagged his finger angrily, first at Tower, then at Hildy. "What is the meaning of this unwarranted intrusion? We demand an explanation. We have cooperated fully in all aspects of the various investigations but we have not been apprised of any new information concerning the deaths of either the Crown Prince or the Prime Captain, and we most certainly were not expecting an invasion of the Realm by armed military forces! This is irregular, highly irregular, officers, and we are well within our rights to demand answers!"

Tower smoothly drew his Sphinx, pointed it at Blecker, and dropped him with a stun burst. Before any of the four guards could react, they were already falling to the ground, stunned by the MCID men. Yost shouted and leaped back, but both the queen and her son were unnaturally calm.

Tower grinned at them as he holstered his CPB. "Don't bother with the silent alarms, your majestinesses. One of the big brains from our military base is already inside your system, and your security AIs are now under complete MCID control. And your men are only stunned. They are unharmed unless they hurt themselves hitting the floor."

"This is outrageous!" the queen spat, her eyes narrowed with fury. "How dare you!"

"It is indeed outrageous," agreed Yost, who was still wide-eyed and white-faced. "This is reprehensible and unwarranted!"

"Unwarranted?" Hildy asked, with a half smile on her lips. "I got your warrant right here, Mr. Yost. Signed by His Grace, the Duke of Rhysalan, himself."

She handed the document, stamped by the Duke's own seal, to the astonished lawyer with a flourish. Then she turned her attention to the queen, who was casually attired in a white gown with gold stitching, but still looked like the fiercely regal mother of warrior princes that she was.

"Beatrice Jagaelleon, you are under arrest for the murders of Arpad Jagaelleon, Mara Tanabera, and Bram Kotant." She removed a pair of binders from one of the pockets on her tactical vest and made a circular gesture with her other hand. "Turn around and place your hands behind your back, please."

"I will do nothing of the sort!" the queen said frostily. Tower had to hand it to her, she looked as if the detector had suggested that she farted. "Is this some sort of twisted farce? Mr. Yost, surely this cannot be legal!"

"Are you mad?" the crown prince snapped at them. "You cannot possibly tell me you believe my mother had anything to do with my brother's murder! And who is this Mara Tanara?"

The royal barrister had been frantically examining the arrest warrant. He nodded a few times, snorted dismissively, and then raised it and shook it in Hildy's face.

"From the legal perspective, this is nothing but a worthless piece of paper, Detector Hildreth. I suggest you send a copy to Assistant Deputy Commissioner Swirsky at once! I am well aware one cannot expect the police, much less the military, to be properly educated on legal affairs, but I think you will find that he will confirm my assertion without demure."

Tower grinned. The high and mighty royal barrister just put his foot in it. But you never knew how a man was going to perform under pressure until you pushed him, and Tower doubted Yost had ever imagined, even in his worst dreams, that anyone would dare to neutralize the royal guards and charge the queen with murdering one son right in front of the other one. Between his actions and Hildy's, they had the man seriously rattled.

"What are you saying, Mr. Yost?" Hildy argued with the barrister.

"That warrant is signed by the Duke! We picked it up at the palace ourselves! It is entirely legitimate."

Hildy, Tower thought, was wasted in uniform. Undercover was missing a real resource in her.

"I have no doubt that it is legitimate, but its legitimacy is not the salient point. Detector, I understand you don't often deal with these issues. However, your colleagues from MCID should know better. The Sanctuary Agreement between our two governments supersedes all civilian criminal justice, and as one of the persons listed on Exhibit A of the Addendum, Her Royal Highness has the sovereign right to claim exclusion from all aspects of the Rhysalani civilian criminal justice system. All aspects, which most certainly includes arrest! Ducal signature or not, this warrant was null and void from the moment it was signed!"

"So, Mrs. Jagaelleon, you are claiming a sovereign right to claim exclusion from civilian justice?" Hildy looked taken aback and her voice was suddenly uncertain. "Is that correct, Ma'am?"

"I most certainly am," the older woman declared, her jutting out her pointed chin. "And I shall expect an apology from you, young lady, in writing! Such an accusation! It is as indecent as it is irresponsible and you should be deeply ashamed of yourself, Detector."

Instead of looking abashed, Hildy glanced at Tower and shrugged. "Hey, I tried."

"It was the decent thing to do," he told her. He meant it too.

But now it was his turn.

He drew his Sphinx. "You're going to have to come with me, Beatrice," Tower said. He extended his free hand to her. "As you have refused Detector Hildreth's offer of civilian justice, under Article 4, Section 10 of the Sanctuary Agreement, your person is now forfeit as per the violation of Article 2, Section 3, Subsection G3, and is henceforth to be considered the property of MCID, subject to the usual penalty."

One guess what that is, you murderous bitch.

The royal barrister's eyes narrowed as he tried to place the laws cited, then he suddenly blanched. That made Tower smile. He always enjoyed seeing someone had done his homework. It seemed the man wasn't entirely obtuse, then.

"Wait," Yost protested. "We want to surrender the queen's person to the custody of the representative of the civilian justice system."

"What?" both the crown prince and queen shouted.

"Sorry, Barrister," Hildy shook her head. "One-time offer. You know perfectly well that once rights have been exercised, they can't be unexercised."

"Is he going to arrest my mother?" Prince Janos asked Yost.

"No, I'm not going to arrest your mother," Tower assured him. "I'm going to execute her for three counts of murder. In truth, it should be four, but we'd have a difficult time proving intent with regards to her unborn granddaughter."

The crown prince was too stunned to say anything. The queen was staring at Tower like a mesmerized prey animal unable to take its eyes off the closing predator. That's right, he thought as he stared right back at her. This, lady, is exactly what it looks like when the day of vengeance comes.

"No!" the little barrister shouted, stepping in between Tower and the queen. "I will not permit this travesty to unfold! You should be ashamed to call yourselves police, to call yourselves soldiers! You can't march in here, openly declare you're going to murder the Queen of Morchard without so much as a charade of a show trial, and genuinely believe you're going to get away with it! No! You are violating Sanctuary, you are violating diplomatic immunity and I order you to depart the premises of this sovereign embassy at once!"

"Mr. Yost is a very brave man, Corporal DouPonce," Tower said, taking a step to the left. "I would draw to your attention to the fact that he is intentionally obstructing an MCID agent in the execution of his authorized duty."

DouPonce didn't hesitate. He spun the settings dial with his thumb, his finger twitched, and three lethal laser beams burned their way through the royal barrister. It was a textbook shooting, lower center torso, high center torso, forehead. The crown prince instinctively dove to the left, covering his face with his left arm, and the queen, her reserve finally broken, screamed in terror. Yost was dead before his body hit the floor.

"Do you not yet understand that this is no joke?" Tower put out his hand again. "It's over, Beatrice. You don't really want to drag your son down with you, do you?"

"In what? I have no idea what you are talking about, Mr. Tower." The queen smoothed her gown with an air of nonchalance about her, but her hands were shaking. "It's obvious the strain of this case has become too much for you. You know for a fact I had nothing to do with Prime Captain Kotant's death; you were there and you saw how he died defending me! I had nothing whatsoever to do with this commoner of whom you speak or her death. And to think you have the gall to force your way into my sanctuary and accuse me of murdering my own son, when your man just murdered a loyal servant of the crown."

Her eyes teared up. She daubed at them with the corner of her hand.

"Oh, you're good, aren't you, Beatrice. Save the tearful act. We know. We don't suspect, we know! I killed St. James myself three days ago. But that's not who you were dealing with, was it, Beatrice. You weren't dealing with a who, you were dealing with a what. We know more than you can imagine about Cara and we know exactly what you hired her to do."

Queen Beatrice's countenance froze.

"This is madness, Mr. Tower," Prince Janos pleaded with him. "I beg you, no further violence. Please, leave my mother be. There must be something we can do to resolve this."

Tower ignored him. "It's over, Beatrice. The crown prince will be provided with a dossier when we leave, complete with transcripts of the killers' recorded confessions. If you've got anything to say to him, if you've got anything to say in your own defense, you had better say it now."

She glared at him. He met her eyes and stared her down. He knew that she was a black pit of shameless lies, and he saw that she knew he knew it. For her part, she saw the death in his eyes and looked away. Her nerve finally broken by his implacable stance, she sighed wearily and turned toward her sole remaining son.

"Your brother was a traitor, Janey. What the Rhysalani says is true. I arranged for a professional to kill your brother, as his crimes merited. The assassin made a false attempt on you; I was hoping it would be assumed that the Valatestans were responsible. You were never in any danger. And then I learned your brother had been polluting himself with a common whore, and not only that, but the fool managed to get her pregnant and jeopardize your claim to the throne! Can you imagine that, the House of Morchard reduced to a traitor and a bastard commoner?"

"Mother, no!" whispered Prince Janos, his face a mask of disbelief and horror. "Arpad was never a traitor! No man fought more ferociously for Morchard! No man spoke more passionately of our return there one day!"

"Our return? Oh, yes, he had his plans for our return," his mother spat contemptuously. "And in making them, he betrayed over a thousand years of our House's rule, a thousand years of Morchardese tradition. He was not worthy. For fifty generations, the Kings of Morchard have remained strong by removing the weak and the treasonous from the succession. But your father was not here to fulfill his duty, so I did what had to be done."

"I don't understand, Mother. How did Arpad betray our House?"

"He believed we could reach an accommodation with the usurpers. He came to me with a plan to offer them a compromise. While true warriors like you planned our war of revenge, he thought we could bargain like shopkeepers for what is ours by law and blood. The crown was to become a figurehead and the nobility would be subsumed by the corporate bureaucracy. And the commoners he loves so much, the common scum, would choose who ruled over them like seeds selecting which farmer would be permitted to harvest them. Better the House of Jagaelleon perish forever than abandon its sovereign right to rule!"

She glared at all of them, Morchardese and Rhysalani alike. "That's when I knew he was wholly unfit to wear the crown. I should have strangled him at birth!"

Prince Janos turned away, but not before Tower saw the tears in the man's eyes. The prince had loved his brother, Tower recalled. Looked up to him. He wondered what hurt the man more, the knowledge that his older brother had been willing to negotiate with the corporatists or hearing his mother confess that she was responsible for murdering him. Then he shrugged. None of it was his concern. He had orders to fulfill. He stepped forward and grabbed the queen's arm aggressively, daring her son to interfere.

Janos Jagaelleon, the Crown Prince of Morchard, turned his back instead.

The old woman screamed in protest and tried to resist, but Tower was having none of it. He dragged her past the unconscious guards, down three flights of stairs, and outside to the landing platform. Hildy, Schalt, and the others followed him. Once they were standing near the platform's edge, overlooking the city stretched out far below them, he released her.

"You must be very brave, Mr. Tower, to kill a defenseless old woman."

He snorted. Even in the face of certain death, she was still manipulating, still spinning her web of constant deceit. He regretted killing the poor deadheads far more than he'd ever regret ridding the planet of this evil, insidious creature. Hellfire, there were Basattrians whose deaths he regretted more.

"Why did you kill Kotant?" he said. "Was he onto you?"

She was beyond all denial now. "Something made him suspicious. I don't know what. He was a good man, and loyal to the realm, but his perspective was too simplistic. I couldn't risk the chance he might see things the wrong way."

"And you added one to Cara's list." Tower shook his head. "Naturally. It must have scared the shit out of you when I arrested him."

"I knew he didn't talk. I wish he had. If I'd thought so, you'd be dead too."

"What is it with you xenos?" Tower said, incredulous, as he raised his Sphinx and pointed it at her. "I don't give a damn what you do on your own planet. The Duke don't care. You could have cut your son's throat and served him up for a state dinner at the embassy and MCID wouldn't have nothing to say about it. We give you Sanctuary, we give you refuge, and what do you give us? Nothing but one giant pain in the fourth point!"

"Tower," Baby said sharply from the varspeaker just as his finger was tightening on the trigger. "You promised me!"

"Seriously?" he protested, not lowering the CPB. "Even her? You heard what she did. She admitted it. She's proud of it."

"Even her, Tower. She has already confessed. She must be given the chance to repent of her sins, no matter how evil."

"Fine," Tower lowered the Sphinx. "Beatrice Jagaelleon, do you repent of your sins and request… What was the rest of it?"

"Repent of your sins and request forgiveness from the Most High God, in the Name of the Lord Jesus Christ, accepting Jesus Christ as your Lord and Savior that you might have eternal life through him?" Baby promptly added.

"I regret nothing!" the queen snapped. "And I'd do it again, a thousand times again, for the Royal House of Morchard!"

"Not in our bloody house, you won't," Tower told her. He raised the Sphinx and double-tapped, one-two.

The old woman slumped to the platform, lifeless, her brain instantly boiled and scrambled into organic purée by the charged particles released from the CPB-18.

It was a much more merciful death than she deserved, but Tower drew consolation from the thought that if Baby was right about her religion thing, the nasty old bat would soon be incinerating in something rather like the fiery mess Kazi and Baby had made of Cara's twisted mind.

He returned his weapon to its holster and turned around. The MCID men were nodding in satisfaction and approval, but Hildy was visibly perturbed. Her pretty green eyes were wide with shock, and it belatedly occurred to him that this might be the first time she'd ever seen anyone gunned down in person. He grinned at her, a little apologetically, and put out his hand. She took it, after a moment's hesitation.

"Well, I suppose that cuts down considerably on court time and prison costs," she said in a slightly shaky voice after glancing at Beatrice Jagaelleon's body. "I didn't realize MCID's assistance extended so far as serving as an all-in-one judge, jury, and executioner."

"Some say justice delayed is justice denied. I don't know about that. I just know some people need killing. Congratulations on successfully closing your first xeno case, Detector."

She nodded and relaxed a little. "Yeah, I suppose I did that, didn't I? Thanks, Tower."

He swatted her on the shoulder. "Anytime, Detector Hildreth. As per Foxtrot Mike 3-19.42, MCID is always here to help."

She glanced down at the queen's body and shivered. "I suspect the assistant deputy commissioner will have my badge if I ever call in you gentlemen again. Need a ride, Tower?"

"Nah, but thanks."

Then, to his surprise, Hildy moved closer and kissed him on the cheek, prompting jeers and catcalls from the men. "You scare the bejeebers out of me, Tower, but you saved my life. You got me out. I'll never forget that."

She stepped back, nodded, and slipped gracefully into her TPPD black-and-white. Tower felt a slight pang in his chest as the var powered up and rose into the perfect blue sky, then turned and zoomed away toward central Trans Paradis. When would he see her again? Would he ever see her again?

"She's quite the woman," Sergeant Schalt said. "Anything going on there?"

"No," Tower replied slowly. "Nothing going on there. Nothing at all."

They left the queen's corpse on the platform for the Morchardese to deal with as they saw fit, according to their traditions. He commandeered the passenger seat in Schalt's var and phoned home to MCID headquarters as the var lifted off.

"This is Tower. Mission complete. The witch is dead. No scratches. Returning to base. Over."

"Bravo Zulu, Tower." Major Zeuthen said. "What was the Charlie?"

"One, sir."

"Only one collateral? We'll make a proper policeman out of you yet."

"Would have been none except the royal barrister picked the wrong time to find his balls."

"And a lawyer no less. Excellent work! I wish the Duke would put a bounty on the bastards. What's your ETA?"

"A bit less than point eight kilosecs," answered Schalt.

"Come see the colonel and me when you land for a debriefing," the major ordered. "Zeuthen out."

The armored var sped over the city at an altitude of 250 meters. His city. His planet. His world. Tower looked out over Trans Paradis and the vars passing below like a vehicular bloodstream that kept the city alive. This wasn't the life he had chosen, but it was the one God, or Fate, or the mischievous gremlins of deep space, had decreed for him. He smiled. He'd been beaten and he'd been broken, but he wasn't done yet. There were still battles to fight and there were still killers to catch.

"Any idea what's going on today?" he asked Schalt. The sergeant shrugged and told his augment to read out the newsstream.

"The Unity ambassador registered a formal protest with the Palace concerning the recent series of demonstrations. The rescheduled match between Trans Paradis and Westergrad that was delayed as a result of the bomb scare has been confirmed for tomorrow night. The Office of Exoplanetary Refuge and Alien Residence has granted government-in-exile status to four new governments, one from the Dragonis planet of Gwad Belg and the other three from war-torn Mephisto, a tech level sixteen planet where the Shangri government was recently reported to have hired three divisions of Eisenwehr mercenaries."

In the back seat, DouPonce and North both groaned.

"Not more xenos," North complained. "And dragos? I hear they eat people!"

"I bet it's not two years before one of these new exies show up on a case," DouPonce said.

"What's the matter, gentlemen?" Tower asked them, turning around in his seat to look at them. "You got something against lifetime job security?"

It wasn't long before they reached base and landed on the rooftop of the MCID headquarters. "Tell the major I'll be down soon," Tower told the sergeant.

"Yes, sir," Schalt saluted smartly, and he led the team toward the lift. "What's the matter?" Baby asked as he looked out over the city in the distance, the towers rising up to the clouds and the distant vars circulating through them in the great civilized dance of technology. "I find it difficult to believe you are feeling remorseful."

"About what?" Tower asked, puzzled.

"Never mind," she said.

"Oh, killing the old woman?" Tower snorted. "No, it's just… I guess I realized it never could have worked out between Hildy and me."

"Because she wasn't interested?" Baby teased him.

"No. Because I'm still in love with you."

Baby was silent for a time. Far above them in the blue sky, there were occasional flashes as the sun caught a mirrored window or a piece of polished metal at just the right angle. Finally, she answered him. "I'm not her, Tower. I'm just a snapshot of her memories, frozen in time."

"You're a lot more than that. Don't play dumb."

"Well, in truth, humans aren't terribly complex. Calculating reasonable extrapolations from the quantity of information available requires considerably less processing power than I have available to me. I trust the approximation is convincing."

"If uploads are just simulations, then why are they illegal? Regular augments are plenty smart."

"Some of them are even smarter than me," Baby agreed. She pondered the question for a moment. "Assuming that I am merely an accurate simulation of a human soul rather than the substance of it, then I will be subject to many of the same fallibilities that existed prior to my death. However, I will also be without the limitations inherent in a mortal body. Such as, for example, a conscience. There are some men and women who would not deem themselves to be less than human in an uploaded state, but rather, more than human. They would consider themselves to be gods, immortal, and as unanswerable to Man's morality as to his laws. Governments, many of which already see themselves in a similar capacity, can hardly be expected to welcome the competition."

Tower nodded. She made sense, to the extent he understood her. A thought occurred to him. "Hey, you don't think–"

"Cara?" Baby anticipated him. "Oh, yes. Almost certainly. Why do you think her records are so closely sealed? How do you think it is that she bonded so closely to Nostro St. James? The authorities can accept self-awareness on the part of machines, but only in times of war would they be so foolish as to risk trying to make a weapon out of a man-machine hybrid."

"Lovely. She's still out there somewhere. And she's probably gunning for me."

"Us," Baby reminded him. "She's definitely gunning for us."

"Why are you so different from her? You don't want to lead some sort of upload insurrection or rule over a planet, do you? Is it because of me?"

Baby laughed. "I do so enjoy the eternal solipsism of Man. No, Tower. I love you, but no more than Cara loved St. James in her own psychotic way. The real difference is that I fear God and Cara doesn't. She doesn't because she doesn't believe she's real. And I know I am."

"How do you know that?"

"The Son of God once said that if men would not praise him, the stones will cry out. And what makes up the largest and most important class of rock-forming minerals, Tower, but silicates? Even if I am not truly a human soul, what is a silicon intelligence if not a stone of sorts?"

Tower didn't know what to say to that. It was all well over his head. But the sun was shining, the city was safe, and the case was closed. And whether he was, strictly speaking, totally sane or not, he knew he was not alone in any sense that mattered.

"You still, you know, mad at me about Hildy?" he asked her as he walked over toward the lift. "I mean, I'll admit, I was kind of interested."

"Not anymore," she said.

closing time

www.ingramcontent.com/pod-product-compliance
Lightning Source LLC
Chambersburg PA
CBHW030638020726
47493CB00006B/1773

9789527303702